OF SEA AND CLOUD

JON KELLER

TYRUS
BOOKS

F+W Media, Inc.

Published by TYRUS BOOKS
an imprint of F+W Media, Inc.
10151 Carver Road, Suite 200
Blue Ash, OH 45242. U.S.A.
www.tyrusbooks.com

ISBN 10: 1-4405-8022-7
ISBN 13: 978-1-4405-8022-2
eISBN 10: 1-4405-8023-5
eISBN 13: 978-1-4405-8023-9

Printed in the United States of America.

10 9 8 7 6 5 4 3 2 1

Library of Congress Cataloging-in-Publication Data
Keller, Jon,
    Of sea and cloud / Jon Keller.
        pages cm
    ISBN 978-1-4405-8022-2 (hc) -- ISBN 1-4405-8022-7 (hc) -- ISBN 978-1-
4405-8023-9 (ebook) -- ISBN 1-4405-8023-5 (ebook)
    1. Lobster fishers--Fiction. 2. Domestic fiction. I. Title.
    PS3611.E4244O37 2014
    813'.6--dc23
                            2014007792

Cover design by Frank Rivera.
Cover images © duplass/123RF.
Author photo by Abi Maxwell.

This book is available at quantity discounts for bulk purchases.
For information, please call 1-800-289-0963.

I've seen the devil and you're not him.

—Oscar Look Jr., lobsterman

E bb tide and fog and three slashes with wooden oars. No land left only the fog and the oars like bones creaked in their locks. A single gull rode the skiff's bow. The tidewater drained fast and the lobster fisherman named Nicolas Graves leaned his shoulder and spun his skiff and rowed stern-first together with the tide and he and the gull both squinted into the fog.

He told himself that his boat was moored here somewhere. He told himself that after a lifetime on the Atlantic he could not be lost in this one small cove. He shipped the oars and ducked his head. He lit a cigarette. Water dripped from the oar blades. His sweatshirt hood was beaded with moisture and his hands were cold and raw. Fog like frost spread atop his gray beard and condensed on his glasses and trickled from the lenses to the coin-sized patches of skin above his beard. From behind him the gull watched and Nicolas turned to the bird and released a lungful of smoke and said, You tell me.

He smoked and allowed the ebb tide to draw him toward the mouth of the cove and when he was finished smoking he dropped the butt into the water. The gull circled and landed. Nicolas took a plastic bag of crackers from his sweatshirt pocket and removed one. He turned fully around on the bench seat to face the gull and held out the cracker in his cracked palm. The gull batted its wings and craned its neck and hopped on one foot.

Come on, Nicolas said. You like them quite well.

The bird flapped its wings in place and jumped into the air and hovered overtop Nicolas for a split second. It landed again on the bow. Nicolas rested his knuckles on the wooden gunwale. He wiggled his fingers. The gull stepped hesitantly from the bow to the gunwale as if understanding this beckoning and it walked the rail and in a quick lunge it took the cracker and returned to the bow. Nicolas smiled to himself and turned in his seat and took up the oars. The gull disappeared into the fog then reappeared like an apparition that hovered six feet above the surface of the sea. A few more slashes with the oars and he saw that the gull was perched on the bow of his moored boat. Then the entire hull shape of the boat emerged like the body of a centaur beneath a gull head.

Nicolas rounded the boat and tied the skiff's painter off to the pot hauler and climbed aboard and thought unremarkably that he'd done this same thing too many times. If he was to add up his hours aboard a lobster boat it would be nearing a quarter of a million and he did not want to think about it. More waking hours at sea than on dry land and he'd heard people say that life is short but he did not believe it to be so. The night previous he'd awoken from a dream with the conviction that death was a rock which he would one day grip and never release. Nicolas did not trust in anything he could not hold in his hands but even so he suspected his wife's death to be somehow behind the dream. She'd been dead for over twenty years and she was the exception to his rule because although he had not held her in so long he still believed wholeheartedly in her presence.

Nicolas fired the engine and let the boat idle. It was a big block diesel with over 600 horsepower and it hummed and growled. He untied the skiff's painter and pulled the skiff along as he walked the washrail around the wheelhouse and onto the bow. Both femurs ground like stone pestles in their sockets. He stooped and pulled the bridle over the bit and freed it from the chocks then tied off the skiff to the bridle and dropped the ropes into the ocean.

He flicked his two-way radio and GPS and radar on and he spun the boat 180 degrees. He piloted still deeper into the fog bank and he counted seconds out loud and veered north at sixty seconds and counted again and veered south at forty-five seconds and south again after seventy more. The seafloor was charted like music in his mind with the boat's movements like steps and he knew each ledge and each rock and he avoided all of them.

Soon he spilled out of the cove and into the gulf. He throttled up and watched his compass and he headed southwest between Two Penny and Ram's Head. He could not see either island through the fog but he watched his instruments and he watched the water. The ebb tide ran hard and stood in curling waves for both the pinching of the islands and the coming of the seas. He steered south around a series of half-tide ledges and watched a flock of purple sandpipers swarm in singular flight with white undersides flashing from rock to rock.

Nicolas glanced at his radar and the islands passed on the monitor. Also on the monitor was another boat which steamed toward him. He paused. It was December and the bulk of the traps were stacked on shore. A handful of lobstermen still fished but they fished their deep-water grounds 35 miles offshore so they left long before daylight. Nicolas himself left late and fished unhurried but he was old and he was a rarity. The dragging season was open for urchins and Nicolas knew there were draggers around but this boat came too fast for a dragger. He watched the scrolling numbers on his GPS. The boat came out of the east. To the south spread open ocean and to the north lay the mouth of a broad sound and further north rolled a river into that sound.

The dots on the radar closed. Nicolas throttled down and lit a cigarette and held it bitten in his front teeth. He stuffed his cold fingers into his armpits. The boat was a quarter mile off. He went to the stern and gazed into the fog. He heard an engine echo across the water and it grew louder and louder and the noise surrounded him and made him feel that he would soon be run over so he charged to the wheelhouse and spun the wheel and rammed the throttle. He faced his boat toward whatever danger came.

He tried to listen as if his ears would do what his eyes could not. He thought quickly of calling on his two-way radio but then suddenly there the boat was just a bow with spray flying and a radar spinning and a circular windshield wiper rotating around Osmond Randolph's face with its black mustache and long black hair. The diesel engine howled and threw smoke black and thick into the air.

The boat circled Nicolas's boat *Cinderella* once and once again and the sea itself rose and surged with the boat's wake. Osmond backed his boat *Sanctity* up so the boats aligned stern to stern. Both sterns were open to the sea so that a man could step easily from one boat to the other. The two men faced each other. Osmond Randolph wore a black oilskin barvel that wrapped his body like a dress. Nicolas had once teased that he looked like a warlock but Osmond was not one to be teased. He stood six and a half feet tall and his entire body was tight and strung hard as rope and right now he tucked his greasy hair behind his ears.

Nicolas, he said.

Osmond.

Decisions regarding the pound are made by the two of us, not by you and you alone.

Nicolas faced the fog. His boat had an underwater exhaust piped out the stern. The exhaust bubbled and belched with the rise and fall of the sea. He had nothing left to say to Osmond Randolph.

Nicolas, Osmond said. I have invested time and energy into negotiations, and only the Lord knows why you have undermined that. I do not understand. We do not want to jeopardize this lifetime. Explain yourself, Nicolas.

Nicolas took his glasses off and worked a section of his shirttail from beneath his belt and wiped the lenses dry. He put them back on. He watched the water begin to shift and roil and spread between the sterns. Osmond watched too then stormed the length of his boat and slid *Sanctity* into reverse and came alongside Nicolas. He dropped two red fenders over his gunwale and tied a line fast between the boats so they were rafted side to side then stepped aboard the *Cinderella*. He stood in front of Nicolas and when Nicolas looked from the fog to the man he saw Osmond's throat with its skin like a turkey neck and he smelled that skin like something reptilian.

Explain yourself, Nicolas. Here and now. I have a family and my family will have a future. Explain what you've done. I cannot change things unless you tell me your reasoning.

Nicolas said nothing. He felt a line of blood leak into his heart as if into a bilge. His heart flexed and his temples throbbed and he wondered if he should be scared but instead he thought of his dead wife. Her name was Jennifer. Jennifer Regan when he'd met her. Next he thought of his son Bill followed by his other son Joshua who he'd not spoken to for so long. But he did not think about the man who stood before him.

Piss off, Nicolas finally muttered.

You have pushed, Nicolas, and I do not recommend you continue to do so.

Osmond stepped forward so their chests nearly touched.

Back up, Nicolas said. His voice was calm. He stepped back and sat on the washrail with his back to the sea. Water sloshed between the hulls and Nicolas's exhaust bubbled and belched with the sea's surges. From time to time the hulls together squeezed a wave and sent a waterspout into the air. A curtain of fog blew between the two men and Nicolas thought he must be very old to allow all of this and the thought was like threading the tail of a rope through a loop and that was it.

The hell with you, Osmond, Nicolas said. I got final say and you know that good and goddamned well. Now get your fucking boat off here before you stove both to shit.

Osmond held a palm out to the sea as if to still it. Nicolas, he said. I have been patient with you for twenty years and for twenty years we have operated as you've wished. We will not survive, not on this coast, not without evolving. That is a fact. I am over seventy years old, Nicolas, and what I do now I do for my grandchildren and for them alone. This is bigger than you and me.

Good, Osmond. Finest kind. Take care of them kids.

Listen to me, Osmond barked. Hear me.

Osmond took a step toward Nicolas and like a crow he loomed. Nicolas felt the hairs on his neck prickle. He stood and said, I won't have it. How many times do I have to tell you that? I seen what will happen to the harbor. He dismissed Osmond with a wave and added, Get off my boat. I got traps to haul.

Osmond's face was blank but he had coal in his eyes.

Nicolas took a mouthful of air and tried to rally the strength that used to exist but his words felt empty. This settles it. This horseshit right here. It's been a long time coming.

Osmond's body quaked. With the heels of his hands he wiped at his cheeks although no tears fell. Nicolas, he said. You must have faith. You must listen. Please.

Osmond's voice was quiet and hurt and Nicolas had never heard anything like hurt from this man. It stopped him. He understood that he was the closest thing to a friend that Osmond had ever had but so too did he understand that to Osmond Randolph friendships were finite whereas bloodlines were not. His was no blood of this man's. He felt bad for Osmond but his pity was scant and brief.

I've had enough, Nicolas said. All your happy horseshit. Enough. You're done. You go piss a ring around someone else.

Osmond looked at his feet. The boats rolled with the sea.

Nicolas said, Get off my boat.

Osmond's voice was a whisper—*Please don't*—but before he finished and before he could pause or hesitate a charge inside of him dropped and he surged toward Nicolas. Nicolas met him and the two collided. Nicolas's two bad hips ground bone to bone. His head reached only to Osmond's chin and Osmond outweighed him half again. Osmond pushed him back until his thighs braced against the washrail and behind him Nicolas felt the stretch of cold empty sea. He swung once at Osmond's face but Osmond caught the fist as if Nicolas were a child and squeezed with a crushing strength that shot pain like blood flow through Nicolas's body. Then Osmond's hand wrapped around Nicolas's throat like a collar too tight. Nicolas saw sudden blackness. He could not breathe. He fought the grip and tried even to scream but could do nothing. He heard Osmond's voice out there—*You will help me, Nicolas*—but Nicolas was conscious only by fury and the pain suddenly vanished so he braced his legs and gritted his teeth and launched himself into Osmond. Osmond was a wall that forced Nicolas backward until Nicolas's feet slipped and his legs went out. The two stumbled but Osmond caught himself as Nicolas flipped into the sea.

That was it. The seawater was 48 degrees Fahrenheit. That crossed Nicolas's mind but not for long because the tide ran like a river and sucked him fast from the rafted lobster boats. He watched Osmond grow smaller aboard his boat. Osmond fell to his knees with his head bowed and his body swayed in anguish and if Nicolas had been closer he would have seen the lips moving and perhaps heard the words of prayer which rose into the air. Then Osmond stood and without a last look at his friend he stepped back aboard his own boat. Nicolas saw black smoke shoot from *Sanctity*'s exhaust as the rafted boats together spun away.

Nicolas's rubber boots and oilgear filled with water and his head dipped. He kicked and thrashed and tried to rip away his boots and jacket and pants but it was already too cold and he was already choking on too much saltwater. He surfaced. That quick and the boats were gone. Osmond was gone. Only seconds and fog surrounded Nicolas and water surrounded Nicolas and from somewhere in his mind came a voice *swim* but something stronger surfaced. It was a scene that for so long he'd held tucked away. Twenty years ago and he held a gaff at his side and watched from his boat as his son Joshua fought the sea. His older son Bill stood beside him and Bill cried and looked up at his father but did not say, *Help him Dad.* The boys' mother had died only weeks before and she'd been the world to all three of them and Nicolas held the gaff and watched Joshua while anger tore him to shreds and he shouted at the drowning boy, *Goddamned poison aboard here is what you are.*

Now Nicolas was in the water himself and death was indeed a rock which he held in his hands. What had Joshua even done? He'd released a day's catch of lobster. Thrown the lobsters overboard one by one every last one but truthfully that was nothing because what was everything was that Joshua would forever be a relentless reminder of the woman who'd died so Nicolas's own hands had lifted his own son and thrown him into the sea and he'd yelled, *My own flesh and blood. You want to throw things overboard?* Then he'd reached the gaff out to Joshua but the boy would not touch it. *Take it,* Nicolas had said and he'd realized hatred in his voice and he'd realized that a part of him wanted his son to die right here and how could a father wish that? How could a father wish for the son to take the mother's place in death?

Take the fucking thing, Nicolas now screamed frantic in the fog but there was nothing to take but the biting of the waves. His head dipped and his body thrashed and Joshua would not take the gaff and there was the older son Bill who was cast in his own image and Bill leaped into the water and swam screaming for his little brother. Nicolas spun the boat and saw the sea surrounding the boys and his wife was dead and buried somewhere on dry land and their two sons were now sinking into this wasteland. Bill who was eleven years old choked on saltwater and caught his younger brother in a weak headlock. Joshua was white and blue by then and already readying himself for a new world but his eyes were still fierce and intent on his father who had thrown him overboard and his father whose miserable depths the boy now understood more completely than Nicolas himself.

Nicolas himself drowning. Saltwater piled into his mouth and out his nose and stomach acid raced up his throat. Small waves piled overtop his head and pressed down like hands. His rubber boots and oilgear jerked him into the deep and Nicolas remembered Bill's long ago scream shrill as a girl's and that scream should have echoed throughout his life but such a thing could not be held. Only now that he was drowning did he realize how weak his own hands were. Twenty years ago with both sons overboard he'd spun his boat in a tight loop and plunged his arm and head and torso overboard and with one hand jerked both children into the boat but now he could not so much as tread water.

He grew colder by the second but he was actually surprised how long death took. Death was indeed a rock pulling him down and like life it took too long. Images he did not care to see splashed through his mind. He wished he could see his friend Virgil Alley because his apology was so overdue and it occurred to him how tragic it was that in a life too long lived a man can find no time to do what matters most. He wondered briefly if this was a taste of hell brought about by a life lived without confronting specific sins.

He did not wonder for what he was thrown into the sea. It was as if his mind understood perfectly that it occupied a man deserving of this death so when the cold penetrated and Nicolas felt the depths call him downward his thoughts rested solely on his son Joshua who all of the fishermen called Jonah. He needed to see the boy one last time. He needed to face his son and he needed to hold his son and whisper to his son because finally as he touched the end Nicolas understood that Jonah would live his life without knowing his father's last truth.

The first drops of rain came. The brothers on the wharf stood and watched the drops fall into the fish blood stream. The flood tide fell to slack and all of the lobster boats and the five draggers swung on their hooks and the younger of the two brothers spat on the filthy oil-soaked wharf planks and said, Where's Virgil gone to?

Christ if I know, Jonah. I wouldn't give a damn anyway.

You wouldn't give a damn? The hell not. What're you gonna do?

You asking me that?

That's what I'm doing.

That ain't what you're asking.

She ain't what I'm talking about, Bill. I'm talking of the price of goddamned lobsters is what I'm talking.

The hell you are.

The two brothers turned at the grind of a new diesel and watched the black truck drive past the fog-worn bait house. The tires splashed through the fish blood. A series of gulls with their asses perched from the wind flew from the swayback roof. The rain came harder.

Here's Virgil all dressed up. See what he says.

You know what he'll say, Jonah. Same as you and same as me.

Virgil parked on the wharf and rolled the window down. His fingers crept like spiders onto the edge of the door and his face stuck out above his fingers. His cheeks hung like paper sacks. He wore a suit coat and a loosely knotted tie. What in clamfuck's the price dropped to now, Jonah?

Two-fifty.

Two-fifty. Virgil turned his gaze to Bill. His head moved slowly. What're you planning on doing, Captain?

Bill shifted on his feet and stood straight. I'm planning on fishing same as you and same as Jonah.

Captain Bill's planning on fishing, Virgil muttered. He leaned back in his seat and looked at the water. He ran his windshield wipers. He had a small dog in the cab with him and the dog climbed onto his lap and licked at its own nose. Virgil said, You boys best get going before you get them fancy suit coats ate by this weather.

Jonah didn't listen. He sat back on a stack of storm-beaten yellow traps and he pulled his collar up and looked out at the end of the harbor where the barren island called Ram's Head rose as if to plug the harbor mouth. He felt a shiver run up his arms and into his shoulders and neck. He looked at the harbor where his father's empty mooring ball leaned with the ebbing tide. Don't look the same, he said.

Ain't nothing the same ever, Virgil said.

Bill leaned against the fuel pump with his back to the water. The wind blew south against the tide and small whitecaps rolled and broke in the harbor. That's so, he said and clenched his jaw in thought. But I got me some plans for the pound.

The Captain's always got plans, Jonah said. That's why he's the Captain of this here coast of America. Me, I got plans too. I might just take myself clamming.

He might take his own self clamming.

Might.

Now that the old man's dead and gone the Downcoast Highliner gives up fishing.

I just might.

That there, Virgil said, is why Nicolas had the good sense to die on us. The world ain't much on spinning the right direction.

Jonah pinched a dead barnacle from the yellow trap wire and crushed it between his fingers and let the powder fall to the wharf plank. He reached through the trap head and pulled a dried starfish

15

out and turned its brittle mass in his wet hands. Erma Lee spins any direction the Captain beckons, he said. Ain't that so, Bill?

Virgil lifted his glass and sipped his drink. Ice clinked and left a smatter of brandy and milk on his mustache. His eyes landed like lead on Bill.

Bill looked at his own big wet hands. We're done late now, he said. He lit a cigarette and shook his wet head and the drops of water beaded on his glasses. For a heartbeat his eyes connected with Virgil's then broke away. Bill walked down the wharf and past the stinking rotting bait house and the rusted thousand-gallon fuel tanks and the clamshell bank.

Jonah heard the truck start and saw Bill drive up the dirt hill to the road.

Guess he's off, Virgil said. You taking your rig up?

I aim to.

Good. I got the mutt here.

Jonah looked around and felt the cold rain on the backs of his hands and he told himself that it was only the chill that made him feel childish. You fishing in the morning, Virgil? he said.

Virgil put his truck in gear. Guess you don't need to go talking dumbshit now, Jonah. Virgil ran his hand down the dog's head and looked back to Jonah. You thinking we should take a day of rest for Nicolas?

I don't know what I'm thinking. Just with the price gone and the old man gone, things ain't right.

That's right, Jonah. Things ain't right. The only thing that is right is that you and me and the Captain are fishing in the morning, same as each man on this coast.

Virgil backed up and turned around the back of the bait house and drove up the hill. Jonah walked to the edge of the wharf and reached overhead to the winchhead gallows and stretched his arms and hung out over the tidewater. Seaweed rushed in the cold salt currents and wrapped around the barnacled hackmatack pilings.

Mussel shells and crab shells and clamshells covered the rock bottom. Jonah hung down low and whispered, Guess you're in there somewhere.

• • •

He drove slowly and bounced north up the peninsula through granite ledges and stunted and tangled maple and alder. The road climbed and rain spattered. At the summit of the hill he turned into the brown dead-grass field which held a dozen trucks and freshly made ruts. A few men stood by their trucks and smoked and drank. Jonah sat for a moment in the warm truck wishing everyone would go home and then got out and nodded to the men. He felt their eyes track him as he crossed the field.

He saw Virgil in his truck with the dog named Chowder in his lap and the wipers flicking. He continued to the pathway and stood alone with rain running down his neck. He lit a cigarette. Some of the women with their black umbrellas and black stockings and black heels covered in wet grass came over and hugged him and stood silent for a moment with their hands on his sleeve and their eyes on his. Then they moved on.

Erma Lee rushed to him and wrapped her skinny arms around his waist and set her head to his chest. He felt her sob and when she looked up at him her chin was red and wrinkled and soft. Tears ran along her nose. I'm so sorry, Jonah, she said.

Fine, Erma Lee. Thanks.

Is Bill okay, Jonah? He don't speak often of his feelings.

He's good.

Oh the Lord, she said.

Oh the Lord, Jonah repeated but he was watching Virgil's wife Celeste and their daughter Charlotte. Celeste smiled at Jonah. The two women waited for Erma Lee to release him and when she was gone Celeste hugged him for a long time. Her hair was gray and her skin was warm. He saw Charlotte over Celeste's shoulder.

She watched him but he closed his eyes. Celeste's touch was like climbing under a blanket and he pinched his tears away as Celeste stepped back.

Charlotte slid her arms around him. She was taller and thinner than her mother but smelled the same like salt and sage and he held her tight until she pulled away.

I'm sorry he won't get out of the truck, Jonah, Celeste said. She nodded toward Virgil.

Jonah smiled and shook his head. I'd think he'd be crawling into that grave himself if he come in here.

Your father would have wanted Osmond to minister this, Celeste said. She reached out and squeezed Jonah's forearm.

I know it. But ministering or not ministering, I ain't got to like him any more'n Virgil does.

He gives me the chills, Charlotte said then looked around as if the man named Osmond Randolph had snuck up behind her.

Come to the house afterward, Jonah, Celeste said. I don't want you going home alone. We have lobster and crab and mincemeat pies and all sorts of things, and there's the extra bedroom if you want.

Charlotte stuck the tip of her tongue out. A bead of water slid down the line of black hair that had fallen from beneath her hood. She raised her eyebrows at him and her eyes were red and somber and Jonah felt them in the pit of his stomach. Celeste grabbed Jonah's arm and the three of them followed the short pathway to the cemetery where Osmond Randolph stood guarding the wrought iron gate. He nodded to Jonah but did not speak. His black hair hung over his shoulders and his black robe clung to his chest and clung to his arms in the ripping wind. His two granddaughters stood at his side.

Once through the gates Celeste leaned close to Jonah and whispered, Charlotte made clam fritters. I'll be damned if she wasn't up early digging clams in the rain. You'll like them, Jonah. Please come over.

Jonah nodded. He noticed Bill making his way around the parked vehicles with a gang of fishermen following him. Bill smoked a cigarette and flicked the butt away and let the smoke ease from his nostrils and the other fishermen took that as a signal and tossed their own cigarettes into the grass. Bill nodded to Osmond and stopped next to Jonah and all of the fishermen found their wives or girlfriends and stood silent and awkward beside them. When the two dozen or more people were in the cemetery Osmond pulled the gate closed.

Strange being orphans, Jonah whispered to Bill.

Bill didn't move and after a pause he said, Guess we are that.

Osmond approached Jonah and Bill. He took them both by the hands and he held tight. Jonah's hand felt small and fragile within Osmond's grip and he fought the need to pull away. Osmond's two granddaughters flanked Osmond as if leashed. Osmond's head hung low and he raised his eyes to Jonah and then to Bill and each eye was a tarn and he said, Virgil will not come inside?

You know that well as we do, Osmond, Jonah said.

Yes. I hoped that this might be different.

Jonah pulled his hand free and his heart rushed. I'm guessing if the situation was reversed you'd be sitting out there too, ain't that so?

Bill glared at Jonah. Bill's hand was still within Osmond's.

Osmond licked his lips. His face was pocked and clean-shaven save for a black mustache. Your father will be missed here on earth, he said. He released Bill's hand and took the two girls with him to the center of the small circle which had formed around the grave hole and the casket.

Celeste and Charlotte moved in beside Jonah and Bill. Erma Lee made her way to Bill's side. Osmond lifted his hands into the rain and the group silenced but as the silence fell a pickup truck slowed on the road and pulled into the field. The truck was glasspack loud and drove fast over the ruts and parked. Osmond pointed a finger like a sword at his grandson Julius and motioned him into the cemetery. Julius slid out of the truck and moved past Virgil without a glance and entered the cemetery. He left the gate open behind him.

Osmond's arms were still in the air and his long fingers were outstretched like feathers and his robe and hair blew in the wind and the rain. Jonah felt his brother shift. Charlotte gripped with two hands the umbrella that she and her mother stood beneath. The rain slashed through the gravestones and rapped on the empty casket with thuds like a distant knocking.

Osmond lowered his arms and bowed his head.

We stand here in the rain, the sons and daughters of this earth, and try to understand what has happened and why it is that our friend and father and partner, Nicolas Alexander Graves, was called from us. We look to the heavens for answer and we look to the earth for reason. We seek redemption, and we find redemption, but we find it within our own private persecution. We blame ourselves—we think this is atonement. But it is not. What could *you* have done? What could *I* have done? We must each understand, *we* do not choose salvation, salvation chooses us, and those choices were made long before this world began.

Jonah turned toward Virgil and saw the glow of Virgil's cigarette and the swipe of the windshield wipers and the small dog on Virgil's lap. Osmond began again but Jonah looked down the hill at the snaking brown river where the falling tide emptied the mud shoals. The south wind hurled against the water and lifted the river into standing breaking waves. He heard Osmond's voice but paid no attention until Osmond silenced.

Wind filled the void. Jonah felt the cold rain pelt his face. He saw Osmond's eyes shift as if the man had forgotten what he'd intended to say. Then as Jonah watched Osmond exhaled long and lifted his arms high and tucked his voice low as if to utter a secret meant for Jonah alone.

I hold no scripture in my hands. I bear no cross about my neck, for I have come here as a man. I have come because Nicolas Graves was called. Nicolas was not a man of the church, and if asked he would have said he worshipped no god. Nicolas Graves was a man of the sea and what he believed in was blood. And I ask you, what is faith but each man's belief in his own blood? Man is of sea and cloud, and like sea and cloud we are not long separated from the Lord. Each death falls like a raindrop into His great palm. Nicolas Graves worked the sea and he loved the sea and at sea he shall remain. So be it. He has rejoined the only eternity he ever believed in, the only eternity he ever sought, for he was blood and blood alone.

• • •

When people lined up at the casket to whisper their goodbyes Jonah slipped through the gate and the wet grass and sat in the truck with Virgil. Virgil handed him the bottle and Jonah drank. As he lowered the bottle he saw Osmond standing beside the casket with one hand where Nicolas's head would have been. Osmond watched Jonah.

The sonofawhore, Virgil said.

Osmond?

Who do you think?

Guess I don't see why the old man was friends with him and you ain't.

I don't trust the sonofawhore is why, Jonah. Same as ever.

Yeah, Jonah said and lit a cigarette. It was humid in the truck and the humidity smelled like nicotine. He rolled the window down.

Forget Osmond. This day's been coming a long time, Jonah. I'm sorry for you to go through this.

Coming ever since Ma died I figure.

That's right. That changed Nicolas something. That'd change any man.

I been thinking about her.

I know it. We all been thinking about her.

Not the Captain.

Captain Bill's been thinking on your mother more than all of us together only he's too chickenbeaked to admit it. That's why he's the Captain because he's a chickenbeak. Look at him with Osmond. Christ Almighty and hally fucking looya. Now the Captain's at Osmond Randolph's beckon. That ain't good.

Jonah nodded and watched the dark sky and felt suddenly that the sky was motionless as the hilltop graveyard spun.

And he done knocked up that little slush Erma Lee now, Virgil said.

Yeah, he done that.

Nicolas wouldn't take to that notion any more than I, Virgil said.

They watched in silence as Bill and Osmond lowered the empty casket into the ground. What'd he say up there, old Osmond?

He didn't say nothing that I know of, Jonah said. Said we're stuck between the flesh and the Lord and the ocean's a big puddle of blood.

Guess I agree with him on that.

The old man didn't love God no matter.

Nicolas didn't love much.

Guess he didn't, Jonah said.

Just lobster fishing.

Like loving a heartrot whore he always said.

Virgil grinned and nodded his head in slow agreement.

Bill came to the window and Jonah rolled it down the rest of the way and handed the brandy bottle to him. Rain blew over the cab and onto Bill's head and pushed his hair down like a bald spot.

Bill took a drink and held the bottle on the windowsill. His jaw was square and clean-shaven and his glasses were wet. You didn't have no last respects to pay our old man, Jonah?

Jonah didn't answer.

Christ, Jonah, said Bill.

That's just an empty box up there with Osmond Randolph standing next to it. You know as well as I do.

It still means something.

That what little Erma Lee been telling you? This means something?

She don't matter. It means something to me.

That's fine, Bill. That's good. It don't to me.

Well something better mean something sometime, Jonah.

You ain't my Pa last I checked.

I'm what you got, Jonah. Me and Virgil here. Bill put his hand on Jonah's shoulder for a second then took it back. Ride on down to the pound with me, Jonah. I'll drop you back here later.

I'll take my rig.

Suit yourself.

I aim to do just that.

Erma Lee crossed the grass and took Bill by the arm. Bill nodded to Jonah and Virgil and walked away. Jonah and Virgil sat in the truck as the rest of the people left the cemetery. Celeste and Charlotte came to the truck and Virgil rolled his window down.

You two will be along soon? Celeste said.

We will, Virgil said.

Celeste looked to Jonah then back to her husband. I don't know which one of you to worry about more.

Him, Virgil said.

Celeste nodded.

Osmond and his three grandchildren came through the cemetery gate last. Osmond closed the gate. He waited until

Celeste and Charlotte left then stepped to Virgil's window. His grandchildren stood in a row behind him.

Virgil, he said.

Osmond.

We will miss Nicolas, Osmond said.

Yes we will. Virgil lifted the bottle from the seat and handed it to Osmond. Osmond twisted the cap off and tipped his head back and took a long drink. He handed the bottle back to Virgil and their eyes connected through the wind and rain. A piece of Osmond's wet hair blew across his cheek. Osmond nodded and left.

Rain hammered on the roof. After a moment Virgil said, The Captain is fucked, Jonah.

I know it. What'll Osmond do to him?

He'll take over the pound is what he'll do.

Jonah shifted in the seat and said, The Captain's tough.

But he ain't smart like Osmond, you know as well as I do.

That night the wind swung around to the east and the sea piled into corkscrews that surged against the outside islands. The spruce and birch trees that surrounded Virgil and Celeste's house creaked and tossed their heads and lifted their root wads and each throw of air carried the smell of salt spray and rockweed and rainwater.

Jonah stood on the porch and smoked a cigarette and passed a bottle of whiskey with the other fishermen. He watched the trees lean and fight and he wondered which would fall first. He felt like an intruder in this house that was nearly his home and in the wake of this death that was his father's. He stood by his brother's side but found no comfort there.

The wind pushed the rain sideways and the eddy of porch air was a swirl laden with moisture and tobacco. A single light hung from the door trim. The food Jonah had eaten churned in his gut. He wondered where Charlotte had gone. He paid little attention to the other fishermen as they argued about lobster prices and diesel engines and reduction gears and after another hour he left without saying goodbye to anyone.

He stuffed his hands in his sweatshirt pocket and pulled his hood down to his eyes as he walked the long driveway toward the harbor. Rain drilled against him and soaked into his sweatshirt and dripped down his neckline. When he came to the road he stopped and looked around the dark village. There were only two dozen farmhouses and twenty of those farmhouses stood empty for the cold months of the year so the only lights Jonah could now see were the lights of his father's final celebration flickering and faltering through the rain and through the trees.

At home he sat at his kitchen table. His trailer rocked and the big spruce in his front yard rocked, too. He spun a scallop shell ashtray in circles across the tabletop. Rain beat the window and rattled the glass in its aluminum framework and he felt the bursts of wet air like screams. This line of storms each one had been followed by a humid stillness that swallowed the horizon and made the sea and sky merge into a single oblivion that did not belong on this bold cold-water coast. It had been eight days since his father disappeared. Eight days filled with boats searching the seas for a body and eight nights filled with Jonah bolt upright in his bed with sweat stapling his forehead like buoy patterns. On each of those nights the arcane dream-image of his father's lobster pound existing as some massive heart had surfaced in his mind and he didn't know what to make of the image and he could not shake the image from his daytime thoughts. In actuality the pound was nothing more than a cove converted into a tidal lobster storage facility but since Nicolas's death it had become synonymous with the man himself.

Another streak of rain and the water pounded like footsteps on his roof. Jonah didn't hear the truck but saw the sweep of headlights. His brother kicked his rubber boots off and came into the small trailer kitchen.

You got coffee hot?

I can, Jonah said.

Get it hot then. I guess I might need a cup.

I imagine that's so. She's blowing a gale.

Bill grunted. Guess ain't none of us fishing in this. Price don't matter if she's blowing too hard to fish anyhow. Hell, Jonah, the tide's right up overtop the wharf, higher'n I ever saw. She's lapping the bait house doors and liable to flood the whole operation. Fuel pumps and all are going under.

Jonah put water in a kettle and turned the burner on. Bill sat down and turned his hands together to dry them. He lit a cigarette. Jonah slid the scallop shell ashtray across the table then opened a beer for himself and he wondered when Bill would mention Erma Lee. He sipped the beer as the water heated.

Neither spoke.

When the coffee was finished Jonah poured a cup and handed it to Bill and said, Hell, Bill, Virgil done knew about her anyhow.

Well you don't see me squealing you out.

That's different.

Different because it's you is why it's different. And how'd Virgil know?

How you think Virgil knew? Same way Virgil knows who's gotta have a shit and who's got crabs and every other goddamned thing under this fogfucked sun.

He don't know one thing.

What's that? Little Erma Lee got twins?

No, she ain't got no twins. She ain't big enough for twins.

She ain't big enough for you.

I'll tell you what neither one you or Virgil knows if you shut your highliner mouth for a breath.

What's that?

The Downcoast Highliner is going into the lobster pound business with his big brother is what.

Like hell.

Like hell is right Mister Man. I know we figured I'd take his share in the pound and you'd get the camp, but I'm thinking on you and me going in half partners and we sell the *Jennifer* and you take the *Cinderella* once we get her back. Now don't you go getting ornery. You need a bigger boat.

I ain't getting ornery, Bill. And I don't need a bigger boat. And I ain't gardening lobsters in that mud hole and counting numbers in books and I especially ain't going in with Osmond fucking Randolph.

You always was good with books, Jonah. You're the Downcoast Highliner by Jesus. You can do any old thing. That pound is worth more'n twice what the camp is worth and so if we go partners with you taking a share of the pound, them numbers can work out. The price ain't shit but all we got to do is feed and hold some lobsters over the winter and by March the price'll be up.

That don't account for Osmond.

The hell with Osmond. We'll buy him out down the road.

The hell so. You got yourself a infant coming. You fixing on marrying her or ain't you?

Bill leaned forward and put his elbows on the table. He held his coffee in both hands. I don't know, he said. I just ain't sure what to do.

Jonah set one hand on the warm kettle. He wasn't used to seeing his brother confused. He said, That girl'll be the ruin of you.

That what Virgil said?

That's what I said.

Well she ain't like that.

The hell she ain't. Get rid of her.

Rid of her? You want me to run her offshore with a cinderblock?

Christ, Bill, you know what I'm saying. If you love her, good. Congratulations. If not, end it before you got ten kids, a pile of food stamps, and more cousins than you can count.

Bill stood up. You want in the pound or not? It's family, Jonah. Always been. We got sixty thousand pounds of lobster in there right now and next summer I'm rebuilding the dam and causeway and dragging that rotten mud out of her and everything. It's called fine tuning, Jonah. She'll hold upward of eighty thousand pounds next year.

It ain't my deal, Bill, and you owe the bank for them sixty thousand pounds.

Bill put his coffee down and stood straight and put his hands in his pockets. The pound's good protection, Jonah. It's security. The price'll change by late winter.

You'll be changing diapers is what'll change. Christ no I don't want in just like you don't want in with Erma Lee Carver or Osmond Randolph.

She ain't what you think. And I can handle Osmond.

I don't give a shit, Captain.

Bill stepped into his rubber boots and opened the door. A gust of wind filled the room and he pulled the door closed without leaving. I know it, Jonah. I know it.

Bill met Jonah's gaze and the two stood like that for a moment and within that moment Jonah wondered how his brother would survive without their father.

Bill continued, But I can't keep away from her is the thing. I think it's them pheromones you spoke of. She's got a full trawl of them.

I imagine that's so.

Bill shuffled his feet in the doorway. And besides, you ever seen a woman shaves down there, Jonah? It's smooth as a frog's belly.

Christ, Captain. Any woman can do that. That ain't just Erma Lee.

It's just Erma Lee for me.

When he left Jonah stood with his back to the door and listened to the trailer rattle in the wind. He was exhausted and wished he could lie down and sleep for twelve hours straight but knew that if he went to bed he'd be alone with the wind and the flexing trailer walls and his father's pound like a heart and he didn't want that. He wanted warmth but more than warmth he wanted time and he couldn't put his finger on why.

He finished his beer and opened another and another set of headlights pulled into his driveway. He peered out the window and saw Virgil's truck and saw Virgil flick his cab light on for Jonah to see who it was then it was dark again. Christ, he muttered. He pulled on a sweatshirt and put the hood up and his rubber boots on and took his beer outside. Virgil put the little dog on his lap when Jonah got in.

I figure this rain as the Lord shitting on Captain Bill, Virgil said. What'd he say?

What'd Bill say?

Yes, Jonah, what'd Bill say?

About what?

About Erma Lee. When Bill was here, what did he say about little Slush?

I guess he said she weren't slushy at all, Virgil. Said she was like a frog's belly is what he said. Fine as frog's hair.

Don't fuck with me, Jonah.

I don't know. I suppose he'll marry her.

Your old man would have laughed his ass off then beat the Captain's ass off. Hell, we knew you'd be trouble before you even come out shittin' and gettin' on the floor, but we had hopes for the Captain.

Guess I ain't been much trouble.

Not so bad as we thought.

Drove the old man a bit mad, Jonah said.

Virgil coughed and lit a cigarette and reached down with one hand and wrapped the fingers around Jonah's wrist. The touch was warm and comforting. Virgil squeezed hard.

Jonah kept his eyes on the pale and shaking hand.

That wasn't you, Jonah. You know that. That wasn't you at all. Virgil squeezed even harder then let go and sipped his glass of brandy and milk. He shut the wipers off and the rain streamed down the windshield. They sat in silence for a minute.

I got a favor for you is why I come by, Virgil said.

A favor.

I got four hundred new traps to sell you. You seen them in my dooryard.

You got four hundred new traps to sell me.

Five footers.

Hell.

Hell is right. You don't need to go clamming or some dumbshit notion. Old Nicolas would want me to instruct you on that. You need a new gang of traps is what you need.

I might go partners in the pound.

Virgil turned his head to Jonah. He scratched the dog's ears. Shut up, Jonah, I'm talking to you. I been thinking about you this night. Your gear's all shit and you don't catch half what me or Bill catch. You're not going into the pound. You'll get that new gang rigged and get you a sternman and you'll fish the *Cinderella* offshore with me and the Captain.

And Osmond.

The hell with Osmond. He's not fishing there yet.

He's all around you though.

But he's not on top of me yet, and he's not ever going to be on top of me. Even if he gets the Captain up his asshole, he's not fishing on me.

Jonah looked out the windshield at his trailer gleaming silver in the headlights. The woods around the trailer were a black wall of spruce and fir. The wind tore over the roof of the truck and everything shook and howled and Jonah figured it would be a quick relief to see his trailer ripped from its pad and flung like a dead gull against the tree line.

The Captain said the wharf's gone under.

Virgil nodded and waited.

Biggest tide he's ever seen, Jonah said.

We're not talking about the tide, Jonah.

My gear's fine and I got all the old man's traps if I want them. Hell, they're already set, just sitting out there full of lobsters right now.

You and me and Bill are taking them up soon's this storm passes. Christ. For a college boy you're not too smart, Jonah. Those traps are getting old anyway.

He done fine fishing. I don't need new traps.

You're not a businessman and you're not a highliner like Nic and the Captain, so you need all you can get.

What am I then? Jonah said. He watched the oil smoke from his furnace rise out of the chimney and flatten in the wind. He felt Virgil staring at him but didn't want to make eye contact.

Virgil sighed out loud and his shoulders drooped and his chin dropped. I haven't told you the deal yet.

There ain't no deal, Virgil.

I'm talking business.

I ain't a businessman. Jonah slumped in the seat and put one foot on the dashboard. He lit a cigarette. He wondered if the confusion he carried like a whirlpool in his gut was something he would ever rid himself of. He said, I don't know what to do right yet. I been thinking on moving out of this shithole and into the old man's camp. The hell with this beer can trailer.

Virgil emptied his drink and reached for the bottle on the floor between his legs. He poured brandy into his glass and pulled a gallon of milk from the floor and sloshed some in. He turned the windshield wipers on and the two watched the rain.

The price will go up, Jonah. I know things aren't right, not now they're not. Nic's gone and the price is fucked. The government's got their fist so far up our asses that I can taste their fucking cuticles. Bait and fuel cost twice what they used to. And the Captain's got Erma Lee waxing his dolphin. We're fucked, Jonah.

So what in hell do I need new traps for?

Virgil took a deep breath and expelled it slowly as though exhausted by the truth of what he was about to say. When he spoke his voice was low and soft. Listen to me, Jonah. This is important. You need to remember what matters here, what really goddamned matters. Price does not matter, not right now. What matters is who we are and what we do. Virgil tapped his chest with the rim of his glass. We got to hang down on her, Jonah. We got to fish hard. We have got to maintain.

I might dig clams.

Virgil shifted his weight in the truck seat. The heater fan ran. Ask Bill about it, he said.

Bill wants me in the pound with him and Osmond. Says we're gonna buy him out.

Virgil glanced surprised and frustrated at Jonah. Bill don't know shit.

Then why ask him?

Virgil put the truck in gear. I'll see you.

When's the storm passing?

Tomorrow. She'll turn around in the morning and blow north and flatten them seas. We'll have a day, day after tomorrow.

Jonah opened the door. You ain't said the business deal yet.

Christ, Jonah. He lurched the truck forward. Just come on and get the sonsofwhores out of my dooryard and shut your highliner mouth.

Jonah shut the door and put his hood up as he crossed to his trailer. He dumped his beer out in the sink and sat at the table. He wished his brother would come back. He sat for an hour then went to bed with a cigarette and watched the rain drip down the window and listened to the roof leak drip into his catch-pot in the bathroom.

Jonah fell asleep but shortly afterward a hand landed on his shoulder blade and the blankets slid back. The hand was joined by another and both hands pressed firmly and moved slowly up the back of his neck. Then bare legs straddled him and the warm weight of Charlotte landed on the small of his back. She tucked herself to him with her mouth beside his ear and both of her hands driven into his hair.

She kissed his neck beneath his ear and said to him, Jonah, wake up, Jonah.

He smiled with his face half buried in the pillow. He rolled his head enough to kiss her.

You have something to tell me, she said into his ear.

He smiled more.

I know you do.

She blew into his ear and moved her hands to his armpits and tickled.

You have to tell me, Jonah.

I don't know what you're talking about.

Bullshit, she said and she tickled and he rolled back and forth and pressed his elbows to his side to pinch her hands in his armpits.

I got nothing, he said.

Charlotte sat up. She flung her hair over her shoulder. A gust of wind hit and shook the trailer and shot over the roof. Charlotte ran a single fingertip up each side of his torso. Then two fingertips. She tickled. Jonah reached with both hands behind his back to stop her but he couldn't catch her fingers so he rolled quickly over and grabbed her by the wrists and held them tight. She smiled. A faint light crossed her body. He sat up and shifted her weight from his abdomen to his hips and pinned her hands behind her back so he could hold them both with one hand and with the other hand he traced his fingertips over her ribs. She laughed and twisted free and they stared at each other for a quick moment.

Tell me. You have to tell me.

He lay back down and landed his hands on her thighs. She wiggled but kept her spine straight. She looked down at him and her hair was a mess now.

Sounds like you already know, he said.

Know what?

Whatever it is you're asking me to tell you.

I don't know any such thing, she said and laughed. I don't know anything you haven't told me, Jonah Graves.

Who told you?

Told me what?

He lifted her up then lowered her down and she started to sigh but lifted herself and said, Nope. I don't know anything yet.

So you want to trade? Is that it?

Yup.

That's prostitution.

No it's not. It's espionage.

Espionage? Jesus.

He lifted her again and shifted. He saw her close her eyes and watched her neck bend and her chin lift. He sat up and ran his arms beneath hers and pulled her body tight to his.

• • •

Later. Jonah lay on his back with Charlotte's cheek on his breast and her fingers in his chest hair and one leg over his legs.

Are you going to tell me now? she said.

Christ, you know as well as I do that he knocked her up.

Who knocked who up?

How do you think it worked? Erma Lee didn't knock Bill up.

I just wanted to hear it from the source.

Jonah laughed. I guess I ain't the source, Charlotte.

Dad says she took serious the thing he poked at her in fun.

Virgil said that? What's he doing spreading that around for?

Charlotte lifted her head and rested her chin on his chest with her face to his. Just to me and Mom. He's excited about kids around here again. He says it's all old people now. He keeps talking about the old days when the school bus came down here and kids rode bicycles and jumped off the wharf and stuff like that.

And you go telling everyone what he tells you.

She pulled his chest hair. Shut up, Jonah. I do not.

Bill ain't going to be happy when he finds out Virgil's been telling everyone.

Everyone knows anyhow. You think Erma Lee isn't proud?

Jonah's fingertips traced her spine. I imagine she's just walking on water all over America.

She is, Charlotte said and laughed and put her cheek back to his chest and her hand on his hip. She's telling folks that he's buying her a sports car.

A sports car?

Yeah.

What in hell kind of sports car, Charlotte?

You know. A Nissan or something foreign.

Jonah shook his head back and forth. Well, he said. Your old man knows about us now, so might be that we're public knowledge too.

Charlotte rose and propped herself up with her elbow. Did he say something?

Gave me four hundred new traps is what he done.

So?

So that's why he gave 'em to me, I figure. Those traps are a hundred fifty bucks a piece.

Charlotte laughed and kissed him then slid her mouth over his nose and gently bit down. Good job figuring, Jonah. You think he's paying you because you're screwing his eighteen-year-old daughter? Charlotte smiled and pulled more chest hair. That's what you're figuring? You aren't too bright sometimes.

The wind rushed against the walls and the trailer shifted and Jonah cupped a hand over the top of her hip and said, I love you.

I love you too. But I'm too young for you. You need a girl your own age.

You'll be my age by the time we're old. When you're eighty I'll only be ninety.

She touched his cheekbone and traced her hand around his jawline. Are you going to be okay, Jonah? I'm worried about you.

I'm fine. I didn't know him that well anyways.

He tucked a flake of her hair behind her ear then set his thumb on her chin.

I know, she said. But he was your father.

Well there's not much to do about it now, is there?

I guess not. But I'm still worried about you.

I'll be fine. Bill's the one we got to worry over.

I know it, Charlotte said and her voice became loud and animated. It's crazy about him and Erma Lee, isn't it?

People get pregnant all the time.

I know. But it's different. I never figured on your brother knocking someone up, you know? He doesn't seem like the type. You, I'd believe that. I could see it if you knocked Erma Lee up.

I bet you could.

Charlotte leaned down and kissed him then went to the bathroom. He heard her piss and heard the toilet flush and she returned and dressed in the darkness. She sat on the bed and pulled the blankets up to his chest and leaned over him with the ends of her hair on his cheeks and said, Are you sure you're going to be all right?

Why don't you stay? I'll deal with Virgil if he says something.

She kissed him for half a minute then said, I can't tonight, Jonah.

T wo days later in the predawn black with a waning moon slung like an anchor in the south sky Jonah fired his boat's engine and the diesel roar echoed across the harbor. He flicked the overhead running lights on. The light bounced off the water. The point glow of his single cigarette moved about the boat deck. The wind blew cold and empty out of the northlands and knocked the high seas down but the broken waves still slopped and slammed against the granite shoreline.

Jonah wore his hood up and he flicked his cigarette overboard. This was the first time since his father disappeared that he'd been on the water and not searching for a body and it felt good. He'd grown up surrounded by talk of deaths at sea so had always known drowning to be a separate and feared form of death and it wasn't just the absence of a body to mourn over that made it so. Since his father's disappearance Jonah had wondered if what separated drowning from other deaths was the sea's claim on the human soul. He'd never been one to believe in the idea of a soul but lately he could not fight the feeling that some remote piece of his father now belonged forever to the sea.

His boat slid through the black water. A few houselights glowed in the small village but most of the coastline was dark land that pinched the harbor like a claw. To the south the open ocean lay empty and calling and every eight seconds the whistler buoy off the western edge of Two Penny Island flashed and seven miles beyond that the light on Drown Boy Rock made its 360-degree sweep.

The air was cold on his face. He tapped the brass throttle lever down with his knuckles and the bow of the *Jennifer* lifted and sprayed. He stomped his feet to warm himself as the boat rocked and pitched in the slop. The island called Ram's Head appeared as a green blob on his radar screen but as he veered westward the actual black island built of cliff and nettle rushed past not ten yards off his port rail.

He passed the red can whistler buoy off Two Penny as the sun wove like a stitch through the horizon. He heard static over the two-way radio then heard Bill's voice, Don't the harbor look empty without the *Jennifer* this morning?

Jonah took his microphone from the roll of duct tape he kept it balanced in. The radio was mounted overhead and it was covered in specks of fish grease. He thumbed the button and said, Guess ain't nobody with a brain would be enduring this for a buck fifty a pound.

Bill laughed into the microphone and Jonah heard the background rumble of Bill's boat *Gale Warnings*. I guess that's so, by Jesus. But I'm thinking this is the first time I ever did see the Highliner's mooring empty. Here it's December and you're geared up to hang down.

Guess I couldn't sleep is all, Jonah said. Or might be that Erma Lee's got you sleeping late.

That might be, Bill said. That just might be.

• • •

As the sun rose the sky and seawater turned blue. The quarter moon arced across the southwest sky. It took Jonah twenty minutes to reach his first traps and by then the moon had stepped and the sky had clouded with a dark bank that faded into the horizon. His boat lifted on its wake and settled. The buoys in front of him were all Styrofoam and the traps below the buoys were vinyl-coated wire but Jonah could remember a time when he and his brother had sat beside the wood stove in his father's trap shop and watched Nicolas paint his wooden buoys with an old brush and build his wooden traps with a hammer and nails. Those had been days of family and the smell of wood chips and fresh paint permeated his memories making them feel somehow gentle but all of those gentle memories ended with the end of his mother.

That was twenty years ago.

Twenty years since Nicolas threw Jonah overboard and hollered, *Goddamned poison aboard here is what you are.* Then pulled him aboard and hugged the boy to his chest while the boat circled and pounded upon its own wake. Nicolas shook and cried and that was the only time Jonah had ever seen his father cry despite a newly dead mother. His father's breaths came heavy and begrudging as if each one were a separate piece of gut that had to be grabbed and jerked from his throat. Jonah clutched the quaking back and stared at the gray water that danced against the hull and this final hug was a goodbye but Jonah understood the opposite.

Nicolas had set Jonah down and put a jacket over him. He hugged Bill briefly and put a jacket over him too. Then Nicolas pointed his boat *Jennifer* north to the harbor and piloted a straight line with the bow pounding an easterly chop. Jonah spent the entire hour forgiving his father but when they hit the harbor Nicolas was gone. He'd sealed himself away and Jonah saw this instantly. Just a kid and with a single glance he understood that his father had gathered himself into a coil that could never be unwound.

• • •

Now the *Jennifer* drifted on the smooth sea surface. Jonah lifted the cover from the bait box and peered in at eight bushels of salted herring. Some of the fish were stiff and some were mashed and all of the dead eyes stared red and loose at him. He breathed the bait air and tasted it like a wave of rot starting in his stomach and cresting within his eyes. He set the cover down and pulled a bucket of nylon mesh bait bags out and stuffed them with fistfuls of baitfish.

Thirty fathoms below lay an undersea badland that was nothing more than the foothills of an ancient mountain range gone to flood and erosion. The *Jennifer* idled and as he worked Jonah pictured the kelp forests and sand canyons below. He pictured his traps on bottom with lobsters and sculpin and wolffish all swarming like flies and so too did he picture his father's dead body down there. He carried a bait bag to the washrail and leaned his weight over the side and stared into the water. He caught himself again feeling that his father's soul was within that of the sea and now after so many years he felt the sudden urge to join him. He looked up at the flights of clouds and tried to laugh at himself and wondered what was happening within his heart to rally such thoughts because never on dry land had he felt such a sheer urge to be with his father.

● ● ●

Later that day and ten miles offshore. Two black and red metal Coast Guard buoys rode the shoal water waves. The water shone alabaster in the slanted end of fall light. His father's big yellow buoys lay on the waves like beacons between the metal buoys. Jonah stared at them thinking that one day soon he would not see those buoys on the water ever again and the thought made the sea seem somehow hollow. As a child before his mother's death he'd spent days and days aboard his father's boat with his eyes trained on the water in search of those yellow buoys. Then later when the *Jennifer* was handed down from Nicolas to Bill to Jonah those yellow buoys became a sign that his father had been there and would be there again. The buoys were footprints that made the ocean familiar and knowable. Now he and Bill and Virgil would bring load after load of Nicolas's traps ashore until all 800 of them were gone and all that would remain would be the relentlessness of wind and wave.

Beneath the buoys spread a stone-flanked seamount broken by canyons and fissures and pits. This was the Leviathan Ground. Jonah steered for his father's first buoy but his eye caught a flash of red that stopped him. He squinted. He waited. A wave train rose like flayed skin and when the train fell Jonah saw a red lobster buoy. His gut dropped. He watched over the sea until he saw a line of ten red buoys.

Osmond's here, Jonah whispered. He couldn't quite believe his own eyes but without thought he spun his boat and gaffed Osmond's first buoy and looped the rope over the stainless block and around the pot hauler discs. He gripped his gaff with his right hand and operated the brass hydraulic hauler lever with his left. The boat spun in a slow circle. Rope faked at his feet.

The buoy and rope both were clean and new and the stiff rope screeched through the pot hauler. There were two traps for the one buoy. They surfaced one by one with seven fathom of float rope between them. Jonah pulled each trap onto the rail with a full-body heave and stood between them with a hand rested on each. His boat idled. The traps were five feet long and looked like small coffins made of gray wire. They held bait bags the size of a man's head in both ends. The bags were still full and the herring fresh and silver. The traps must have been set only the day before but already they held a few lobsters each.

Jonah felt a nauseous stirring. His father's body was still lost at sea and Osmond Randolph had already set traps on the Leviathan and if there is one thing a fisherman does not do it is this. He thought of calling Virgil and Bill on the radio but decided against it. He pulled a glove off and spilled his pack of cigarettes onto the bulkhead. He pulled one from the pile and twisted it in his fingers while his heart pounded.

He ducked his head and lit the cigarette. He blew a pile of smoke out. He squinted at several boats working in the distance. What if he cut Osmond's ropes and tossed the buoys overboard and left Osmond's traps lost like trash on the seafloor? Then Osmond would cut Jonah's traps off and Jonah would have to cut more of Osmond's traps off and soon someone's boat would sink in the middle of the night and not long afterward someone would get shot.

Jonah looked at the water and said, What do I do, Old Man? You tell me. He was your friend.

But all Jonah could imagine his father doing was turning blood red in the face as he silently hurt somebody. Or sent their boat to bottom. Nicolas had been fishing the Leviathan since before Jonah was born and territory was lineage. Osmond knew that. Osmond was of the old guard so he existed by the old rules but the rules went both ways.

Jonah walked to the stern and back then tossed the lighter on the fiberglass bulkhead and nodded to himself as if finally agreeing with his own thoughts. His father was gone and he was here and to hell with Osmond. If he let Osmond fish his territory then he may as well not fish at all. He knew what Bill would do if he was here. He would cut every damned buoy that was not his own because nobody would fuck with Bill. But Bill was not here and neither was Nicolas. It was just Jonah and he spat and grabbed his knife from the bulkhead and he said out loud, Come on and get me, Osmond.

He worked his way down the string. He hauled each trap and cut the nylon heads open so the traps would not continue to fish. Then he cut each buoy off and tossed the mess overboard and he watched as lobsters and traps and ropes together disappeared to the deep. He'd never before done such a thing to another fisherman but never before had another fisherman tried to fish his ground. Of course he'd heard stories over and over again about trap wars with fishermen carrying rifles and shotguns aboard their boats and the sounds of gunfire echoing over the sea and this right here was how those wars started but whether Jonah was ready for that to come down or not he did not know.

• • •

An hour later he gaffed the first of his father's yellow buoys. He turned it in his hands like a quarterback would a football. The buoy was clean but the paint was slightly faded by sunlight and seawater and bleach. He tried not to think about Osmond so instead he thought of his brother but that didn't last long. He could have warned Osmond. He could have taken some time and settled the fuck down and maybe tied a knot in Osmond's ropes or cut out a few trap heads like a normal fisherman and thereby given Osmond a chance to move the traps.

But not him. Not Jonah Graves.

Jesus Christ, he said out loud. I did it now.

He'd destroyed nearly five thousand dollars' worth of gear and that didn't include Osmond's time or the catch Osmond wouldn't have. He tried to silence his mind and its fear as he worked his way around the Leviathan and he kept muttering, Fuck Osmond but that did little to reassure him. He stacked his father's traps aboard his boat and he told himself that his father would have done exactly what he'd just done but the more he thought about it the less certain he was and the more certain he became that he'd just started something he could not finish.

When he had a load of traps aboard he steamed north toward home and he kept saying fuck, fuck, fuck and he couldn't see any land except a single mountaintop which rose sprawling in the western sky as if to hold sway over the seawater and he wished something so powerful would hold sway over him.

Virgil and Bill in their bigger boats caught up with Jonah as he neared the coastline. Each boat was stacked high with Nicolas's traps and flocks of sea ducks like firecrackers burst from the water and flew before the boats. Together with the birds the three boats steamed into the harbor like a funeral procession with Bill in the lead and Virgil at the tail and the three men were silent on their radios as each thought his own thoughts about Nicolas and about the ocean which was different than it had ever been before.

When the boats were unloaded they trailered Nicolas's traps to the pound and parked in the small field that backed up to the marsh. A twisting section of tidal stream ran through the middle of the brown grass and beyond it stretched a thick patch of alder. The light faded and the sea lay flat calm in the twilight. A band of eiders bobbed in the surf and far offshore the clouds and sea fell to a deep blue and disappeared.

The pound was a three-acre body of water shaped like a horseshoe. At its head stood a causeway which at one time had been only a gravel bar but now held tons of blast rock that Nicolas had hauled from the upriver quarry. The causeway led to a small island called Burnt and causeway and island together formed one edge of the horseshoe. From the tip of Burnt Island a slat wood dam crossed to the mainland and thus closed the mouth of the horseshoe like a row of teeth. The tidewater came and went through these teeth every six hours but the lobsters that Nicolas and Osmond had put in the pound were there to stay. The base of the dam was solid concrete like a giant gum beneath the teeth that held at least six feet of water at low tide.

Jonah climbed onto the trailer and didn't speak as he handed the traps to Bill. Bill stacked them five high. Virgil watched in his mirror and pulled the truck forward when they needed room for another row. When they finished stacking the traps Bill and Jonah stood next to Virgil's window and listened to the engine idle as the smooth rolling waves whapped the riprap causeway and the ghost calls of the eiders filled the air.

Chowder rose up on her ass with her front paws on the truck door.

Frigging dog, said Jonah.

Virgil eyed the gulf. He played with Chowder's ears. Bill kicked at a rock with his rubber boot and when he freed it from the ground he kicked it across the dead grass.

Jonah gathered himself and cleared his throat. I hauled a string of Osmond's out on the Leviathan today.

Bill peered at Jonah for a second then said, A whole string? Oh, fuck me.

Virgil waited.

Five footers and double baited. He must've set them yesterday or the day before. Hell, he had to average three pounds a trap.

That's a hell of a day to set a offshore string, Bill said. She was blowing a gale and them seas would've been breaking over that mountain all the day long. Bill rubbed his eyes with frustration. How in hell'd he set them, from a chopper? Don't tell me he was out there in a boat. And I'm guessing them bait bags weren't small. Fuckachrist, that's a half bushel of bait per pair.

That's right, said Jonah.

That's over a grand a day in bait alone, Bill said. He's got to be landing a ton of bugs a day to make a day's pay. He's burning five hundred in fuel easy. How's he landing a ton a day?

He sold his soul is what he done, Virgil said.

Bill worked a glaze of moisture from Virgil's rearview mirror and flicked it off the edge of his palm. I don't know how he does it, the cocksucker. But he'd be better off with forty-three-and-a-half-inch traps on that bottom. A single parlor'll fish better there.

Guess not, Jonah said. The old man's strings didn't have shit.

Bill ignored him.

Where's he at on the mountain, Jonah? Virgil said.

Off the southwest ridge.

Bill blinked. He scratched his temple. You hauled them? All of them? Oh shit. What'd you do? Don't tell me you cut them.

Don't you go fretting all over the place with yourself.

I ain't fretting. What'd you do? Fuck me, you did, didn't you? You cut off a string of Osmond's? A whole string? Of Osmond Randolph's?

Virgil lifted a single surprised eyebrow at Jonah.

Jonah couldn't look at either one. He gazed offshore and his chest smacked and he nodded once so both understood what he'd done and both took a moment to realize the ramifications.

Goddamned right you did, Virgil finally muttered. He forced a smile onto his face but Jonah could see it framed by worry like a touch of sun surrounded by cloud and even as Jonah watched him the smile disappeared.

Goddamned right? said Bill. His voice trembled. Goddamned right? Now the two of you are going to have to explain to me one goddamned right thing about cutting Osmond's gear. You think he isn't going to start a fucking war over this? Jesus, Jonah, I know you don't give a shit about your boat or gear but I got to make a living for Christ's sake. I can't afford to lose any traps, let alone my boat or any other fucking thing. And Christ, Jonah, I'm his partner now. I got to work with him.

Jonah lit a cigarette. He glared at Bill. Well why don't you tell me what the fuck it is you would've done, Captain? Because what I should of done is stuffed Osmond's ass in a trap and sent him to hell and bottom.

You do that, Jonah, Bill said. His face was red. You do that. You dumbass. You been to college and you're so fucking smart so you got options but this is it for me. Fishing lobsters and now running this pound. I lose my gear or my boat and I'm done, Jonah. Finished. If I break my damned leg it's over for me. You get that? It's fucking welfare and coupons for me. I can't be fucking around in some trap war that your highliner ass started for no damned logical reason.

Jonah held his cigarette hidden in his hand at his hip and smoke curled from between his fingers. He'd only seen his brother scared once before and that was twenty years ago. A small gust of wind rippled across the pound and a pair of eagles circled far overhead. A single bright star popped out of the western sky.

Virgil cleared his throat but didn't speak for a few more seconds. He leaned over to the passenger side of his truck and came up with a bottle of brandy. He took a swig and put the bottle between his legs and in a voice strangely humid said, Settle down, Captain. You wanting to let Osmond fish the Leviathan, that what you're saying?

Bill shook his head no. But—, he started.

Don't *but* nothing, Captain. The Highliner might've been a bit rash out there but he did what he did and that's it. Now we deal with it. Osmond fucked up and he'll pay. He started this shit, and by Jesus we'll finish it and do it together, you got that?

It took Bill a while to answer. Yeah, I got that. But fuckachrist, cutting all his traps, Jonah? Holy shit. I didn't think you had the balls.

Yeah, said Jonah and he was tempted to say, *I didn't either*. Or, *I don't have the balls*.

Virgil twisted the brandy cap back and forth with the weight of his palm. Nobody spoke for several minutes.

Well, Bill finally said. I'm going on home to rest up. I don't want to be too tired when my boat gets sunk and my gear gets cut.

It will be all right, Virgil said. Just go on home.

Yeah, you got Erma Lee to tend, said Jonah. That's some serious tending. Not much rest there.

Bill stared at Jonah and his lips and nostrils quivered. Jesus, you started a goddamned war, Jonah, and now you want to make jokes? What the holy hell ails you?

Jonah started to respond but Virgil cut in. Leave it be. Both of you.

Bill shook his head from side to side.

Erma Lee staying down to your place? Virgil said.

For now she is, Bill said. Till we get this settled.

Settled? Jonah said. She ain't a debt, Captain.

I understand that.

Well good, Captain, Virgil said. Erma Lee might be a wild one but that ain't all bad either. I'm glad to see you doing what's right. Little Slush might just surprise us all. Celeste seems to have taken a fast liking to her, and Celeste isn't typically wrong.

Yeah, said Bill. She ain't what you two think. Maybe she fucked up some but who ain't fucked up some? Sure as shit us three have.

Clifford Beal though, Bill? That's a tough act to follow.

Fuck off, Jonah, okay? Case you ain't noticed, there ain't many virgins left on this piece of coast, and I really don't give a shit.

That's right, Bill, Virgil said. We've all got skeletons. But I'm curious about something else here. Did Nic ever give you any paperwork for the pound? Did he have a will or anything?

He didn't have a will, no. But Osmond'll have the pound paperwork. That'll be easy.

Easy? Virgil gazed out to sea before continuing. What'll be easy is for Osmond to pull your pants up over that head of yours and bend you over to doomsday. You think with him intending to fish the Leviathan and his gear all cut that he's going to do anything easy? Or even without his gear cut?

Virgil's voice was hard and that surprised Jonah.

I guess he ain't going to bend me over too easy. And wasn't I just saying that the fucking Highliner shouldn't of cut his goddamned gear?

Well if he does bend you over, Jonah said, just poke him in the eye, Bill. That'll get him off you.

Shut up, Jonah. You fucked up enough shit today. Bill paused as if catching his balance then they all three turned when they heard a red pickup ease down the two track.

The truck stopped beside them. It was muddy and the man inside was old. The window rolled down and the old man stuck his bald hatless head out and looked from one brother to the other and then to Virgil.

My goddamned friend Royal James, Virgil said. Imagine that. Just when shit can't get worse, he shows up.

Boys, Royal said. His face was red from a lifetime of wind and work and liquor. He settled back into the truck cab and studied the trap pile.

Bill said, You been egging?

Royal glanced at the truck bed where a dozen fish trays were stacked full of spiny green sea urchins. It smelled to Jonah as if the ocean itself were stuffed into the truck bed.

Royal rubbed his fingers together. Uni, he said and he had to push the word from his mouth. Then he continued. I seen you boys out there today and figured you was fetching loads of Nic's gear. I put my boat on her mooring, thought might be I'd come down and check on progress.

Royal paused and stared at Virgil as if to say something more to him alone but only his big ears rose up and down. He turned his look back to Bill. His voice was deep and sincere. I'm sorry about your father, Nicolas. And sorry I missed his funeral, by Jesus. I suppose the only funeral I ever do attend'll be my own and I'd soon miss that one.

It's fine, said Bill. Thanks.

Royal nodded again and put his truck in gear but held his foot on the brake pedal. He seemed to think for half a minute then spoke. Virgil, come on by the house tonight. I got something for you. Come on by.

I don't need any of your poached deer, Virgil said.

I ain't done that for years, said Royal. His ears twitched like flags.

Virgil nodded.

Royal's eyes focused straight ahead and he let his foot off the brake and did a slow U-turn.

That there is one odd duck, Bill said.

What'd you think he wants? said Jonah.

Hell, I don't know, Jonah, said Virgil. He probably wants company. But I kind of like the old coot, don't you?

He's odd, Bill repeated.

You think anyone who ain't you is odd.

That's right. Only two good things ever come out of this town. That road right there and me. We'll see you.

Bill got in his truck without another word and left.

Jonah picked up a rock and flipped it in his hand then chucked it at the pound but it didn't go far enough and landed clattering on the riprap. He rounded the front of the truck and got in. Chowder climbed onto his lap and Virgil eased the truck down the dirt road. Jonah rubbed the dog's fat belly and her hind leg drummed.

They drove to the end of the pound road then followed the harbor's eastern shore. Silence hung like a noose and Jonah struggled to think of something to say but he kept thinking about sending trap after trap to bottom.

The road went by.

I thought Osmond was a priest, Jonah said. That just don't seem to add up. Him being such a asshole and all.

Calvinist minister is what he was. But he gave it all up for a woman.

Jonah felt himself relax but could not have said why. What woman?

Laura was her name. She was married to his brother Orrin. Her and Osmond got together while Orrin was in Korea. She got pregnant and they had a daughter, then she died of cancer not too long after. Their daughter died of cancer too, but not till she had Julius and them two twin girls.

I can't imagine Osmond Randolph and a woman, Jonah said. Or a woman with him.

We're people, Jonah. We all fall in love and it might be with a rose or a pile of bait. Laura changed things for Osmond while she was around, but then she died and their daughter died. Osmond went off the deep end. Your old man was probably the only one who knew Osmond for sure.

Jonah wanted a drink and he looked at the bottle between Virgil's legs but didn't want to reach for it. He looked out the window.

You want a bubble? Virgil said and handed the bottle to him. Jonah tipped it back and swallowed the thick coffee syrup.

I don't know how you drink so much of that shit.

Like a gorilla, said Virgil. He pulled into Jonah's dooryard and stopped the truck and they sat silent for a long moment. Then Virgil spoke. His voice was hushed. I don't like this, Jonah.

What?

Virgil swallowed. The Coast Guard finds Nic's boat out past Spencer Ledges, but no Nic anywhere. Not tangled in some trap warp or floating or nothing. Then Osmond sets gear on the Leviathan? He thinks he can do that? He really thinks he can do that to us? I don't like this.

Yeah, Jonah said. His voice was noncommittal and Virgil didn't appear to have heard him.

I don't trust Osmond, Jonah. Something's not right. Something doesn't add up. Virgil took a deep breath and squeezed the steering wheel with both hands as he released the breath. Anyway, supper'll be on if you got nothing for dinner.

I'm just having a sandwich and going to bed I think, Virgil. Thanks anyway.

Jonah opened the door and climbed out but before he shut the door Virgil stopped him. Jonah, he said and turned his face so their eyes met. You did good today. Got me? The hell with Osmond Randolph.

Erma Lee was standing on the couch when Bill opened the door. She wore a tight pair of jeans and a pink sweater. She held a hammer in one hand and a nail in the other and she pounded the nail into the Sheetrock and missed. Half-moons speckled the wall. Sheetrock dust lay scattered across the couch cushions.

The room was different than it had been that morning. Pictures of her parents and grandparents and cousins and friends hung on the wall. All of the pictures were framed and most of the shots were posed with blue or gray backdrops.

By Jesus, Erma Lee. What're you doing?

Don't talk like that to me. She walked across the cushions with her feet in pink ankle socks and stood on the armrest and said, Catch me. She jumped and he caught her and with her came the smell that he loved. It was her hair or her skin, he didn't know which. She wrapped her arms and legs around him and wrapped her mouth over his earlobe and he felt a shiver in his side as she softly bit down.

He carried her across the room and put his lunchbox on the counter and glimpsed the pictures covering the refrigerator and the ornaments on the windowsill and the line of stuffed animals on top of the cabinets. She still had his earlobe in her mouth.

You been busy, he said.

I'm getting busier, Captain.

Seems so. He rested his hands on her waist and pushed softly but she didn't budge.

I'm a monkey.

You ain't a monkey, he said. He pushed harder. You know I hate monkeys.

You don't either, Bill. She kissed down his neck and around his jawline.

Down to Argentina they got guided monkey hunts.

No they don't either. You can't kill no monkey, Bill.

They got monkeys all round the equator. I'd like just to beat one once.

Argentina ain't the equator, and you can't beat no monkey, Bill. They're too cute.

They got bald asses.

That's a baboon with a bald ass.

I hate them too. He sat down on the couch with her on his lap and she leaned back so they could look at each other. What's that smell?

That smell is dinner.

What is it?

Erma Lee was small and her weight on his thighs was barely noticeable.

It's casserole, she said.

We just had casserole.

And we didn't finish it, so this night we got us a casserole made of a casserole.

A casserole casserole?

She nodded and smiled and wiggled. Her cheeks were red and her eyes dark and her hair curled down over her neck. Bill smiled as he looked at her and he put his hand on the back of her neck. She frowned and her chin grew a neat cluster of wrinkles.

Don't you like what I done with the house? Ain't it a home now, Bill?

Erma Lee, he started but didn't know what to say.

And I got more to do, but that's enough for today.

More? No more pictures I'm hoping.

That's my family, Bill, and you and them are going to be like you and Jonah are.

I don't know about that.

You will because we got a infant coming and my family's that infant's family. And speaking of family, I got a question for you that's been nagging, Bill.

I would imagine you do.

It's not funny, she said and her voice was serious and her face concerned. It's how come Jonah's called the Highliner when you say he don't catch nothing?

Bill laughed. He took his glasses off and wiped his eyes and shook his head from side to side. Jesus Christ, Erma Lee, he said.

What's funny about that?

He catches some. He does all right.

But why's he called the Highliner?

It's just a joke. Like calling a fat guy Slim or something. Jonah's just kind of lazy. He don't hang down.

Well don't laugh at me. I didn't know, she said and she paused and looked at him with her head tilted to the side. What? Ain't you happy I got moved in quick?

He put his glasses on and ran his hands up her sides. It's just that I didn't know you was moving in. I thought you were staying here for a bit. Like a trial.

A trial.

Yeah. Ain't that what we discussed? A trial.

Me getting knocked up weren't a trial, Bill. And this is a trial? I can't have a trial without feeling like I'm home or ain't nothing'll work.

Christ. So long as we're clear.

We're clear all right, Captain. But I got more news for you. Ain't you happy?

What is it? You done found that sports car you're buying with your mystery money?

No. I want for you to guess. She slid off his lap and dropped down to her knees in front of him and set her chin on his knee.

I ain't guessing about nothing. I guess all day on the boat and now I'll be guessing down to the pound and what I want is to come home and be damned sure about every damned thing in my house. If I ain't damned sure about my home then I ain't coming home.

Aren't you tough? She hissed like a cat and ran her pink nails across his cheek. You good and well better be sure about things, Bill.

Not with this guessing horseshit I ain't.

Well then I won't have you guess no more. That smell coming from the oven is a tuna casserole and a fresh chicken flavor mixed in for tonight.

Christ, Erma Lee, I didn't know I was guessing as to your casserole.

Erma Lee laughed to herself. There's other news too, she said and smiled at him. I made friends with Celeste and Charlotte today. Celeste was awful pleased with us living together.

All I said is we could have us a fucking trial, not that we were living together.

When you done this, she said and leaned back and jutted her pelvis out, when you done this you said a lot and if you ain't ready for it then tough because you got no choice now.

That? Hell. Bill ran his hands through his hair and breathed in and out to settle himself. Well I need some help feeding down to the pound.

Now?

Yeah now. Them lobsters'll eat each other before dawn.

I got a casserole in.

You always got a casserole doing something. Just put the fucker on warm, Erma Lee. I need help.

Fine, she said. I'm only here to help you, my liege.

What?

Nothing. Is Osmond going to be there? It's spooky you being partners with him, Bill.

Why's it spooky?

Bill pictured Jonah cutting Osmond's traps.

Why's it spooky, Bill? I heard he can dream things. Erma Lee lowered her voice and her head lowered at the same time so she looked at Bill through the tops of her eyes. She spread her hands across her cheeks like a child hiding behind them and said, His eyes get moving when he dreams and when he wakes up he knows everything we do.

Dreams things? He dream up the things you and me do? He dream that thing we done in the truck the other night? He dream that?

She hit him on the chest. Ain't nobody knows about that, Bill. Just you and me.

That's right, excepting Osmond who dreamt about Erma Lee Carver doing that. His eyes would've been moving like a tilt-a-whirl at the fair he dreamt that.

Erma Lee glared at him.

Hell, he'd want you for his own if he dreamt you doing them things you done with me.

That ain't funny at all, Bill. Not one bit. There's a line you're crossing and I'm not taking any of your bullshit. Just like Celeste said.

My bullshit?

Erma Lee nodded.

Bill thought it over and nodded and said, Fine.

. . .

The air was thick with salt and seaweed. A cold breeze blew across the harbor and the wharf light bounced on the ripples. The moon had yet to rise and the sky was black but shot with stars. They drove in silence past Virgil's house and past Jonah's trailer and down the rough pound road and parked in front of the building. They could see the dark mouth of the harbor on their right and the open ocean out beyond the Burnt Island causeway.

They sat in the truck with the radio on. They held hands with their fingers spliced. The wind was increasing and gusts of air drove across the Atlantic and rose over the island and causeway. The small trees on the island swayed and the pound water stood in rips like the curl of reaching hands.

I used to feed with the old man, Bill said. I been here only a couple times since he went. I suppose I could've got Jonah to help feed earlier, but I didn't. I just didn't.

Erma Lee pulled her hand from his and placed it on his thigh and squeezed. I'm sorry about your dad, Bill. I know you two was best friends too.

Bill rocked his head from side to side. The pound was dark but in the distance he could see the open shining gut of sea. It wasn't far across. Just through the mouth of the Bay of Fundy and there was Nova Scotia. On certain days when he was far offshore he could see a cloudbank hovering over Nova Scotia and sometimes the ocean wasn't that big.

Bill blinked. He remembered what they were there for. They got out of the truck and Erma Lee stood above the black pound water while Bill slid the pound house door open. The room smelled pungent and sweet like salt cod. He flipped a breaker and a series of overhead lights turned on. The building was twenty by forty and stuffed full of plastic fish trays holding 100 pounds each of cod racks. The racks were all that remained of the fish after being processed for fillets in the Canadian fish houses and they were dried and salted like jerky. Bill flicked a breaker and the floodlights outside illuminated the driveway and water and dam. Erma Lee stepped inside as he slid a side door open and they both looked across the pound water.

You ever been in love before, Bill? Before me I mean?

Bill took a steel rod with a handle on one end and a hook on the other from the wall and hooked a blue fish tray and dragged it loud and scratching across the dry concrete floor and out the door to the ledge above the pound. The tide was down and it was a fifteen-foot drop to the feed scow. The scow was an eight-foot-by-eight-foot raft with an outboard motor bolted to the stern. He tipped the tray over the edge and dumped the fish racks. The scow bucked and settled. He went for another tray.

Bill? I asked you something.

I know it, he said. He slid a tray from a stack six high and he hooked it and dragged it across the floor. I'm thinking, he said.

How much you got to think about that? I know you was with Bobbi-Jo for a full year or more.

Bill dumped the fish out and tossed the tray on top of the first one. So?

Well I'm asking if you loved her.

I don't know, Erma Lee, hell. Did you love Randy or Clifford or any of them boys?

That ain't fair, Bill. That ain't fair at all.

He stopped in front of her and held the hook with the fish tray in tow. Sweat trickled down his temple and he wiped it with his shoulder. Now you're going to have to spell out to me why that ain't fair.

They was just quick boyfriends. Not real loves.

So Bobbi-Jo Norton was a real love and Clifford Beal weren't?

I knew it, she said.

Bill dragged the tray outside and dumped it on the scow. When he turned around he said, I thought I loved her but I was a kid.

It was only a year ago, Bill.

I done grew quick. Now shut up about it and do something.

What should I do?

See that dark spot on the wall? He pointed. Where the knot's at on the wood?

Yeah, I see it.

Lean your forehead on it till I'm ready for you.

Ain't you gonna pay for that, she said and turned so red that he had to smile. She backed away as he approached her and when she'd backed against the wall her eyes darkened. She held her elbows out as he hugged her and she turned her cheek when he tried to kiss her.

I do love you, he said.

You better love me. You're a baboon about it though.

She watched him in silence as he dragged six more trays across the room and dumped them onto the scow. He grabbed a shovel from the wall and said, Come on down.

He climbed down the wooden ladder to the scow. He pulled the pin on the outboard and lowered the prop into the water and turned the fuel on and opened the air valve on the gas tank and choked it and pulled it three times before it started.

Erma Lee followed him down and stepped hesitantly onto the wooden scow. The stern sank and water came up to their ankles with both of them on it. Bill throttled the engine to keep it running as a cloud of blue two-stroke smoke rose around him.

Untie her, he said.

She worked the knot on the stern free and Bill left the outboard and walked with the shovel over the pile of fish racks and untied the bow. He pushed it off and said, Okay, you drive.

I can't drive this thing, Bill.

Twist the throttle and point where you want to go.

She twisted the throttle and the engine wound hard but they didn't move.

Hold on, Bill yelled. Hold on.

The engine wound at full throttle.

Christ, he yelled and climbed back over the fish and turned the throttle down. The engine quieted. Be gentle, he said, and he turned it partway. Like a car. You ain't got to have her in the bucket the whole time. Go slow.

We didn't go nowhere.

You got to put it in gear. He flicked a small lever and turned the throttle and they motored away from the wall.

Well you neglected that information.

He went back to the bow. Now just go slow around the pound and don't run her aground.

Where's the ground?

The fucking edge. Don't hit the edge. Keep her in the water.

Well I never got to drive one before.

You'll be a pro in a few minutes. He pushed the fish racks into the water a few at a time as they circled. They made one lap around the pound and he pointed her to the center and she steered toward a small lobster buoy. Bill set his shovel on the fish racks and stooped over and pulled the buoy out of the water. Small waves lapped over the scow edge. Everything was dark except the small body of water. Bill hauled up a big mesh bait bag and pulled it inside out. It was empty.

They're hungry, he said. He broke a few tails off the racks and threw the heads overboard and put the tails in the bag.

What's that? Erma Lee said.

He straightened. This here's a feedbag. When it's empty you figure they need fed. If it's full they still got enough to eat.

How many you got in here, Bill?

A set of headlights came out of the woods and stopped behind Bill's truck. Bill watched and from within the glow of the pound's floodlights he could just make out a black truck. It looked like Osmond Randolph's and he waited to be sure but couldn't tell. His heart raced. He thought about Jonah cutting Osmond's gear on the Leviathan.

That Osmond? he said.

Erma Lee turned. I don't know. It looks like him. Oh the Lord I'm scared of that man, Bill.

Let's finish this feeding, Bill said. Make another few rounds and we'll be done.

They finished feeding and as they motored back Bill put his weight on the bow to drive it underwater. When it dove he walked to the stern and the bow rose and a curtain of water rushed over the deck and rinsed the salt and flecks of fish flesh from the wood. When they got closer he saw Osmond step out of the truck and walk into the building.

Bill tied the scow to a pylon and Erma Lee whispered into is ear, I'm scared, Bill.

Jesus, he muttered as she climbed the ladder but then he looked up and saw Osmond silhouetted and looming as if stepping from the floodlight. He reminded himself that it was just that morning that Jonah had cut the traps off so Osmond could not know but that fact felt somehow irrelevant.

Erma Lee climbed slowly and Osmond reached his hand down and helped her up. Bill took a breath and climbed the ladder and straightened himself in front of Osmond. Osmond stood four inches taller than Bill and thicker all around.

William, Osmond said. He reached his hand out and Bill took it. Osmond.

You are picking up where your father left off?

I guess I been helping the old man feed these bugs long enough to do it. Bill hooked the stack of empty fish trays that were nested together and dragged them across the floor to the corner of the room. Erma Lee stood beside the scale.

William, Osmond said. He took a cod rack from one of the trays and turned it and smelled it and tossed it back. Your father was one of the few men I've ever respected.

That's good. Me too.

Osmond rubbed his hands together. I'm fifteen years older than he was. I've always assumed that I would go before he did. Do you understand?

Bill tried to hold Osmond's gaze but he felt hot and the room felt tight and pinched and maybe he did understand but he didn't know. He blinked several times. Understand what?

Just then the waning moon crested the waterline and shone through the single dirty window and cast a fray of light over

Osmond like a flare. Osmond's eyes held Bill. I haven't been expecting this, he said and moved his hands across a waist-high plain as if removing the creases from a sheet.

Me neither, Bill said. He wasn't sure what Osmond was talking about unless it was the Leviathan but he could not know about the Leviathan. Bill turned his gaze to the end of the building where large blue plastic feed bins held a ton of feed each.

Osmond took a step toward Bill. His face was lined with vertical wheals of skin that seemed to glow in the dirty moonlight. That feed won't last long.

The old man always done the feed. We been feeding a thousand pounds every two days so we got enough for another two weeks. But they'll slow down once this temperature drops, Bill said. He wiped a sheen of sweat from his forehead and looked at Erma Lee. She picked at a loose thread on her jeans.

Osmond's eyes followed Bill's to Erma Lee then shifted back to Bill. Has the insurance company contacted you, William?

What insurance company?

Osmond held his hands together at his waist. It was a long time before he responded. I believe you and your brother are due a settlement.

I ain't heard a thing, Bill said.

Let me know when you do. I will help if you need it.

Thanks, Bill said. I figure I can handle her.

Osmond's face softened and he settled on his feet. The Lord recognizes his own, William Graves.

The following morning and three miles to the southeast and just before dawn Osmond rowed his skiff with his three grandchildren in it through the ink-black water and rushing tide to his boat *Sanctity*. He lifted the twin girls one by one over the washrail. The boy Julius held the skiff as Osmond climbed aboard. Wind poured from the sky. The two little girls both wore hoods over their blond braids. They were half-asleep and he carried them below one at a time and put them in the small forward bunks.

Do you want earplugs in, girls?

I do.

Does Rhonda?

She never does. She doesn't care, Grandfather.

Osmond twisted a piece of paper towel and wetted it on his tongue and slid a wedge into each of Dolly's ears. He went to Rhonda. She was asleep already and he kneeled next to her and his hair fell along the sides of his face. Rhonda's chest rose and fell in quick breaths and a small gargling came from her throat. He stuffed the wetted paper into her ears and she stirred and wiped at his hands and at her ears but he waited with one hand pressed like a spade atop her chest and soon she slept. When he came up Julius was standing on the bow with the wind in his face. He wore orange oilgear. His hood was up. He was twenty years old and his skin was dark and smooth and an arrowhead patch of hair grew beneath his lips.

Osmond fired the engine and let it idle as he wiped the inside of the Plexiglas windows down with paper towel. He tossed the towels overboard. He nodded and Julius bent and heaved on the bridle and worked it over the bit and out of the chocks and dropped it overboard then walked down the washrail. He gripped the steel davit and swung himself into the wheelhouse and landed with a thud.

Soon you'll have your own boat, Osmond said.

Julius peered out over the running tide and chop. Yeah, and I'm gonna be the biggest sonofawhore lobsterman in all of America.

Osmond turned the circular windshield wiper on then shut it off. Watch your language, Julius, he said and turned the boat and headed through the mouth of the reach.

The islands were crow black in the morning. He cut inside a green Coast Guard buoy which flashed and groaned as they passed. The moon moved through the southern sky and somehow reminded him of Nicolas but then again everything now reminded him of Nicolas. In the distance he could see the lighthouse on Drown Boy Rock and beyond the lighthouse the last stars of Orion plunged into the sea just as Nicolas had plunged into the sea and Osmond reminded himself that one act was not separate from the other for both were acts of the heavens long since conceived.

The biggest in all of the U-S-of-A, Julius said again.

Listen, Julius. You are a strong young man now and you will have your own boat soon but you are still nothing on this earth. Look around you. Osmond spread his arms one to the sea and one to the stars. We are so small.

Julius rubbed the arrowhead of hair and said, My sled ain't small. Soon as she's splashed I ain't setting foot on this boat.

That's fine. Osmond worked the wheel with one hand as he stepped into his black oilskin barvel. But that won't be for another few weeks and God rest Neveah Elaine's soul I swore an oath to her.

I guess I'm raised.

You've done well, Osmond said. He veered east and ran along a line of spruce-covered islands rimmed with slabs of pink granite like foreheads. They passed Spencer Ledges and hit the open sea.

Julius chewed on his bottom lip. I got them lazy bastards working nights on my sled. She'll be done soon. Just buy them beer and they'll work.

Osmond glanced at the boy through the sides of his eyes and felt a rip of muscle drive up his sides and into his hands. He squeezed the boat wheel. Don't rush a boat like that, Julius. You won't get a chance for a new boat again soon.

I aim to get me a new boat whenever I damned well please, Julius said as he opened the stainless steel baitbox and peered into the twenty bushels of salted herring resting in their own septic grease.

You won't always have that kind of money.

Julius ignored him and pulled a plug on the baitbox and drained the blood and oil into a plastic five-gallon bucket and dumped it overboard.

• • •

The eastern sky lit an apron of clouds. Thirty minutes later the sun lifted from the water. The sea turned blue and clear. Julius stood stuffed tight to Osmond's side and Osmond stole a glance at Julius's serious face and the boy didn't scare him but the fact that he even thought of fear was troublesome. After Julius's mother had died and his father had left Osmond had adopted his three grandchildren. He'd rearranged his life for them and rebuilt his home for them and soon everything had become for them.

Osmond breathed the salt air. He held it in his lungs until they burned. He gripped the steering wheel tight and steamed offshore for another hour. There were no other boats on the water. Julius baited bags and piled them on one side of the baitbox and when they neared the first ten-trap trawl Osmond throttled back and went below.

Do you girls want to get up and help fish these traps?

They didn't move and he shook Dolly's leg. It was thin and light in his grip. He shook it again. Dolly? Are you alive down here?

She woke up and pinched the paper towel from her ears. The steady banging of pistons within cylinders filled the fiberglass hull.

You want to help fish these traps?

Okay. I'm coming but let me get Rhonda up too. Dolly rubbed her eyes with her fists and pushed the blankets off and woke Rhonda. Rhonda shook her head and wouldn't look at Osmond. He waited.

You want to help your old grandfather catch lobsters Rhonda? I'm too old to do it without your help.

The girl looked at Dolly with empty eyes.

Come on up here quick. We'll get you some cocoa to keep you warm.

Are there any whales out today, Grandfather? Dolly said.

No, not today.

I want to see one.

You'll see one again sometime soon. They've all gone on vacation, but they'll be back.

Osmond climbed the three steps back up to the wheelhouse and saw Julius holding the wheel in one hand and with the other hand he held the gaff over the side like a trident. Osmond watched the boy for a moment then stacked six fish trays into two piles. When the girls came up he lifted them into the trays. Their legs hung out as the boat rode the chop and swell.

That comfortable?

I'm cold.

You'll warm up soon, he said and spread their blanket over the both of them.

He took the gaff from Julius and set it on the washrail. He stared at the horizon and as he did so he felt calmness rising like warm water. He knew this feeling to be faith and he knew the ocean to be the only external source of faith he had left but nevertheless Nicolas dug at his heart. He breathed in and out with slow methodic breaths until he felt Nicolas rest.

Look over the sea, Osmond whispered to his grandchildren.

Look at what, Grandfather? Dolly said.

Julius leaned against the washrail opposite Osmond. He wants us to see the Lord out there is what. Same as ever.

That is right, Julius, Osmond said.

I don't see a thing, Julius said.

You must be still long enough, Julius. Faith is something you must learn and accept. Watch the water. Everything there is to know can be found on the water. Osmond watched the sea in silence for three full minutes then looked at his grandchildren and nodded.

He steered the boat to his first buoy and gaffed it and hauled it aboard. The rope coiled at his feet. The boat surged up and down and spiraled around the rising rope as if untangling it from the whirlwind. Julius stayed at the bait tub with his hands resting on its steel rim. The traps rose one at a time until he had ten lined on the washrail and Osmond ran his hand down the wooden runner beneath a trap and held it before Julius. The orange rubber glove was covered with dark stinking mud and crushed shell.

Do you see that?

I see that, said Julius.

You have got to understand the bottom you're fishing.

It's mud.

Osmond rubbed the mud around his palm with his thumb. It's soft mud and shell. No clay in it.

Julius nodded.

Tell me what that means, Julius.

Means if there's bugs there and traps there you might catch one.

We're in sixty fathom of water so soft mud means summer and early fall fishing, Julius. That is what it means.

Yeah, said Julius. 'Cept we fish this canyon year-round.

Osmond grinned and held a gloved hand in the air as if to silence the wind while he said, That is our secret. Lobsters like it here, and I cannot tell you why. That is something only the Lord knows.

Julius picked the traps and baited them and set them at the stern. Osmond watched his depth finder as he maneuvered over the narrow underwater canyon and he nodded to Julius and Julius pushed the first trap overboard as Osmond followed the canyon and one by one all ten traps pulled each other into the sea.

They hauled nineteen more trawls then steamed north and the coast rose like a black nebula disconnected from anything below. They ran for an hour before Osmond spotted the red and black metal buoys marking the Leviathan. This had been Nicolas's territory but Nicolas was gone now and here came fear riding the thought of Nicolas like a parasite and what had he done? *What had he done?* Osmond looked at his hands as if they alone had betrayed him but he knew they had not. He told himself that the death of Nicolas Graves did not belong to him any more than the life of Nicolas Graves had.

He focused on the Leviathan Ground. His eyes scanned the water for buoys he could not find. Slowly the fact that they were gone penetrated his thoughts. He slowed his boat to a stop.

What the fuck is this? Julius said. Where the fuck are our traps?

Osmond did not hear the boy. He stared at the empty water.

Dolly and Rhonda watched from their perches.

They cut *our* traps? Those sonsofbitches cut our traps? Julius said. The voice to Osmond held sound but no meaning and Osmond stared and his fists pumped and flexed then released and again and again until his arms and shoulders and entire torso pumped and flexed.

Julius saw this flexing and stepped backward.

Ten minutes passed.

Fifteen.

Twenty and Dolly looked to Julius wondering if all would be all right but she did not dare ask and he gave her no sign because he himself did not know.

Thirty minutes and the engine idled and Osmond reached down and lifted his gaff and in a single motion swung it like a baseball bat into the side of the wheelhouse. The wood shattered and the iron hook on the gaff's end hurled across the bow of the boat and skipped over the water before sinking. Julius bent his knees to brace himself and to duck what might come. Rhonda screamed. Dolly pinched her eyes closed and shrank into the fish tray. Osmond beat the wooden gaff handle against the washrail until it was only a pile of splinters littering the boat and water alike. He tossed the piece that remained in his fist overboard and grabbed a length of rope and worked it like a bullwhip over his shoulder.

With the first snap of the rope Julius moved to the open stern. One more step and he'd be in the sea. Rhonda screamed shrill until she was out of breath then began again. Osmond approached Julius with the line coiled around his fist like a boxing glove. Julius ducked and moved past him and tucked himself beside his sisters as Osmond stood alone at the open stern of the boat and uncoiled the rope. His hair fell in ravels. He braced his legs and paused for seconds then began to whip the tip of the rope against the surface of the sea until sweat rolled from his face and his frame slumped in exhaustion.

Then slowly and without a word to his grandchildren he steered the boat for home.

• • •

Now darkness. Osmond back on the water but alone this time. To the north he could see the lights of the harbor and in their homes slept Virgil and Jonah and Bill and one of them had cut his traps. Or all of them. He didn't know which and he didn't much care which. He steamed south over black water and rolling swell and as he steamed he felt Jonah Graves step into his mind as if into an empty room. He allowed himself a slight grin.

He'd known Jonah as a child when he and Nicolas had first partnered together but that was long ago. Jonah's mother had only recently died and Nicolas had been unable to deal with life after her death. He'd stopped fathering and stopped fishing and would have lost the pound but Osmond had stepped in with money and faith and counsel. Nicolas had not listened but their partnership had worked. The only explanation was that Osmond had lost a wife only months before Nicolas and so mutual but unspoken grief had brought and held the two men together.

Osmond flicked his overhead lights on and lit a fifty-yard stretch of water before him. Swell silver in the light slashed through his field of vision. He watched the numbers on his GPS and soon enough he saw the first of Jonah's strings. He throttled down and circled one of Jonah's buoys then gaffed it and dropped it on his washrail as the traps rose. He pulled the two traps in. The tailer trap was empty but the head trap held a female the size of his forearm with a cluster of black eggs tucked beneath her tail. She was green and black and her shell chipped and worn by too many fights and too many storms. Barnacles grew from her claws and bits of seaweed hung from her shell. She backed into a corner of the trap and lifted her claws over her head to fight and she curled her tail tight around her eggs.

Osmond paid her no attention.

Both traps were small and old and basically junk. Osmond took his knife from the bulkhead but paused before he cut the ropes. His body felt numb. He looked at the knife in his hand as if some unknown force had placed it there. His boat turned and rolled with its beam to the swell and the head trap tumbled from the washrail to the deck. Osmond thought of his cut-off gear. A shock ran through him. He lifted his leg and slammed his foot into the bridge that spanned the center of the trap and his foot broke easily through the old wire. He slammed his foot through again then again and pounded the wire and the lobster both until he'd stamped the entire cage flat. He stepped back and saw the egged female mixed within the breakage with her useless claws and useless armor and all of her now only a pile of eggs and meat and shell.

Without cutting any ropes he threw both traps overboard and shoved the throttle down full. The rope hissed as the boat and traps separated. The buoy and float shot from the washrail into the night. Osmond took the deck hose and washed the lobster remains out through the scuppers but the eggs stuck to the deck like gnats that he had to scrub away with his deck brush. He headed *Sanctity* south at full throttle. The engine surged and only a single time did he make a fist and raise it into the air and bring it down slow and silent onto the bulkhead as the name Jonah escaped his lips.

It was after one in the morning by the time he slowed and turned north toward home. He cruised at three-quarters throttle and let his eyes close for minutes at a time but each time he snapped them open when Nicolas or Jonah or Virgil or Bill appeared. He told himself this was not guilt but weakness but he could not explain where the weakness had come from.

At home he made coffee. He sat at a wooden table in the dark. He watched the working of the sea through the sliding glass door. He wondered what they knew. He imagined crows circling the near distance. He waited.

Celeste woke when Virgil pulled into the driveway. She rolled over and looked at the clock. She heard the front door open and close and she heard the gentle creak of the railing as he pulled his body up the steps. She closed her eyes when he entered the room. She smelled seawater on him and sensed a presence that she could only equate with death but what it meant she had no idea. She tried to swallow the ink-like taste that suddenly trickled down the back of her throat but her tongue had gone dry.

Virgil showered then sat in the chair beside the bed and she heard him pause and lean back. She listened to his breathing heavy through the darkness. After a while she could tell that he was trying to match the pace of his breaths with her own which was something he did when he could not sleep as if her calmness could transmit to him through patterns of lung and air. But now his breathing ran askew and he quieted and if she had looked at her husband she would have seen him close his eyes and she might have known that he wanted only to listen as her breath filled his chest.

Celeste opened her eyes. The faint light from the sea beamed through the window and lit her gray hair. She didn't move but she felt Virgil's eyes on her. She swallowed the ink taste and said, Go on and tell me, Virgil, since I'm awake.

He didn't speak.

Virgil, tell me. It's after one in the morning.

Virgil quietly clapped his hands together. As he rubbed them Celeste heard the scraping of his rough skin. She sat up and leaned against the headboard and let the sheet and blanket stay at her waist. She wore a white nightgown that absorbed the sea light. She saw the silhouette of her husband's forehead and cheek and nose and jaw and she tried to fight the impression that he was returning from someplace horrible.

He moved naked into the bed beside her and their arms and hips touched and she shuddered involuntarily and for the first time in over thirty years of marriage she found herself wondering who her husband was. Or what he was capable of. She didn't know what was giving her these impressions and she didn't know why her skin felt like a layer of cold wax had suddenly cloaked it.

You're frozen, she said and covered him with the blankets. Oh God, Virgil, are you all right? She rubbed his bicep with both hands and looked him over in the blue moonlight. Are you okay, Virgil?

Finest kind, he said but he shook and he did not stop. He rubbed his face with both hands. His words were slow and frigid and they scared her. Just been up visiting with Royal.

Visiting with Royal and what?

I'm scared, Celeste.

She dug her nails into the loose skin on his arm as if to awaken him. She swallowed more ink and kissed his cheek then shifted her face into his field of vision and said, Scared of what?

I don't know. That's it—I just don't know. Jonah cut a string of Osmond's gear off. Out on the Leviathan. But that's not it. Something's gone wrong.

What do you mean something's gone wrong? Your best friend died, that's what went wrong.

Not that. Something just ain't right, Celeste. It doesn't add up. Nic dying like that, and now Osmond trying to fish the Leviathan, and Jonah cutting him off. It's just not right.

Do you need help? What were you doing with Royal James?

Riding around, Virgil said but as he spoke he looked at his own hands as if surprised to find them empty.

Celeste pulled the covers to Virgil's throat and rubbed his arms then leaned back so her head touched the wall. Her eyes remained wide open. She said, Is there anything I can do?

Virgil coughed.

Oh God, Virgil, she whispered again and she put her hand on his thigh and he covered it with his own. You're shaking, and you're freezing. Do you need a doctor? What happened, Virgil?

Nothing happened. I can't make sense of it.

You can't make sense of what?

This.

This is madness, she whispered.

Trust me, he said. Just trust me.

An hour passed in silence. Then Celeste rolled over and without opening her eyes said, What have you done?

I'm not sure, he said and his voice creaked. He took a moment to try to compose himself but he could not. He continued, I can't tell you yet. I can't, Celeste. Just not yet.

She wrapped her arms around him and laced a leg between his legs and his entire body felt cold and wet. She spread her hand over his back and gripped the skin and she opened her mouth over his shoulder and she stared at the wall.

harlotte noticed the flower as soon as she stepped out of the building. She glanced from side to side. The wind pressed a tuft of her hair beneath her jaw and she rolled her head to free it. She crossed the parking lot and other students dodged around her and climbed into their cars but she paid them no attention. The flower was tucked beneath her windshield wiper in the same way they all had been. She'd counted seventeen flowers in the last two months and they never came with cards and at first she'd thought they were from Jonah but one day her friend saw Julius Wesley pull into the parking lot and slip a flower onto her windshield. That was number five. Julius hadn't called her until number twelve but she doubted he'd kept count and she'd learned by then that the flowers came only on bad weather days when he wasn't on the boat. By the time he called her she'd already begun listening to the marine forecast before bed. When she'd once lain awake dreaming about Jonah she now thought about this boy Julius and listened to the forecast and silently hoped for the winds that would bring another flower.

She paused and looked at the flower for a moment. It was a white rose just like all of them. She'd done the research and it was a forty-five-minute drive to the nearest store that sold white roses. That was an hour and a half of driving when he could have bought a red rose at the local grocery. She let her book bag slide to the pavement and she lifted the wiper enough to release the flower but this time there was a small white card folded around the stem. She opened it and read the one line and smiled and bounced once on her toes. She read the line again and pocketed the card. With two fingers she held the flower beneath her nose and closed her eyes as she breathed its scent.

• • •

An hour later she pulled into Jonah's driveway. She went inside and Jonah was at the table. She crossed the kitchen in a few quick steps and sat with her jacket still on and her small purse in her lap. Darkness gathered like a swarm through the windows. She stared tight-lipped at him. I'm sorry about not staying longer the other night, she said.

It's fine.

She looked down at her purse and picked at her nails then flicked her eyes back to Jonah. I might be leaving, Jonah.

Leaving?

For college.

I know.

No you don't. I got a letter yesterday. I was accepted early to one in Idaho.

Good, he said. That's good. Congratulations. He got up and took a beer from the refrigerator and opened it and drank down half of it before sitting back down. He lit a cigarette and said, You don't look too overly enthused.

Neither do you.

I been to college already.

Well I'm excited about going, Jonah.

You don't look it.

Are you going to give me a beer?

He nodded and got up and gave her one. He watched as she took a sip.

Jonah, I don't know what to do.

He leaned his head forward and ran his hands through his hair. Do whatever you want, he said.

She rotated her beer can on the tabletop. I don't know what that is.

He waited.

I don't think we should keep going, Jonah.

Okay.

She waited and he didn't say anything else. Is that it?

I don't know what else to say right now, Charlotte. I'm sorry.

Can't you say something? Jesus.

I got nothing to say, he said. I hope you do well.

She took another sip of her beer and he stared at her small hand on the can and in that instant he wished she would just go. For a moment he wished everyone he knew and loved would just go.

She stood up. She held her purse against her stomach. I'm sorry, Jonah. It's not easy for me either. I love you but I'm graduating and going to college. I want to be happy about that.

You should be.

Her eyes dulled and the lids closed slightly. You were the one that kept telling me to apply to colleges. I wanted to stay here.

I know it. He flattened his hand on the table then lifted it a few inches and swatted down as if to kill a fly. When he spoke his voice was quiet the way it was late at night. I know it, Charlotte. That's good. I'm proud of you.

She stepped toward him. Are you okay, Jonah?

Fine. I'm fine.

She rounded the table and set her purse down then took his head in both of her hands and turned it so he faced her. His face was pale. She bent down and kissed his lips and said, I'm worried about you, Jonah. You seem so—I don't know. Cold or angry or something.

Imagine, he said.

She held his cheeks in her hands. She blinked. Look at your brother and Erma Lee, Jonah. I don't want to be like that.

They're happy.

She's not happy. Me and Mom went and saw her the other day and she was sitting in that house all alone bawling her eyes out. That's not happy, and I wouldn't be either. And neither would you. I love you, Jonah, but I'm going away and that's that.

That's that, Jonah repeated and as he heard his own words cross the room like a pair of flies he felt something inside him tamp the sadness down like dirt. Charlotte still stood in front of him with her hands on his shoulders. He gripped her thin wrists. He felt bones. He slid his hands along her arms and shoulders and down her rib cage to her hips. Then he pulled her forward lightly but she braced herself and stared down at him. He forced a grin. He unzipped her jacket and spread it open and lifted the side of her shirt to expose the top of her hip. He leaned his head in and kissed the skin.

Jonah, she said.

He reached up and worked her jacket from her shoulders. It dropped quickly to the floor. Her hair hung past her cheeks and shrouded her face. Her eyes were narrow and dark.

Jonah, she said again.

Jonah leaned back in his chair. He crossed his legs at the ankles and lit a fresh cigarette. What? he said.

She straightened her shirt and straightened her hair and lifted her jacket from the floor. She faced him and said, Please, Jonah. Don't.

He reached out and rolled the ashes from the tip of his cigarette onto the edge of the scallop shell ashtray then abandoned the cigarette and stood. A twist of smoke cut the air. He cupped his left hand around the back of her neck and after a pause with their eyes locked together she took a step to him. She closed her eyes and so did he. He pressed his lips softly against her forehead.

• • •

He stood in the window and watched her walk away. He felt a fist in his chest clench and he took his breaths one by one as if reminding himself to do so. He watched until she was gone and he watched until it was full dark hoping she'd reappear but he knew her too well for that. In his cupboard he found a half bottle and he took one quick swig then went out the door. He walked slowly to the wharf. Two trucks passed him and the fishermen waved at him but he didn't wave back. He kept one hand in his pocket while the other held the bottle tight to his hip and there seemed to be yet a third hand still clenched fast in his chest.

Aboard his boat he fired the engine and idled his way out of the harbor with his running lights aglow. He held a course due south. He sipped the whiskey. He passed Ram's Head and Two Penny without a glance and continued on through the up and down of the sea and into the smooth black darkness. Slowly as the few scattered lights of the coastline dimmed behind him he tapped the throttle lever down and the boat lifted to a plane and disappeared into the night.

He drummed the bottle against the bulkhead. He did not look back for a long time and when he finally did he could see no lights at all. He continued on and swallowed more and finally when his knees began to feel the warmth he reached down and turned the key off so the boat rose atop its own running wake and came to a lurching halt. Everything fell silent save for the last tumble of the wake which dissipated fast. He stood there at the wheel and looked at black sea and sky all around him. After a moment he swung his legs over the side and sat on the washrail and faced the sea as if facing the long void of his own future.

He took a final haul off the bottle and threw it and watched it glint through the starshine then heard it splash. He lit a cigarette. His entire body quivered with fear but what exactly he was scared of he wasn't sure. He leaned forward and squinted at the water and whispered as if the wrong person might hear, Fuck you, Dad.

Then leaned forward a bit more and felt a line which all he had to do was teeter over and he'd plunge headfirst into the water. He leaned back to safety. Then forward and he hit the line and felt a rush of solidity. His father was gone and Charlotte was gone and he'd started a trap war with Osmond Randolph and Virgil and Bill may as well be gone and what else was there? Only the line and the water beneath the line.

He leaned forward again and the sky swung and the water felt close and concave in the darkness. The davit for his pot hauler hung beside his head for him to hold on to but he did not. He only leaned into that line across which lay the same cold waters that held his father. He stayed there for full seconds willing and uncaring with his boat beneath him riding up and down on each piece of swell.

Then shut his eyes and fell.

The noise of the water around his ears shocked him awake and the cold came next. His clothes and rubber boots were heavy and his boat loomed above him silent and still with its old chips and grooves from thousands of traps banging against the hull on their way up from the seafloor. But he himself was on his way down. The story of an old-timer falling overboard flashed through his mind. The man's wedding ring had caught a screw head on the splash rail and there the man had dangled until someone heard his shouts. But that was in the harbor. Jonah was out here alone with no wedding ring to save him and the side of his boat came up and down and he grabbed but could not reach the gunwale and there was nothing else. He was not frantic but the cold was biting deeper and his teeth felt brittle beneath his jaw's tight lock.

The gunwale rose on a wave then dipped and he reached and missed and the next time he nearly got it but his hands were too cold to hold. Again and nothing and one more time because that was all he would have. This time he locked a single row of fingertips onto the brass coaming. He gripped and his hand tried to betray him but he held and the boat rocked and lifted him out of the water to his thighs then dunked him again. On the next rise he got his other hand up and he dunked then pulled and got his chest over the washrail and there he locked his elbows and hung his head into the boat and breathed.

Once in the wheelhouse his fingers would not turn the key. His entire body shook as if somebody's angry hands were upon him. He slammed open the door and dropped below and pressed his hands onto the engine block. He could not tell if it was too hot or not but he heard no skin sizzle so held his hands there despite. Finally his hands began to ache then burn and as the pain ran up his forearms he was able to pull his wet clothing off. He started the engine and went back below and stood naked in the small space and the bright light with oil and tools. The engine chugged and banged all around him. He found a dirty sweatshirt and a pair of oil pants but that was all. He put them on and stayed below with the noise of the engine loud but all of his thoughts and fears stunningly silent.

· · ·

He went that night to his father's camp. He was too cold to start a fire but buried himself in the old bed with piles of wool blankets.

He lay on his side with his hands between his thighs. His entire body shuddered. From time to time the trembling slowed enough for him to wonder if he would survive and to wonder at what he'd just done out there on the ocean. He knew he had not meant to go overboard but the fact that he hadn't cared one way or the other shocked him. He gripped his hands together. He trembled and cried.

• • •

The camp was a single-story cedar shake cottage with a wood cookstove and a small bedroom. Propane lanterns lined the ceiling and a propane refrigerator rusted in the corner. A water line ran from a boiling spring into a soapstone sink and when the ocean was calm the smooth overflow of spring water filled the air.

The camp sat perched atop a slab of pink granite ledge at the end of the peninsula. A mile-long skid road led east along the southern edge of the peninsula from the pound to the camp but the path was overgrown and rarely used. A small cove shimmered below and spruces towered above. Stone Island protected the cove from wind and surf but the height of the ledge enabled Jonah to see overtop the island and far out to sea. In the morning he searched through some of his father's things and was surprised to recall that his father had bought the pound and built the camp after Vietnam.

The previous night echoed in him like a distant memory but no matter the distance it still shook him how close he'd been to the end. He told himself that he'd been drunk and that tale worked only in increments because like a blade came the truth to his chest that for a moment he'd not cared what happened out there.

• • •

Later that day he moved some of his things by boat into the camp. He started a fire in the wood stove and waited as the flames caught and grew. His father's old Winchester 30.06 hung from a nail on the wall and he took the rifle down and turned it in his hands. It smelled of oil. The stock was scratched and gouged but worn smooth. He opened the bolt and it was empty so he closed it and sighted out the window at a rock on Stone Island. He dry fired once then hung the rifle back from the nail.

He fed the fire and unpacked his things then took two bottles of beer with him to the wharf and sat on the end with his legs dangling. He watched the cool flight of gulls above Stone Island. The *Jennifer* was moored in the small cove before him. The water was clear green and he could see the shadow shapes of boulders and the tall sway of old growth kelp. In the warm months those kelp beds held fleets of lobsters living lives built on an ancient and simple pattern. In the fall the lobsters fled the icy inshore waters for the relative comfort of the offshore depths. Then returned in the summer as the shoal waters warmed and in those warm shallows they dug their mud caves and shed their old shells only to emerge new and soft and vulnerable. These migrations were huge and the seafloor would seethe as the lobsters fanned like cavalries across open flats then piled atop each other to enter underwater corridors or skirt mountainsides and anything that was in their way was either food or not food and all they did was fight to eat and fight to breed. Fight to live and fight to die.

That night Jonah lay in his father's bed listening to the waves touching the rocks and the distant grinding of the sea. The bed smelled like his father even though he'd changed the sheets. The smell was Nicolas despite the fact that Jonah couldn't remember his father ever smelling like anything but lobster bait and diesel fuel and cigarette tobacco. And occasionally bourbon. Now this familiar and strange scent made him feel suddenly close to a man he'd thought in many ways to be a stranger. In that smell he was six years old again and it was a good feeling but not one he was ready to surrender himself to.

He ran his hands over his face and blinked in the darkness. He thought of armor and claws. He thought of underwater caves and of shedding a shell. He reached to the bed stand and searched for his cigarettes. He knocked one out onto his bare chest and dropped the pack onto his stomach and reached for the lighter.

One week later. Julius Wesley stood at the boat landing with the wind blowing the water into breaking curls that piled against the steel pylons. The sky was blue and trains of clouds rode the offshore winds. Julius's sisters stood one on each side of him. He held their hands. They both wore dirty pink jackets with the hoods down and their braids hanging. Dolly wore a small backpack and from time to time she looked up at her big brother. Osmond stood next to them with his oiled hair tucked behind his ears. He was a head taller than Julius.

The truck and trailer carrying the new 42-foot boat *Dolly Rhonda* turned in the parking lot and backed down the slick pavement. Julius and Osmond and the girls walked up the galvanized float ramp and Julius ran his hand over the mirror black gel coat on the boat's hull. Osmond eased a stepladder from the bed of his truck.

This sure is big, said Dolly. It's beautiful, Julius.

They stopped at the stern. I know it is. And so are you two. Here are your names, right here, he said as he traced his finger over the white letters.

That's us, Dolly said. Do you see, Rhonda? It says, *Dolly Rhonda*. You and me.

Rhonda stared openmouthed at the stern.

Can we fish with you? Dolly said.

No, he said. No you two better keep fishing with Grandfather. He needs your help. You're his new sternman, aren't you?

Dolly nodded uncertainly.

We'll see, Osmond said as he propped the ladder against the boat. You better get aboard.

You coming? Julius asked him.

We're coming, Osmond said. But you go first.

Julius adjusted the ladder and climbed aboard the boat and ran his hand over the bulkhead. He smelled fresh fiberglass resin. He leaned over the washrail and Osmond handed the girls up one at a time then climbed the ladder himself. He began to pull the ladder up.

Don't bring that aboard here, Julius said.

Osmond stopped.

I don't want that up here.

Why not?

I don't want shit like that aboard is why.

It will be fine, Julius.

Just throw it, Julius said.

Osmond shook his head and swung a leg over the rail and climbed down the ladder and carried the ladder to his truck. Julius watched him for a moment then went to the wheel. The truck lurched and the boat backed down into the water. Bubbles seethed from the hollow trailer frame and the wheels slowly disappeared underwater. The truck stopped and the driver climbed out of the truck and took a control box from its mount. Julius felt the boat drop into the water as the driver worked the individual hydraulic lifts. Each lift made a loud mechanical whir. When the boat was afloat Julius turned the key and the big diesel roared and he smiled at Dolly and she smiled back.

It sounds like thunder, said Dolly.

Seven hundred and fifty horses beneath our feet is what that is. John Deere power.

Oh, said Dolly.

Osmond sat in his truck with the heater running. His daughter had been dead for four years and he'd held her hand in the hospital bed and he'd sunk to the bed and wrapped his arms around her as she died. Her name was Neveah Elaine and she had trusted her father to die for her children but Julius was something beyond him. He rolled the window up and watched as Julius eased the boat up to the float and gaffed a rope. Dolly climbed out and stood on the steel grate float and waved Osmond down. Osmond didn't move. Then Julius leaned out and Osmond saw that the boy's face was red and could not tell if it was happiness or sadness or pain but he opened the door and walked down the float and got on the boat.

Too bad Pa ain't here, said Julius.

Yes, said Osmond. He put his hand on Julius's shoulder and gently squeezed the muscle and sinew. You should be proud.

I ain't proud. I got no time for that.

Osmond lifted Dolly and Rhonda onto the shining stainless steel baitbox so they could see out the windshield. He turned back to Julius. You can stay at the house, Julius. There's the mooring there for you.

I got a mooring going in today.

I know you do. But so you know.

I don't need a thing but this boat.

Fine, Julius. But you're always welcome.

Julius revved the engine and pulled away from the float and eased her up to speed as he crossed the bay. Thunder, he said to Osmond with a grin. I sound like thunder.

Jonah stayed at his father's cabin on the end of the peninsula. His head slowly began to clear. Each day the moon rose after midnight and set after dawn. The loud ocean silence descended upon him and that silence felt good. He spent long periods of time watching the sea and its curious combination of motion and stillness. The clouds drifting overhead had the same quiet movement and he wondered why humans after thousands of years of studying sea and cloud had not learned such lessons.

One night while sitting on the end of the wharf with a scattering of constellations rising over the waters and his feet dangling above those same waters it occurred to him that with this move he'd done something nobody had expected him to do. It was a simple realization but for Jonah it had been a long time coming. This was the first time in as long as he could remember that he'd made a decision and done it despite what Virgil or Bill or Charlotte or anybody else said. Even an action as rash as cutting Osmond's traps had been done in part out of the mistaken certainty that those he respected would have wanted him to do so. Then he'd nearly died out on the water when in reality he'd wanted the opposite of death. He'd wanted to feel something and perhaps he had. Perhaps the waters had changed him. He'd packed his things and moved to the camp and it didn't make sense because he should have stayed home and talked to Charlotte and it didn't make sense because winter loomed and he would be so alone but moving was something he wanted and something he needed and it was something he did.

• • •

It had snowed wet and heavy the previous night and through that day. Six inches of slop covered the ground. Now the snow quit and the sun set and the coastline went red and fibrous as open flesh. Jonah heated a basin of water and carried it barefoot outside and dumped it steaming over himself in thick lava-like surges that melted a circle around his feet.

Back inside he dressed. He paused at the window as the sun dropped over the horizon. The chain of islands southeast from Mason's Island to Spencer Ledges dropped black and the sea dropped black but far off in the west beyond Two Penny and Drown Boy Rock and beyond the line of coastal mountains remnant shreds of sunlight clung to the earth rim. A final blood-red surge flushed over the darkness.

He pictured Charlotte. The strips of muscle on the back of her neck. The black curls of hair that he used to tuck behind her ear. The gentle rasp in her voice and the cluster of freckles like a constellation on her shoulder and as the spruce fire crackled he was reminded of the late-night patter of her bare feet on his kitchen floor.

He shook his head. He put his jacket on and blew out the lantern and went outside and down the trail. Thoughts of her lifted and crashed like the action of waves. The two of them picking apples in the old peninsula orchard. Her so much younger. Days on his boat. Days along the shore. The two of them catching snowflakes in their mouths. Heads back. Throats arched. The first time she came to his house alone. Just walked in seventeen years old and stood in front of him and said his name. Jonah.

He pushed the skiff across the frosted planks and into the black water. The last of the tide rushed out like a cloth pulled from beneath him. A gull from somewhere unseen swooped and landed on the bow of the skiff and watched him as he rowed. It batted its wings and stamped its feet. A hush descended and the timeless clatter of wood and water and boat rose into the night sky.

Jonah tied the skiff off to his boat and checked the oil and turned the key and the engine ground to life. He ran the bilge pump and watched the oil and water piss from the chine. It was cold and getting colder and he stuffed his hands into his pockets and hopped up and down as the engine settled into its deep rhythm. The deck hose was frozen and he cursed and went below and removed the belt from the pulley so the rubber impeller wouldn't thrash itself to pieces any more than it already had. His fingers went numb with the cold wrenches and the cold grease and the cold oil.

His wake sparkled white and phosphorescent. The stars glinted. He imagined returning to the camp with Charlotte beside him. He imagined her to be pregnant. He imagined the smooth sea-swell of her body. He listened to his engine pound the shoreline only to drive back at him like fists. Perhaps going to find her was a mistake but he was beyond that so he continued on and rounded the ledges and entered the harbor. The tide turned to flood and the Big Dipper lifted above the harbor as if ladling saltwater into the sky. The pound slid by in the night light with its wood slat dam like baleen and Jonah had the instantaneous image of his father building the dam and he felt a pang for the simplicity of those days.

A half mile ahead of him he could see the small wharf with its single light bulb hanging from an old wooden post. A lean-to hut was built on the float below. Inside the lean-to was a single stool and a scale for weighing crates of lobsters and a shelf stacked with rusted wrenches and dirty gloves. The seawater around the wharf and float shifted in the light and as Jonah approached he could make out the familiar and comforting shape of the bait house with its swayback roof and rotted cedar shake siding.

He tied off to the float and climbed the ladder beneath the light. His gloves stuck to each wooden rung and he heard them peel back the chilled yellow herring grease as he climbed. Rusted and broken lobster traps and dirty bait buckets and fish totes and coils of rope were piled haphazardly around the wharf and Jonah had the fleeting childhood memory of afternoons spent jigging for mackerel with his brother and mother while they waited for Nicolas to return from a day on the water.

• • •

Snow banks lined the road and the village was dark save for a few porch lights shining orange on the snowpack. He walked down the center of the empty road. The birches lining Virgil's driveway stood white and still. Virgil's truck and Celeste's car were both parked in the driveway but Charlotte's car was not. Its absence hit Jonah like a swallowed stone.

He stepped into the yard and stood beneath her window. Her bedroom was dark. He shivered. His breath rose into the night and he reached for his cigarettes and all of the calmness he'd accumulated over the last week disappeared. He felt occupied by vacancy. He heard Chowder bark. He lit a cigarette. He wondered what he was doing. He packed a small circle in the snow like walls to hold him and he watched Charlotte's dark window as if hoping she would let her hair down but instead the door opened and Celeste peered into the darkness. She wore a short sleeve shirt and a red and white striped apron. The dog kept barking.

Jonah said, Celeste. It's me.

Jonah, she said. What are you doing? Come inside.

He crossed the lawn and stamped the snow from his boots and stepped onto the porch. She pulled him in by the arm and shut the door. The house smelled like heat and like sugar. He hadn't been there since his father's service and despite Charlotte's absence it was comforting to be there now. He kicked his rubber boots off.

How are you?

I'm good, Celeste. Fine.

He stood with his back tight to the door. His cigarette burned in his fingers.

Come in, she said. Virgil's in the kitchen.

Jonah heard classical music as he followed Celeste down the hallway. He looked into the living room and up the staircase for Charlotte but she was not there.

Virgil turned on his stool when they entered the kitchen. Jonah. I thought you'd run off on us.

Virgil looked like he'd aged years in the last week. His back was stooped and his skin was loose as clam meat. His eyes were sallow and cavernous. Jonah put his hand on Virgil's shoulder in an awkward one-arm hug then stepped back.

Good to see you, Jonah said. He felt like he was visiting Virgil in a hospital room though the room itself was warm and comfortable and smelled like ginger and sugar.

Celeste's making us some Christmas cookies here, Virgil said. We were aiming on bringing a batch out to camp for you.

I forgot it was even Christmas coming up, he said.

Sit down, Jonah, Celeste said. Do you want a beer or something?

Give him the gorilla milk. He needs it.

I think you've had enough for everybody, Celeste said. She took a beer out of the refrigerator. Maybe he'll listen to you, Jonah. Look at him. He looks like he got run over by a truck, doesn't he?

A little bit, Jonah said and tried to laugh as though it would be an apology.

Virgil scoffed. The hell with you both.

Celeste tipped the mixer up and wiped the blades with her finger. It's that brandy he sucks on like he's a tiger.

Gorilla.

The Captain hates gorillas, Jonah said. He sipped his beer. He had the feeling that something had happened between Virgil and Celeste but he couldn't figure out what it was or why he felt that way.

The Captain's been knuckle-dragging and mouth-breathing all over town, said Virgil. He ain't right. They're taking lobsters out of the pound in the morning. Him and Osmond.

Celeste disengaged the mixer blades and held one out to Jonah. Do you want that?

Jonah took the blade and cleaned it with his finger and licked his finger then began on the blade itself.

Virgil rocked on his stool. You don't hear shit out there at camp. You saw Nic's boat on its mooring. The Coasties finally gave that back. You'll be wanting to sell the *Jennifer* and use the *Cinderella*.

I don't know, Jonah said. He wondered how it was that he hadn't even noticed his father's boat.

And the wharf is up for sale, Virgil said.

What? The wharf? Benji's going to sell? Holy shit.

He ain't been well, Jonah. I visited him today.

Benji ain't been well for years. But sell the wharf? He can't do that.

He's dying, Jonah. He can't get up, can't piss, can't eat, can't do a thing but be a peckerhead like he's always been. He says he wants to see the wharf go before he's dead. He doesn't care about the fishermen or the harbor anymore. Says that's what gave him the cancer. Now he wants it to go before he goes.

Why would it be so bad if it sold? Celeste said. What else is going to happen to it?

Would it be bad to get bought up by one of these Boston conglomerates? Christ yes, it'll be bad. Sell it to a local outfit.

There aren't any local outfits.

Sure there are. Their pockets just aren't as deep. The big money guys are buying wharves up and down the coast. If they own the wharves, then they'll own the fishermen. Then we get pushed out.

They ain't going to buy all the wharves, Jonah said.

The hell they ain't, Jonah. Look around you. Look down the coast a hundred miles. What do you see? You see a handful of outfits buying everybody and everything up. When they get enough wharves then they control the price. Then we're fucked.

We're already fucked, Jonah said. He sipped his beer and held the mixer blade in the air. He tried to imagine the wharf being run by some company out of Boston or New York but it seemed ridiculous. A small harbor wharf was the center of family and community and he recalled only an hour ago climbing the wharf ladder and thinking about his mother and his brother and his father. He said, But the price is supply and demand, just like anything. You said so yourself.

Virgil grunted. It is for now. But that's what the big boys want to change. They want to control the price. That's when the lights go out. They did it with shrimp in the Gulf and they did it with crab in Alaska and over and over again. All the fisheries are fucked. We're the last one, damn near.

Celeste went to the counter and flopped the ball of dough out of the mixer and onto a breadboard.

Jonah pushed his seat back and crossed his legs. I'd hate to see it gone but who's gonna buy it? Hell, it'll cost half a million just to clean her up.

Virgil shifted his weight. I'll tell you who it is but you don't go telling a soul.

If it's a big secret I don't need to hear it.

Virgil ignored him. I'll tell you but don't go whistling it into the Captain's ear either.

I won't. You going into the bait trade?

You've heard the name Jason Jackson.

I heard of him. He bought from the old man and Osmond.

Virgil nodded. A rogue outfit is what Jason is. He's not aligned with any of the big seafood buyers. He works on his own. Jason's a ruthless sonofawhore but at least he understands quality. So guess who's cozy with Jason Jackson?

Erma Lee Carver?

Virgil's eyes crimped and his face went suddenly red. When he spoke his voice had turned hard. Shut up, Jonah. I'm trying to teach you something but you're too goddamned foolish. Your damned father's dead and you still sit there making kid jokes. Get yourself together.

Fuck, said Jonah and lit another cigarette. His chest began to lurch and his knees shook and he felt as though Virgil had sucker-punched him. It took a while for him to respond and even then his voice wasn't as strong as he wished. Together like you, Virgil? Drunk by dawn type of together?

Okay, Celeste said. Tell him what you want to tell him, Virgil. And Jonah, he's right. It's high time you took something seriously. And Virgil, he's right. You've been nothing but drunk and mean lately. And you are worrying me.

Jonah watched the grease-blackened etchings on his own thumb and forefinger as he twisted the brown cigarette filter back and forth. He drew on the cigarette and concentrated. He felt a choking in his throat and heat in the backs of his eyes. His face burned with embarrassment. He knew Virgil was right but still wanted to say, *You don't know me*, but if he spoke his voice would fall apart.

He began to push his chair back but Virgil sighed and dropped his shoulders and spoke. I'm sorry, Jonah. It's fine. This is hard on all of us. We all have to deal with our pain. I drink and you make jokes. Finest kind. Virgil cleared his throat and held his drink up in a short silent toast. What's going to happen is this. Jason Jackson and Osmond Randolph are going to buddy right up. Mark my words. Jason's bought from the pound for years now. He's going to drop the money and buy out Benji so they'll have the wharf and pound both. You wait. They'll run this harbor and it won't be long till they get even bigger.

So if Jason Jackson and Osmond work together, they're not going to want Bill around, is that what you're saying? That's what you keep worrying about?

Virgil's eyes narrowed and his voice turned low. The price of lobsters goes up twenty-five cents in Japan and your father gets killed is what I'm saying. Some clamfuck restaurant chain in Tokyo decides to put lobster on their lunch menu and our world shifts like someone slapped the Jell-O is what. They call Jason Jackson, he sees an opportunity and he calls Osmond and Osmond sees an opportunity. But your father doesn't like that shit so all of a sudden he's in the way. Bam.

Killed? Christ, Jonah said and looked away from Virgil but something slowly dawned on him. There was a moment of silence before he spoke. You think Osmond killed the old man?

Virgil stared like a snake black-eyed.

You think Osmond wanted to go into business with Jason Jackson but the old man didn't? So Osmond killed him for the pound? That's fucking crazy, Virgil. Osmond's a asshole but he ain't that bad. Besides, the Captain's gonna get his half of the pound and he wouldn't go for something the old man wouldn't of gone for anyway.

Osmond ain't that bad? He thinks he talks to God.

Celeste turned to Virgil and her face was filled with disgust. Well you think you are God. Lots of people think they talk to God. That doesn't mean they're murderers. And the price of lobster in Tokyo, Virgil? My God.

She squeezed her fingers together with her hand as if she'd lost the flow of blood. She said, You may think all of the insane thoughts you want, but do not, and I mean do not, speak them out loud.

Virgil ignored her but he looked pained. He said, Osmond damn near killed his brother and would've if I hadn't of caught the sonofawhore.

That's not true and if it was true it's still irrelevant, she said.

The hell it's not true. Virgil turned to Jonah. I told you before, about Osmond and Laura. She was his brother's wife. Julius's grandmother.

I remember.

Celeste spoke up. Osmond isn't such a bad man, Jonah. He's just different, and maybe a little creepy, but that's not for us to judge. He's good to his grandchildren, and I promise you that there are plenty of men around here that would not be so good to theirs. Anyway, Osmond fell in love with Orrin's wife while Orrin was over in Korea. Orrin is his brother. Osmond left the church for her but she went back to Orrin when Orrin came home. Orrin had been injured in the war.

So Osmond goes ratshit batshit, Virgil said and fluttered his fingers in the air. He gets thinking the heavenly Lord's sitting on both his shoulders, and he beats all hell out of Orrin and takes baby Neveah Elaine for his own. Beat the shit right out of his own fucked-up war vet brother. I mean beat him to a pulp, Jonah. So I'm over buying boat parts when Laura comes screaming that Osmond killed Orrin, Osmond killed Orrin. And I end up damned near breaking Osmond's neck so Laura can take her kid back. The only reason I got the drop on the big bastard is he was holding that baby Neveah so tight with both arms that I could just latch myself right around the bastard's neck. And he was big then but he was damned close to unconscious by the time he started struggling. Hell, I was only a teenager or something and that there's why me and him don't take to one another. I'd of killed him too and I well should've.

Why didn't you? Celeste said but she didn't want an answer.

Mercy. That's why. I had mercy on the whoreson.

Celeste turned back to her cookies and no one spoke. The deep thrum of the cello on the radio filled the room. Virgil made circles on the table with the condensation from his glass. Everything that had been said slopped around the room like tank water and every once in a while the water overtook Jonah. He tried to follow Virgil's logic but all that he could believe was that his father had been pulled overboard like thousands of fishermen before him and thousands of fishermen after him and of course it was tragic but tragic was all it was. Anyone who paid attention knew that big business was taking over fishing just like it had everything else. But to think it was worth killing someone? They weren't dealing with cocaine or diamonds. They were dealing with lobsters. Bugs that crawled around the seafloor and hid in mud holes and rock caves and ate each other or any other piece of sea rot they could find.

Celeste interrupted his thoughts. Jonah, do you want to use the shower?

I washed up some earlier.

Use the shower, Jonah. It's nice to have a hot shower once in a while even if you don't need it. Dinner's not for a while yet and Virgil needs to cool down.

Sure, Jonah said. Sure.

You know where it is.

Is Charlotte up there?

Virgil turned. In the shower?

Upstairs.

She's not here, Virgil said. Just go on the Christ and take a shower.

I'll get you a towel, Celeste said.

Jonah followed her up the stairs. She set out a blue towel for him and paused in the hallway. The space was shadowed and her face was half lit by the bathroom light and her hair was tucked behind her ear.

Jonah, she said. Don't think about that stuff with Osmond and lobster prices. You know how Virgil gets. He doesn't deal well with things, especially death. He needs to blame someone and losing your father has been very hard on him. He doesn't have many real friends—not that any of that is an excuse for the things he said.

I know it, Jonah said. Osmond was good to the old man. No one else, but he was good to the old man.

Celeste closed her eyes then opened them. Yes. Yes, he was.

Jonah hesitated then spoke in a hushed voice. Virgil doesn't look too good, Celeste.

He's drinking more than ever and he won't sleep. I don't think he's slept since you moved out of the trailer.

Maybe I should come back. For a while or something.

No. She shook her head from side to side. You take care of you. He just drives around and watches the harbor like he's waiting for your father to come home. He says he's looking for whales is what he says. And yesterday after they brought your father's boat back, he wouldn't come home. He just sat in his truck down at the wharf looking at Nicolas's boat.

She turned to go but stopped. She took a moment as if deciding whether or not to speak. Then said, Yes, I am worried about him, Jonah. He's been acting—I don't know how to explain it. He's not himself anymore, and I don't think it's all because of your father's death. I don't know what's happened. And now this conspiracy theory of his—.

Her voice trailed off. She bit her lower lip and Jonah thought she would cry. He gripped her hands in his and they were cold and dry.

He'll be fine, he said.

She pulled her hands free and hugged him. It's good·to have you here. If you get tired of being alone, stay here as long as you want. There's the extra bedroom and no one will bother you. Just come in and make yourself at home.

I'm fine, Celeste. I like it out there. It's quiet. He paused. Then, Where's Charlotte? I haven't seen her in a long time.

Celeste didn't answer at first. She gave him a sympathetic look. Maybe she'll talk to you. She always wanted a big brother and you and Bill were like that for her.

He watched her walk down the hallway. He shut the door and turned the shower on.

. . .

Virgil shook his head slowly. I don't know what the hell that was. I shouldn't of told him that shit about Osmond and Jason Jackson. Now I lit a fire under his highliner ass. I got blathering like the Captain.

Celeste held a star-shaped cookie cutter in her hand and she pressed it into the sheet of dough. She didn't want to look at her husband. She'd always had absolute faith in him but that faith was fraying. You got blathering all right, she said without looking up. I haven't got any idea if what you said has any grounding in reality or not, Virgil, but if it does—if it has any grounding at all—then you need to go to the police right now. And whatever it is that you did that's made you go insane, I don't know. Just fix it for crying out loud.

Virgil didn't appear to hear her. Now Jonah's up there thinking all the things he's going to do to Osmond Randolph and what he's going to do is get his highliner self killed if he does anything but set his ass home. Now I got to watch over him.

Yes, you do have to watch him. What were you thinking? What are you going to do if he starts making accusations? Or worse? What's going to happen when he tells Bill? Don't you have any idea that he listens to you?

Virgil stood up and rounded the table and took Celeste in his arms. She held her dough-covered hands out to the side and moved her head away from his but still she breathed his brandy breath.

She stepped from his grip and squared herself in front of him.

Virgil's hands hung at his sides. He spoke in a feverish voice. Trust me. Just trust me. I know I'm coming off crazy but goddamn it, Celeste, trust me. Jonah won't do anything stupid, but don't you go talking to the Captain about this. He'll come off pissing fury and we don't need him on the warpath. I'll make sure the Highliner don't open his mouth.

Celeste leaned against the counter. Jonah's fine and the only one thinking about Osmond is you and you had no right whatsoever telling him that his father was murdered. Do you have any idea how crazy that is, Virgil? Any idea whatsoever? You just told a young man that his father was fucking murdered. I can't even believe it myself. I just can't fathom it. We're lucky he's more worried about Charlotte right now than he is about all your talk.

Christ. I am too.

Celeste turned and stamped a few more cookies and moved them onto a tray and they were perfect. Neither spoke for a moment then without facing her husband Celeste said, What happened that night, Virgil? That night you came home so late and you couldn't stop shaking? What did you do? I need you to tell me.

She heard him breathing.

He stood up and circled the kitchen like a nervous dog then stopped in front of the window and gazed off into the night for so long that she wondered if he intended to answer her or not. Then he spoke. Remember when we got married?

Of course I remember.

He cleared his throat and swallowed. Well you said that you'd share everything you possibly could with me.

He turned to her and she to him and she nodded.

And you said that sometimes there would be some things that would be impossible for you to share. Well, this is one of those things right now for me.

She studied his face with its drooping cheeks and clear sad eyes then nodded again and turned back to her dough.

After several minutes passed Virgil sat back down on his stool and said, I figured the Highliner was over all that Charlotte stuff.

Celeste paused and looked at the wall and held her breath for several beats and said, He's in love, Virgil. He's not going to get over it that easy.

Charlotte met Julius at the Irving station. He went inside while she waited in the truck. She examined her fingernails and tried not to think about Jonah. A part of her wondered what she was doing with Julius but since the moment she'd discovered that it was he who'd left the flowers she'd wanted to find out who he was for herself. She'd met Osmond and she'd met the twin girls but she'd never actually met Julius. She'd heard rumors around the school and the wharf but that's all she thought they were. Rumors. Julius was a drug dealer and Julius tried to drown his sister and Julius's father was in prison and Julius should be in prison too.

She didn't believe the worst of it but if she was wrong then she'd handle him just like she'd handled everything else in her life.

Julius returned with a bag of hard candies and a twelve-pack of colas. They crossed the river and he sucked on a candy. The tide was ebb and slabs of salt ice broke free of the frozen river and floated downstream to the bay while the rocks and seaweed along the shoreline stayed wrapped in the smooth ice sheets. Snow lined the banks above the high water mark and geese fed in the field and the coastline spread like a hand with its fingertips pressing deep into the gulf.

They drove in awkward silence along the knuckles of land and came into a town that lay at the crux of two peninsulas separated by a river and bay. They turned down the western peninsula. Julius ran his thumb and forefinger over his arrowhead patch of hair and glanced at Charlotte out of the sides of his eyes. He grabbed a cola and opened the can and drank long but he did not speak.

Charlotte pulled one foot onto the seat. She wrapped her arms around her knee and watched him as he drove. His eyes and hair and skin were all dark. Your father's in prison?

Yeah, he's there.

Is it true what he did?

I don't know, Julius said and grinned. What'd he do?

They rounded a corner and saw a lobster pound. In the middle of the pound two men on a scow shoveled antibiotic feed pellets the size of dog food into the water. Several aerators bubbled around the men and a row of refrigerated trucks lined a new tank house. Beyond the pound the inshore islands appeared like black spots in the evening light and miles across the bay on the parallel peninsula Charlotte glimpsed the mouth of her home harbor and the rise of Ram's Head at its mouth.

People say he smuggled drugs.

Yeah, that's what they say, Julius said.

But he didn't?

His eyes shot to her. I didn't say he did or didn't.

Well, said Charlotte. If you don't want to talk about it, that's okay. I was just curious.

He put another candy in his mouth and when it was gone he said, I'm fine talking about it. I don't give a shit.

You're fine talking about what?

Julius grinned. His eyes narrowed. We ran some stuff. That's what we done. It's no big deal now.

Did your grandfather too?

Grandfather? Hell no. He's too religious for the real deal.

The road led them away from the water and over a small knoll then back down to the water. They followed the edge of the bay and a half mile across the bay stretched the island called Numbers. Several old houses and an overgrown orchard and an abandoned schoolhouse and a collapsing church were visible on the western shore. A few deer stood in the snow beneath an apple tree and pawed at the ground.

Your father's name is Chimney?

Yeah, Chimney Wesley. He's a pirate is what he is. He was the one gave me the name Julius. Julius Caesar Wesley. My dad's a real pirate. What we'd do is meet them big boats offshore and load our holds with weed or coke or hash or whatever. Then we'd pack lobster crates with it and put lobsters on top and the truck met me and him right there at the landing in front of everyone and all those dumb bastards thought we were just selling lobsters. I'll tell you what else I done before. Me and my dad Chimney crated up lobsters and shipped them overseas to the Netherlands or Denmark or something. Amsterdam. Them Frogs over there'd put a bunch of shit in the crate and pack the lobsters back around it. Course by then the lobsters would be dead so they'd put stickers saying *Dead Seafood* or some shit in there and return it all to the sender. So me and my dad got the crates back full of stinky-ass dead bugs but in there was the good stuff.

How long's he in jail for?

Ten or twenty, I don't know. He'll go back to court. He runs the show. He lives good up there.

Charlotte wet her lips and looked out the window. She thought and then she spoke. Why aren't you in prison too, then?

She watched Julius's eyes narrow. She wondered if she'd gone too far.

Finally he said, Because my old man covered for me is why and don't you ever forget it because I won't. Not ever. You get that? Never.

Charlotte started to respond but his face had turned angry so she turned away and crimped her mouth into a thin hidden line and wondered about him. The road left the water again and wound up a small plateau sided by blueberries. Neither spoke and Charlotte could feel scorn filling the cab like exhaust and she wondered if her friends at school were right that this boy named Julius was *psycho*. She kept herself from looking at him. She wanted suddenly to be out of the truck and in her car or in her home but it was not that simple. She gripped the door handle. Julius drove fast and for the moment at least he was still a magnet from which she could not pull away.

Why'd you leave me those flowers? she said.

Me?

Yeah, you. Why'd you leave me flowers?

She waited and watched the snowy fields rail by.

Because, he said. Because you helped Rhonda that time. At the store.

All I did was help her up off the floor.

Well all I did was give you some flowers.

They neared the end of the plateau and the sea spread forth and blended with the sky and the two together formed a cosmos that the truck sped into. The light became bright red and pulsed and gleamed over the snow-covered peninsula and the bays and rivers with all of their islands like studs sparkled crimson in the sunset. Straight offshore the Drown Boy Rock lighthouse rose tall and cylindrical out of a submerged granite peak and if the water had been calm they might have seen the great mountain's flanks and ridges disappearing into the soundless depths. They dropped down the hill into the thick gloom of spruce and fir and parked at a small brown church.

You been here before? he said.

Not for a long time.

Julius stepped out of the truck and shut his door. Charlotte held the door handle and tried to ignore the fear she'd felt moments ago. The trees surrounding them were thick and crowded. Something about the situation didn't feel real as if it were not her here with Julius but another girl who she had seen but never met and one day she would hear stories about that girl and shake her head and say, *I remember her, foolish girl.*

She tried to forget that other girl. The door opened and she stepped out. Julius was there. He gripped her hand and swung the door closed. He pulled her toward the church. The snow came to her shins and as she followed him she caught herself thinking that this boy could do anything he wanted to her.

He'd of gotten away with it too, Julius said with a voice soft and nearly sweet. Pa would've.

If what? Charlotte stopped herself from walking and pulled her hand away. He turned to her and they saw each other as shapes in the darkness.

If that offshore tug with them fucking Puerto Ricans hadn't of got lost. That's when they threw all our hash overboard while the Coasties were chasing 'em down and all the dumbass urchin divers and scallop draggers on the coast were coming home with steel tubes full of our hash. Sea hash is what they call it.

And the Puerto Ricans told on your father?

He didn't turn himself in.

Charlotte forced a laugh. Do you miss him?

Chimney? He's only been in for six months.

She waited for more and nothing came so she followed the snow pathway to the steps. The church was small and sided with rough cut pine boards stained brown. The hipped roof and fieldstone bell tower stood framed by a break in the timber. She stood at its base and gazed up at the smooth rounding of rocks and the stars that were beginning to come out like eyes spying. She felt Julius's hands on her hips. She didn't move at first then turned.

It's beautiful, she said.

I know.

She laughed. You know everything.

Damn close to it.

He still had his hands on her hips.

She put her hands on his hands then pulled away. She opened the big door to the church. The door swung slowly and creaked through the small chapel and bell tower. Charlotte could see the black lines of the pews and the black line of the altar and the big stained glass window behind it. She walked down the aisle and her footsteps were loud on the wooden floor and the room was a cavern filled by echo and it did not feel like a place of refuge or a place of worship. She shivered. She put her hands in her pockets and she felt her spine tingle.

She stood at the altar as Julius stepped in. She turned and she saw him. A shadow in the doorway. He eased the door shut and latched it. The creaking seemed to stay in the room even after the door was closed and she couldn't see him anymore but heard his breathing and then his steps one by one by one. She searched the darkness for him. She held her breath. She felt the fine hairs on the back of her neck rise and she felt once again that another girl had come and why would that girl do such a thing?

His footfalls echoed around the chamber. She thought of Jonah. She turned in the darkness and looked for a place to go but there was nowhere. She reached out to grab something or fend something off but found only air. Then he flicked his lighter and the church lit and he stared through the flame. His eyes were dark slits like wings. His nose like a hawk's. The flame went out and in the flash she saw the hawk nose and the arrowhead of hair and the wingspread eyes. Her neck pulsed.

Suddenly he filled the space in front of her.

She smelled candy on his breath. She waited for something but nothing came. He stood motionless. She forced a small and nervous laugh then gripped both of his biceps. His arms were lean and hard like stretched bricks and she smelled his skin and breath like sugar and she brushed her lips over his then said, This is a church.

I know.

Why'd you bring me here? Her hands climbed his biceps then rested on the back of his neck.

I knew you'd like it.

I'm going to kiss you, she said.

You like it, don't you?

It's fine, she said but suddenly she felt off balance and didn't know why. She told herself that Julius was standing there harmlessly but her precariousness came from within and she wasn't sure if she liked the feeling or not.

You like it, don't you?

His voice shot into her eardrum and she felt vibrations prance along her ribs. It took her a moment to realize that he was talking about the church.

It's fine, she said.

You trust me, don't you?

She nodded.

Don't you?

Yes, she whispered. Yes.

She saw him smile through the darkness and her heart thudded. She couldn't swallow because her heart seemed to fill her throat. Her hands were still on his neck and she slid them down over his arms and wrists to his hands. She pinched the wedge of skin at the base of his thumb then pressed his hands onto her hips and held them there.

She placed her fingertips on the tops of his hands then lifted herself onto her toes and pressed her lips briefly into his. She moved his hands to the front of her belt and with their fingers laced together she flipped her belt open and coached his fingers as they worked her button free then slid the zipper down.

A shock of cold air landed on the beam of her bare pelvis and her knees felt loose and weak. She set a hand on the altar to balance herself and her other hand stayed slack atop his. She could hear a heart beating but didn't know who it belonged to. She shifted her hips as he pulled her jeans and underpants down. He worked his fingers slowly into her and they were hard and cold.

She heard him groan.

She put a hand on his shoulder as they backed to the wall. With the one hand he lifted her to her toes. She kissed him on the neck and then their mouths met and she slid her tongue into his mouth. His tongue was sugary and fast. She reached for his belt and beyond but quickly he released her and caught her hand.

He cleared his throat and coughed. He took her in his arms and hugged her to the length of his body. She stared up at the dark church rafters and it took a few seconds to realize that the trembling she felt came from him. He held her tight with his hands fisted in her sweatshirt and his face stuffed against her neck. She felt the hot breath from his mouth and nostrils on her skin.

She didn't move and tried barely to breathe.

Then he cleared his throat and snorted loose snot. Her pants and underpants were stuck at her thighs. Her ass was cold and she shivered and tried to release him but he burrowed his face still deeper and squeezed tighter. Finally he lifted his mouth to her ear and she felt cold tearstains and heard his whisper deep in her ear, I'm so sorry.

Then he was out of her arms and out of the church. Charlotte's hands were left awkward in front of her with her arms slightly bent at the elbows as if she was readying to play a piano. Her fingers and wrists moved and curled and pumped. She had no strength in her legs so she slid slowly down the wall and landed with her bare ass on the cold floor.

After what felt like both too long and not long enough she lifted her hips from the floorboards and pulled her underpants back up. She waited and caught her breath then pulled her pants up but she did not zip or button them until she was standing. Whether or not to cry came in waves that she fought off each time and by the time her belt was latched she'd stopped shaking. Thoughts of Jonah piled in her mind.

She walked down the aisle and opened the door. Tall spruces loomed over her head. At first she did not see him in the night but a motion caught her eye. He was a silhouette in the trees to the right of where she stood on the church step. He kicked at something over and over then as she watched he lifted whatever it was and swung it against a tree with a scream as high and frightening as a coyote's.

He screamed once more but in a deeper pitch. More like a wolf. Charlotte looked around as if searching for help but they were alone. After a minute Julius stilled and stood with his back to her. When he made no more noise she approached him with one hand held out in front of her. She didn't know what he'd swung against the tree but found herself preparing for an animal the size of a dog. Her outstretched hand landed on his back and she paused. His body heaved. His muscles jumped. She pressed her hands against him and looked beyond him and on the ground she saw a broken and splintered log spread over the snowpack.

She exhaled.

Julius, she said. Julius, it's okay.

His back was covered in wet snow but she felt sweat rising through his sweatshirt. He didn't respond so she took another step then another and she put her arms around his body and gripped his rib cage tight and his trembles became her own so she leaned her head against the back of his neck and held.

When Jonah finished his shower he opened the door and went down the hallway. He carried his socks in his pocket. His bare feet touched quietly on the carpet. The door to Charlotte's room was open and he paused on the threshold then went in. The porch lights lit the driveway and the yard below and cast a glow into the room. He could see the birches outside lined like ramparts.

The room smelled like her. Like honey and sage and summer wind and he looked at the bed and the bureau and the vanity and the pile of jeans and T-shirts and bras in the corner. Pictures of her friends hung on the wall above the bureau and Jonah stepped closer and set his hands on the bureau top. It was covered in bracelets and necklaces and rings and barrettes and he recognized some of them. He began to feel strange among her things but couldn't pull himself away. He resisted the urge to open a drawer. He lifted a silver necklace and let it dangle and flash from his fingers and wished Charlotte were there with him. He set the necklace down.

She had two pictures of him and his brother on the mirror and one of Nicolas and Virgil when they were younger. Virgil was lean but still had the big shoulders and big cheeks. Jonah stared for a long time at the young version of his father and wondered what the man had been like.

His earliest clear memories were of Sundays spent fishing on the lakes and rivers to the north. Bill and Nicolas fished relentlessly but Jonah was more interested in watching birds or clouds or currents. Sometimes Bill would hook one and hand his rod to Jonah and Jonah would feign excitement. Bill's excitement was rampant and by the time any fish was in the boat Nicolas would have to bark at him to sit down before he tipped them all over. At noontime they'd land their boat and start a fire. This was Jonah's favorite part. He'd collect twigs and leaves and grasses and Nicolas would give him only a single match no matter the weather. Sometimes Nicolas brought a package of hotdogs with them but usually they'd spear their trout with alder branches and hold the fish over the coals until the skin peeled back. Nicolas carried a tin of salt in the pocket of his fishing vest so the boys would hold their fish out for Nicolas to sift a pinch of salt onto. They'd eat the fish like corn on the cob and then they'd toss the guts and bones into the fire.

Jonah stared at the photo on Charlotte's mirror then said out loud, What the hell happened out there? What's Virgil talking about? How'd you go overboard, Dad?

Then he realized that although he did not believe Virgil was right he did not believe he was wrong either. He tried to piece together some altercation between his father and Osmond but he could only see his father with a foot wrapped in a rope and the weight of the traps tugging him over the stern of his boat while his fingernails raked first the floor then the stern then the water. Teeth grinding. Legs kicking. Throat screaming and Jonah knew that very same cold water and he reached out and pressed his fingertips against his father's chest as if to test for a heartbeat but found only his own racing pulse. He blinked and was surprised to find himself in Charlotte's bedroom. He went down the stairs.

Get another beer, Virgil said. We got a long night.

Long night of what?

None of your business.

Celeste put dinner on the table and Jonah opened a beer and sat down. He thought of his cold trailer and the cold camp and neither felt like home but this suddenly did. He couldn't remember his father ever cooking a dinner. He drank down half of the beer and picked at the placemat. He smelled garlic and shrimp.

You stewing on Charlotte? Virgil said without looking.

Jonah's eyes shot up to Virgil then down to the table.

Well she's out with a friend.

She's got to make her own mistakes, Celeste said as if she'd said it a thousand times already.

Jonah clenched. He felt as if his blood had drained down his torso and legs and pooled in his feet. A friend who?

That little clamfuck is who. Julius fucking Wesley is who.

Celeste paused at the far side of the table. She stood shoulder to shoulder with Virgil. She held a place setting with both hands. Jonah, she said and as she watched him he knew that she saw a weakness within him that he wanted to keep hidden. Hidden even from himself.

She set down the place settings and rounded the table and gripped him by the forearm and her grip was strong. You need to remember that she's smart and she's tough and she's got some growing to do. I don't like that boy Julius either but she's got to decide for herself. Virgil thinks she's still a little girl and she is in some ways but it's hard on her having her father knowing her whole life.

Yeah, said Jonah. He was about to cry right there in front of them and he hoped Celeste would either leave him alone or say something to fill the hole growing within him. He blurted, It's just sudden.

Virgil ate a few shrimp from the pan of risotto and wiped his hands on his shirt. I'll take care of it, he said.

Celeste stepped back so she could see Virgil better and slowly the implications of what he said dawned on her and her eyes opened then narrowed and the muscles in her face tightened. Oh no you don't, Mister Man.

Don't what? Virgil said.

You won't take care of it. What are you going to do?

The clamfuck, he said. His cheeks were white and wrinkled with shadow.

You are not leaving this house tonight, Celeste said.

The hell I'm not.

And you too, Jonah. You're sleeping here or I swear to God I will never speak to either of you again.

God save the king, Virgil said.

Jonah slugged the rest of his beer and lit a cigarette and placed the pack on the table and spun the lighter in a circle on top of it. He thought about Charlotte and Julius and wished he had not come.

You don't have to worry, Celeste.

You bet I don't have to worry because you two aren't leaving this house. Blood rushed her cheeks. Jonah had never seen her so angry.

The hell we're not, Virgil said. He rocked on his heels as if losing his balance then settled as Celeste stepped in front of him. She grabbed the waistband on his pants and pulled him toward her and at the same time she slapped him across the cheek loud and sharp. Jonah coughed out a lungful of smoke as if he'd been hit.

Virgil caught Celeste's hands and he pulled her arms around him and hugged her. Her entire body shook. She rapped her hands against his back and Jonah heard her say, I won't take this anymore.

Virgil hugged her tighter and set his head on her shoulder. He faced Jonah but his eyes were closed. Don't worry, he said. Don't worry about anything.

Jonah tried to look away but he couldn't. Virgil held her until she calmed and when they finally parted she said, I'll not have you two touch that boy.

I'm not aiming to, Jonah said.

Don't lie to me. He is, she said, and you'd go with him if he went. If Julius so much as hurts a hair on my daughter then so help me God I'll take care of him myself. But you two will stay away from him until Charlotte says otherwise and you will let the police deal with Osmond if he needs to be dealt with.

She's scared of Osmond, Virgil said and tried to smile but it wasn't funny.

Yes, she said. Yes I am. And you would be too if you'd sober up.

I ain't scared of Osmond, Virgil said. He's just Judas with rubber boots. But I am scared of that lad who's got your daughter with him right now. If I believed in that religious crabshit I'd say that boy's Lucifer if there ever was one and I'd bet my boat that Osmond'd tell you the same.

Leave it be, Celeste said. We're eating dinner then we're watching some dumb football game then Jonah is sleeping in the guest bed.

That'd be fine, said Jonah.

That'd be fine, Virgil mocked.

Jonah lay awake thinking about Julius and Charlotte until he heard a car pull into the driveway. He rolled over and slid the curtain back and peered through the edge of the window. He saw Charlotte climb out of her car and shut the door. She wore a blue sweatshirt and lifted the hood over her head as she walked. She glanced up and he slid away from the window and stared at the ceiling. He heard the door open and close and heard keys jingle and then her footsteps fast on the stairs. The door to her room opened and closed. He didn't hear another thing.

He waited and expected her knock on his door but it did not come. He'd been foolish to expect it. After ten minutes he stood and pulled his pants on and slipped out of the room and across the hall and opened her door.

He saw the shape of her body huddled beneath her comforter. He crossed the room and sat on the edge of her bed and when he put his hand on her thigh she jerked away and said in a voice that sent a chill down his spine, Don't touch me. Get the fuck out of here.

Jesus, Jonah said. He stood up angry and crossed the room to leave but stopped. Are you okay, Charlotte?

She didn't answer.

Charlotte? He took two slow steps back toward her. Are you okay?

He heard her sniffle. Fine, she said. I'm fine. Please just leave me alone.

Something in her voice made him feel like he could not help but cry so he pinched his nose closed with a finger and thumb and pinched his eyes shut until it passed. Then he looked up. Charlotte? Are you okay? What happened to you?

She sat up and threw the blankets from herself. She was still fully clothed. She sat cross-legged on the bed and faced him in the half dark. Her look and her voice were not her own. What do you want from me? What the hell are you doing here? You want to screw, is that it, little Jonah? Fine, you can screw me right now. I don't care.

He stood there in the middle of the room. He hadn't put a shirt on and felt suddenly naked. I'm sorry, he said. I just came for dinner but your mom wanted me to stay.

Why would she want you to stay? Your shitty trailer's only like ten feet away.

She was worried I'd go after Julius.

Oh Jesus Christ, Charlotte said. She stood up. This is crap. So you were waiting in the window spying on me?

I just heard you drive in. I didn't want to stay here.

You could've left. She didn't tie you up.

She slapped the shit out of your dad though.

No she didn't.

The hell not. Cuffed him right across the face.

What'd he do? Get shitfaced and turn into a prick?

What? No, he didn't do a goddamned thing and you know that. Jesus Christ. What's wrong? What happened with him, Charlotte? Did he hurt you?

No, she said. Her voice was flat and cold and held a finality he recognized. She stared through him for a moment then spoke again and her voice had calmed. I'm just having a hard time right now, Jonah. You wouldn't understand. But I'm fine, so don't worry about it.

Jonah rubbed his arms for warmth. What are you doing with him, Charlotte? A week or two ago things with us were good.

I can do whatever I want, Jonah. You don't own me. You said everything was fine, didn't you? Isn't that what you said? Fine?

I don't want to own you.

Yes you do. And they want you to.

Hell. I told you right along that you'd be better off with a boyfriend your age. You know that.

And now that I got one you're pissed.

He's your boyfriend?

What's it matter what he is? You don't get it, Jonah. I'm not going to live here and be some boring woman like Erma Lee. I want to see things and go places and meet people.

Christ, Charlotte. I get that. But that don't explain Julius Wesley. He's bad and besides, that's a awful fast change. Me then Julius.

She interlaced her fingers and held them to her waistline. It's not sudden. I was going to talk to you before but then your father died.

So you figured you'd wait?

She looked exasperated. Do you think I wanted to break up with you the day your father drowned? I'm sorry, Jonah. But Julius is not what you think. You don't know him. He's got problems, but he's nice.

Maybe you don't know him. Maybe you shouldn't be so fucking naive.

You're an asshole, Jonah. Just a little baby asshole, she said. Get out of here now.

Julius and Osmond were at the pound when Bill showed up. It was early morning and a thin line of clouds split the sky in two so that the sun shone bright on the offshore waters while the inshore waters still lay tucked in shadow. Bill parked his truck and watched as a half dozen crows abandoned the causeway leaving the broken shells of several lobsters scattered about the rocks.

He crossed the driveway and entered the salt-fish air in the pound building and crossed the concrete floor. He remembered that Jonah had cut Osmond's traps. He dismissed the thought and went out the far door and climbed down the ladder to the floathouse. The house was a twenty-foot-by-twenty-foot lean-to with a metal roof and ten inches of flotation foam in the floor.

Osmond stood in the scow bolting the 25-horsepower outboard to the fiberglass transom.

Julius leaned against the wall and watched and he didn't appear to notice Bill.

Bill looked across the water at the causeway. The rocks were pink and gray and void of snow. You see them crows over there? he said.

Osmond straightened and looked at the water. There were no crows in sight. No, he said.

They been feeding awful on these bugs.

I haven't noticed, Osmond said.

Bill squatted on his heels. What's your loss here? Ten percent ain't it?

Seven to fifteen has been typical.

I'd say them crows make up a good portion of that.

Osmond looked at Bill as if being patient with an adolescent. The crows don't go in the water, William. They only feed on the dead at low water.

Where do the dead come from? The fucking gulls I'd say. I seen them blackbacks dive in two feet of water for a lobster.

So the gulls feed them to the crows, William?

That is right. They eat the tomalley then the crows get the rest.

Osmond hooked the gas tank up to the outboard and turned the gas on and choked it and started it. He left the choke on and the engine ran fast and spat blue smoke. Osmond watched until it began cycling water then shut the choke off and left it at idle.

He stepped out of the scow. He looked bigger now as he towered over Julius. He crossed the floathouse to where Bill stood. We don't kill crows, William, he said.

Bill pushed his glasses up his nose bridge. He could smell Osmond like wet fur. It ain't just the crows by Jesus. We got otter and coons and who the hell all knows what.

What would you do?

That's a lot of shrinkage, Bill said. He lit a cigarette and blew the smoke out of the side of his mouth. Even on this shitass market, ten percent of eighty thousand pounds is costing us thirty-two grand.

Two crows circled the causeway and landed on an exposed rock.

We don't have eighty thousand pounds in here, Bill. We never have.

We will next year. Bill looked at Julius and Julius caught his eye as if Bill had finally said something that interested him.

Osmond laughed. Nicolas always said you were a planner. We need to get the crates down here. We can discuss shrinkage later.

Fine, said Bill. But I'm getting me a crow call and I'll be damned if I ain't going to kill everything that spits, shits, flies, or crawls from here to Canada. He turned around and climbed the ladder. His breath came quick and he wondered why and he reminded himself that he had not cut Osmond's traps but still he felt his pulse slam like an ill-timed engine. He thought of his father and wondered if he was watching from wherever the dead go and he hoped he was not because he did not feel like Nicolas Graves's son right then.

The crates were lined up beneath a lean-to on the far side of the building. Ten rows of ten and Bill dragged the first row into the building and across the concrete floor and the plastic grated loud on the dry concrete. He peered down at the floathouse where Osmond threaded twine through the torn dragnet. He wished his father were there. Just one more day working at the pound to help him prepare for Osmond. Just one more day to help him prepare for life on dry land.

He dragged the rest of the crates over then climbed down the ladder. Julius still leaned against the wall. The sun which had crested the chain of islands now glimmered off the pound water.

Osmond hooked the drag to the scow.

Give me a hand with these, Bill said to Julius.

Julius turned slowly and stared at Bill. You can't get them?

It'd be faster with us both.

Christ, said Julius. I can get the fuckers myself.

Bill stepped back as Julius passed him and Osmond stopped what he was doing and watched. Julius reached up and pulled at the stack of crates. The bottom of the stack was two feet over his head and the top another eight feet above that.

I'll lower 'em down to you, Bill said.

The fuck you will.

Julius, Osmond barked and his voice was big and stopped Julius. He will help you.

I don't need his help.

But you will have it.

I could be fishing right now.

Bill climbed back up the ladder and separated the crates into fives then lowered the stacks down by their beckets and Julius restacked them against the floathouse wall. As they worked Osmond throttled the outboard forward and pulled the drag overboard. The drag was six feet wide with iron runners on each end and a nylon mesh bag in the middle. Osmond circled the pound with the drag running over the smooth bottom while the lobsters tumbled and piled into the mesh bag. He circled twice and headed to the floathouse and he rammed the bow of the scow into the float and unclipped the drag rope and handed it to Bill. Bill ran the line through a block that hung from a rafter. Osmond flipped the outboard into reverse and throttled back and the rope reeled through the block as the drag slowly rose out of the water.

The outboard whined. Bill and Julius each took an iron runner and heaved back. The drag rose onto the floathouse floor. The mesh bag held 500 pounds of lobsters piled with strands of rockweed and twists of kelp. Osmond helped them dump the catch onto the floor then Julius and Bill flipped the drag over and lined it up at the edge of the deck as Osmond motored off again. The line tightened and the drag dropped into the water and the salt swished and sparkled in the wintertime light.

Osmond circled the pound with the drag as they crated the lobsters and weighed them out and strung the crates into a line that floated serpentine in the pound water. Bill and Julius worked in silence until the third drag when Bill pulled a skull out of the pile of lobsters and held it in the air and the world stopped.

Fuck, he said and his knees sagged and his back bent as if he could no longer hold himself up.

The skull was eaten clean of flesh and had been turned beige by the salt. The jaw and teeth were loose but intact. Julius stood straight-legged and stared. Osmond on the scow turned and saw the skull as if the presence of such a thing could impact a man a hundred yards off and he ran the scow into the floathouse and stepped out and took the skull from Bill.

Osmond's hair fell over his cheeks. He held the skull at arm's length and he whispered, Lord.

Who the hell is it? Julius said. Unlucky sonofawhore.

It's my father, Bill said. He tried to straighten his body but he could not and he felt himself sink into the float as if the wood beneath his feet had suddenly rotted. He took his glasses off and he put them back on and he stepped to Osmond and took the skull from him and held it to his stomach like a woman embracing her pregnancy. He looked around the floathouse and the walls pressed against him. Julius sat on a crate and breathed slowly and didn't say anything. He stared at the skull for a long time. When Bill finally noticed Julius's gaze he wanted to hide the skull but he saw something in Julius's eyes or the way Julius held his head slightly cocked that made him hold the skull up as if out of sympathy or childish camaraderie. All was quiet save for the swish and lap of the tidewater on the pound dam. One of the bottom canine teeth was gold and Bill pinched it between thumb and forefinger as if testing the root's strength.

Julius stared. His mouth fell open and his nostrils flared and his eyes held a light that Bill would have thought the boy incapable of. He couldn't stop watching Julius as Julius watched the skull as if it were the only thing in this world that he cherished.

That's your father, Julius finally said and the words came slow and didn't sound like Julius's voice.

Bill nodded and he felt Osmond behind him. Osmond took a step forward.

How'd he get in here? Julius sounded like he'd lost something that truly mattered.

Osmond brushed past Bill and took the skull and walked to the outer edge of the floathouse and flung it sidearm over the dam. It landed with a splash in the tidewater.

Bill stood dumbfounded. His hands felt empty. He turned them palm-up to be sure the skull was gone from them.

The Lord shall tend to such things, William.

Bill blinked. The Lord?

Yes. He shall cross to the other side.

The other side?

Bill noticed Julius standing beside him. It was a comforting presence.

Osmond stepped back into the scow.

Is the rest of him in there? Julius asked Osmond.

Osmond's face was pale and it took him a moment to speak. Horse and rider he has thrown into the sea. Now crate those bugs before they freeze.

Osmond pulled the cord and started the outboard.

Bill dropped to his knees with a crate beside him and began filling it. He worked slowly and methodically. He turned each lobster in his hands as if any one of them could be another part of his father. He concentrated on each breath. When that crate was full he slid another one over and looked at Julius. Julius was sucking on a hard candy and staring at his own palm.

You working today? Bill said.

Julius made a fist. That was your father? You sure?

Bill pulled one glove off and lit a cigarette and clenched the lighter in his trembling hand. He drew on the cigarette hard enough to cave the filter. How many gold-toothed dead guys you know of?

How'd he get in here?

I got no clue.

I thought he died offshore.

Somewhere out there. Not in here, I know that much.

• • •

A few hours later the dirty white refrigerated truck backed up to the loading dock at the pound. The driver got out and tied his cheap leather work boots and straightened. He was short and stocky with curly blond hair and wide blue eyes. Osmond approached him and they shook hands.

Osmond, he said and nodded.

Osmond clenched the man's hand. Daniel.

Daniel opened the backdoor of the truck and slid the rows of empty crates out to Bill and Julius. They stacked them alongside the building.

Osmond operated the winchhead as Julius hooked the lobster crates with two steel hooks. Bill stood on the loading dock and unhooked the crates as they rose dripping and spinning from the seawater. He dragged the crates into the cold metal truck and he and Daniel stacked them five high atop pallets. As he worked his father's skull hung in his mind and like a gull circling a dead fish that it didn't dare approach Bill couldn't quite grasp that he'd held his father's skull in his hands. Held it in his hands then watched Osmond throw it overboard. He wasn't certain if what was going on around him was actually happening or not and uncertainty wasn't something Bill was used to. The crates couldn't rise fast enough and any time Bill spent waiting he spent hiding his shaking hands and clenching his thigh muscles to keep his knees taught.

When they finally got the hundred crates loaded Daniel took out a book of checks and receipts and wrote a check out to Osmond. They stood next to the truck.

Jason sends his regards, Daniel said.

Osmond nodded.

He was in Japan then Honolulu. He'll be back tonight. He's expecting you.

Osmond looked up. That's right.

Good, said Daniel.

Bill stood next to them and listened but all he could concentrate on was the skull and his own shakes.

This is Nicolas's son, Osmond explained then cast a look at Bill that said with the hard weight of stone, *Keep your mouth shut.*

Yeah, said Daniel. I was sorry to hear of his death. He was a good man. Jason respected him.

Thanks, Bill muttered.

Daniel handed the check to Osmond. I'll see you soon.

Yes. Osmond folded the paper into his breast pocket.

I'm off, said Daniel and he shook their hands and untied his boots and climbed into the truck and left.

Bill looked around and felt the wind in his nostrils. It didn't feel like any wind he'd ever known. He looked at Osmond and said, You going there for business?

Osmond blinked his eyes once and the lids were thick folds that remained closed for a couple of seconds. When they opened he was looking at Bill. Yes, William, I am. I am going on my business and my business alone.

If it's pound business it's my business too.

A raft of pintails lifted off the harbor and looped out of sight.

I'm getting a crow call, Bill said.

Osmond opened the door to his truck. I wouldn't if I was you, William.

Why's that?

Killing crows is bad luck.

Hell, said Bill. My old man killed them all his life.

Osmond raised his eyebrows but Bill was back to thinking about the skull.

Osmond sat in his truck with the door open. His face appeared to contort into an expression that it had never before known. He spoke slow. About your father, William. I wish that had not happened and I know it must be hard on you. How did he end up in here? In this pound? I do not understand.

I got no clue, Bill said.

Neither do I. Osmond took a moment to think. His face regained its composure and the vertical wrinkles once again stretched across the skin. Do not mention this to anyone. Not a soul, William. We don't want anything going on around here. If the police find out they will drain this pound down to mud and kill every bug in here. We will lose everything. We will go out of business and this pound will be sold. We will lose our boats and our homes and everything, William. This pound will go bankrupt. We will go bankrupt. Let your father go the way the Lord intended. That is what he would like.

We got to do something, Bill said but even as he said it he knew that Osmond was right. His father had spent sleepless nights pacing the kitchen and even puking into the sink with anxiety over the pound. Pounding lobsters was always a gamble and each and every poundman on the coast would take one hell of a beating before he removed any more than a cupful of water from his pound.

Bill pictured his boat being driven out of the harbor with some other fisherman at the helm and he nodded consent to Osmond and Osmond nodded in return.

Bill watched him drive away and he went back to the doorway and leaned against the doorframe. He pulled his glasses off and wiped at his eyes which were raw as if salt burned.

Julius came up behind him and stood in the opposite side of the doorway. Neither said anything then Julius hacked and spat and said, Can't believe we found a fucking skull in there.

Bill turned his head slowly to Julius and looked the boy up and down then went back to looking at the driveway and the harbor mouth. A few gulls bobbed in the water and a crow rose from a spruce snag. It circled once then landed in the same tree.

You moving somewhere? Bill said.

I moved already.

Where to?

Up the east side. The old Smith house.

Bill nodded. He felt like everything had gone strange on him and the only thing that connected him to what he understood was Julius Wesley. That made him feel even stranger. He didn't want Julius to leave. His head throbbed. He wished he was on his boat.

How's the new boat?

Like fucking thunder, Julius said.

You got a new trap gang too?

Who said that?

Nobody.

Then why you asking?

I'm not, Bill said. He looked down and kicked at the ground with his rubber boot then walked to his truck and left. He drove slowly down the road and bashed his palm against the steering wheel and said, Fuck, Dad, but he didn't know why he said it and he almost said, *I can't do it,* but he didn't know what exactly it was that he couldn't do so he held the words crunched in his teeth like a piece of shell he planned to spit out.

Charlotte didn't come down for breakfast. Jonah and Virgil sat at the table without talking. Celeste made waffles. The classical music station played in the background. When the waffles were finished Celeste called up to Charlotte but didn't get an answer. She looked at Virgil and Jonah and neither spoke.

I'll get her, Virgil said.

Just leave her be, said Celeste. She'll come down when she's ready.

I should go, Jonah said. She don't want me around here and that's fine. I shouldn't be here anyhow.

He stood up and pushed his chair in.

You sit your highliner self back down, Virgil said. Celeste didn't make all these waffles for the two of us. Hell, we'd be fine with coffee.

Sit down, Jonah, Celeste said.

This Julius business, said Virgil. This ain't good.

You cool your jets, she said.

Virgil took a minute. He focused on Jonah. The price went up this morning. We got an extra quarter.

A quarter?

That's right. Now we're getting closer to half what it was last year.

I wonder how they'll do with them pounded lobsters.

They'll do fine on them. Jason Jackson's a mean bastard but he pays for what he wants.

Celeste put a plate of blueberry waffles and a glass pitcher of maple syrup and two sliced grapefruits on the table and she set out juice glasses and a carafe of orange juice. She forked thick slabs of bacon onto brown paper to drain and set it on the table and the smell of wood smoke and pepper and maple sugar filled the room.

Virgil stood up and said, I'm getting Charlotte.

Celeste and Jonah watched him hobble down the hallway and heard him slowly climb the stairs and heard his hard breathing and heard his feet make their way down the upstairs hallway.

• • •

Charlotte was dressed and sitting on her bed with a book. Virgil shut the door and sat on the bed next to her.

You okay, honey?

I'm fine.

The sun was bright on the snow through the window. There was a faint breeze on the cove and waves of sea smoke rose from the water. A dozen black ducks worked the currents and three gulls stood perched atop a rock. Sheets of yellowed tide ice lined the shore.

We have waffles ready downstairs.

I'm not hungry.

What's going on?

Nothing.

Look, Virgil said. I know this is because you and Jonah had something, but now you're impressed by Julius.

Charlotte turned away. She examined her fingers. All you want is for me to marry a lobsterman like Jonah and get pregnant.

We want you to be happy. But I want to talk about Julius and I'm not going to mess around. I don't like him because he's a bad human being. He scares me, Charlotte. He doesn't care about anything and if you think he's going to care for you then you're wrong.

How do you know so much about him? You just think you do.

I pay attention. Why don't you ask him why it is that little sister of his isn't right in the head?

I pay attention too, she said. And those are just rumors about his sister.

Fine, Virgil said. I said what I had to say and you can do what you want, okay? Be careful with him. But now it's breakfast time and Jonah's down there and he's family and in case you've forgotten his father just died. So get your ass down there.

Virgil put his hand on the back of her head and pulled her head into his stomach. She dropped the book and wrapped her arms around his torso.

I don't think Jonah wants to see me right now.

Why not?

I yelled at him last night. And I've been mean to him but can't help it. All of a sudden I just can't help it.

He's the Downcoast Highliner, Charlotte. He's a tough whoreson.

No he's not either. He's sensitive.

Either way, said Virgil. Come eat a waffle with him.

• • •

Bill drove down the long dirt road that followed the harbor line and parked on the end of the wharf. There wasn't anybody around. He got out and lit a cigarette. He peered down through the timbers at the swirling waters. Seaweed hung from the pylons and a red bushel onion bag of periwinkles rotted on bottom.

He sat on the wooden bench and leaned his forearms onto his thighs and let his head hang. He still felt the shape of his father's skull in his hands. The grainy texture and the salt-polished teeth and the single shining gold tooth. The flesh and cartilage and the brains eaten clean by swarms of lobsters so thick a man's hand wouldn't fit on bottom. That was his father.

The cold air carried the faint smell of bait. The wooden float below was slick with ice. The two trapdoors that opened to seawater storage for lobster crates were open and water swished and tossed in the empty compartments. Bill ran his hands over his head and felt the divots and roundings of his skull and wondered how similar it was to his father's.

He held his cigarette clenched in his teeth and puffed on it. The smoke rose out of his nose and burned his eyes. His boat and his brother's boat and his father's boat were all moored a hundred yards out. A boat made sense. A few weeks ago the whole world had made sense. He put bait in traps and put traps in the ocean and he caught lobsters and sold lobsters. That was it. Now he felt like his feet were tangled in a trap warp and the weight of the traps was slowly jerking him overboard. There was just no way in the world that his father's skull could end up in the pound without someone having put it there.

He gripped the cold bench with both hands as if to hold himself above water. He breathed slowly. He felt as if his brain had an itch. If he knew his father had been killed that would be one thing. If he knew who it was that killed his father that would be another thing and with both of those things together Bill would take his rifle and find the man and the man would be crow shit in under a week. But he didn't know either one and all that not knowing was enough to make him question a life that had previously been unquestionable.

After twenty minutes he got up and drove through the village to Virgil's house. Virgil's truck wasn't there and Bill turned around to leave but Jonah opened the door and waved at him and waited on the porch as Bill parked and got out. Bill tried to swallow but his mouth was too dry.

Jonah? Bill said as if not believing that it was really him.

What'n hell you doing? I seen Jason Jackson's truck go by.

We sold a load of bugs, Jonah.

Good. Celeste's got coffee on inside if you want some.

Hold on, Jonah. I got something we need to discuss.

You getting yourself a divorce?

It's about the old man, Jonah.

What about him?

Bill lit a cigarette and offered the pack to Jonah. We found him in the pound today, Jonah. Found his skull anyhow.

Jonah worked a cigarette out of Bill's pack. He held the cigarette loose in his fist and it took a moment for the fist to begin to tremble. You found his skull in the fucking pound? In the lobster pound?

Yeah, we found his skull in the pound, Jonah.

Jonah lit the cigarette. He watched the smoke ease out of his mouth. A shiver circled his torso and rose through his head and dissipated like vapor. He felt strangely calm as if entering some dream space and he was aware of this calmness and it worried him.

Ain't you gonna say something? Bill said.

What am I gonna say?

Bill blinked. I don't know.

Jonah thought of Virgil. It seemed that the last few weeks could not have happened. It seemed that his father must be out at his camp drinking beer and Charlotte must be inside writing a note that says, *I'll be over tonight* and it seemed that he was not about to be in the middle of a trap war with Osmond Randolph and Julius Wesley. But what did *seems* mean anyway? Everything *seemed* this way or that way. He remembered tumbling off his boat so far offshore and he wanted that again. He wanted again for the sea to open up and drag him into the world.

He blinked and said, How'd his boat end up offshore and him in the pound, Bill?

Hell if I know.

You tell Virgil?

That's why I'm here. To tell Virgil. Where's he gone to?

He's uptown running errands, Jonah said.

Bill blinked several times. He watched Jonah for a moment then said, Things ain't right, Jonah. I can't stop shaking.

I know it. I know it. Let's go on inside then.

Things ain't right, Bill repeated.

He followed Jonah into the house. Charlotte and Celeste were at the table.

Jonah avoided their eyes.

Celeste got up and poured a cup of coffee for Bill. How are you, Bill?

I'm good.

You don't look like you feel very good.

I don't feel good. No. I ain't good.

Are you okay? You and Osmond sold some lobsters out of the pound, didn't you?

Yeah. Ten thousand pounds this morning.

It must have been hard there without having your father with you.

Bill concentrated on the tabletop as he sipped his coffee.

We got leftover waffles if you're hungry, Bill.

Sure, said Bill. He looked defeated and repeated himself. Sure.

Celeste gave him a plate with waffles. She stood behind him and put her hand on his shoulder and squeezed the muscle. How's Erma Lee faring? Is she at home?

She's good, Celeste. Thanks for asking. Bill lifted his fork but didn't touch the waffles. He held the fork in front of himself as if examining its tines for trueness.

They heard a truck park and soon Virgil ambled down the hall and into the kitchen with Chowder following him. Captain Bill. You eating my waffles?

I guess I am, Virgil.

Good, said Virgil. Celeste still had her hand on Bill's shoulder and Virgil put his hand on the other shoulder and squeezed. A big happy family right here. He went to the cupboard and took out a bottle of coffee brandy and filled a glass with ice and poured the brandy. Celeste watched as he sloshed some milk into it.

Goddamn it, Virgil, she said.

Virgil didn't respond. He took a sip and put the drink in front of Bill. He mixed another drink and put it in front of Jonah then lit a cigarette. Jonah took a swallow and bent and lifted Chowder onto his lap and the dog licked at Jonah's mouth and ears.

Bill said, We found the old man today.

You found the old man, Virgil said and grunted and his big cheeks shook.

Celeste stared at her husband.

Yeah, Bill said. He held his drink with both hands as if the cold liquid would warm his fingers. On the third tow the drag come up with his skull in it.

The room dropped silent.

You found your father's skull? Charlotte said.

Bill nodded. Third tow.

How'd you know it was his?

Bill blinked several times. His gold tooth is how. But you could tell anyway.

Celeste stared at Virgil. Her face drained and when Virgil saw this he crossed the room and took her in his arms. His cheek brushed her cheek. Then his voice thick and warm as blood shot down her ear and she was the only one to hear him say *please trust me.* His voice was honest and urgent and his thumbs brushed her cheekbones and pressed the soft pockets of skin below her eyelids and she gave him a slight nod but said, We need to call the police.

He kissed her forehead and said, No. Not yet.

Virgil went to the cupboard and took out a third and fourth glass and mixed two drinks. He put one in front of Charlotte. He leaned against the counter with one palm down. He exhaled for a long time and when he spoke he spoke slow. Tell me, what'd Osmond do?

What'd he do? Bill said. He threw the skull over the dam into the harbor is what he did. Hell if I ever expected that. Threw it half a mile near and told me to keep it quiet. He don't want cops and such down there and I don't blame him for that.

He threw the skull. Virgil swirled the ice around his glass and sipped it and wiped the brandy and milk from his mustache. Good.

Good? Bill said. How's that good? How'n hell'd the old man get in there unless someone put him in there? He didn't go and jump in the pound and his boat somehow run itself half to France. It don't make a goddamn bit of sense.

Most likely not, Captain, said Virgil. Where's Erma Lee at?

She's home or over to her cousin's or something. I don't know. Why?

Just wondering.

I'm heading there now, said Bill. I'm getting my dive suit on and I'm going in that fucking pound and I'm seeing what I find and I'm bringing the Highliner with me too, whether he likes it or not.

Jonah looked around the room. He heard his brother and Virgil talking but the voices sounded like they came through intercoms. He held Chowder with both arms and the dog licked at his mouth and he didn't stop her and he didn't stop the image of his father's skeleton from occupying his mind. Other thoughts drifted by and he saw himself getting in his truck and driving through some desert landscape or shutting himself up at the camp for a very long time. Then he saw himself holding Julius by the throat.

One second, Virgil said. Tell me about Jason Jackson, Captain.

Jason? What the fuck for? Enough with the fucking questions, Virgil. I don't know nothing you don't know. I met his driver Daniel. They said Jason's over in godfuck Japan then he's going to Hawaii and then Osmond's visiting him is all I heard today. I asked Osmond if it was pound business but he said it was his business and his alone. Now I got to go.

Virgil dropped silent. His cheeks hung and his eyelids drooped.

Virgil? said Bill.

I'm thinking—Did he mention Benji?

No.

Okay, said Virgil. You go ahead and dive on him then. That'll work fine.

Work fine? Celeste said. She held her hands up at the sides of her head as if she would pull her own hair out. Her voice was angry and frantic. I've heard enough. This is absolutely ridiculous. It's frightening. I'm going to call the police and I don't give a shit what else.

She stepped to the wall and took the phone from the hook but before she could dial Virgil was at her side clicking the phone off with his finger. When he spoke his voice was kind and it was understanding. Celeste, he said. Think about this. If you call the police they are going to drain that pound out. It will be a total loss. Those lobsters in there were paid for on credit and Bill and Jonah and Osmond owe on them. And there's the mortgage on the pound itself. There's just no possible way to drain that pound and have these boys not go absolutely bankrupt. If it was just Osmond, that would be fine by me. But Bill and Jonah have a stake in this. If they lose those lobsters that are in there right now, the pound will be sold. They will lose everything they have. Houses and boats and all of it. Period. Maybe the buyer will use it as a lobster pound but chances are that we'll see a summer home put right there. Is that what we want? Is that what Nic would want?

Celeste's face quivered. Her eyes darted around as if she couldn't focus.

Bill rounded the table and put his hand on her shoulder. I know it, Celeste. I want to call them as bad as you, believe me. It's my dad in there. But Virgil's right. There just ain't no way.

Celeste still held the phone in her fist and Virgil still held his finger over the button. She turned and looked to Jonah as if to plead her case to him. She saw on his face that he agreed with Virgil and

Bill. She slowly hung up. Again Virgil took her in his arms but she held her hands out to the side and would not touch him.

When he released her she said, Why not have police divers, then? If Bill can dive in there, the police could too.

Jonah spoke up. They're right, Celeste. The cops won't be happy with just diving. One thing will lead to another. I agree with them.

Virgil gazed at Jonah and they locked eyes and Virgil nodded once to him.

Bill said, Good then. I'm gone.

Jonah stood up to go.

Can I come? said Charlotte.

No, said Celeste. No you don't. You stay here.

It's fine, Mom, Charlotte said. I want to go.

And see Nicolas's dead body or skeleton or whatever they find? I don't think so.

I can go, Charlotte said.

Celeste turned the faucet on and held her hand under the stream until the water came hot. Do whatever you want, she said and squeezed dish soap into the sink. All of you. Just do whatever the fuck you want. I'll make your fucking dinner.

• • •

Jonah and Charlotte waited in the truck outside Bill's house. Jonah felt his leg and hip against hers and he suddenly forgot all else and remembered a moment months ago when all was good and she'd climbed into his bed with only her thin yellow underwear on. How dark her summertime skin had been and how bright the yellow was against the skin. He forced himself to look out the window but all he saw was yellow fabric and smooth skin and all he felt was the heat of her hip against his.

Snow covered the roofs and yards of the dozen or so farmhouses around them. Everything was quiet except for an urchin dragger idling in the harbor. He glanced at Charlotte and her lips were crimped tight and she looked as furious as she had the night before.

Are you okay? he asked. His voice was quiet. Did something happen last night?

No, she said. I'm fine. Just leave me alone about it. Please.

• • •

Minutes later. Bill turned the truck around and began toward the pound.

You think someone killed your father, Bill? Erma Lee said as they drove. She sat wedged between Jonah and the door.

I don't know.

Jonah didn't say anything for a while and he thought about the things Virgil had told him then said, Seems a bit like it. I mean, how the fuck else would he end up in there?

Yeah, Erma Lee said. What do you think, Bill?

I don't know.

That's what makes sense though, Erma Lee said. Don't it?

I just flat out don't know. For fuckachrist's sake. I don't know. Now everyone shut up. Please.

Jesus fucking Christ, Jonah said. He shifted his legs and hips and tried to make more room but all four of them were stuffed across the bench seat. All he could smell was Erma Lee's perfume and all he could see was Charlotte's angry face. The windshield felt too close as if gradually descending. His skin was tight and itching and sweating and trees blinked by one by one. He felt near panic. He fought the urge to elbow his way out of the moving truck and dive into a snow bank. He wrapped his fingers around themselves and drove his feet into the floor panel and sighed.

Charlotte looked over at him with disapproval and disgust and said, God.

It felt like it took an hour to reach the pound. Bill backed the truck up to the building and parked. He left the engine running and no one moved. Then Jonah said, Open the goddamned doors someone.

Erma Lee got out and Jonah piled out next and he walked over the snow bank and down the rocks to the water and he splashed his face and looked out over the harbor mouth. He breathed in and out several times. The names Osmond Randolph and Jason Jackson and Julius Wesley surged and confusion spread like sea foam in his head. He bent and splashed his face once more. He tasted the saltwater on his lips. It seemed that everything Virgil had said was true and every reason he could now think of to not call the police seemed petty and trite but even so he'd rather shoot Osmond himself and go to prison himself than be the one to make the call.

When he turned around he saw Charlotte standing on the bank above him. Her hands were locked at her waist and she lifted them toward Jonah in a gesture which he could not interpret. Virgil had arrived and she got in the truck with him. He had a cigarette going and he lifted his glass and drank.

Jonah crouched on the rocks and put his head in his hands. He spat salty white spittle onto the rocks. He pinched his eyes closed and said, Fucking Julius Wesley.

He climbed the bank and helped Bill pull his tank and weight belt on. Bill slipped into the water and fitted his mask over his face. Snow ringed the pound above the high water mark. He tested his air then dipped beneath the water and Jonah and Erma Lee watched his silhouette move like a bird through the water. They lost sight of him but followed his air bubble trail as he circled then he stood and said, I can't see shit. We got her all mudded up from dragging and them bugs are right riled. Give me that light.

Jonah fished Bill's dive light out of the bag and handed it to Bill. The tide poured out through the dam.

Tides going fast, Jonah said.

Bill glanced at the dam and nodded. He squeezed the dive light trigger and looked at the beam and pulled his mask down and dipped into the water.

After twenty minutes he came up with two leg bones. The bones were clean and beige like the skull and Bill said, She's clearing up some now.

He went back under and Jonah didn't touch the bones but stared at them and after another ten minutes Bill found the pelvis and torso. Erma Lee climbed up the ladder and walked past Charlotte and Virgil and disappeared down the road without looking back.

Bill stopped when he had what he figured to be his father's entire skeleton except for the skull. He pulled the weight belt and tank off and handed them to Jonah and pulled himself up onto the float.

This ain't right, he said.

Them lobsters you sold are half the old man, huh, said Jonah. He felt seasick but kept talking. Someone's gonna find a finger in their goddamned tomalley. That'd be enough reason for them to drain her out right there. Lobsters eating people ain't exactly appetizing.

Bill's eyeballs were big and round without his glasses on. That ain't exactly what I was thinking weren't right. He took a moment to breathe then said, You think we should call the cops, Jonah? Just let them drain her out? The gulls didn't drop him in here.

I know that. But what'n hell the cops going to do?

I don't know. Whatever cops do. Look for a weapon.

They already looked at his boat with a fucking magnifying lens.

We could call the FBI, Bill said.

Yeah, and like you said, they'll drain this whole thing and we'll be fucked. You want to lose your boat? You want to lose this pound?

I don't know. I just don't know anymore.

See what Virgil says.

Virgil's right ignorant drunk. He couldn't pull a sick whore off a pisspot.

Might be, said Jonah. Hell, I don't know.

Bill loaded his dive gear into the bed of his truck. Jonah stayed on the float. Their father's bones were piled on the wooden deck. Jonah stared at the bones and had a hard time understanding that the dismembered skeleton was his father and not some coyote-ravaged deer carcass.

When Bill returned he said, What'd you want to do with him, Jonah?

Jonah thought for a few seconds. Put him in his coffin? Next to Mom?

We ain't digging up a grave.

I guess not. I don't know, Jonah said and as he gazed at the bones the fact that this was his father suddenly penetrated and he fell to his knees and vomited.

Are you okay, Jonah? Virgil said. He stood behind Bill with a glass in his hand and a cigarette burning. Charlotte was still in the truck.

Yeah, said Jonah. He wiped at his lips and nostrils and tears flooded from his eyes. His entire head throbbed. Just puking.

Let's get him in a tote or something, Captain. Jonah, are you sure you're okay?

Yeah. I'm fine.

This is hard stuff, I know, and I'm sorry for that. You two shouldn't have to go through this. But someone needs to come back at low water tonight and see if that skull's out there somewhere and I'm too old and fat and crippled to get over those rocks. We'll take Nic offshore tomorrow and give him a proper burial.

I can do it, said Jonah and hacked and spat and stifled a sob. I can do it, he said again. He thought for a few seconds before continuing. But you really think he was killed, Virgil?

Bill pulled on a pair of blue rubber gloves and waited for Virgil's response.

Virgil swished his drink in his mouth and swallowed and his voice turned angry. What in the clamfuck sort of question is that? Why don't you tell me all the ways you think he might not of been killed?

I don't know.

Virgil breathed in and out. He closed his eyes then opened them and his voice was once more gentle when he spoke. Neither do I, he said. Neither do I.

I don't get it. Jonah blew his nose into the water then leaned down and sucked a mouthful of water and gargled the salt and spat it out. You think it's like you said, Virgil? With Japan and Jason Jackson and Osmond?

What's that? Bill said.

Nothing, Virgil said.

Nothing what? What's Jason Jackson and Japan got to do with anything?

Nothing, Virgil said again.

Fine then, Bill said as he put the bones into two fish trays. He moved slowly and the bones thudded against the hard plastic.

Virgil shook his head at Jonah then walked away.

Fuck you, Jonah whispered to the spot Virgil had occupied. He watched the empty doorway. Bill stood next to him. What's Virgil talking about, Jonah? Jason Jackson?

I don't know. He had some bullshit notion that Osmond done it.

I'd say bullshit is right. I'm more concerned for Virgil than Osmond anyhow, Bill said. He's drunk as hell lately. He ain't well.

I know it. I know it.

Bill and Jonah each carried a fish tray full of bones to the truck and as they crossed the driveway Jonah saw Charlotte in Virgil's truck watching him. She looked angry but she made no sign that she saw him and he didn't care at all.

• • •

That evening Jonah drove to the pound. He sat in his truck watching dusk settle as the tide receded and the last light flushed like dying embers over the rock and sand and seaweed. Even inside the cab he could feel the air turning colder. He smelled the saltwater and he watched the western sky. He closed his eyes and listened to the gentle work of waves on the shoreline. The methodic beat brought to mind the image of the pound as a heart only now his mind allowed the image to sculpt itself into a body that surrounded the heart. The body was neither man nor beast but a living coastline of rock and water and sky and Jonah saw himself and his brother and the memory of their father stuck within that cold flesh.

He made his way down the riprap and rockweed slope then over a patchwork of sand and boulders. A tongue of water poured out of the sluiceway in the center of the dam and ran in a small river into the harbor. The earth spun and darkness approached and far out at sea the tide shifted beneath the moon. Jonah waded across the tidal river and walked aimlessly among the rocks in search of his father's skull. He felt stuck within that body he'd imagined and it was solid and it was real. Every few minutes he'd look up at the line of sea and remind himself that he was actually out there on the rocks searching for a lost part of his father.

He paused at the tidemark and stood ankle-deep in the water. He faced the open ocean. He watched the crescent moon set in the southwest and all faded to black. The Two Penny buoy flashed and Drown Boy Rock spun and suddenly the ocean receded and left Jonah on bare rock. He looked around wondering where the water had gone and as he did so the sea surged back and nearly filled his boots but then again it receded as if the entirety of the

Atlantic was subject to the maelstrom of humanity and not the strict order of the universe. Jonah whispered the word *Dad* out loud and his voice disappeared into the air. He followed the tidemark toward Burnt Island and climbed the ledges gone purple in the darkness. He turned toward the pound and as he crossed a bank of dead rockweed he saw the skull. He stood over it for a full minute before picking it up. The bone felt as if it had been at sea for years.

He slumped down onto the heap of seaweed and perched the skull on his knee and balanced it upright with one hand. He quickly remembered so long ago gripping that head in his arms as he bounced upon his father's back to the ringing of his mother's laughter. The skull glowed white and the eye sockets loomed like black holes large enough to encompass a fist. For much of his life Jonah had rehearsed the blows he would deal his father but now nothing would come as if the skull held the same power as the man. Jonah stared at the skull and wished he were stronger than he was.

The house was quiet when Jonah returned. He went straight to the guest room and stripped his clothes off and climbed into bed. He lay awake with images of skulls and lobsters and waves crashing through his head but soon the crashing ceased and the frenzied sound of thousands of feeding lobsters erupted like an infestation in his eardrums. He rolled and folded the pillow over his head but that was no help so he shoved a finger into his ear and wished he could sink it to the knuckle.

Finally he fell asleep but after only an hour he awoke to Virgil's horn. He dressed and when he opened his door Charlotte stepped out of her bedroom. She wore white flannel pajamas and her hair was in a ponytail and her skin was pale and blotched with sleep. Both stopped but neither spoke. He caught her eye for a moment and when she shifted he thought she would speak but instead she stepped into the bathroom and shut the door.

He heard the shower turn on. He grabbed the doorknob and was about to turn it when he heard Celeste yell for Virgil to stop honking.

Get the Highliner out here, Virgil hollered.

I'm coming, Jonah yelled down the steps.

He listened to the shower and heard the splashes as Charlotte moved. He opened the door and stepped inside. He shut the door. He crossed the room full of steam and stood next to the curtain and said, Charlotte.

Jesus Christ, Jonah.

He pulled the curtain back a few inches and saw a slice of her body.

Get the fuck out of here.

He started to say something but she cut him off.

I don't care. Get out before I scream.

The lid was down on the toilet and he sat on it. I'm sorry, he said. His voice was gentle. Charlotte stuck her head out from behind the curtain and peered at him then stepped out of the shower and wrapped a towel around herself. She put her hand on Jonah's head and dug her fingers into his hair.

Jonah, she said. Look at me.

He tipped his head back so he could see her. Her skin was red from the heat of the shower. Her hair was slicked back. Beads of water slid down her forehead. He saw the shape of her hips beneath the white towel and he reached his hand up and set it on her waist and pulled her to him. She took a step and their knees touched. He leaned his head into her breastbone. He shut his eyes. She put her other hand on his head and held him pinned to her.

The shower was still running and the room was hot with steam. The windows were fogged and outside lay full dark. He coughed and choked several times and when he settled she stepped back and lifted his chin and kissed his forehead. I'm sorry about your father, Jonah. And about us.

I don't get it.

You're ten years older than I am.

You got to give it a chance to change, Charlotte. He still had his hand on her hip and he put the other hand on her other hip.

I'd rather have you as a big brother again.

What?

I miss being friends, Jonah. I miss feeling like you and the Captain are my big brothers. Like when I was little.

Christ, Jonah said. He heard the whir of the exhaust fan as if it were within his head and he looked around the bathroom and he looked back up at her. You're not little anymore and things aren't always going to be the same.

I know you don't understand, she said.

Understand what?

We'll talk later, Jonah. I love you but I'm leaving and right now I just need a friend. She rubbed his shoulders and kissed his forehead again. You need a friend too. Aren't you scared, Jonah? About your father and stuff?

The hell with it, he said. We're going to dump him overboard right now.

Charlotte's head tilted to the side as she looked at him.

I found his skull last night, Charlotte. Down below the pound.

Charlotte settled onto her knees so that her face was level with his. She refitted the fold of her towel between her breasts. She ran her hand over his cheek and held the back of his neck and he leaned his head into the hand as if it would hold all of him.

I always wanted to yell at him, he said. I planned the shit I'd say but never did. I thought I'd find that skull and smash it but I just held it like a little fucking kid.

Jesus, Jonah, Charlotte said. Maybe you need someone to talk to. Like a counselor or therapist to talk to about this stuff. It's too much for anybody.

I need you.

Charlotte stood up. Jonah, this is serious. You need help. You should call the police.

Fuck that, Jonah said. He stood up and put his hand on the doorknob. And don't you go whispering a word about this to a soul. And that means Julius too even though he ain't got one.

* * *

He didn't see Celeste when he went downstairs. He met Virgil at the truck.

Get the hell in here, Jonah. We got work to do.

A layer of ice covered the driveway. The wind blew steady from the southeast and rocked the birches in long sways.

Jonah got in the truck. I guess we're having another funeral, he said.

That's right.

The truck cab smelled like old tobacco and brandy and Virgil had stains down the front of his gray sweatshirt. The heater was on and the truck was hot. All that remained of Nicholas Graves was in the truck bed.

Virgil looked over at Jonah. Are you okay?

I'm fine.

Virgil sighed. He went silent as the truck idled. When he spoke his voice was so quiet that Jonah had to struggle to hear him. You don't have to do this. I know it's hard, and I know it's wrong.

Jonah looked out the window.

Jonah, Virgil said and he reached over and gripped Jonah's wrist. Jonah, this is something that no one should ever have to go through and I'm sorry for that. You can stay here and Bill can stay too. Neither one of you should have to do this. I'll do it. Nicolas wasn't my father.

I know it. I just want all this to be done.

Virgil held his grip on Jonah's wrist. Stay here, Jonah. Go take a shower and get in bed. Eat something. I'll tell Bill the same thing. This isn't the sort of thing that leaves a man once it's finished. You've already been through too much.

Thanks, Jonah said. Tears pooled in his eyes. He envisioned his brother handing his father's bones out of the pound one at a time and the skull set in a bed of seaweed and then he envisioned Charlotte and he said, I'm going.

Bill was waiting in his truck when they pulled onto the wharf. His face was pale and bags hung like bruises beneath his eyes. The rotted and paint-chipped bait house doors were closed and locked and the bait buckets and lobster crates were inside and the ropes had been taken off the winchhead gallows. Most of the lobster fleet had been hauled out although three boats had makeshift plywood and sheet plastic houses built over the work decks for tending winter urchin divers. A half dozen other boats had been rigged with drag gear for either scallops or urchins. The three quahog draggers hadn't moved in days and a handful of offshore draggers both gypsy and local had arrived for the season and their rigging tinked and slapped metallic in the cold air.

Nicolas's mooring was the closest to them and the *Cinderella*'s white hull was lit by the small wharf light so the boat looked somehow alone among the harbor fleet. Jonah and Bill both took a moment to look at the boat then loaded the fish trays full of bones. The three of them steamed out of the harbor in Virgil's boat *Charlotte & Celeste*. Bill stood next to Virgil with his arms on the bulkhead. They both smoked and they both looked as if they'd already survived something they should not have. The sky was still dark and the head of the cape was a black arm grasping at the water and the rocks were fingernails slicked with salt ice and starlight. A half mile out Ram's Head rose above them in a sheer cliff face.

Jonah sat on the stern with his sweatshirt hood up and his orange oil jacket hood on top of that. He held his hands together in his sweatshirt pocket and his chin tucked against the cold hard wind. He watched the black water slide by and he listened to the boat's splash and he told himself that this was what his father would have wanted. The sea was heavy and came southeast and Jonah felt a shadow that would haunt the three of them for the rest of their lives forming but he saw no alternative.

The abandoned lighthouse on Two Penny looked like the remnants of a stormed castle and once past the island there was no more protection from the Atlantic. The boat rocked and heaved and Jonah caught a shield of water across his body. He went to the wheelhouse with Virgil and Bill and grabbed the bulkhead and fit himself between Bill and the port wall. They crested a wave and a line of spray drove into the windshield and poured over the house.

Jonah looked to Virgil. Virgil was lit by the scant wheelhouse light. Jonah said, You okay, Virgil?

Finest.

You don't seem so good, Bill said.

I ain't the best, Captain. And you ain't either.

I'm fine. Considering.

Virgil turned his head to Bill. The bow dove into a wave trough and shuddered against a wall of green water. They rose with a surge. Explain to me this pound business with you and Osmond.

There ain't no business. We sold a truckload. We'll run things the same as he did with the old man.

Did he give you any paperwork yet?

No.

That's not right. You need a title. He should have given you a title by now.

Bill rubbed his eyes and adjusted his glasses and wiped his hand along his jawline.

Osmond isn't in this to be partnering with you, Bill.

How do you know that?

How do I know that? Because I pay attention, and because I know Osmond.

So you think Osmond shoved the old man in the pound thinking he'd own it free and clear?

I'm not sure what happened yet, Captain.

Bill rapped his knuckles on the fiberglass bulkhead. That's bullshit. Osmond's not got shit to do with it.

Virgil nodded. He turned and grabbed Bill's head with both hands. Bill tried to shrug him off but could not and Virgil turned Bill's head to face the stern of the boat and the boneyard held there. Look at that, Captain. That is your dead father. Right there. That is your father.

Then Virgil released him. He held the spoked wheel with one hand and his cigarette butt in the other. His head hung as if held by vertebrae alone. The sun was beginning to rise off to the east. In front of them a dark spread of clouds crossed the horizon but far offshore the sea and sky together shone as a single light.

Virgil spoke again. Things aren't as black and white as you want them to be, Bill. You got to get used to that. It's okay to not know something. You understand me?

Bill continued to stare at his father's broken skeleton. Jonah put a hand on his brother's shoulder. Bill turned to him and the look in his eyes wasn't the brotherly look Jonah had expected so he removed the hand. Bill's eyes were red and his pupils were tiny black puddles.

Fucking Jonah the Highliner, Bill said. You standing there smiling at the old man being gone? You think this is all so fucking funny?

The bow rose on a wave crest then piled downward and drove through the next wave and green water poured over the boat and cascaded down the washrails and filled the stern. The diesel engine groaned. The bone fish trays went afloat and slid to the starboard rail as the water drained out the scuppers.

Bill stared at Jonah. You always hated him, ain't that right? Ever since Mom died you hated him.

Jonah didn't say anything. He watched a wave crest and break as the *Charlotte & Celeste* heaved. He felt everything inside of him collapsing but a surge of adrenaline kept him afloat like a life vest.

You done blamed him his whole life for that, Bill said. And you're too chickenshit to say anything when he's living.

The hell I blamed him for that. I blamed him for near drowning me is what I blamed him for. And you near drowned yourself, or you forgotten that fact?

You blamed him for Mom and he knew it. That's why he threw you overboard.

She died in a fucking car wreck, Bill. How the hell would I blame that on him?

You wouldn't even so much as visit him when he was living right down the way and when he up and dies you think it's a big joke is what you do.

You think he ever visited me? Ever once? You think he ever set foot in my trailer, all the times he drove by? I'll tell you how many, Captain. Not one single time. Six years I been there and not one time did he knock on the fucking door. So fuck you, Bill.

You don't know shit, Jonah. Just because you run off to some prep-boy college don't mean you know shit. I stayed home and fished with the old man.

That done you a lot of good, Captain. Lucky you ain't on the stern with him.

Bill took a step back and slammed both hands against Jonah's chest and drove him against the port wall. Jonah's head rapped the Plexiglas window behind him and Bill held him pinned there.

Easy, said Virgil.

Bill's eyes blinked and his lips quivered. Jonah felt his brother's whole body shake but he stood calm. Virgil let go of the wheel and grabbed Bill by the hood and pulled him stumbling back and as he did Jonah pushed off the wall and into Bill. He drove Bill to the floor and landed on him and hit him over and over until Virgil pulled him away. With Virgil gone from the wheel the boat turned sideways in a wave trough and dipped a washrail. Water filled the stern. Virgil lunged for the wheel and gunned the engine and the bow lifted into the air as if they'd go over backward. Black water rushed out the scuppers and across the stern. Jonah stood against the window and shook and watched with disbelief as the boat drained and settled. The sun wasn't visible but it lit the world as if someone had polished the gray dawn silver.

Bill got up. He looked like he'd been underwater. His mouth and nose bled. His glasses were bent on his face and he took them off and tried to bend them back but couldn't keep his balance or settle his hands. A wave crested next to them and Bill squatted like a wrestler as the water drove over his back.

He crawled up between Virgil and Jonah and said, You got my cigarettes soaked.

Now adrenaline shook Jonah. A part of him wanted to keep hitting Bill and another part wanted to hug him. He watched Bill try to rebend his thick glasses. The skin around Bill's eyes was soft and white from being hidden behind the glasses his entire life and suddenly the whole of Bill's face looked like a child's and everything Jonah felt about his brother turned to a single and sheer feeling of empathy as if he was his brother's keeper.

I'm sorry, Jonah said.

It's fine.

You two try that shit again and you'll drown us all. We're going to bury your father out here because that is what he would've wanted and that is what we want.

Jonah expected Virgil to say something more but he didn't. Both brothers nodded and for a few minutes all they heard were the workings of water and diesel. Jonah watched the water and felt a motion within like the first touch of seasickness.

Virgil looked at Bill. You going to freeze to death or do you need to go below and dry off?

I ain't going down there, Bill said. Hell.

• • •

They heard the Leviathan before they could see it. It was a roar and a crash like the smash of steel and glass and as they crested the swells they glimpsed spray and foam hanging in the atmosphere like the discharge of a seawater inferno. Soon they saw the first of the waves and it rose twenty feet in the air and broke like thunder over the four-fathom shoal. White foam tumbled and shook the ocean. Everywhere was whitewater and curling waves and they could not see the sky for the spray and foam and the smooth glass rising of the next swell.

Virgil worked the boat around the edge of the breakers.

Jesus Christ, Virgil, Jonah yelled and he looked for something to hold on to but found nothing. He watched a comber loom twice the height of the boat and curl and break next to them and the spray piled into them like hits from a shotgun.

Bill watched the breakers wide-eyed and yelled to Jonah without looking away, He's going to fucking kill us.

Another wave broke and the *Charlotte & Celeste* skated sideways.

Okay, Virgil yelled. Ashes to ashes. Say what you got to say and get him overboard.

Jonah looked to Bill and Bill looked to Jonah and neither moved.

Get him the Christ overboard, Virgil yelled as he worked the boat away from the breakers and into the smoother swells. Bill and Jonah kept their eyes on the tempest as if it were a poorly shackled beast and the beast's open maw rang in their ears and filled their heads. Virgil's face was red and grim. Chilled sweat combined with seawater and streamed down his cheeks. The boat pitched and rolled and heaved and the waves came in walls that eclipsed the sky. The breakers broke. Jonah's mouth was dry and his tongue leather and his entire body soaked. He tried to swallow but could not.

Jesus fucking Christ, Bill yelled into the wind. He went to the stern and grabbed a fish tray and lifted it to the washrail. He held it on the rail and he tried to keep his balance as water drilled against him and broke against the gunwales.

Hurry the fuck up, Virgil shouted. He maneuvered farther into the swell and the bow dove and surfaced with a shower of water over the house and onto Bill and it nearly knocked him over. Jonah pushed past Virgil and went to the stern and grabbed the skull from the tray and dropped it overboard and it disappeared too fast. Water poured over both brothers and they faced each other as each silently beseeched the other. Then Bill reached into the tray and dropped a bone overboard. Jonah did so as well and they stood there on the stern with the ocean churning and seething as they tossed their father into the chop bone by bone by bone and Virgil glanced back and bit his cheeks with his molars and pinched his eyes closed and said out loud, God help us.

Celeste sat on the edge of the bed and placed her hand on Virgil's foot. The skin was damp and the foot swollen. Veins rose black beneath the skin and Celeste thought for the thousandth time that her husband had spent more waking hours at sea than on dry land. His body proved that. Hundreds of thousands of hours squinting over wave and through fog or into sun and it was no wonder that his reality was so different from her own.

Through the window she could see the small cove and the old towering spruces and the chunks of salt ice that scoured the shoreline. Virgil shivered beneath the blankets. He lit a cigarette then rolled onto his back and set the ashtray on his stomach. He smoked the cigarette down as Celeste watched.

She swallowed. She couldn't tell if she was angry or scared or disgusted. She said, I don't know what you're doing, and frankly I don't care. You're killing yourself and you're taking Jonah with you. If you want to hurt yourself then goddamn it don't do it around your family and don't do it around Jonah. Just crawl off into the bushes and die on your own.

Maybe I will.

I will not allow you to drag Jonah down with you. And I will not allow you to go down. Nicolas died by accident. Even the Coast Guard said so. I'm sorry, but people die and we all have to deal with that. And Osmond Randolph might be a strange man or a bad man but he's no murderer. And if he is that's up to the cops. Not you.

Nic wouldn't get caught in a trap warp. It's not right.

Then call the cops. Call the FBI. I don't know what happened and neither do you.

It ain't right, Virgil said. They found his boat out past Spencer Ledges. His boat shouldn't have been out that far.

Virgil's voice drifted off and he closed his eyes. Celeste heard the deliberation in his breaths. She brought her legs up onto the bed and crossed them ankle to ankle. She looked up at the ceiling white and shadowless. Her voice was soft when she spoke. You can't call the police now, can you? It's too late, isn't it? You dumped his body. That's what you three were doing today. Now it's done, at least.

Virgil opened his eyes.

She leaned forward and kissed him. Her lips lingered on the big loose cheek. She whispered into his ear, I'm proud of you for that, Virgil. Nicolas would have wanted you and his sons to do that. I'm scared of what is going to happen, but goddamn it I believe you did the right thing today.

Virgil's pupils shifted back and forth. Celeste wondered with a feeling like a waterspout pressing her chest if her husband was right about all of it. She could feel his heart thumping against the silence then a series of muscle spasms shook the mattress and Virgil lifted his torso from the bed.

Celeste put her hand on his forehead. I'm calling a doctor.

I'm fine. Tired is all.

You are not fine. You have a fever and you're shivering, Virgil. She ran her hand down the side of his neck and onto his bicep. And you're soaked.

It got cold out there.

If you don't look better in the morning, I'm calling a doctor.

Fine.

I know you miss Nicolas, she said. But this isn't helping. Whatever this is. I told you that I trust you and I believe in what you did today, but that is as far as I go. This madness has got to end because my trust is about to.

O smond crossed the bridge over the river. The traffic was fast and steady and streamed in patterns he had trouble discerning. He stole glimpses at the barges and the tugs and the murky water below. He dipped into the tunnel and it glistened and howled like a wolf throat and when he came up he was in the city. He turned off the interstate and took several turns and drove through an industrial area on a wide empty street with dark puddles and piles of dirty snow. He parked beside a warehouse lined with refrigerated trucks and dumpsters and a stack of wooden pallets and three broken-down ice machines.

Daniel sat at a desk and smoked a cigarette and wore a suit and tie. He stood when Osmond came in. He was a foot shorter than Osmond but he was stocky and muscled. They shook hands.

I'm glad you came down here. How was the drive? New bridge. New tunnel.

Fine. You've done well, Osmond said as if Daniel himself had built the bridge and tunnel.

Check this out, Daniel said. He opened the large metal door and led Osmond into a tank room which held one swimming pool–sized tank and other smaller tanks along the periphery. Stacks of blue and gray lobster crates lined one wall. A man on a forklift sped by. The sound of running and bubbling water and exhaust fans echoed throughout the warehouse. The room smelled like saltwater and bleach.

Here it is, said Daniel.

Osmond peered into the new tank. The sides came to his waist. The bottom was clear blue like a swimming pool and lined with metal aerators. Cables spanned the tank creating lanes that held neat rows of submerged lobster crates. Osmond put his hand into the water and swished it around.

Good, he said.

The forklift shut off and the man who'd been operating it crossed the wet concrete floor and stood in front of Osmond. He was Osmond's height and had a round stomach which hung from beneath his white laboratory jacket. He wore cutoff sweatpants and rubber boots and his beard was gray and white and his nose was big and round.

Osmond my man, he said. His voice was loud.

Jason. How are you?

Staying the course, Osmond.

I'm glad to hear it.

And you're joining me tonight?

That is the plan, Osmond said.

I'm happy, said Jason. Come with me.

The three men walked around the tank and into a smaller refrigerated room. The smooth wet concrete floor was covered in pallets and the pallets were covered in big eye and skipjack tuna and broadbill swordfish and striped marlin. Each fish had a wedge of meat cut from its tail and the wedges were set atop the fish.

I bought these in Honolulu yesterday, Jason said. He bent over and shoved his hand into a big eye's gills and nodded at the temperature. He took the wedges of meat from two big eyes and held them next to each other. Both pieces were red but one was dark and cherry as new blood. The other looked like cheap beef.

See that, Jason said. That's a three-dollar-a-pound difference right there.

He drew a knife out of a plastic scabbard attached to his boot and sliced deeper into the dark tuna and cut off an additional wedge of meat.

Open up, Jason said.

Osmond opened his mouth and Jason placed the meat on Osmond's tongue.

Osmond let it dissolve for a second then chewed. He nodded his approval.

All longlined down there. It's all Japanese run in Hawaii. The Japs know what they have. They know how to treat a fish, unlike these poor Italian bastards around here. The Mediterranean is beautiful and the people are beautiful but they are slobs, Osmond. Absolute fucking slobs.

Jason looked at his watch and said, We're getting set for an auction in a few minutes. Stick around. This is our first time buying from Honolulu.

Osmond stood against the back wall and sipped a cup of coffee as fifteen men and women arrived and examined the fish. Daniel poured himself a cup of coffee and stood next to Osmond. This is how they do it in Japan. One fish at a time.

I've seen it done, Osmond said.

In Japan?

Portland used to do it.

Yes, said Daniel. We don't get enough fish here but Jason will start a line with Honolulu. Honolulu is skeptical but you know Jason.

Yes, said Osmond with a nod.

The buyers all held clipboards and Jason led them up and down the aisles of pallets. He started the bidding on each fish and the process was fast and Osmond couldn't understand the quick and thick Boston accents. When the bidding stopped Jason wrote the buyer's name and the price on a tag and set it atop the fish. The buyers were chefs and restaurateurs and specialty marketers and purveyors.

When the auction was finished Jason gave his clipboard to Daniel and took Osmond by the elbow and led him back into the tank room. Jason was sweating and his shirt was unbuttoned at

the collar and his laboratory jacket flopped open. They climbed
a set of stairs to Jason's office which had a window viewing the
lobster tanks and one facing the harbor. The walls were dark
mahogany. Osmond sat on a black leather couch. Jason went to
a small glass bar and poured two glasses of sake and handed one
to Osmond.

He sat at his desk. To a good year, he said.

To a good year, Osmond repeated.

Jason licked his lips. It's hard to get good sake in this city, he
said. There's mostly Chinese here.

You have friends in Japan.

This is from Honolulu, and I wouldn't call them friends. I have
what they want so they give me what I want. You know how it is.
Those little ratfuckers would as soon eat my balls off my ass as toro
off a mermaid.

He put his glass down and eased his weight onto his elbows.
His lab coat stretched across his back and shoulders. How much
product is left in your pound?

Fifty minus shrinkage.

Which is what? Ten percent?

Roughly. Eight to fifteen lately.

That's a lot of loss.

Osmond nodded and he thought of Bill's intention to kill all
of the crows. It is not an arc. It's a pound. We deal with the otters
and gulls.

Fucking raccoons, said Jason.

Yes, the raccoons as well.

I'm sorry about Nicolas. He was a solid man.

Yes, said Osmond and he moved forward as if to bow and he
remembered the weight of Nicolas's skull as he heaved it over the
dam and again he wondered how the skull had ended up in the
pound. He'd tried over and over to imagine the body floating its
way into the pound but he knew that to be impossible and he

knew the notion of accident to be nothing more than a naive explanation of an action that began when the world began so the question was simply *who?*

But Nicolas was not always easy to deal with, said Jason. The last time I spoke with him, things did not go well. He had no interest in our plans. I trust your mind has not changed?

Osmond waited for his pulse to slow. My mind has not changed.

Jason leaned his weight back. He finished his drink. Good, he said. Now tell me if what I say is mistaken. Jason waited for a response and when Osmond nodded his consent Jason continued. The pound is incorporated and you and Nicolas carried a key man policy. With Nicolas gone all of his shares revert to you, leaving you the sole owner.

Osmond nodded and said, Yes.

But Daniel tells me that Nicolas's son was there for the pickup.

Captain Bill, said Osmond.

Are you thinking of selling Nicolas's shares to William?

He's a good man. He's honest and he works hard, Osmond said. He paused and considered what he would say then said, He believes that he is part owner already.

Jason slid his chair back and stretched his legs out and crossed the rubber boots at the ankles. He reached down and pulled the knife and its scabbard from his boot and set it on his desk. He put his hands in his lab coat pockets. How does he believe that?

Apparently Nicolas never told him about the policy.

And neither have you.

No, Osmond said.

Because you aren't sure what you will do yet?

I am sure of myself.

What will you do?

I will run the pound.

Jason straightened in his chair and lifted his shoulders up near his earlobes then settled. Nicolas's son lacks vision?

He lacks vision, yes. He's a fisherman. Good fishermen are simple and they are greedy. Like sharks. They have to be.

Nicolas's death seems to benefit you, Osmond, Jason said and waited for Osmond to respond.

After a full minute Osmond said, Don't.

All right. Forget that for now. I'll tell you what, Jason said and stood and looked out the window at the harbor. What if we stop all of that loss? It was Nicolas who hated change, wasn't it?

Osmond sipped his drink.

What we do is drain it and dredge it and rebuild it. We wire in aerators and we make it the nicest lobster pound in the fucking world. You have big tides there, plenty of clean water and not a drop of fresh water. What limits us is size and size is always negotiable.

Osmond stared at him.

Here's the other thing, Jason said. What's wrong with the market? The price is gone, right? That's because there's too much product, plain and simple. All this talk about Icelandic banks pulling processor funding from the Canadians, and the goddamned cruise lines cutting back—that shit's all well and good, but that doesn't matter to me. What matters to me is basic economics. Supply and demand. You highlining bastards catch a ton of lobster or more a day. Maybe two or three tons. You can't expect the demand to keep up with that, Icelandic banks and cruise ships or not. You got all these agencies and promotion councils spending all your money on marketing and bullshit when all you need to do is slow down. But you won't do that because your ball-size depends on how many bugs you catch.

Jason wiped his forehead.

But what exists in this shitty market are little niches, Osmond. Little niches that pay as well as ever. You'll always get top dollar for top quality. Period. That's a word you never, ever hear in the fisheries. *Quality*. Most guys catch a ton of product and three quarters of them are hollow and their tomalley tastes like mud. That won't sell, especially with the Canadian processors offline.

Osmond crossed his arms. You're rattling, Jason. Say what you need to say.

Jason smiled.

Good pound lobsters are a premium, but you knew that.

Osmond waited. He thought about Julius. He thought about the future and this was it.

Jason looked around and lifted his arms in the air and his voice was a whisper. It's about water, Osmond. Clean, cold water. That's where the market is. Here we have no space and we have no water. You have the water and the room and you have the catch coming in. I talked with Benji Beal. I can buy his wharf right now. We can rebuild the pound and build a seawater tank house next to it. We grade our own product. Top to bottom. We run the show on that coast. Fuck Iceland. Fuck Canada.

Osmond swirled the sake around his glass and finished it in a gulp.

I just visited my buyer in Japan, Jason said. I can move some high-end lobsters, Osmond, but they want to know those bugs come straight out of the fucking seawater. They don't like these swimming pool pump house bugs. My man says he can taste the fake saltwater in them. He says the tomalley sucks. They want cold saltwater product but they want a lot of it and they want it to be consistent and perfect. The Chinese are the same. They want to slap a spiny little two-claw bastard on a plate and say that Osmond Randolph caught this thing yesterday and it's still wet as a happy whore.

Osmond stood and looked out the opposite window. Rows of crates strung together by their beckets filled the tank below. He wondered about Benji selling the wharf and he wondered about Nicolas and he wondered about the strange unrolling of the future but as he did so he saw his own destiny and that of his grandchildren together align like a star cluster turned constellation. I wouldn't want to eat these tanked lobsters either, he said.

Jason crossed the room and stood next to him and clapped his hand on Osmond's back. Neither would I, my man. Neither would I. Think it over.

The fishermen in that harbor won't like the idea. Not one bit of it.

Why not? At the very least, they'll get the same price as any other wharf.

It's change, Jason. They don't trust change. Especially from someone from away. They'll never trust you.

Not until I pay them half again as much as the next guy.

Osmond nodded. They won't like it. If you pay them more they'll think you're setting them up for something. It's always the same story. Good promises then a good fucking.

But you, Osmond? Do you like it?

I wouldn't say that.

Jason sat back down and swiveled his chair around so he faced Osmond. There's a new crowd of fishermen out there, Osmond. The younger generation. They got a hot nut to catch product and they got a hot nut to sell at top price. Their allegiance isn't the same as their fathers'. They go where the money is. Money talks to these guys. They have big boats and they watch too much television.

Osmond looked around the room. He sighed. I know it, he said. They've lost faith, and it is a shame. But in the harbor they listen to Virgil and Captain Bill and those two have faith in things that no longer exist.

Much like yourself.

Yes. Like myself, Jason. I don't like change but I accept it. Technology has changed and the market has changed so we must change. Virgil and Bill, they will fight it. They think we are still an isolated harbor surrounded by an endless sea. They don't know this is a global economy. They do not know the world exists. Their faith evolved from their grandfathers and earlier and they hold on to that because it is what they understand. And in a manner, I envy them. But my faith is in something larger than history or tradition.

Jason grunted. What is your faith in, Osmond?

Osmond rolled his shirtsleeve up and exposed a white arm and he clenched the arm with his hand and the fingers were long and strong and he squeezed the arm until his veins rose into ridges beneath the skin. There, he said. There is my faith, Jason. Blood and blood alone.

Jason yawned and scratched the inside of his thighs. Daniel will take you to your hotel. Leave your rig here. And one more thing.

Osmond rolled his sleeve down. He felt empty as if he'd sold something he treasured.

This thing with the skull in the pound—whatever the fuck it is, I don't care. But I want to know this: Did your grandson harm Nicolas? Julius Wesley. I'll find out for myself but I want to hear it from you. I like to understand my business partners.

Osmond stood. He placed his glass on Jason's desk. He left the room and went down the steep metal staircase and found Daniel in the front office. Daniel drove him into the city to a hotel and let Osmond out on the sidewalk. He handed Osmond a keycard.

They'll pick you up at six.

Yes, said Osmond and as he watched Daniel enter traffic and disappear into the city's corridors he pictured an underwater landscape built of ledge and cave and canyon and he pictured lobsters rushing about the streets.

He stepped into the building.

There was an atrium in the lobby with several fountains surrounded by artificial aspen trees. Water noise echoed throughout the room. Osmond carried a single black leather bag and wore a black overcoat. He took the elevator up six flights and went down the hallway and opened the door.

The shower was running and he could hear the exhaust fan. He shut the door and set his bag down and took off his boots and coat. He went to the window. The curtain was open and the view was over the south side and he saw old brick buildings and stone churches. He stood looking out over the cold city and watching the steam and smoke rising in tendrils from the rooftops until the shower stopped and the bathroom door opened.

Osmond didn't turn around. He felt her arms wrap around his waist and her head lean against his spine as her fingers dug into his stomach. He looked down at the long thin fingers so dark brown they were nearly black.

Do you remember what you said to me the last time we saw each other? she said.

Of course I do.

I didn't think you would.

You are the only woman left in the world, he said.

You're so full of shit, she said and smiled as she turned him around. She was six feet tall and her forehead came only to his lips. Her hair was long and wet and brushed straight back over her scalp and she was naked. Beads of water remained on her shoulders. She didn't wear any jewelry except a silver chain above her hips which held a silver pendant below her navel.

Osmond set his hands on her shoulders and ran them down her arms and rib cage and followed the silver chain with his thumb and middle finger. He gripped the pendant. Below his fingers lay a thin strip of black hair.

I'm happy you still have this, he said and released the pendant.

She unbuttoned his shirt and worked it down over his shoulders and arms. She pulled his T-shirt off and his skin was like salt next to her dark skin and his chest and shoulders were covered in thick gray hair. His back was torn with old scars and she traced her fingers over the scars and he had the brief memory of kneeling shoulder to shoulder beside his brother with their father behind them holding the small flagellum and he twisted his shoulders away from her touch. She undid his pants and kneeled down and pulled them over his feet. She stood and her mouth was slightly open so he could see her white teeth and pink gums and the red tip of her tongue.

He gripped her hips and ran his hand over her stomach and breasts and around her waistline and down her ass and he lifted her to her tiptoes and kissed her chin. Then released her. Her nostrils flared. She ran her hand between his legs and gripped and she searched his face for what was wrong and he said, Later.

He pulled the blankets off the bed and lay down and she stretched out next to him.

• • •

Osmond and Renee met Jason outside the hotel. Jason held his arm around a Japanese-Hawaiian woman he introduced as Turtle. She wore a silver fur coat and hid her chin and mouth in the collar. It was dark but the city lights were bright against the wet pavement and their breath rose like street vent steam.

Turtle stuck her hand out for Osmond to shake. He took it and she squeezed him harder than he would have thought possible. She looked him in the eyes and said, You're a big bastard too, aren't you?

Osmond held her small hand and looked at Jason and Jason laughed.

Jason had a car waiting and they climbed into it. Jason didn't say anything to the driver. They sped through the city and turned down an alleyway and stopped beside a dumpster. They climbed out and the driver opened an oversized metal door and they walked into a wooden hallway stained dark with tobacco. There was no door on the men's bathroom and they could smell urine and see the stainless steel trough that lined the wall. The trough was filled with pissed-over ice and cigarette butts. An Elvis poster hung on the wall but it had long since been tattooed with graffiti.

Jason led them down the hallway and past a kitchen with a service window. The barroom was crowded and filled with smoke and the walls were lined with photos of old men like wainscoting and on the wall beside the service window hung a breakfast-all-day menu. A young man who looked to be a weightlifter leaned on his elbows in the window. He wore a tank top and a bandana drenched in sweat.

Jason passed before the weightlifter's field of vision and the man nodded and came out a side door and pushed through the crowd then unlocked a door that led to a wide wooden staircase. The step treads were covered in rubber mats. The weightlifter held the door as the four descended the stairs then shut it behind them. Osmond heard the lock slide home. The staircase was lit by a single dirty bulb hanging from an overhead wire.

At the bottom of the stairs Jason opened a door and they entered a small speakeasy with a bar in one corner and several round black tables. The back of the bar was the glass wall of a pool-sized fish tank. A topless woman dressed as a mermaid swam back and forth and took periodic breaths from a tube camouflaged as seaweed. Underwater bulbs shone blue from the tank and lit the room in waves of light.

The bartender walked around the bar and took their coats. Renee's midriff and silver pendant flashed as she sat down.

Jason still wore his cutoff sweatpants and white lab coat and rubber boots.

The bartender brought two bottles of sake. She set them in front of Jason and he grabbed her by the hip and pulled her to him. She wore a black cocktail dress. She bent to hear what he was saying then nodded and left. Turtle leaned over to Jason and gripped his thigh in her fist and whispered, Easy with the hands there, Big Man.

Jason nodded. He pulled her fist from his thigh and held it in his hands.

Minutes later the bartender returned with a platter of tilefish taquitos. The taquitos were slices of fish the size of silver dollars pounded flat with rice flour then fried until they curled. Raw tilefish was piled inside each curled slice then topped with pickled cucumber and jalapeño slaw.

Jason ate one. He licked his thumb and forefinger. As I was saying, Osmond, he said. This is the thing. The Japanese are the market. Right now the Italians have them. They have the lobsters and the fish so they have the Japanese market. But the Japanese don't like to deal with them.

But they like you.

Right now a few of them do and as long as I provide the best product it will stay that way. They only want one thing and that's quality. The Italians don't understand that. They're slobs. They eat too much sauce to understand. They have the fish but they manhandle them. They ruin their tuna and swords and then they soak the battered pricks in olive oil and tomato sauce like it's fucking gnocchi or something. They have no sensitivities. The Japs are venomous pricks, and the more venomous a creature is, the more sensitive it is. Wouldn't you agree, Turtle?

I would, she said. She grinned and wiped a sliver of cucumber from her chin. But that doesn't mean that you're not full of shit, Big Man.

Jason laughed and his laugh was a boom like a backfire that filled the empty room. Easy, Tiger, he said.

Easy? Turtle said. Easy? You bring me to a fucking strip joint and tell me to be easy?

This isn't a strip joint.

Turtle turned and looked at the mermaid. She held her hand out with the palm up and the wrist arched and the bracelets dangling. What the hell is that then, a fucking dolphin? Fucking Flipper with tits?

Osmond wrapped both hands around his drink and glanced at Renee. Her face looked to be smiling but her lips were set. She lifted one eyebrow at him. She picked at the tilefish.

Jason reached into the air and waved once and the bartender came over. He motioned for her to come closer and he said, Get that girl out of the water and give her some clothes.

The bartender looked around the room as if confused. Turtle pushed her chair back. Get that skinny bitch out of there or I'll get her myself.

The bartender grinned. Will you need a swimsuit?

Jason grunted. Here. Give her this and tell her to go home. He handed the bartender some bills. She nodded at Turtle and took the money. She went behind the bar and through a doorway and Osmond watched as the mermaid surfaced and climbed from his field of vision.

There, Jason said. How's that?

It's still a fucking strip joint, Turtle said.

Jason waited.

Osmond lifted a taquito between two fingers and ate it in a single bite. The fried fish shell crunched then dissolved in his mouth. Who sets the price? he said.

I do, Jason said.

Osmond leaned back in his chair and put his hand on Renee's leg and pulled the hem of her dress up so his hand was on bare skin. He felt the muscle twitch. I don't believe that, he said to Jason.

Jason laughed again. Good, he said. We'd be fools if we did. But I will tell you this. My price doesn't come from Tsukiji. It comes from my man. Japan buys one in every ten fish caught in the world. In the whole world, Osmond. You catch ten goldfish in your granddad's pond, you have to sell one of them to a Jap. The fish at the Tsukiji market are some of the best in the world, but that don't mean shit to a lobster. You know why? Because lobsters are alive, Osmond. Those haiku cocksuckers don't understand a living thing.

I'm not interested, Osmond said.

You will be. Jason ate three taquitos in a row then licked his fingers. China is emerging as a major lobster buyer. They think they want the same quality as Japan, but they're still in the dark in a lot of ways. They might have developed infrastructure, but they haven't developed taste. So we'll deal with Japan and China. The top goes to Japan, the second run goes to China. We go from there.

It's my pound, Jason, and I have no intention of giving it to you.

I don't want it. If I wanted a pound I'd buy a pound. Hell, I'd buy yours. What I want is you.

Those who conquer, Osmond said.

Yes, Jason said. They eat from the tree of life. But we aren't out to conquer, only to eat.

The bartender brought another bottle of sake and two plates of Arctic char crudo. The Arctic char came folded in layers of bright orange atop beds of shining green sea lettuce. Brown dots of miso and strips of shaved radish circled the plates. The bartender left and returned with a plate of steamed buns. In the center of each was a deep-fried lobster the size of a thumb. Jason tugged his sleeve up so his hairy wrist was exposed. He reached for a bun and packed the spilling pickled red onions and cabbage back into it. He ate it in two bites and the entire table heard his chewing.

Osmond eyed Jason. He lifted a bun and peered at the baby lobster and said, Any fisherman back home would cut your hands off for this.

The lobster? Don't eat it then, Jason said.

Osmond glanced at Jason then put the lobster bun in his mouth and chewed and swallowed. He sipped the sake and all of it was good but he had no appetite for it. He watched as Turtle ate down the lobster then the pickled vegetables then the bun.

Renee pushed the baby lobster aside and ate the bun together with a slice of the char.

Tell me this, friend, Jason said. He sipped his sake. Why haven't you discussed the situation with Nicolas's son? I am confused.

Don't worry about it.

I'm not worried, Jason said. I'm confused.

Osmond pushed his chair back. He looked at the hoops that Turtle wore in her ears and the red lipstick. How old are you? he asked her.

Jason grinned big at Osmond.

Guess, Turtle said.

I don't guess.

I don't tell.

Osmond's jaw clenched then relaxed and he squeezed Renee's thigh.

Turtle ran a finger over the corner of her mouth as if to wipe away a crumb or hide a smile. The bartender returned and Turtle said, Can I get a cheeseburger and fries? Rare.

A cheeseburger and fries, the bartender said. She looked at Jason then to Turtle.

Yeah, a cheeseburger and fries.

The bartender nodded but didn't move.

Jason pushed his chair back as if to stand but stayed seated. I should have introduced you, he said. This is Turtle. She used to manage the fish exchange in Honolulu. Now she's with me. She gets whatever she wants. Turtle, this is Kate. She's the best bartender in the city so don't give her any of your pidgin bullshit.

There was a moment of silence before Kate said, A cheeseburger? Rare. With fries.

Kate nodded and left.

Jason cleared his throat and turned to Osmond. He fingered several pieces of Arctic char into his mouth followed by a pinch of sea lettuce. Nicolas's son, Osmond?

Osmond folded his hands in his lap. Nicolas was my friend, he began. I have not discussed things with William because I initially thought we were on the same page. Now I understand that we are not, and I will talk to him.

Why wouldn't Nicolas tell him you were insured?

Osmond looked over his shoulder at the vacant tank as if searching for solace in water then said, So you buy the bugs from me same as ever?

Same as ever.

And you pay for the facility.

Yes.

Who runs the wharf? And the tank house? Who runs the trucks and pays the maintenance? Who gets fucked when the power goes out?

We'll have a manager that works for me but answers to you.

I don't believe you, Jason, Osmond said.

I don't expect you to. That's why you are here.

Osmond blinked. *That's why I am here*, he thought and once again he saw his friend Nicolas Graves alive in the sea and he felt suddenly that he would lose his bowels. He clenched every muscle in his body to keep hold of whatever remained within him. He stood. He saw Nicolas's eyes ready to go down. He excused himself and hurried to the restroom and into a stall where he braced both hands flat on the wall and saw Nicolas later only a skull flung to the sea. Osmond's hair hung beyond his cheeks. He stared at the water in the porcelain bowl. A bead of sweat fell and landed in the toilet and he closed his eyes.

Goddamn you, Osmond whispered. Goddamn you.

The next evening. Osmond sat at the end of the bar in his house. Rhonda and Dolly were in their bedroom and he could hear Dolly's constant chatter. He held a glass of scotch in his hand. An open bible lay on the bar and there had been a time when the men in those pages were the men in his life and miracles were commonplace and belief and truth were one but belief was no longer truth and the time of miracles was over. Faith was forever and Osmond's faith was in his ability to navigate a world as empty and chaotic as the whirlwind but now suddenly he felt that faith cracking.

He sipped his scotch. The south wall of his house was built of floor-to-ceiling picture windows that framed his wharf and boat and beyond that the reach and the bridge that arched across to Mason's Island. To the southwest an archipelago stretched offshore to Spencer Ledges and the sea-swell rolled and heaved against the outside ledges. White spray hung in the air.

On the wall opposite Osmond stood an eight-foot-long saltwater fish tank with a lobster the size of his leg lying motionless in it. Osmond drank his scotch and looked to the lobster. There you are, he whispered. I see you waiting.

He went back to his reading and read several verses and as he read his lips mouthed the words and his right hand slid a check in circles on the bar top. The check was for $35,000. Ten thousand pounds of lobster at three fifty a pound. Osmond pressed it into the bar top to still it. If Nicolas were alive he would deposit the check into the business account and split it down the middle. Any expenses incurred throughout the year would be likewise split.

But Osmond's world had shifted.

Chimney was in prison and Nicolas was dead and Julius had bought a new boat and moved out. Whether Julius was to be trusted or not Osmond had no idea. Osmond had simultaneously abandoned his brother and his beliefs for a woman and he'd lost both her and their child. And he'd later sacrificed Nicolas his only friend with his own hands. Osmond understood these three deaths to be elements of providence and he understood that fear and fragility came in apocalyptic waves which rose and fell with the corrosive power of tides and what remained when fear finished was love and faith and love and faith together meant blood.

But I have this against you, Osmond whispered as if speaking to the lobster. That you, you have abandoned love.

And here he sat about to abandon Nicolas's son William. But that was not a choice of his. That was a choice he and Nicolas made together and they had never once doubted that decision but neither Nicolas nor Osmond had ever doubted who would die first. Nicolas had not been the sort of man to die. But Osmond was not the sort of man to abandon his family. Not again. After Laura died he'd spent years believing her death to be his punishment for abandoning the church and the only way he'd survived was to accept his punishment and accept life as a consciousness dissolved within predestination like salt within water. There existed a God who was neither good nor evil and that God saved those souls chosen regardless of sin or sacrifice. A man must walk this earth with steps true and sure but now and always now was Nicolas Graves.

Osmond wished briefly that he had been the one to drown. To feel the cold waves. But even as the wish formed he threw it away like a coin down a well and focused instead on the question, How the hell had Nicolas Graves ended up a skeleton within the pound?

There was no explanation. None save for a man's hands but whose hands and how?

Julius's truck tore through his thoughts and down the driveway and soon Julius came into the house. He went first to the girls' room and Osmond heard him talk to his sisters and ten minutes later he sat on a stool at the bar and faced the lobster tank. Behind him the sea rose and fell in smooth gun-gray swell. Osmond watched the boy as if seeking evidence of his own blood.

Osmond didn't speak. He sipped his drink and spun the melting ice cubes around the glass. He stood and took a piece of salt cod from a glass jar and dropped it into the fish tank. The lobster backed into its cave with its two claws sticking out and waited as the fish settled to the bottom.

We have to make some decisions, Julius. About our future.

I got my future decided. I got my boat and that's it.

Osmond reached his long arm slowly across the bar and gripped Julius's hand and squeezed it until he saw the muscles work in Julius's face. The blood rushed up Julius's neck and pulsed in a lightning bolt vein across his temple and forehead and beneath his ear. Osmond relaxed his grip. No, that is not it. Nicolas is gone. What happens from this point on is our decision. You have a long way to go. You have been spoiled, Julius.

I earned every cent I got.

Osmond put his hand back on his own drink. How have you earned it?

Working for the old man. Hell I know his operation in and out and ran half of it myself.

So why aren't you in prison as well?

I'm careful.

You're careful? A careful man considers his future. The pound has a lot of potential, but it is a lot of work, Julius. It will take commitment and perseverance.

I ain't a pound man. I'm a fisherman, plain and simple. You can do whatever you want.

Osmond stood fast from his seat. His hair swung in a swish like a cape as he grabbed Julius by the back of the neck and squeezed. He bent over and the heat and moisture of Osmond's mouth shot into Julius's ear.

This pound is not for me, Julius. This pound is for this family. It is for you. It is for your future and that of your family, and it is for your sisters' future, and I have sacrificed myself for those futures. I have sacrificed myself, he repeated slowly as his free hand landed first on Julius's chest then moved to his throat where the fingers wrapped the tender skin.

Do you understand?

Julius didn't answer. Osmond pinched the neck harder and Julius's back arched scorpion-like and his feet kicked and air escaped his mouth and he gagged. Osmond released him and sat on the barstool beside him then reached over and pushed gently on Julius's lips as if to silence the boy. Julius's breath evened and Osmond ran his hand through Julius's hair.

That pound ain't shit, Julius said.

Osmond gripped the jugular in his fingers. He saw Nicolas in the water and he squeezed and the jugular was a grape in his grip as Nicolas thrashed and Julius squirmed. Nicolas went under for this boy who did not even care. Osmond ground his teeth and squeezed harder and tears spilled from the sides of each man's eyes and Julius dug his fingernails into his palms and his mouth flattened into a line. His back arched again.

Osmond released him and slowly nodded. He finished his drink and placed the glass upside down in Julius's palm as if marking the boy. He looked out the window at his boat on the mooring and the gray ripples on the ocean. He ran a finger over his mustache and said, The question now is what changes will be made at the pound.

Julius gripped the glass. He closed his eyes. I'd say it's going to need quite a few changes, he said.

Things already are changing, Julius. Nicolas is gone.

Julius stood and steadied himself against a chair and breathed heavily. His eyes met his grandfather's then he went behind the bar and took a cola out of the refrigerator. He put ice in a cup and filled it.

Osmond lifted the bible. He who conquers shall be blessed. He held the book in front of himself like a wineglass. So tell me, young Julius, what is your future?

Julius held the glass of iced cola in his fist. With his tongue he knocked an ice cube around his mouth then crunched and swallowed it. This, he finally said.

Louder.

This is my future.

Osmond nodded chin to clavicle and back. He heard Dolly instruct Rhonda on something. Waves piled on the shore. He felt his grandson's eyes upon him. A line of sweat streamed down his spine and something within his skull pounded. The lobster in the tank moved from its small cave and dragged the piece of fish back into the darkness.

Osmond spoke quietly. The pound is a lot of work, Julius. And it will only grow from here. This is the beginning. When Jason Jackson gets involved with us we are going to be committed. He is negotiating with Benji to purchase the wharf but that purchase will be contingent on us. He will make sure we do well but there is no room for mistakes.

I know that.

The boat price on lobsters is gone and it won't come back. It might go up some, but it won't come back. Not unless something happens to the catch.

So?

So speak.

Bill ain't going to give up the pound.

Osmond slammed his palm onto the bar top and Dolly's voice from the other room silenced. Bill no longer has anything to do with the pound, Osmond said. It is over for him. The Lord has struck.

Charlotte parked her car at the Irving station and climbed into Julius's truck. She wore a blue hooded sweatshirt and jeans and an aqua blue skullcap. Her hair hung in a ponytail from beneath the skullcap. The truck smelled like air fresheners and cologne. Julius had parked with the front wheels stuffed deep into the snow bank so the tires spun as he reversed.

They pulled out of the parking lot and turned west and crossed the river. The truck rumbled. The tide was coming and filling the frozen mud channel with brown seawater. A layer of snow covered the dead sea grass.

I can't wait to be done with school, Charlotte said.

I'll tell you what school's for, said Julius. It's for nothing.

She felt a charge in her throat. Well, high school maybe. But I'm moving out west soon. I got into college in Idaho.

I like it right here.

Charlotte smiled at him. You've probably never been anywhere else.

He turned onto a side road that passed a wreath factory and crossed a discontinued set of railroad tracks and he put his foot down on the gas and the truck roared over the tracks and began up a long hill.

The hell I ain't, he said. I been everywhere.

You haven't either.

The hill turned to dirt with potholes and frozen washboard. The truck bounced over the roadbed and Charlotte held one hand on the seat beside her and one on the handle above the window.

Where've you been? she said.

Julius pursed his lips and drew them into his mouth. She watched him scratch his arrowhead patch of hair. He looked innocent or naive but she could see the sinew and muscle in his neck and shoulders and hands and she could see a light like a

179

black spark deep in his eyes that made her want to press her eye directly to his. It occurred to her that his entire body held this sort of spark and she wanted to encompass it like a stove would a coal.

He ran his finger and thumb over his mouth then touched the back of his head as if feeling a bruise but he didn't answer her.

The hill grew steeper. They climbed out of the oaks and maples and the blueberry barrens spread before them. Thousands of acres of blueberries and ponds and brooks and rivers covering a single vast deposit of sand and gravel left behind by the glaciers that had ages ago calved and melted into the sea. The early winter winds had blown the snow from the barrens and exposed the blueberry shoots that were blistered red from cold as if the fields were afire. Around the fields the windblown snow was packed into tight drifts set against the oaks and rocks.

I wouldn't go, Julius said.

I don't have any real reason to stay.

Consider it, he said. A careful person considers the future.

Charlotte laughed at the caution in his voice. I have thought it over. And I am careful, thank you. I don't like the smell of bait, I don't like everyone knowing everything about me, and I don't like the fog. I looked on the computer and Idaho gets as much sun as Florida and way less rain.

Julius crunched on a candy and didn't respond. He turned onto a rough dirt road that followed the edge of the plateau and from there they looked north over the barrens and south over the sea. The sun hovered over the mountains to the west. Outside the truck window the barrens whizzed by.

Charlotte turned in the seat and leaned against the door and put one foot on the seat with her knee bent up to her chest. She watched Julius through a long silence. After a few miles he pulled off the road and parked. They walked across the frozen ankle-high bushes toward a car-sized boulder that sat alone among the blueberries. Traces of snow lay in webs on the ground. A waist-deep drift filled the lee of the rock and they climbed the rock and Charlotte sat in the orange radiating glow. Julius stood straight atop the rock's crest and the quarter moon appeared due south. There was no wind and it was silent and cold and Charlotte shivered and rubbed heat with her hands into her thighs.

I hear you moved, she said.

Where'd you hear that to?

School. Just the kids talking.

Kids? Ain't no one knows me.

Charlotte smiled. Everyone knows you.

The hell they do.

Julius's face was serious and the sunset was red on his dark skin. She thought he looked like a statue. She watched his face and he didn't blink or waver just stared into the light strict and intent as if the last rags of sun depended on him alone. Then he raised one arm to the moon and the other arm to the sun to become the vertex of a 90-degree angle between star and moon. Small tides now, he whispered.

Charlotte watched him for a few seconds. You got it figured out, don't you?

He didn't blink. Yes, he said. He lowered his arms. You can tell the tides by where the sun and moon are. I bet you didn't know that, did you? Grandfather's the one told me. He might be a weird motherfucker but he knows some shit no one else does. See, the sun's in the west and the moon's in the south so they're pulling the water different ways. That's why the tides are small. You got to pay attention. A careful man pays attention.

I didn't know that, Charlotte said and her voice held traces of sarcasm like barbs on wire. What else do you know?

He waited a few seconds then sat down beside her. Leave it alone, he warned.

All you men around here think you know everything just because you have big lobster boats.

Them boys don't know shit.

What boys?

Them ones you know. Bunch of pussies is what they are. They think they're tough cutting off a bunch of Grandfather's traps, but they'll see. They'll get their own. I got a boat now.

Charlotte laughed. What about your grandfather?

What about him?

You're moving, and I thought you two were inseparable.

I got my boat. That's all I need.

What about your sisters?

Rhonda and Dolly? Rhonda's only half there. They say the other half of her smarts is extra for Dolly. She's a smart shit.

Charlotte considered what to say. Then, What happened to Rhonda? Was she born like that?

Julius curled his lower lip into his mouth and bit down on it. He didn't answer at first then said, No. She fell off the wharf is what happened. No one saw until it was almost too late.

Oh my God, said Charlotte. That's horrible. Who found her?

I did.

Charlotte didn't know what to say. Thoughts tumbled. She said, Well, it's a good thing you were there. I'm glad you have them. I'm an only child.

I know it.

Except I got Jonah and Bill to look out for me. So watch out.

Julius leaned forward and pressed a slight spray of saliva through the gap in his front teeth.

Charlotte pulled her skullcap off and stretched it overtop her knee. How come you don't get along?

Me and them?

Yeah.

They're a couple of pussies and I don't get along with nobody is why.

You get along with me, don't you?

He looked at her and sucked in his lip just slightly and said, You tell me.

I will tell you, she said. You can get along with me anytime you want. But I wouldn't go calling Bill a pussy.

Hell. I seen him near cry the other day when we pulled that head out of the pound. That ain't pussy I don't know what is.

I'd have cried if I found my dad's head, Charlotte said and scratched at her jeans with her fingernails and concentrated on the rock beneath her. I went down there with them when Bill was looking for the other bones. All of this is crazy. I haven't slept at all. I just can't stop thinking about it. It just doesn't seem real, you know?

Julius leaned to the side and shoved his hand into his pocket then pulled the hand slowly out and held it closed tight before Charlotte. Close your eyes, he said in a whisper that sounded more like it came from a hole in the ground than a mouth.

Charlotte eyed him and considered what to do then closed her eyes. She felt his hand grip hers. She bit her cheeks without meaning to. Julius pressed his closed fist into hers and dropped something hard onto her palm. He closed her hand around the object and said, Keep your eyes closed.

She did keep her eyes closed and a smile appeared on her lips.

He leaned closer. He still held her hand in his. Tell me this. Can I trust you, Charlotte?

She nodded. Yes.

No, he said and squeezed her fist. Can I *trust* you?

Yes, she said. Yes, you can trust me.

With anything?

She nodded. Anything.

You won't tell a soul about me? Who I am?

His mouth was very close to her ear and she could feel his voice like insects. I won't tell a soul, Julius. I trust you. So you should trust me, right?

He slid his hand up her arm and shoulder and over her neck and threaded his fingers into her ponytail and pulled her face to his and their lips brushed. Really?

Really, she said and she leaned toward his lips but he held her back by her hair until her eyes opened and searched. Then he kissed her heavily on the mouth and she felt his tongue on her own and she breathed in the taste of hard candy and wrapped her arms around him still holding whatever it was clenched safe and fast in her fist. He cradled her shoulders and head and eased her backward and the rock cold beneath her held her pinned as if designed to hold a girl supine. Now on her back she opened her eyes and glimpsed the sky behind Julius clutching and dying dark.

She closed her eyes again. She felt him maneuver. He kissed her ear then neck then down farther and he pulled her sweatshirt and shirt up to expose her belly then pulled her belt buckle and the thin frilled rim of pink cloth down to expose the bare spread of her pelvis and the first touches of hair. He ran his tongue in a slow flat line from those hairs to her belly button then released her. She didn't move and she didn't open her eyes and she felt the cold air on the wet track of his tongue. She waited uncertain if she were waiting for more or simply allowing her heart to slow and skin to adjust. When nothing more came and her heart slowed she sat up.

Can I look? she said and held her fist out.

If you trust me.

I do, she said.

She opened her fist and there in her palm was a single tooth gray as gravestone. She started to speak but failed because already she knew from where the tooth came. She shook it from her hand as if it could still bite and it rattled onto the rock and caught in a tuft of frozen moss.

Julius reached down and lifted the tooth between thumb and forefinger. He held it in the air to examine it for damage. He smiled in a way that she'd not seen him smile before and she couldn't tell if he looked like a toddler with a toy or a man with a weapon.

What the fuck? she said. She pulled her sweatshirt and shirt down to cover her exposed tissue. She could still feel the wet trace of his tongue.

Julius turned the smile on her. He held the tooth in front of her as if to show her its true power like some crystal which would soon refract the slight night's light and thereby tell her something of her future but really it was only the dead tooth.

Bill didn't see me so I got to keep it, he said and blinked his eyes several times in a row. It just fell off the skull, down at the pound. I didn't even need to pull it out. You ever touched a dead man's tooth before? Probably not.

What the fuck? she said again. Her throat felt like his fingers were on it or even in it. The moon slid across the southwest sky. In the distance the sea flamed purple as the barrens fell black. The wind picked up and Charlotte shivered.

Julius rose and looked straight down on her. You trust me, he said. I'm glad.

He reached down toward her but she winced and turned her face away. He held his hand in front of her face as if to show her that it held no weapon then removed it. You trust me, he said. I only want to touch your cheek.

Their eyes connected. Then he jumped off the rock and crossed the stretch of barrens to his truck. She watched him walk and she felt sweat like betrayal on her spine. Again she adjusted her clothing. She refitted her ponytail and put her skullcap back on. She tried to tell herself it was only a tooth but it was Jonah's father's tooth and Julius had held the thing before her like a jewel with that coal glowing in his eyes.

She gazed at the emptiness surrounding her. She stood and pressed her fingers against her pelvis and with a smile she wiped the coolness of his tongue away.

Did it even matter if she trusted him?

She rubbed her palms together. She slid off the rock and crossed to the truck. It was already moving as she swung in and closed the door and together she and Julius Caesar Wesley raced across the barren rim as the world hurled itself into darkness.

When Charlotte got home Jonah was sitting at the table with her parents. They'd finished dinner but their plates were still on the table.

Jonah sipped his beer.

Charlotte hugged Celeste and kissed Virgil on the cheek.

Do you want some dinner, honey? Celeste said.

There was a place set for her.

I have homework.

You can sit down with us, Virgil said. He had Chowder in his lap. He sipped his brandy and milk.

Charlotte took her sweatshirt and hat off and sat down.

You should eat something, Celeste said. Did you have any dinner?

I'll have a sandwich later.

Where've you been? Virgil said.

Just out with some friends.

What friends?

Charlotte didn't answer.

Virgil grunted. What friends?

She looked at Jonah then away and he felt a bolt like a taproot run down his chest and stomach and his stomach cramped. He finished his beer and waited. He knew what she would say. He felt the bolt drive into his groin and his knees began to shake. He flexed his thighs and calves but that didn't stop his knees.

Julius, Charlotte said. We went up to the barrens since there's not much snow up there yet. The new burns are still pretty red now.

Virgil didn't say anything.

Jonah peeled the label off his beer. Blood pumped like hydraulic fluid in his ears. He set the empty bottle on the wooden table next to his placemat and spun it. Fucking Julius, he said. He stood from the table and went down the hallway and out the door. He rubbed his hands hard in his hair and felt the pull on his scalp. He stepped from the porch and started down the driveway.

Fucking Julius is right, Virgil said and he looked at his daughter in a way he'd never looked at her before with his eyes dark and half closed and his mouth tight. Celeste had seen the look before but never directed at their family. The look chilled her but Charlotte endured it.

Celeste went after Jonah and called to him from the porch. He turned and waited and lit a cigarette as she crossed the driveway. She caught him beneath the birch trees. The branches were framed like finger bones against the porch light.

Celeste crossed her arms for warmth.

I'm sorry for that, he said to her.

Jonah, she said. Stay here for a while. I made an apple pie.

I don't need pie, he said.

Stay here tonight.

I don't think so. Don't worry about it, he said and smiled but the smile made Celeste worry.

You won't do anything will you?

What do you mean?

To Julius.

Christ, Celeste. I just want to be alone.

● ● ●

Virgil stared at Charlotte until she stood up and asked him, What?

Fucking Julius Wesley? My daughter is looking at the clamfucked new burn foliage in the middle of winter with Julius Wesley.

I wasn't fucking Julius Wesley.

Virgil waited.

He's nice. I know he acts tough and stuff. But he's just a scared boy is all and at least he's not drunk all the time. I'd be scared too if you and Jonah and Bill were after me.

Virgil didn't respond. He ruffled Chowder's ears. Celeste came back inside and she was pale and exhausted. She took her wineglass into the kitchen and poured a full glass and came back into the dining room.

I told you why I don't like Julius and it's not about fishing, Virgil finally said.

That's not true.

You don't know what you're talking about, Virgil said. You're just a spoiled little girl.

Well you're just a drunk old man that everyone thinks is crazy. Do you even know that?

Virgil stood up and did so more quickly than either Celeste or Charlotte thought possible. He stepped in front of Charlotte so close that she could taste his brandy in the back of her throat. She looked down at her feet but he lifted her chin and she heard her mother say, Virgil, but he said, You have no idea, Charlotte. I keep things to myself so they don't touch you. But this is about Julius. That boy is dangerous.

His voice was gentle and was kind and was the voice of her father. She relaxed but he was still so close. He is a bad man, Charlotte. You will not ride around with him and you will not see him, do you understand that? Did you ask him about that sister of his? Did you ask how long he held her underwater? Did he tell you what he did for his father?

Yes, I did ask him. And yes, I know what his father did but Julius just wants to fish lobster like you guys.

Virgil stepped away and Charlotte glanced at her mother then went up the stairs. Virgil sat down. Sweat dotted his chin and nose and he wiped at it but missed. He finished his drink and set the glass on the table. Fuck, he said.

You need to stop drinking, Celeste said. Now.

I just buried Nicolas.

I don't care what you just did. You want to know why she likes Julius? Because he's not you is why. You can't understand that?

I understand fine.

They sat for several minutes then Celeste said, Is Jonah going to do something?

I imagine he will. Jonah ain't much till he gets his get going. Then he's a mean fighting sonofawhore. He beat the shit out of the Captain on the boat till I pulled him off.

That's what I'm worried about.

I'll get him.

I don't have to go with you do I?

To chaperone?

Yes.

I guess not.

• • •

Celeste climbed the stairs and stopped outside Charlotte's door. Her breath came long and sluggish and out of sync with the thudding of her heart. She took two deep breaths and tucked her hair behind her ears. She set her hand on the door frame. Her fingers were pale and cracked and they shook and she caught herself thinking all of this to be testament to her own failure but she knew it was not.

She forced her knuckles against the door wood. Charlotte told her to come in and Celeste opened the door and shut it behind her. Charlotte was in her bed with a book. The bedside lamp glowed like a spotlight. Celeste turned the desk chair around and sat down and crossed her legs and ran both hands over her thighs and wondered why the room and daughter both felt so unfamiliar.

Are you okay, honey?

Charlotte tipped her book against her chest and held her page with her thumbs. She sucked her lips in and said, I hate him. He's fat and drunk all the time, Mom.

The muscles on Celeste's back and stomach tightened. She stopped herself from defending her husband. I don't know what to do, she confessed.

He was like this before Jonah's dad died and now he's worse. They found a body, Mom. Doesn't anybody think that's crazy? Why won't you call the police? Why doesn't someone call the police? Why don't the police even know?

How could they know? Celeste said. As far as anyone but your father's concerned, Nicolas died by accident and that was that. I don't know what happened, but you have to believe me that your father's mind isn't like ours. We have to trust him, I think. I know I sound crazy to you, honey. But at least trust me.

It's like Mexico or something around here. I can't wait to move.

I know you can't. It'll come soon.

I just want to get out of here, Mom. Charlotte hit the mattress with the side of her fist like a slowly swung gavel. Tears streamed down her face and she sniffled and the face that had looked more and more like an adult's now looked like a child's. Her back shook. I want to get away from Dad and Jonah and all of this. Jonah's going to grow up to be just like Dad. What if one of them dies, Mom? What if Jonah dies?

Celeste stood from the desk chair and moved to the bed and sat with her hip against her daughter's. She put her arm around Charlotte. Jonah will be fine. They both care about you, honey. Don't take that for granted. I'm going to talk to your father.

I don't know why you put up with him. I'd divorce him if it was me. Why don't you make him stop? Just make him stop. Charlotte's voice sounded like it came from far away. I'm not going to live here and wait for Jonah all day long and get fat and watch television and change diapers and hope he's not going to be dead because of some stupid lobster traps. I saw Nicolas. I just keep thinking that it could have been Dad. Why don't you call the police, Mom?

Celeste nodded and separated herself from Charlotte. She tried to clear her throat but it had constricted. She felt a bead of sweat drop from her armpit and trickle down her rib cage. She forced herself to speak. You mean you don't want to be like me? Fat and waiting for my husband? Just a docile wife?

Charlotte's face calmed. That's not what I mean, Mom.

I'll tell you something, Charlotte. I am happy with my life. It's not perfect but nobody's life is. Your father is an alcoholic. I'm sorry for that. But he's got a kind heart and he doesn't mean anyone harm. He loves the two of us and he loves Jonah and Bill and he will do anything for any of us. Don't you forget that. There're a lot of people out there that would do anything for a father like you have.

I don't see why he won't drink less.

He can't stop is why. Celeste took a deep breath and ran her hands over her thighs and stretched her back then relaxed.

Charlotte put a bookmark in her book and set it down. She wiped at her tearstained face and scratched her arm. I can't stand this. I hate this.

I hope your father knows what he's doing, Celeste said.

They sat together without talking for a few minutes then Celeste said, Charlotte, what are you doing with Julius?

I'm having fun. He's nice and he doesn't want to get married and he doesn't drink. We can just talk. He's sweet down deep, Mom. Sometimes I think Jonah's the opposite. He's sweet on the outside but mad and mean down deep.

He's a handsome boy, Celeste said.

Charlotte smiled and touched her fingertips to her neck. She thought of the black spark in Julius's eyes and the cold wind on her wet skin but somehow not of the tooth.

Don't confuse those things, Celeste said.

What things?

You know damned well what things. I see you smiling, honey. Just be careful. Celeste paused and looked around the room. And I don't know what went on with you and Jonah, but you at least owe him respect. Are you sure you're not trying to upset him? Or trying to upset your father?

Dad's just so drunk all the time. I can't stand it.

Neither can I.

You need to get him to stop.

Well, Celeste said and patted Charlotte's arm and stood up. I don't know if anyone can do that.

. . .

Jonah piloted his boat through the night. He watched the numbers on his GPS and he watched the shadows of islands shift and orbit like planets as the space spread before him. The bow spray splashed white against the boat's chines and Jonah thought that perhaps Charlotte had been right and he did need help but he knew not from what direction. He thought about distance. He could point the boat south and run until he ran out of fuel and then he'd bob atop the waters and drift wherever the sea took him. There were countries out there. Continents. If he sailed due south and never ran out of fuel he'd hit Venezuela but he would run out of fuel and he would run out of water and he'd sit down and close his eyes and that would be it until the gulls arrived.

He shook his head at his own thoughts. He wished life would open up and swallow him. He wanted to feel the sink of teeth and the slide of throat and the burn of stomach acid. He hung his head over the side and hollered. He hollered until his voice was hoarse and when he silenced he found himself wanting only to face his father as if the sea would unfold and allow Nicolas one more earthbound moment.

Jonah looked up at his GPS. He was nearing Stone Island. He squinted into the darkness and soon made out the familiar shape of the island then the cove and camp. He felt a revitalizing blast of air. He moored his boat and rowed to the small wharf. He dragged the skiff out of the water and flipped it onto its gunwales and tied the painter to a ringbolt. He didn't have a flashlight and the spruce canopy stretched like cloud cover across the sky and blocked any possible light. Jonah held his hand in front of his face and couldn't see it and the attempt made him dizzy. He made his way along the trail by feeling the packed snow with his feet and now and again he stumbled from the path and lost his footing in the deep sideline snow but each time he regained the trail.

When he reached the camp he carried an armload of wood inside with him. He fired the propane lights and their hum filled the room. The light was gentle and orange on the wooden walls. He took a deep breath of the cabin air. He made a fire in the wood stove and set a kettle of water to heat. He stepped outside and listened to the ocean as he pissed off the ledge.

He made coffee and sat with his back to the stove. His heart clicked as his eyes landed on his father's rifle. The word *revenge* shot through his mind. He imagined himself taking that gun and loading it and aiming it at a living man. Settling the crosshairs and pulling the trigger. That was easy enough to imagine but what he could not imagine was what would come next. He looked down at his palms as if to judge their capabilities. He squinted his eyes closed and suddenly heard Osmond Randolph's voice like the creaking of an old hull. *Blood and blood alone.* Jonah crimped his hands into fists and thought of his father in the pound and of throwing the bones overboard. With his eyes still closed he silenced Osmond's voice and silenced his own mind and listened as waves stretched and broke across the entire coastline.

Nearly forty-eight hours since he'd buried his father at sea and still Bill couldn't concentrate. He took a cold shower but his skin burned and his jaw clenched. He paced the house over and over again. He didn't know where Erma Lee was but that wasn't what bothered him. He drove east around the bay and up Osmond Randolph's long arcing clamshell driveway.

Osmond opened the door and let him in. The house smelled like garlic and shrimp. Bill heard a television. Osmond led him down a hallway and through the kitchen to a bar where a football game played on the overhead screen. A bowl of whole shrimp and another of raw scallops sat on the bar top. Next to it was a small bowl of vinegar and olive oil with a halved head of roasted garlic in it.

Osmond dipped a scallop and ate it. He pushed the bowl of shrimp toward Bill. Noise from another television set came from a back room.

Go ahead, William. Eat.

Bill tore the head from a shrimp and peeled the shell and tail off and ate it.

Fresh today, Osmond said. Rough weather for being on the water, wouldn't you say? I wouldn't want to be out in this, would you?

Bill shook his head no and thought back to the waves breaking over the Leviathan and his father's severed bones tumbling across the seafloor.

What happened to you, William? You're hurt.

Bill rubbed his cheek where Jonah had hit him. I'm fine, he said. He took his glasses off and looked at the bent frames and put them back on.

Did you get in a fight?

I'm fine. I come to talk about this pound business.

Good. I've been thinking it over myself.

Bill ate a scallop without dipping it in the oil. He swallowed and said, Can I get a drink?

Osmond stood and hooked his long oily hair behind his ears. Of course. I'm sorry for not offering. He stooped down behind the bar and came up with a bottle of scotch. He set the bottle on the bar and took a glass from the shelf and put three ice cubes in it. He dumped the melted ice out of his own glass and refitted it with fresh ice. He filled each to the rim with scotch and left the bottle on the bar and slid the glass to Bill.

That's a big buck, Bill said as the lobster in the tank turned in a circle.

He's been here fourteen years. He was barely legal when I caught him. He shed every year for a while but now he hasn't shed in three years. I'd thought he would shed again soon, but that might be as big as he can get in that tank. He's limited, you see.

That might be so. Bill sipped his drink and watched the lobster. But I come to talk about the pound.

Good, said Osmond. Good. Have you lined up feed yet? We're nearly out.

Yeah. I got some coming day after tomorrow.

How much?

Twenty ton of haddock racks in pickle.

Haddock racks in pickle.

That's all I could get. They'll winter on it fine.

I think so too, Osmond said. Good. Osmond tapped his glass on the marble bar top. Have you heard from the insurance company yet?

No, Bill said. I ain't heard a thing.

Osmond held his finger in the air. One second, William.

Bill nodded and Osmond left the room and returned with a manila folder which he put in front of Bill. Take a look, he said.

While Bill opened the folder Osmond took his checkbook out and wrote a check. Bill flipped through the papers. What's this? he finally said.

That's called a key man policy. That's the insurance policy your father and I had at the pound. You see, William, we're incorporated. That means we have shares, half of which I own and half of which Nicolas owned.

Yeah, said Bill. I know that.

I can imagine, Osmond said. He hooked his hair behind his ear again and thought for a few seconds. There are a lot of changes when a loved one dies, especially when it is so sudden. I lost my daughter and I lost her mother but both were expected. Not that expectation offers consolation.

I heard, Bill said. He smelled Osmond's breath like diesel exhaust.

But I do have a question for you, William, and I hope you don't take it the wrong way. You see, I have Julius and the two girls and that is all I have. This is a long life to live. I'm over seventy and only the Lord knows what lies ahead. My question is this, If you were in your father's shoes, what would you have wanted to happen to the pound if one of us were to die? What sort of insurance would you want?

Osmond watched Bill through the sides of his eyes.

If I died, I'd want it to go to Jonah, Bill said. He reached into his sweatshirt pocket with both hands and worked a cigarette out of the pack and brought it up to the bar top. He held it in his fingers.

What if I died? Would you want to be partners with Julius forever?

I can't say, Bill said.

You have to say, William.

No offense, Bill said. But I don't think so.

I don't blame you. You see, Osmond said as he reached across the bar and slid the folder over and picked it up. You see, your father thought the same thing. He assumed that he would outlive me, and he didn't want to share the pound with Julius.

So?

So, William, what we decided was this. Osmond held a hand out across the bar as if to hold Bill back although Bill made no move. We took out a key man insurance policy, which means that if one of us dies, all of the dead man's shares go to the survivor. In this case, me.

Bill was silent. He lit his cigarette.

And what you get, William, is a settlement from the insurance company. Technically, the settlement should go to the business, but we made arrangements to protect our families. Over the years, we've paid in on insurance for one half of the equity in the pound.

Come again?

You and your brother will receive a check for one half of the value of the pound is what I'm saying.

And the pound's yours?

The pound is mine, William. One hundred percent. I'm sorry. I thought that your father would have explained that to you a long time ago. Then I realized you were unaware.

Bill stood up and spoke fast. Unaware? My old man started that pound before you even knew it was there. He was a good friend to you. Only sonofabitch on the coast who could stand you.

Osmond nodded. That pound was there long before either of your parents arrived on this coast, William. Your father merely rebuilt it and brought it into this century. But never mind that. I accepted your father just as I've accepted you—and yes, it is true that he was the only sonofabitch who could stand me, just as he was the only sonofabitch who I could stand. Things will work out for you, William. Don't worry about that. I am sorry about the disappointment. I know the pound means a lot to you, and I've written you a check for the work you've done.

No, said Bill as if he could simply reject the past. He looked at Osmond for a moment then drank the scotch down in a single swallow. He refilled his glass and stepped back. He took a shrimp out of the bowl and examined its shell and legs and ate it shell and legs and all.

One more thing, Osmond said. He didn't take his eyes from the television. Have you thought more about how Nicolas ended up in the pound?

I been just now figuring on asking you the same thing.

You found more of Nicolas's skeleton. I know you went offshore with it. He should have been given a proper burial.

You're the one chucked his fucking head over the dam.

Osmond bowed his head. That is true. Forgive me. That was rash. But that doesn't explain how he got in the pound in the first place. Understand that I am granting a lot of latitude here, Bill. I would like to find your father's murderer as much as you would.

Who said he got murdered?

How else would you explain it?

I ain't in the explaining business but right now it seems you had yourself a pound to gain.

Bill, Osmond said. Think before you speak. Do not forget that you and Jonah had several hundred thousand dollars to gain. You are Nicolas's son and so I will grant you leeway here, but tread softly.

Softly, Bill said. He drank down his glass of scotch and refilled it and said, He sure as shit didn't go in on his own free will, Osmond.

No, I don't suspect so. I haven't any idea how he got in there, William, but I will look into it. I have a few contacts.

What contacts? Chimney? He's liable to have done it himself.

Chimney is in prison. He could not have. And he is not a murderer.

The hell he ain't. And Julius ain't any better. If it weren't you and weren't Chimney it was that little whore's egg Julius is my way of thinking. We all know for fact that he's experienced at drowning folks. Or half drowning anyway.

You may leave now, William, Osmond said. He tore a check out of his book and held it out to Bill. Here is your check for the work you've done. I appreciate your help.

Bill ignored the check. He turned with his glass of scotch in his hand and faced the darkness behind the windows and when Osmond didn't say anything he walked through the kitchen and out the door. He drank his scotch as he crossed the driveway and he tossed the glass into the trees.

• • •

When he got home Erma Lee was waiting at the dinner table. You been drinking, Bill?

He pulled a chair out and sat down. Goddamned right.

Erma Lee rounded the table and put her hands on his shoulders and told him to push back. He backed his chair up and she sat astraddle him and she examined his bruised face.

What happened, Bill?

Nothing.

She pulled his glasses off. Is your eye feeling better, Bill?

It's fine, Erma Lee. It's fine. But Osmond owns the pound. I ain't got none of it.

You got in a fight with Osmond?

No. He owns the pound is what I'm saying.

Oh the Lord. You got in another fight. I'll get you some ice for that eye.

Are you listening to me? The whole pound's fucking lost. Gone. We got none of it.

She didn't say anything for a while then, Ain't you got a copy of your father's will?

No. He didn't have a will and it wouldn't help no-how.

Her chin wrinkled and her forehead furrowed. She cupped his face in her hands. I'm so sorry, Bill.

I got to get all the pound paperwork. And I might have to get a lawyer down here. I don't know, but I ain't backing out of the old man's pound.

Is it the income you need? We'll be fine without the pound, Bill.

I know it. But I'm gonna have it. I catch enough on the boat, Bill said and as he spoke it dawned on him that they could have called the police. He and Jonah had no part in the pound. They could have drained it and let Osmond deal with the fallout. There could have been a real police investigation but it was far too late for that now and he and Jonah and Virgil were the ones who had made it too late.

Bill shut the thoughts out. He said, I been thinking of taking you on sternman. That way we keep all our earnings in the household.

Not while I'm pregnant you ain't.

No kidding, Erma Lee. After.

After, Bill? This infant ain't going away once it's born.

We'll get a sitter.

A sitter, Bill? We ain't having some drunk woman raise our infant. I'm staying right put. You got a hundred different folks you can pick sternmen from.

Well. You ain't big enough or fast enough anyhow. A trap weighs more'n you.

Erma Lee stood up. I'm getting dinner.

She came back into the room with a bowl of mussels and some melted butter and she put it on the table. She went back into the kitchen and returned with a quiche.

What the hell is that? Bill said.

That's crab quiche, Bill.

Crab what?

Quiche.

Looks like baby puke to me. And where'd you get them mussels?

I picked them at low water, Bill. And cooked them in white wine and parsley with garlic and onions. Try them, Bill. You'll like them.

Garlic? Quiche?

Just try it. It's from a cookbook of Celeste's that she's lent me.

Oh God. Now we'll be eating that weird shit she feeds Virgil all the time. Jonah likes that shit.

It ain't weird and it ain't shit, Bill. It's good.

Where'd you get crab meat to?

Celeste had some frozen that she gave me. Is that okay with you?

Ain't you two just buddy-buddy.

Yes, Bill, yes we are. She's come to visit, and it's nice. We've even been talking of making a Christmas dinner together.

Bill sliced a piece of the quiche and loaded it onto his plate. Erma Lee watched as he tried it. He took another bite and looked up at her while he chewed and he smiled and quiche spread from between his teeth and he said, That's good.

Try them mussels, Bill. They're good too.

He ate mussel after mussel and the shells clinked in the shell bowl each time he threw one. Ain't you eating?

Not now, she said. I ain't hungry now on account of the infant.

Everything's on account of the infant.

Erma Lee ignored him. You eat. I had fun making it all.

Fun cooking. I couldn't stand just sitting around the house.

It weren't sitting to make that.

I know you weren't sitting, Bill said. Not doing nothing is how I meant it.

You mean cooking for you ain't doing nothing, Bill? I'm gonna learn to cook good like Celeste. And get us a garden going too.

I'd just heat up something. It don't take all day.

Erma Lee stood up and leaned against the counter and folded her arms. What about once the baby comes? What would you do then?

I told you. I'd get you a sitter and go sternman. Any old woman could raise a kid. The kid don't know who's who. You'd make enough on a boat to pay a sitter and buy groceries and have money left over.

Oh my God, Erma Lee said.

Oh my God what?

Erma Lee stared at him and she trembled slightly. You actually think any old woman could raise our kid, Bill? You think that?

No, Erma Lee. I don't think that. I know that. It's a fact.

She tried to cover her abdomen with her hands. A fact?

You don't think so? Bill said.

She spoke softly. No, Bill. No I don't.

His face went red and his jaw muscles flexed. So you intend to spend eighteen years sitting on your ass with that kid doing nothing all day long while I'm on the water? Well I'll tell you what, me and Jonah grew up fine without a mother sitting on her ass next to us. We done good. You think you know it all sitting around in the kitchen and talking about goddamned quiche and diapers, Erma Lee? Well you don't know shit.

She shook her head no without meaning to.

You can get a job and I don't care if it's pumping gas or lugging bait but that kid can grow up just like I done. That's another fact.

There's more than one way of doing things.

What? Yeah, Erma Lee, that's right. There's two ways. There's my way and there's the goddamned wrong way and I won't have you doing things the wrong way all the fucking time.

Erma Lee took two steps back then turned. She walked down the hallway and into the bedroom and shut the door and Bill put his head in his hands and ground his teeth and pulled on his own hair.

F our days later. Christmas morning. Snow covered the islands like shells and the water in the cove lay flat calm. Jonah held a cup of coffee steaming between his thighs and rowed across the cove to his boat. The gull who he now recognized as a beggar bird rode his skiff's bow. He tossed a cracker into the water and the bird circled then scooped it from the water and carried it to a nearby ledge. He climbed aboard and ground the diesel to life. Blue-black smoke coughed into the cold salt air and waste oil and bilge water pissed from the chine and spread in an uncoiling rainbow across the sea surface.

He steamed out of the cove and the entire ocean was forever blue before him. Eiders and pintails and buffleheads squawked and parted and flew. He followed the coastline around Burnt Island. He slipped between a ledge and the red nun buoy that marked the entrance to the harbor. The tide was up and water lapped the pound's slat-wood dam.

Jonah idled his boat into the shallows beside the dam. The pound house rose above him. The seafloor was green in the cold light and he'd found his father's skull in this very spot and that memory struck him hard. In the days since Bill told him about losing the pound Jonah had convinced himself that this was not hallowed ground but now at the pound with the waves pumping and swishing like systoles it seemed that the coastline had indeed become something more than landscape.

The *Jennifer* idled in the shoal green water. Jonah watched the rockweed below swing in the currents and he watched the shape of the water reverberating off the dam. He thought of his father's skeleton awash amid endless seawater. He was beginning to suspect that with this life came a harsh fragility that endured well beyond death.

He motored away and craned his head around and watched the slat-wood dam framed in the V of his wake. He was suddenly angry and he whispered, Fucking Osmond, although just then he felt that it was not Osmond but he himself who deserved the curse.

The air was clean and crisp and it stung his lungs but did little to clear the confusion from his head. He took a skiff from the wharf float and put his boat on his mooring then rowed back to the float. He walked through the small empty wintertime village. Road salt crunched beneath his feet. He found Virgil watching television. Celeste was in the kitchen and she wore an apron with a Christmas tree embroidered on the front. Charlotte was in her bedroom. Jonah sat at the kitchen table and ate homemade potato donuts dipped in maple syrup and drank coffee and after an hour he went into the living room and sat on the couch and watched television with Virgil but neither spoke.

Two hours later Bill arrived. His skin was raw and he looked like he hadn't slept in days. Jonah met him in the hallway and said, You ain't made up with Erma Lee yet? I thought that was your Christmas Eve plan. To make up with her.

Bill shook his head no but he didn't speak. Jonah got the feeling that if Bill did speak he'd cry.

What happened now?

Bill shook his head again. Nothing, he finally said. She's just bonkers is all. Flat out gone-fuck bonkers. I had enough, Jonah. Enough. I told her last night to either one get her damned head screwed on straight or get the fuck out.

Celeste came down the hallway. She stopped when she saw Bill. Bill looked away from her like a guilty dog but she approached him anyway. Merry Christmas, Bill.

Merry Christmas, he mumbled.

Where's Erma Lee?

She ain't coming.

I thought she was.

Well she ain't.

Celeste faced Bill. Bill's sweatshirt was unzipped. He took his hand from the pocket and it already held a can of beer and he drank.

What did you do?

Nothing. She's just a bit mad about our arrangement.

What arrangement is that, Bill? Your trial?

Bill blinked and looked at Celeste then away. That's right.

I love you, Bill, but you are so stupid sometimes that I want to strangle you. Go in there and sit down. I'll be right back.

Celeste, Bill said as she pulled her jacket on.

She looked at him. What?

Nothing.

Nothing. Is that what you said to her? Nothing? Celeste stepped forward and tried to stand face to face with Bill but he was half a foot taller. Do you realize that she is scared out of her mind, Bill? That she's all alone and has a baby growing inside of her? A human baby that you helped put there. You, Bill.

I get it. He stepped back as if she were going to hit him but she went out the door. Jonah stood on the far side of the hall with his back to the wall. Before he could say anything Bill said, Shut up, Jonah.

● ● ●

Celeste didn't knock. She opened the door and stepped inside. Two stuffed full black trash bags sat in the middle of the room. One was torn on the side and a framed picture stuck out.

She looked around and the walls were empty. The sheetrock was speckled with nails and nail holes. She heard a rustling from down the hall and she said, Erma Lee? It's me.

Thanks but I'm all set, Erma Lee said.

Celeste went down the hall and stopped in the bedroom doorway. Across the room a sliding glass door led to a patio facing the harbor. The afternoon sun shone bright and Celeste squinted her eyes. Erma Lee held a trash bag which she loaded clothing into.

Erma Lee, she said.

I'm fine.

I know that. But it's Christmas.

Erma Lee straightened and faced Celeste. Her chin was wrinkled but Celeste was surprised to see her face so clear and dry. Thanks for everything, Celeste. The cookbook and things.

Keep it, Celeste said.

I feel good, Erma Lee said.

You feel good?

It dawned on me of a sudden. He don't love me and he don't love anyone. I got a baby and I'm happy. I can do it. And you know what? It weren't even that I was scared of doing it alone. I was just scared to go crawling back to my cousin's like a failure.

What happened?

Nothing happened. Erma Lee rolled a pair of jeans up and stuffed them in the bag. There was a pile of clothes on the floor at her feet where she'd dumped the dresser drawer out. She bent down and grabbed more clothes and stuffed them in. When she straightened she held a small pair of black lace panties in her hand. She held them up for Celeste to see. I wear this stuff for him, she said. And he don't care. He don't care about nothing but lobsters and boats. Well he can get some other girl to wear them.

She shoved the panties under the pillow.

It's none of my business, Erma Lee. I know. I'll leave if you want.

Erma Lee wiped her nose and nodded. She tried to pick up the trash bag but she'd filled it too full and the bag was too weak and her hands tore through it. She coughed and sat on the bed.

Celeste sat down next to her. What'd he do that was so bad?

He's just changed. Or maybe he ain't changed but everything else has. I'm pregnant and we got a baby coming and he don't realize that. He won't say nothing about this baby other than it don't need a mother and nothing about me but me needing to get off my ass. Why can't he just say that he understands or something? Or that he wants this baby? Or maybe he don't want it. Anything. He got mean. All he done all along was make fun of me for it like I made a big mistake on my own. Like caring for a baby is wasting time or something.

Celeste slid over and put her arm around Erma Lee. I wish I could tell you something good, but that sounds like Bill. If it helps, I can tell you that he's different inside. His mother died when he was nine and he took care of Jonah but he never stopped being a scared little boy stuck inside that big body of his. He was always supposed to not feel a thing.

Erma Lee nodded. Well, she said. That don't mean he's got to treat me like he done. I grew up like shit too.

You're right, Celeste said. She rubbed Erma Lee's back. Where are you going? For dinner?

Down to my cousin's. Where I should've gone in the first place. But Bill wanted me to join your family. And things were going good. Then Osmond and the pound—he changed of a sudden. I know he lost his dad and all that, but don't he know I can help him? I didn't do this on purpose but it's done.

I know it, Celeste said. I know it. You didn't do anything wrong. The first time I got pregnant I was scared out of my wits. But I was lucky because Virgil was there the whole time and he was so happy and eager for our baby. I think he wished he could carry it instead of me.

I wish Bill was that way. I done everything I know to do.

He might feel it, Erma Lee. He probably does. But he doesn't know how to say what he feels. He just shuts himself off. And right now things are especially hard for him.

Erma Lee coughed again. I know they are. But don't he know I can help? It's hard but still that don't mean he can take it out on me or a unborn infant. That ain't right no matter what.

That's right, Celeste said.

Erma Lee wiped her eyes. You got pregnant more than once?

Celeste looked surprised. What?

You said the first time was when you was scared.

Celeste nodded. Yes. I miscarried the next one and that was it. We never did try again. Sometimes I wish we had. For Charlotte's sake. I think she'd be better with people if she had a sibling.

She's nice.

Celeste laughed. She can be. But she's selfish because she never had to share. Her best friend was always Jonah and he was always in love with her so he gave her anything she wanted. And she took anything she wanted. She still takes anything she wants and doesn't think about anything else. Not even her own future. But she'll do well. She's smart enough.

Erma Lee nodded and stood up. I best get these things together. My cousins is all waiting and it's Christmas.

Are you sure you won't change your mind? I stuffed those cabbages I told you about, and I roasted a bunch of root vegetables. There's sourdough rolls and cranberry sauce with horseradish— please come over. Everything's from the garden, and there's still some cooking you can help me with.

Erma Lee thought for a moment. I might change my mind about Bill if he changes his own mind. I know I can help him but he's got to allow that. I ain't lagging around no more just because I'm scared of being on my own. Me and this kid can make do fine. I always made do growing up with my mom drunk and my dad who knows where, and I can make do now.

Celeste set dinner on the table and opened two bottles of wine and everyone sat down. The meal was quiet and awkward. No one mentioned Nicolas and no one mentioned Osmond and no one mentioned the lobster pound. After dinner Virgil made everyone watch *The Sound of Music* and Jonah and Bill and Celeste sat on the couch and Virgil sat in his chair and Charlotte lay on the floor hidden beneath a blanket.

Bill declared the movie to be Erma Lee's type of horseshit but sat and watched it without stirring. Jonah spent the night in the guest room. A few minutes after he was in bed he heard Charlotte move about in her bedroom. He heard her dresser drawer open and close and he knew she was taking her clothes off and putting her pajamas on. Her sheets rustled and he knew she was climbing into bed so he put his fingers in his ears to block the images the sounds carried.

Bill picked him up the next day. Neither spoke until they were out of the driveway and headed toward the wharf. Jonah said, You call Erma Lee last night?

Not yet I ain't but I want to, Jonah. That's the thing. I do miss her.

Tell that to her, not me.

Who said I ain't told her?

You did. You just said you didn't call her.

Bill thought for a moment. What if she ain't the right one, Jonah? That ever occur to you? Women always know they got the right one, but with us guys it's different. We got a harder time telling. By Jesus, Jonah, if I tell her something like I been missing her, then that's it. Like stepping in wet concrete on a hot day is what it is.

Now how in hell you figure that? She's a woman, Bill. She ain't a fucking pile of concrete and she ain't a boat either.

Well it weren't too long ago you were telling me to run her offshore with a cinderblock if I remember correct, Jonah.

Well, I don't know what to say. I'm getting to like her.

Bill nodded. Jonah examined his brother's face with its square jaw and thin red lips and big cheekbones and eyes so gentle and innocent that Jonah had trouble equating the face with the words that tended to spill from its mouth. He half expected Bill to say, *I wish she was a boat.*

They eased down the frozen hill to the wharf. Virgil's truck was already parked out on the wharf. Diesel exhaust drifted from the tailpipe.

Bill sucked his cigarette hard and his cheeks caved and he said, Maybe we should go down to Florida or something. You ever think of that? Get the hell out of here? Go down there and get a skiff and do some sport fishing on them flats? Or hell, we could just run the *Jennifer* down there and do some real fishing. Chase some tuna and marlin or swords around.

Jonah nodded but didn't answer. He watched Virgil's truck reverse and turn around and pull alongside.

Virgil rolled his window down and put one hand on the windowsill.

I see Julius's boat ain't on the hook, Bill said.

Virgil locked his gaze on Bill. He took a deep breath that bulged his cheeks like a saxophone player. He blew out a pile of air. What in the clamfuck makes you think I ain't noticed that, Bill?

Just saying.

Just saying. Fuckall, Captain. Why don't you just say where in hell he's gone to with a hundred new traps he loaded aboard this morning.

I'd say he took them outside and set them right on top of your favorite little fishing spot, Virgil, Bill said.

Virgil sipped his drink. I'd say that's right astute of you, William. You apologize to Erma Lee yet?

Bill ran his hands around the steering wheel. A hundred traps? That's a lot of gear to be putting down in winter. Hell, the price ain't even over three bucks yet. He'll lose half that gear in a month's time. Better on the bottom line to stay on shore these days. Christ, damned near like getting paid not to haul. Even in a good winter who in hell sets fresh gear?

He knows Jonah cut that gang of Osmond's off out on the Leviathan. My guess is he wants to test us again. That new boat's got him fierce, and he'll fish hard. Lucky little prick's got Celeste looking over his shoulder like a damned angel, and he don't even know it. We mess with him and I'll be living with the two of you boys.

Julius just can't help it, I'm guessing, Bill said with a slow up and down nod.

Virgil revved the engine. He can fish the bay and the sound— and hell, all the way out in any direction his black heart desires. But he is not fishing the Leviathan. The Leviathan is ours.

· · ·

That night Celeste got into bed by herself. A football game played on the television downstairs and after a while she heard it shut off and heard the front door open and close. She shivered as though a shell of cold air had climbed the staircase and crawled down the hallway into her bedroom and into her body. She waited and soon enough Virgil's truck started and idled.

After an hour of the truck idling she put her bathrobe and slippers on and went outside. Virgil had a gallon of milk and a bottle of brandy with him. Chowder rested her head on his thigh and her tongue hung out. The heater blasted. The moon was big but tucked behind a thin layer of clouds and the cloud cover diffused the light over the snow and water and mud and turned the night bright. The tide was low and the frozen mudflats were slick chrome.

Virgil rotated his head atop his neck like the twist of a socket drive and said, Julius set a gang of traps on the Leviathan this morning.

Celeste sighed. That's why you're sitting out here pouting in the middle of the night?

No. It's Osmond.

Osmond? Celeste's voice was exasperated. She rotated in the seat and gazed at Virgil with her mouth half open. She felt like she'd spent her life believing in the wrong thing. She stared at him in the shadow of the truck. The shadow made him look older and paler than usual.

You really think Osmond would kill Nicolas over the pound? That doesn't make sense. The pound's not worth that, even to him.

The pound is worth it. Jason Jackson changes things. Benji selling the wharf changes things. The wharf is a buying station. The pound is a storage facility. The two combined are worth a hell of a lot more than the two separate. Osmond understands that, but that's not all his reasoning. The real reason is Julius. Osmond's scared that without the income from the pound, his only male blood would be a pirate drug dealer his whole life and end up like Chimney or worse. And he knew with Nic in the pound, Julius couldn't be a part of it because Nic had two sons and the pound don't split that many ways. Osmond probably would've died first and Julius would've gotten the insurance, not the pound. Then Chimney would've gotten his paws on that money. Osmond was set upon this earth to have dominion over the sea, not to smuggle dope.

Virgil paused and his heavy breathing filled the cab. When he caught his breath he continued.

With Jason Jackson on the scene, things are going to change and change fast. Benji's wharf's the first step. We don't see the rest yet, Celeste, but Nic was the end.

Celeste suppressed the urge to scream. She said, Oh my God, Virgil, I am sick of this kind of talk. The end of what, for heaven's sake?

The end of the ocean is what it is.

Celeste scoffed. The end of the ocean? She gazed at the pale night outside the truck. We've always shipped lobsters out. That's how we survive.

That's right. We made enough to get by. Now it's big money and big boats. We aren't trucking lobsters to little markets in Boston anymore. We're shipping around the globe so now we got the attention of some big money. Whatever happens in global markets happens to us but in a different way. Virgil put his hand on hers and his voice calmed and took on a new sensitivity. It's important that you understand this, Celeste. This is about money for them, but it's about life for us. If we sit back and let this stuff happen, we lose who we are. Isn't that worth something? Isn't that worth everything?

Without meaning to Celeste whispered, Nicolas. Then thought, *I'm going crazy too.*

Virgil nodded and his voice resumed its previous fervor. And it ripples down. The demand for lobsters in Asia goes up so the price goes up. All of a sudden this coast is worth something. Nicolas doesn't like it so he gets killed. Then Jonah bottoms out so Charlotte dumps him and Erma Lee gets knocked up and Julius gets our daughter and on and on. Those markets fuck our lives, and it ain't right, and it'll get worse. Look at scallops or groundfish or salmon or crab. Big business runs the government so they make the regulations. That's how they win. Now they have fish farms that run on computers and drift across the Atlantic. No people aboard at all. Just floating computerized factories. That's what it's coming to. Imagine looking out there and seeing a city of floating farms run by robots feeding corn to genetically engineered salmon. It's real and it's coming. Jason Jackson isn't as bad as the big corporations, but he's the first step and we need to fight now and we got to do it our way.

Virgil gazed blankly through the windshield. When he spoke again his voice was soft and easy as if begging something of her. We are smart enough to do this, aren't we?

What is *this*?

This life. We are smart enough for this life, aren't we? For this world? To live here?

I don't know, she said. She put her hand on the door handle. I love you, Virgil, and I agree with some of what you said. But that is no excuse for what you're doing to yourself or to us. I swore to stand by you and by God I will, but you made the same fucking promise to me.

She opened the door and stepped out of the truck. She shut the door quietly and pulled her robe tight to her chest. She walked through the cold night air and went inside and up the steps and paused outside Charlotte's room and listened to her daughter's slight breath and wished momentarily for her adolescence. Hers and Charlotte's.

Virgil and Jonah met Bill at the wharf in the morning. The moon hung over the western edge of the harbor. The wharf light shone yellow in the blue dawn. The air smelled of ice and wintertime wind. One of the urchin draggers idled on its hook and its overhead lights flooded the deck space where Royal James worked and smoked. The three of them took a moment and watched Royal move about the boat deck then Jonah spoke.

You heading straight offshore, Virgil? I'm guessing you are.

I'm heading to find Julius's traps. Every single last one of those hundred sonsofwhores.

Jonah coughed and hacked up a pile of phlegm and spat it onto the wharf plank. He cocked his head and looked at Virgil. Even in the half-light he could see Virgil's sunken eyes and caved cheeks and slumped shoulders. You don't look so good, Virgil. You doing okay?

Finger licking, Virgil said.

You sure? What're you going to do? You aiming to cut each one?

Just the ones I don't like.

They walked down the ramp. It was covered with asphalt shingles for traction and Virgil hung on to both rails and grunted with each awkward step. Two gulls quit the float. Jonah held Virgil's skiff alongside as Virgil climbed in. They wiped the snow from the seats and sat and pushed themselves off and rowed to their boats.

The three boats ran single file out of the harbor and when they reached open water they fanned out side by side by side and all three boats cast wakes like the flight patterns of geese. The boats

215

spread farther and farther apart until each one became nothing but an isolated dot on the horizon. As Jonah watched this separation he felt a pang like twilight in his chest and he wished he could save them all but he didn't know what from.

He steamed south to his first string. He hauled the pairs of traps and piled them on the stern and he was on his way to his next string when Virgil came on the radio.

Jonah, you might want to come out here and lend me a hand. I got boat troubles.

What is it?

Jonah spun his boat south and the *Jennifer* lifted and planed through the water.

I ain't sure. She's just upset I'm thinking.

Bill's voice came on the radio, You okay, Virgil? What's up?

I'm fine, Virgil said. The Highliner can give me a hand. You keep on fishing.

Where're you at, Virgil? Jonah said. The Leviathan?

That's right.

Let me know if you need a hand, Bill said but Virgil didn't answer him.

Twenty minutes later Jonah pulled alongside him and both boats lifted and settled with the charge of water. Virgil walked to the stern and faced Jonah. He pointed at two of his strings. Jonah looked to the south and to the west and saw Julius's buoys side by side with Virgil's. Jonah's mind followed the ropes to the seafloor and he saw Julius's traps stacked atop Virgil's.

Jonah looked at Virgil. Fuckachrist, Virgil.

I don't know, Jonah. I just don't know.

That ain't right.

No shit that ain't right. Did the Captain send Erma Lee any flowers yet?

Not yet he ain't.

He better do something, Virgil said. Goddamned Julius set atop me each and every one of them bastards. Virgil looked at his boat deck and swung his head back and forth in a gradual arc. It makes me sad is all I can say. What does that boy think, Jonah?

Jonah worked his gloves off and clasped his hands beneath the bib of his oil pants. He could feel the layer of sea air rising into the cold winter sky.

Julius don't respect a thing, Jonah said.

Virgil held his breath and released it. If that's how he wants to play.

What's that?

He's just lucky I'm too old to get mad anymore. Ten years ago I'd hang that sonofawhore high. Instead I'm taking the Highliner and the Captain sternman tonight.

Tonight?

That's right.

Maybe we should let Osmond take care of Julius. He wouldn't approve of this any more than we do. I see he ain't set a string back here since we cut him off.

Virgil picked a herring out of the baitbox and tossed it over the stern. A half dozen gulls dove and fought for it. *We* cut him off, Jonah? *You* cut him off. Don't forget that because I guarantee Osmond hasn't. Just because he's been quiet about it doesn't mean he's forgotten. He's just waiting. And I agree that he might not take to Julius's behavior. We don't like each other but he understands lobster fishing and he knows the rules, even if he breaks them once in a while. But I'll be goddamned if either one of us goes crying to him. Julius's got to learn some manners and my guess is he won't listen to Osmond any more'n he listens to anyone else. Osmond had his time with Julius and it added up to nothing. Now it's our time.

It was midmorning when Osmond dropped the two girls off at day-care and gave the woman two hundred dollars and said he wouldn't be back until the following afternoon. The woman folded the money into her apron and nodded. Osmond peeled another hundred from his billfold and said, They are my life.

I know it, the woman said. We get on good, don't we Dolly?

Yes, said Dolly.

Osmond knelt down and hugged them both and kissed each one on the cheek and held his hands on the backs of their heads. I'll be back before you know it.

He drove to Julius's and Julius was waiting in the driveway with a small gym bag in his hand. He climbed into the truck and shut the door and said, Hell, I could've set five strings this morning if I'd known it would be this late.

Osmond glanced at him. I thought I said to dress well.

Julius wore black sweatpants and a gray sweatshirt. I ain't exactly flush with tuxedos.

Never mind, Osmond said. We'll take care of it.

Where we going?

To get you acquainted.

Acquainted with who?

With whom? With your future partners. We're going to the city. To Boston.

The fucking city?

Osmond reached over and grabbed Julius's bicep and squeezed it. You will mind your manners, Julius. Until the time is right to not mind them anymore, but until that time, you will.

When's that time?

You must learn to pay attention to people. You are going into business now. Even in your father's business, he had to be a judge of people.

Yeah. Or he'd get his ass shot off.

As may you.

It was six hours before they crossed the bridge and dipped into the clean new tunnel. Julius was wide-eyed and held one hand on the door and the other on the dash. Traffic echoed.

Sonofawhore, he said.

Osmond grinned.

They emerged near the train station and financial sector and the skyscrapers pincushioned the sky. They exited and veered east toward the water and parked outside Jason's warehouse. Patches of snow and ice missed by plows dotted the pavement and the sky was gray and the air was heavy and cold and raw and smelled of heating oil and traffic.

The steel door echoed. Daniel smiled and stood up and shook Osmond's hand.

This is my grandson, Julius Wesley. You met at the pound.

Daniel nodded. I remember. Follow me.

They followed Daniel into the tank room. Julius stopped at the doorway and looked around. Holy shit, he said.

Osmond gave him a sharp look and Julius caught the look.

Daniel explained the operation to Julius until Jason came down the steps from his office. He wore Hawaiian shorts and rubber boots and his white laboratory coat. His gut hung out over the waistband of the shorts.

Julius looked up at him and the man was nearly as tall as his grandfather.

You are Julius? Jason said.

Yeah.

It's a pleasure. Jason reached out and they shook hands. Come upstairs. We can talk there.

They followed Jason up the metal stairway. Daniel went back to the front desk. Osmond and Julius sat side by side on the leather couch and Jason poured sake for both of them and one for himself then sat at his desk.

How was your drive?

Fine, said Osmond.

We have a lot to talk about, Jason said. He held his glass in the air and tipped it toward them then drank.

Like what? said Julius.

Jason smiled. I heard you were the ornery one.

I ain't ornery.

Jason smiled bigger. No, I was wrong, he said. I apologize.

Jason stood up and faced the window that looked down over the tank room. Julius, he said. Come look with me. He held his hand out toward Julius and Julius joined him at the window.

You see this? This operation holds thirty thousand pounds of lobsters. That's not much.

No, that ain't much at all, Julius said.

Jason and Osmond exchanged glances and Jason turned back to Julius. No, that is not much. What we do here is hold lobsters for a matter of days. We get them in from operations such as yours, and we resell them to certain buyers. The highest-quality product goes to the highest bidder, obviously. The culls go to the processor. Most often, our highest bidder is my Japanese buyer. Very soon now, he will be the only bidder.

Julius peered out the window as if bored. He drank down the sake and set the glass on the sill. Jason took the glass and refilled it at the bar and returned to the window and handed the glass to Julius.

Now Julius, what I have discussed with Osmond is the possibility of building a new operation like this one at your pound. He tells me that you will be receiving half of the shares and replacing Nicolas, so any decisions involving the pound involve you.

Julius didn't say anything. He ran his fingers over his arrowhead of hair then reached into his pocket and gripped Nicolas's tooth as if it were his talisman.

We got a pound. What would we want a swimming pool for?

Fair enough. I'll buy the wharf and remodel the pound to nearly double the capacity, and cut your shrinkage. Then we'll build a seawater tank house like this but three times the size. Four times the size.

Which is it?

Jason laughed again and slapped his hand on Julius's shoulder. That is for us to decide.

You got no market there. You got no airport there. If you're shipping them bugs to Japan you need to get them out of the water and on the plane. You'll have six hours on a truck before they get on the plane, same as now. Why the fuss?

That's right, Julius, Jason said. Unless we fly out of a different airport. But we'll get to that. Osmond didn't tell me you were a businessman.

I ain't. I'm a lobsterman and I know lobster.

What sort of business were you in before lobsters?

Julius looked away and didn't answer. He released the tooth and in his other pocket with his other hand found a hard candy. He unwrapped the candy and put it in his mouth. He sipped the sake.

What we would do, Jason said, is we could still use this operation in the same way we do now, only we won't be dependent on it, and you won't be dependent on us. We'll combine our efforts and get bigger and more efficient. You won't need to sit around hoping your lobsters won't die in the pound before the price rises. Your fishermen will get paid according to the quality of their catch. You bring in good product, we pay good money. That simple. If we have top product we'll have top price.

It'll still go up and down.

Of course it will. But pound lobsters are a different product than run lobsters. Pound lobsters travel. The weak have already been culled. We can harden off the softshells over the summer and sell them in the fall for a real price, instead of sending them all to some Canadian processor for jack shit. We can make that pound *work*. Not just fill it once a year. We'll fill it at least three times a year. And like I told your grandfather, the Japanese will pay for lobsters that have never seen tank water. They want to taste that seawater. And what we're talking about is everything, Julius. We're talking about the wharf and all of it.

Huh, said Julius. He went back and sat down next to Osmond. He crunched his candy in his teeth. They wouldn't know tank water from seawater no how, he said.

Maybe not, Jason said. But they'll pay for it. He moved some papers around his desk. I have some things to finish up. I'll see you at the hotel?

Yes, said Osmond.

Daniel will take you.

Fine.

Jason opened the door and he shook Julius's and Osmond's hands. Osmond paused in the doorway. Julius climbed down the steps and looked into the tank.

We need to find clothing for Julius, Osmond said.

Jason nodded. I'll have Daniel take care of it.

Daniel led them to the black car. Osmond sat in the back seat and Julius rode in the passenger seat. He spun his head to see everything as they passed through Chinatown and beyond. He hunkered low with his chin to the dash to see the tops of buildings. Daniel gave them keycards to two rooms and dropped them at the hotel and the porter opened the door for them and they crossed the atrium and got in the elevator. Julius had never been in an elevator and he spread his legs wide and held his arms out for balance and he smiled like a little boy on his first bicycle ride.

Their rooms were side by side. Osmond handed one of the keycards to Julius and Julius opened the door and went in. He dropped his bag on the floor and started across the room to the line of windows and stopped. A blond woman sat in a chair in the corner. She wore a loose flannel shirt and faded blue jeans and held a book folded over her thigh.

Julius, she said.

He looked out the window at the city.

I'm Gwen, she said. She shifted in the chair and uncrossed her legs. She held the page of her book with a finger. You're a lobsterman?

What're you doing here?

Jason Jackson wanted us to meet. I work for him. She stood up and held the book at her side and faced the windows. She put one hand on the glass pane and peered down to the street. She was tall and thin and her tight jeans were tucked into tall boots made of brown leather.

She turned back and faced Julius. He felt himself blush.

You work for Jason Jackson, he said. Doing what?

Sometimes I'm a chef and sometimes I'm a consultant. I do what I want and I charge what I want and Jason doesn't argue.

What're you doing here then?

I told you. Jason wanted us to meet.

My old man always said a hooker's just a homeless whore.

Excuse me? She took a step toward him.

You heard me.

She took two more steps and stood with her face nearly touching his. Are you calling me a whore?

Julius backed up a step. I'm calling you a hooker. And I got a girlfriend so get the fuck out of here. He pulled a hard candy out of his pocket and unwrapped it and put it in his mouth.

Gwen walked past him. He smelled her slight perfume as she moved and he felt a crimp in his gut but he ignored it. He looked out the windows over the sea of brick buildings with smoke and steam rising in waves. He heard the door open and he felt her pause. He turned around. She'd put a ball cap on and as she stood there he was surprised at her beauty.

She crossed the floor and stood in front of him and said, You're an ignorant little prick, aren't you?

She walked out the door.

Julius watched television for several hours and then someone knocked on the door and he answered. It was a porter with two paper shopping bags with twine handles and he handed them to Julius.

He dumped the bags out and looked at the clothes. There was a black silk shirt and black slacks and a pair of sharkskin cowboy boots and a belt with a silver buckle shaped like a harpoon and a long black trench coat. Julius took a shower and shaved and dressed. He used the styling gel that was in the bathroom to slick his black hair back and he looked in the full-length mirror and he looked good.

Another knock came on the door and he opened it. It was Osmond and with him was a tall black woman wearing a shining black fur coat and Julius had never seen his grandfather with a woman and this woman held Osmond's arm. Osmond said, This is Renee.

Renee nodded to Julius and Julius looked at Osmond.

Where is Gwen? Osmond said.

Kicked her ass out, Julius said.

What?

I don't need a hooker.

The wrinkles on Osmond's face rose like a tectonic shift. He turned to Renee and whispered into her ear. She nodded. He stepped into the room with Julius and shut the door. Osmond hit him in the diaphragm and Julius bent over and struggled to breathe but couldn't. Osmond righted him. Julius couldn't catch his breath and his face went instantly purple. Osmond held him by his armpit with his thumb driven deep into the joint. He leaned in close to Julius's ear and gently whispered, You may make decisions in this life, Julius, but you will never again disrespect either me or those with whom I am associated.

Julius couldn't breathe and his mouth worked itself open and closed like a frog's. He told his chest to breathe but it would not listen. A ring of black circled his vision. He needed air and needed it right away. The black closed tighter and tighter until finally Osmond said, You may breathe now, and let go of Julius. Julius sank to the floor and his breath came and he sucked at the air with small gulps that were all his body would allow.

Julius worked his way to his feet.

Do you understand, Julius?

Julius stared him in the eyes and Osmond repeated, Do you understand?

I got a girlfriend.

You got a girlfriend.

Julius nodded.

And exactly what does that have to do with a thing in this world, Julius? Nothing, that is what. Not a thing. Do you understand?

Yes.

Now Jason is going to find you a date for tonight and you will treat her with respect and if you embarrass me one more time, Julius, I shall punish you. You understand that, don't you?

Julius nodded.

Good, Osmond said. After a moment he said, Who is this girlfriend?

Charlotte Alley.

Charlotte Alley?

Yeah, Julius grunted.

Osmond peered at Julius as if searching for the truth and he saw something in Julius's eyes that satisfied him. He nodded his approval and ran a hand over Julius's shoulder to smooth the bunched coat.

Together with Renee between them they walked down the hallway. Both Osmond and Julius wore long black trench coats and black slacks and they both wore their black hair greased back. They took the elevator down.

Jason stood in the atrium with Turtle holding his arm. He still wore his rubber boots and Hawaiian shorts and lab coat and he smiled and crossed the room. He went straight to Julius and took Julius's hand and squeezed it with a strength that made Julius's knees hurt. He pulled Julius close. Julius smelled aftershave and cologne but beyond that the simple smell of flesh.

I understand that you had some misunderstanding with a dear friend of mine.

Julius saw Gwen stand up from the couch she'd been sitting on. She wore a black evening dress and carried a jacket folded in her arm. She wore very little makeup. He was again shocked by her but the pain that stemmed from his hand worked like a sliver through his abdomen and spread to his shoulders and neck and his head involuntarily tilted to the side to alleviate the pain.

Jason leaned in again. Are things cleared up, son?

Now Julius leaned into Jason's ear and the pain vanished and he said, Things are clear but do not ever call me your son again or I will cut you from your balls to your chin. Is that cleared up?

Jason laughed as if no other response would have been appropriate and he released Julius's hand. Yes, that is perfectly clear. I apologize. And now you may make your apologies to my friend, and we will go.

Julius stepped away from Jason but Jason stopped him and said, And Julius. You look good.

Julius crossed the room and approached Gwen. She held his eye as he approached her. He stopped in front of her. I apologize, he said. I have no reason to think I am better than you.

Gwen smiled. We'll see, won't we?

T he tide poured into the cove in a smooth skin rush. Jonah sat at what had become his usual place on the wharf. His legs dangled over the water. He held a beer between his knees and from time to time he fed a cracker by finger to the beggar gull. The wharf planks were dried gray and worn smooth and fibrous and when the bird flew off Jonah shifted and rested his back against a pylon. The wind had stopped. The sun reflected off the water. He watched the swish and sparkle and he tried to imagine that this was the same water that swished and sparkled against the shores of Europe or Africa but he couldn't fathom that. He pictured a fisherman drinking a beer on a wharf in Ireland with his legs hanging over the same ocean but the image ran afoul as if blurred by weather. It was easy to understand that if you sailed east for long enough you'd hit Europe but it seemed more complex than pointing a boat and going.

The kelp forests swayed underwater. Waves climbed the ledges and stirred the rockweed and the rockweed crinkled with cold. He remembered sitting in Virgil's truck watching Bill and Osmond lower his father's empty casket into the ground and no matter how he reasoned through things he always came back to Osmond. He thought of his father's rifle hanging in the camp and the cartridges he'd found in the drawer. It would be so easy to load those cartridges into that rifle and aim that rifle and all would end.

Or all would begin and for what? That was the question. For what?

He looked back over his shoulder at the camp. He was tired. His adult life had been spent searching for a context in which to live but he'd found nothing. Bill had lobster fishing but for Jonah it was not so simple. At his college he'd been the lobsterman and at home he was the college boy but in truth he was both or he was neither. He just did not know.

He heard a boat and cocked his head to listen. It was approaching the south side of Stone Island. The exhaust came in spells that echoed off the islands and shoals and the depth and duration of the echoes shifted as the boat worked the sea-swell. Jonah shut his eyes. He soon recognized the throaty drum of the exhaust like a howitzer and five minutes later Virgil rounded the tip of the island and maneuvered through the shoals. Jonah stood up and finished his beer and stuffed the bottle in the head of an old wooden lobster trap.

Virgil pulled up to the wharf and said, Get in. His eyes swam in alcohol and his voice came from far away. We're going to get Julius's boat. We're getting his gear off the Leviathan.

His boat? Jesus Christ.

We're going to take his traps up for him. A favor for a friend.

With his boat? Are you fucking nuts, Virgil?

Just get in the boat, Jonah.

Jesus, Virgil. I ain't even had dinner yet. We could have a beer.

Bring your beer, Jonah.

You want to come in, Virgil? See the place?

We don't have time for that shit, Virgil slurred. Grab a beer and can of sardines. We got to catch slack water and that's in two hours.

• • •

Thirty minutes later Jonah and Virgil and Bill left the harbor aboard Julius's boat *Dolly Rhonda*. Virgil clutched the shining new spoked captain's wheel in his right hand. Jonah and Bill exchanged nervous glances. Bill grunted and stamped his feet and cleared his throat and said, This is a bad idea, Virgil. This ain't funny.

And any of this has been funny? Virgil said. He peered out of the sides of his eyes at the sea as if his neck hurt. He pulled a flat brandy bottle from his oilskins and set it on the bulkhead. He switched the bottom finder and the chart plotter on. All of Julius's traps were marked on the plotter screen and Jonah recognized the Leviathan canyons and wondered what Virgil was thinking. Over thirty years ago Virgil and Nicolas had found those canyons and still no chart showed them and no fishermen knew of them save for those three aboard that boat. Now Julius was seeking out their traps and marking the canyons on his plotter and just looking at the screen made Jonah feel a touch of trespass that he knew Virgil felt tenfold.

The boy needs a bullet, Virgil muttered as if responding to Jonah's thoughts. Hell, he's *asking* for a bullet.

They steamed offshore for an hour and a half with the moon nearly full climbing from the east and by the time they reached the Leviathan the moon had flooded the sea silver. Despite the moon Bill flicked on Julius's overhead lights together with a set of deck lights that lit the boat's shadowed workspace. Virgil gaffed Julius's first buoy and the traps rose through the water and burst into the light. He slid the first trap back to Bill and the next one to Jonah.

What're we doing? Jonah said.

Taking them up for our friend. He needs the help, Virgil said. Stuff the fucking rope in there and let's go. Virgil kicked the pile of rope that had coiled at his feet back to Jonah and Jonah kicked it back to Bill. Bill began to untie the bowline that held the tailer warp to the mainline but Virgil said, Cut the fucking thing, Captain. For Christ's sake.

Bill cut the rope just below the knot. What about the bugs?

Each trap had several lobsters in it.

Throw the fuckers back, Virgil said. We ain't thieves.

Bill tossed several lobsters overboard and their shining wet carapaces flashed in the moonlight. He lifted the mass of wet rope into the trap and set the trap on the stern. Jonah put the tailer warp in his trap and stacked the trap on top of Bill's. Another pair of traps rose and they stacked those while Virgil continued down the string.

When the last pair of traps was aboard Virgil cut the wheel toward the harbor. They stood three in a row at the bulkhead with Virgil at the wheel and not one of them spoke and no voices came over the radio. The only noise they heard was the drone of the diesel engine and the smooth spray of water splashing from the chines. Virgil shut the overhead lights off and the moon lit everything and that boat alone out on the water sliced across the sea leaving behind only a sparkling wake that soon ended.

Jonah watched the water slide by. He felt that they were such a small spot surrounded by a universe that he alone could not fathom and in that moment he looked up in hopeful search of the heavens and the consolations found there but he saw nothing beyond the moon. He shivered and stamped his cold wet feet.

The restaurant was a crowded bar with a back room that held a dozen tables. All were full except the largest which had been reserved for Jason Jackson. The waiter led them through the throng of patrons and seated them.

Jason held Turtle at his side and pulled a chair out for her. She kissed his cheek and said into his ear, At least it's not a strip joint.

The waiter brought three bottles of wine. Jason held his glass up and the others did the same. The barroom was filled with smoke and voices and laughter.

To the restless, Jason said.

Osmond gave him a look as if weighing the words.

Julius drank down the glass of wine and held it empty in his fist. Gwen gave him a shy smile and poured him another glass. Take it slow, Cowboy, she said. It's worth it.

I don't do nothing slow.

I understand, she said.

Jason watched from across the table.

The waiter returned and Gwen spoke into his ear. He nodded and nodded again. Soon he brought plates of mussels and fries and a platter of roasted veal short ribs with roasted tomato espagnole and garlic confit. The ribs were the color of caramel with bits of fat still bursting from the heat of recent wood flames.

Turtle stood up and reached across the table and took a fistful of fries. She ladled a heap of ketchup onto her plate and dunked the fries one at a time and didn't look up until they were finished. Then she took another handful.

Jason ate a dozen mussels then forked ribs onto his plate and ate them without looking up. Finally he wiped sauce and juice from his face and looked across the table at Julius. I have two questions for you.

Shoot, said Julius.

First, Jason said and placed his elbows on the table and held his fingertips together. First I'd like to know what you dream about.

At night?

Yes, at night.

Julius looked for a moment at Osmond then turned his attention back to Jason. He ran his fingers over his arrowhead and hid his grin and said, That ain't a fuckbit of your business. You better try the next question.

Jason clapped his hands together and leaned back and laughed and slapped the table. Good God, he said. My next question is different. Tell me our biggest problem. I mean, in our venture. What is our biggest problem?

Transportation but that don't count. The market's flooded is the matter with your plans. We got them Canadians coming into their season when we wind up so that's direct competition for you.

For us, Julius.

See, continued Julius, they're tubing those bugs up there. They got eight million pounds on hold right now just hoping the price'll come about. One guy alone's got four million in tubes. Even the fishermen are tubing bugs on their own up there. They're filling traps with PVC tubes and sinking them in the harbors while they hope the price changes. The problem with what you're doing is market. There just ain't a market. Ten years ago we caught forty million pounds and now we catch over seventy-five. Next year it'll be over ninety. That's a lot of product. We can't expect the market to support that.

Jason leaned back and sipped his wine as he listened to Julius. When Julius was finished the table was quiet. Jason grunted and picked the meat from a mussel and tossed it into his mouth then scraped the abductor muscle from the shell with his thumbnail and ate that as well. So why did you buy a new boat, Julius?

Because fishing's my business is why. Pounds and shit ain't. I'll get by.

I see, Jason said. He glanced at Osmond then tore a piece of the baguette off and ran it through the espagnole.

Julius felt Gwen's hand grip his thigh. She moved close. He smelled her skin and breath. His spine tingled as he watched her lips move. She whispered, What's tubing lobsters?

It's live storage. They shove them end to end in plastic pipes and cycle cold water through the pipes. It's like the lobsters are hibernating or something. They don't feed or nothing. Just sit in them pipes but in there they don't get grassed up with seaweed, so you don't have to scrub each one.

Gwen nodded and sipped her wine.

Jason drank down his glass of wine. He returned to Julius. What's happening now, Julius, and you may be aware of this, is that the Italians are expanding. You have two or three players that run the show. They each operate under multiple names, and they're not just around here anymore. They're in Canada. St. John, and Shediac. They're flying overseas directly from up there. Anything goes wrong, they start throwing cash at it until it's fixed or it's buried.

Julius listened. Gwen's hand drifted down to his knee then she let go and ripped a piece of baguette off and forked caramelized veal and garlic confit onto it and ate.

Osmond ate little and listened to Jason and Julius. He had his arm around the back of Renee's chair and his fingers traced the edges of her dress. Julius paid no attention to him.

There's a lot of pounds might not get rid of their product this year, Jason said. Those lobsters will be growing moss like swamp-fighters until June. They'll be nearly worthless.

So what's the point? Julius said.

Jason hefted his sleeves up over his hairy forearms and leaned onto his elbows. Here's the point. The Italians are heading for a nosedive is what. They got too big too quick. They have money to get themselves out of trouble, but they're fucking slobs. What we need to do is provide quality, pure and simple. The douchebag Canadians aren't much better. Those tubed bugs have a shelf life of what, Osmond? Two or three days once they're pulled from the water. A good pounded lobster will go weeks. And they aren't grading before they tube them. Global warming's changing things. The water's warming up so they're catching a few shedders these days and they aren't used to that. They're trying to tube goddamned softshells. They just shove the weak in with the top product because they think they're being smart and making some cash. The Japs savvy that. They hate the Canadians because the Canadians are cheap bastards.

Even the Chinese are getting on board. A few major things are happening for us in China. One, there's some serious money now and they want live seafood and they want to know it came from clean water and they want to know it's sustainably caught. The Japs are the same—Americans are the only ones who don't want clean fucking water. Nobody else wants a lobster that's been fed antibiotic feed, and that's what a lot of pounds are turning to these days. But you guys don't need that because you have the water. You know what that antibiotic feed's got in it? Oxytetracycline. The same shit they feed you if you get the clap, and these rough bastards are feeding it to lobsters.

Second, up until the last few years China hasn't had the infrastructure to handle live product, but they're on the way and as a consequence they hate the word *frozen* even more than ever. The word *frozen* to them means trash. It means the past and they want to forget the past. Now they have refrigeration and they have a decent transportation network. The Agricultural Trade Office in Beijing has gotten on board. Third is that the Australians used to have a corner on that market with their crappy-ass spiny lobsters, but their catch limits have put a dent in the trade. We can step in if we do it fast and we'll show them the best fucking product they ever saw. We'll sell the best fucking bugs and that's that. That's your market. Small, quiet, and perfect. Look at the fish I buy in Hawaii. I could buy fucking skipjack or marlin from anywhere in the world but I buy it from Turtle's exchange in Honolulu, and I pay extra for it. That market is tiny but they handle as much cash as markets twice, three times their size. That means they sell expensive fish.

The best fish in the world, Turtle said. She had smears of ketchup on her chin and nose and she held a fry in her fingers. You think you got water? We got water. Your fries are better than your junk-ass shellfish.

Julius glared at her and pinched his arrowhead between his fingers.

Turtle wagged the fry at Julius and ate it and said, What're you looking at, you fucking goon?

Julius looked away.

Enough, Jason said.

Turtle laughed. She grasped Jason's head in both of her hands and turned his face toward her and wiped a crumb from his beard. He shook her off and said, You have ketchup on your face.

Then he turned to Julius. The Italians sell a lot for a little. We'll do the opposite. The Australians and New Zealanders savvy that. They get near twenty bucks a pound for their product. The Irish do too. We're just too damned American here. We want a lot for a little. You fishermen think your nut size depends on your haul size. Well it doesn't, Julius. You got to be smart. I've been up and down the coast and you guys get the best-quality lobsters in the world, plain and simple. You have good water and good fishing bottom up there but you got no sense. That's the point.

The waiter returned. He listened to Gwen. Shortly afterward he brought a black steel pan that held a bone-in monkfish tail the size of Gwen's thigh. The fish had been roasted hot in brown butter and thyme and surrounded by sunchokes and golden beets and whole cloves of garlic. Gwen reached out and skimmed a crispy piece of fish off and slid it through the nut-dark sauce. She closed her eyes and murmured as she swallowed. She looked to Julius with a smile and said, I wish I had taste buds all the way down to my belly.

• • •

Later that night in the hotel they sat in two armchairs facing the window with the city lights glittering beyond and Gwen said, Jason told me that you found a body in your lobster pound. Your grandfather's partner?

Julius ran a finger over the arrowhead of hair. He took a few seconds to respond. We found his skull. Just bones was all there was left of him.

How'd he get in there? ·

Julius squinted. No one knows.

Why would someone kill him?

Julius grinned. He was a asshole.

Gwen yawned and pulled two glasses and a bottle of wine and a corkscrew from her handbag. She opened the bottle. The glasses were wrapped in cloth and she unwrapped them and wiped them down. Is it true that the mafia is involved in the lobster industry up there?

Yeah, that's true. One of the pounds near us owed them mafia guys money for some bait or feed or something and he didn't pay on time. They went and watched him load a truck with a hundred crates to sell and then they just backed their truck up to it and loaded the crates onto their truck. Ten thousand pounds of lobsters all crated up and they just drove off and the guy never said a single word. Just went into his kitchen and shot himself in the chin. Now one of them Italian seafood companies owns that pound and five or six other pounds too. These big operations want the pounds so they can control the price through the winter. In the summer the lobsters come from boat landings but in winter most of them up our way are pounded.

Gwen poured the wine and handed a glass to Julius. He put the glass on the table beside him. But the mafia didn't do anything to your grandfather's partner, though?

No.

Jason said that your father is in prison.

Julius darted a glance at her and without meaning to she looked away. She sipped her wine. He took a hard candy from his pocket and unwrapped it and held the candy in his fingers. Sounds like Jason said a lot of things.

We eat dinner together a lot. I'm his de facto private chef, and he's like my de facto uncle or something.

Well it's none of Jason's goddamned business where my father is, Julius said. He put the candy in his mouth and crunched it once with his molars before sucking the shards.

Tell that to Jason.

I will, Julius said.

She reached over and squeezed his thigh and smiled softly then took her hand back and wrapped it together with her other hand around the wineglass. Do you ever see him? Your father?

No.

Do you hear from him? Like in the movies when you see them lined up to make phone calls?

Again Julius spun his head toward her but this time the move was measured and a blackness sparked in his eye like the flashing of a crow wing.

She bit the inside of her cheek. She looked out the window for a full minute then said, So what do you dream?

He didn't answer. She leaned close to him and whispered into his ear and he felt the heat of her breath.

What do you dream about, Julius?

He pursed his lips as if chewing. What do you dream about? he asked her.

Me? I dream about all sorts of things. I dream about when I was a little girl and my mother would take me apple picking up north and then we'd make cider in the barn at the orchard. I dream that a lot. The cider streams down my chin and all over me and I drink gallons of it. And I dream about the two autumns I spent working in the vineyards in California. Maybe I dream about fruit. I never thought of that before. Fruit. But sometimes I dream about other things, mostly food though. Isn't that strange? I love food but maybe I was starved when I was little.

I dream about water, said Julius.

Saltwater?

That's what water is. Saltwater.

What's the water doing? You dream about working on a lobster boat?

No. Never. Just water.

Are you in it?

No.

I don't understand, she said.

Just fucking water.

Are you seeing it from above?

Oh, he said as if he hadn't understood the question. He slouched in the chair so that the back of his head rested on the chair back. He thought for a moment and said, I guess it's like I'm in it. It's like when I fall asleep I'm surrounded by water instead of air until I wake up. That's all. No people or boats in it. Just water all around.

Can you hear anything? Like bubbles?

No, he said. His voice was harsh. I don't dream I'm a fucking whale.

She forced a short laugh as if the noise would pry the room open.

Julius turned his head. The back of his skull stayed pressed to the chair. It's not funny, Gwen.

She remembered Turtle calling Julius a *goon* and laughing as if he were a little boy. She tensed the muscles in her back and stomach and sipped her wine. She told herself that Turtle was right but it didn't feel right. She said, I'm sorry. Your dream sounds beautiful. I'd trade you my fruit for your water.

Sure, he said. Whenever.

Maybe you dream you're in the womb again. Maybe you're scared of this world and want to return to that safe place.

I ain't scared of nothing. He paused then said, What the fuck is a womb?

Don't worry about it, she said.

I don't worry about a thing.

She finished her glass of wine and went to the bathroom and faced the mirror. It occurred to her to go out the door and take a cab to her apartment and lock the door. Her heart raced. Behind Julius's eyes she'd seen a light that scared her and part of what scared her was that she simply could not figure him out. He was tough then an instant later fragile and lost but there was something more. Something that frightened her deep down and the fact that she couldn't place it made her distrust her instincts.

She swallowed. She mouthed the words *you can do this* into the mirror. She took three deep breaths. She ran two fingers across her lips. She tucked a strand of hair behind her ear and she lifted the thin straps of her dress over her shoulders and let the dress slide to the floor. She stepped over the black cloth. She looked again to the mirror. Her heart had slowed and she reached behind her back and unclasped her bra and let it slide. She bent and pulled her underwear over her thighs and knees and ankles and kicked free. She took three more breaths and opened the door.

A blade of city light cut Julius in half. She crossed the carpeted floor. She pulled him to his feet and was relieved to see that his knees shook. She kissed his neck and the skin was hot and dry. She unbuttoned his shirt and spread the silk over his shoulders and ran her fingers over his chest. A tattoo of a black lobster with red eyes covered his breast and she pushed the red eyes like buttons. She kneeled down and held his kneecaps in her palms. She looked up at him and said, Are you nervous?

I got a girlfriend, he said. His voice was a coarse whisper from a sand-filled throat.

So? She reached up to his belt and unhooked the harpoon buckle. He put his hands on hers to stop her but his hands had no strength. She popped the button on his pants. She stood and gripped his thin hips and pushed him back until he sat on the edge of the bed. His eyes glazed. She lifted one leg and her legs were long. She set a foot on the bed next to his hip and set her hands on his shoulders. I'll show you some things that will make your girlfriend's eyes roll into the back of her head.

His chest pinched like a claw crushing a piece of bait. He thought of Charlotte.

Are you scared? She dug her fingertips into his shoulders. He felt the nails bite his skin and the biting shot down his spine and up his neck.

I ain't scared of nothing.

What makes you such a good lobsterman, Julius? You are good, aren't you?

I hang down on her is why.

You hang down on her?

Yeah. I hang down and don't ever slow down.

She backed up and bent over so her mouth was very close to his and her spine was a long flat tabletop. She held his eyes. Would your father like me, Julius?

The words were lost somewhere like a buoy in fog.

What would your father do? Right now, if he was you, what would Chimney Wesley do? Chimney, isn't that his name? Chimney Wesley? I'll bet he *hangs down on her*, doesn't he, Julius?

Julius didn't answer her. His father's name filled his head as if she were saying it over and over. She had no right to say his name but she would not stop.

Lines of adrenaline seared in his head. He couldn't tell if he was hearing her voice or some voice inside his own head but either way he needed for the voice to stop.

What would your father do? Wouldn't he hang down?

Julius's muscles latched. He blinked. It was a deliberate blink and when his eyes opened Gwen saw an emptiness that made her shudder. She stepped away from him and studied him to be sure that she hadn't imagined something. She looked for something to cover herself with but found nothing. She told herself to relax. She went to the table and drank hard from the wine bottle and looked out the window at the city lights. She held the bottle like a club at her hip.

Her hands shook. She felt him step behind her. She drank more. His hands slipped around her rib cage and gripped her breasts. She shivered. She pulled one of his hands free and put the wine bottle in it. She heard his swallows close to her ear and glimpsed the roll of his throat like a snake feeding. She looked down at his hand on her breast and the fingers gripped so hard she thought the tissue would tear.

She breathed in short blasts. She turned and faced him. The city lay down behind them. Julius looked as if his body were the only part of him in the room and he pushed in close and grabbed her shoulders and spun her around. He grabbed a fistful of her hair and shoved her head down to the picture window. She had to brace herself with her hands on the glass and her neck bent so her cheekbone and jaw and ear smeared against the glass. She caught a quick glimpse of Julius's reflection breached amid the city lights. Her hair was still wrapped tight and hard in his fist. He shifted behind her. A squeak piled and clogged in her throat. She closed her eyes and every bit of strength she ever had disappeared. She saw an image of her mother lying in bed white and dying and Gwen was a teenager then but before she untangled the squeak that was about to become a scream she felt first his hand then his body go limp.

Then he released her.

She gathered herself for a quick moment against the window. She didn't want to see him but she forced herself to turn and look. He sat cross-legged on the floor. His back was curved so that his face was buried beside his ankles. She watched and soon he began to pound the sides of his head with the heels of his hands as if trying to free something within.

She dodged around him. She heard him choke. She grabbed her purse from the table then in the bathroom she locked the door and wrapped a robe around herself. She ignored the reflection in the mirror. She splashed her face with cold water. She sat on the tub edge until the shaking stopped.

There was a fresh layer of snow on the ground when Julius stepped out of Osmond's truck. He crossed the driveway and went inside and took a cola from the refrigerator and went back out the door. He drove down to the harbor and parked and looked out over the water and sipped his cola. The wintertime dragger fleet was in the harbor and his own traps were stacked aboard the *Dolly Rhonda* and it took him a moment to realize that he hadn't put them there.

He held the can of cola to his chest and squeezed it with both hands. He thought about Bill and Jonah and Virgil. He stared at the neat pile of traps. Not only had they taken his gear up but they'd stolen his boat. His new boat. He put his truck in gear and slowly backed away as if the sight was more than he could handle.

He drove past his house and into the blueberry barrens until he hit unplowed roads. He turned around. He dropped off the barrens. He didn't know what to do. The image of Virgil or Bill or Jonah on his boat was painful and once again he slapped the side of his head with the heel of his hand as if to beat something away.

Anything but fuck with his new boat. It couldn't have been Virgil alone. He was too old and fat to take up that much gear in a day. He would've had to be offshore to find the gear. Then he'd have to come back in and steal the *Dolly Rhonda*. But they could have loaded their boats and offloaded the traps onto his boat. No. They wouldn't do that. The only question was whether or not Captain Bill had a part in it. He knew damned well Jonah had.

• • •

It was the edge of dark when Julius pulled into Bill's driveway. He waited in his truck until Bill stepped out of the house and crossed the dooryard. Julius rolled his window down.

Julius, said Bill.

You have anything to do with it? Yes or no.

To do with what?

Don't.

I ain't exactly in the mood for your shit, Julius. Bill pushed his glasses up on his nose and lit a cigarette.

Yes or no, Captain. Did you have anything to do with it?

I don't know what you're blathering about and like I said, I ain't in the mood for your shit.

Julius put his truck in gear and backed away. He spun his tires until they smoked and peeled down the road. Bill waited in the dooryard and watched Julius pull into Virgil's driveway and disappear through the birches.

Julius parked his truck next to Virgil's and waited and rubbed his cheeks and honked his horn. Virgil's passenger side window rolled down. Julius saw Virgil sitting in his truck and it startled him.

Julius, Virgil said. What can I do for you?

Julius had a lump in his throat. He felt like he was trying to balance on an edge that some force kept knocking him from.

Nothing, Julius said.

Good. Now get the fuck out of my driveway.

Julius gripped the steering wheel and looked straight ahead. You been messing with my boat?

Messing with your boat? Virgil patted Chowder's head. How do you mean?

Yes or no.

Oui or non?

You been messing with my boat? Yes or no?

You look good today, Virgil said.

This is it, said Julius and put his truck in reverse and backed out of the driveway.

244

He sat in his truck at the wharf for an hour. He watched the boats on their moorings and he watched darkness spill over the water. He took the talisman tooth from his pocket and rattled it in his closed hand as if readying to make a wish. He ate several hard candies and would have cried but he swallowed the need like something that didn't quite fit down his throat.

He ran his forearm across his nose. There were fingernail scratches on the underside of the forearm from Gwen's grip and he looked at them and smiled to himself and pinched the sudden image of Charlotte from his mind. Who the fuck did either of them think they were?

Someday, he thought. Someday all of them would understand who he was. He wasn't his father or his grandfather. He was something different altogether. He was Julius Caesar Wesley and his boat was thunder so fuck the ocean because he'd walk right across it.

Let them see. Just let them see.

He thought of Gwen rearing against his hips with her face smeared against the windowpane. Her hair in his fist. She dreamed of fruit and she had wanted to trade her dreams with him. He felt suddenly nauseous. He wished for a split second that he could hold his grandfather by the hair and slam that face into something more solid than a window.

The hell with running the pound. Spend his life on the wharf and sell crates of lobsters and talk with bait sellers and truck drivers and run around on a forklift and stack lobsters in big swimming pools. Goddamned Jason Jackson with his white coat and big talk and Jap girl. Quality was good and Jason knew some stuff but he wasn't a fisherman. He didn't understand that it wasn't about marketing or shipping or product. It was about something bigger. It was about leaving the world behind.

Julius slammed his hand against the steering wheel. He looked out across the harbor. The sky was choked in cloud and a few flakes of snow began to fall and they stuck to his windshield like dead moths. He could make out the ghostlike draggers on their moorings and for a quick second he wished he was in jail with his father so they could run the show there together.

But he didn't need his father.

He got out of his truck. The wharf was lit by a single overhead light and the light shone down on dirty snow banks and empty beer cans and gas station food wrappers. He climbed into the truck bed and opened his toolbox. He sorted through the tools and came out with a rusty fish knife and a flashlight. He shut the box and walked down the asphalt shingle ramp and untied his skiff. He turned the gas on and pulled the choke and started the small outboard.

He rounded the dark head of Burnt Island and cut between the ledges. Small waves opened like incisions in the sea. Ram's Head and Two Penny were both black pits. The Drown Boy light circled like a watchtower.

Once through the rocks he twisted the throttle and sped east and before him surfaced the moon's pale face. Snowflakes melted against his chin and cheeks. Thoughts of Charlotte welled up from somewhere and they were fringed with guilt but he had no time for guilt. He hadn't done anything wrong. He wasn't married to Charlotte and Gwen had got what she'd come for. He tensed his back muscles and stretched the skin and he grinned. Charlotte. Just a little girl is what she was. Maybe he'd show her. Teach her something Jonah never could. Make her eyes roll into the back of her head.

In fifteen minutes he shut the engine down and lifted the prop from the water and locked it in place. He took out his oars and turned up the oarlocks and they knocked and splashed in the silent night. Cloud cover cloaked the moon and the sea turned black and Julius rowed across the black sea.

He made his way into the cove and nearly ran into Jonah's boat before he saw its shadowed hull shape. Two radio antennas rose fifteen feet from the wheelhouse. He tied his skiff off and climbed aboard. He opened the hatch and shined the light down forward. He had to bend over to stand. The engine filled most of the bow space and the rest of the space was old junk and Julius said out loud, What a fucking slob, and as he said it he thought of Charlotte with Jonah.

Let them see.

He shined the light around the bottom and found the through-hull where the seawater was pumped into the coolant system. He wedged himself between the engine block and the pipe and reached out with the knife and worked its serrated edge against the thick rubber hose. He cut the hose clean off and water gushed in. He stood and watched the flooding bilge and only then did he wonder about a high water alarm. He looked around and found an old fish hatchet and swung it against the battery cable. The blade sliced through the cable and into the battery revealing the acid ventricles.

He dropped the hatchet and climbed above and shut the hatch and swung into his skiff and pushed off. He rowed until he was almost out of sight of the boat then paused to watch. His skiff bobbed in the cove. Everything was black and the ocean beyond the cove had a hollow echo like a moan. It was twenty minutes before the bow dove and half that before the stern rose and the boat dropped into the sea.

Jonah heard the far-off running of the outboard as he read a book in bed. He wondered why a skiff would be running at night but the noise stopped. He tried to concentrate on his book but his mind was scattered. He turned the lantern off and rolled over and folded his pillow in half and opened the window. He tasted saltwater. He slept and awoke in the middle of the night and stepped outside to piss. Several inches of new snow had fallen and more was falling so hard and thick that he couldn't see his wharf or the water below. He shivered and went back to bed and lay with his eyes open to the heavy darkness. His future was out there and he felt as though a tunnel extended from his chest to the long ocean chasm and some unseen force at the end of the tunnel was drawing him in limb by limb.

He fell asleep then woke to a hard blue sky. It was ten degrees and a cloudbank lay piled at the end of the ocean as if swept offshore by the coming dawn. He stood in the window and looked over the sea. Deepwater swells broke white against the ledges and flags of water vapor rose like smoke. Everything was clear and everything was quiet but the *Jennifer* was nowhere in sight. His heart clanked as his eyes searched and he wondered if he'd left her in the harbor but knew he had not.

The nighttime ringing of the outboard came back to him like a jarring of the head. He pulled his clothes and jacket on and stuffed his feet into his boots and jogged through the snow-covered woods. The spruce branches hung low and looked like white wings that showered him with snow as he passed. He stepped onto the wharf and looked again for his boat but it was gone. He flipped his skiff over and slid it into the water.

The wind gusted and the rising sun slid across the sky and burned white atop the sea smoke. A loon surfaced beside him then shat and dove again. Jonah leaned his head over and scanned the bottom as he rowed. He saw the loon dart by like a torpedo. He made three passes before he saw the white shape of the hull ten feet down. He wondered how he'd missed it. He could see the boat perfectly and everything was intact in what looked like a silent and still world. A shudder wrapped his spine.

Sonofabitch, he said out loud.

The boat lay careened over on its washrail and the mooring ball floated like a drowned seagull just below the water's surface. He rowed against the tide and drifted back and peered through the green water and he slapped the water with an oar then did so again and again. He dropped the oars and let himself drift with the tide toward the mouth of the cove. He saw blue gloves and orange oil pants and orange mesh bait bags and buckets washed ashore and he left them there. He took up the oars again and rowed as hard as he could out into the gulf and the small skiff rose and fell in the sea-swell.

A flock of pintails beat against the water then launched. Eiders honked in the distance. The shoreline was white with snow and blasts of wind lifted the snow from the spruce tops and flung it into the air as if the trees themselves were afire. He gripped the oars tight in his hands. He gazed out to sea to where the cloudbank rested on the horizon. The ocean was blue. He rubbed his face with one hand. It wasn't Julius's fault and it was too bad he couldn't forget this. He remembered the feeling of cutting off Osmond's traps and he felt that returning. He felt suddenly calm.

He released the oars and they hung in their locks. He looked around. Scarves of sea smoke like ghosts surrounded him and he felt the icy vapor on his skin and in his lungs. The skiff rose and fell with the rolling waves. The temperature had continued to drop and his hands and feet were numb. A fine slick of ice coated the gunwales and oars and floor. Beyond the sea smoke he could see no land. The only thing between him and the late December water was the small and fragile wooden skiff. Only boat and ocean remained. Wood and water and rock and he bowed his head with the cold and pranced his numb fingers on the oars and he rowed on.

The mouth of the harbor finally appeared. The water was deep green and he glimpsed a group of sandpipers feeding atop a ledge. Wood smoke rose from a few farmhouse chimneys. Jonah rowed hard against the ebb tide and fixed his eyes fast on the horizon. As he neared the boats he swung the skiff about and rowed stern-first toward the rundown wharf and the beat-up dragger fleet and he breathed the sharp stink of wintertime diesel and this all was his home.

Virgil's right, Jonah whispered. He's goddamned right.

He pulled his skiff onto the iced float and flipped it over and tied the painter off to a ringbolt. He climbed the ladder and crossed the snow-covered wharf. He saw a gull's tracks and the impression of its wingtips where the bird had left the ground. He stopped and stared at the strange snow striations. He took long breaths that he felt ripple through his entire body like fresh blood. He stared for so long at the marks and felt so newly curious at his world that when he looked up the light had shifted and the harbor looked just a little bit different.

I been thinking about you, Virgil said when Bill and Jonah stepped into the kitchen. He was drinking a cup of coffee and picking at a bowl of oatmeal. Celeste sat next to him with an orange on her plate and a knife in her hand. The Captain and the Downcoast Highliner, Virgil muttered.

My boat's on bottom, Jonah said. That sonofawhore sunk her on her mooring.

Virgil took a bite of the oatmeal and swallowed it. He sipped his coffee. Celeste says I've got to shape up, he said. She seems to be of the mind that a man can't live off brandy and milk. I told her I get a hotdog fixed with chopped onion each time I'm up to the Irving. Onion's good for the prostate.

Your boat sunk? Celeste asked Jonah. Are you okay?

Fine.

What happened?

Virgil looked up at Celeste. What do you think happened?

I don't know. She quartered the orange. I hoped that maybe it sprung a leak.

Sprung a leak all right, said Bill. Right through a through-hull hose would be my guess. Numbnuts Downcoast Highliner wakes up and hears something and thinks it's some pillhead out picking periwinkles.

Jonah, said Virgil in a scolding tone.

You think I was up expecting him to come put my boat on bottom? Hell. All I did was stack his traps for him. I didn't have anything doing with him. Not until now.

Except he stole your girl, said Virgil.

Okay, said Celeste. She's no one's girl and not something that gets stolen. Get that straight. So what I want to know is what happens now.

Me too, said Bill. I'm thinking the Highliner here's going to kick her into high gear. I been here waiting my whole life to see little brother put her in the bucket. Full throttle, hammer down, boom-boom. Bill took his glasses off and cleaned them on his T-shirt and smirked at himself as he did so.

Ain't you something proud, Jonah said. Just hugging yourself right across America.

Shut up, Jonah, Bill said.

High gear, Bill? In the bucket? What is that? said Celeste.

The boots, said Bill.

The boots? Bill, I've known you since you were born and I love you but I'm getting close to kicking you out of my home for the second time this week.

I'm sorry, Celeste.

She held his eye. Have you talked with Erma Lee yet?

I left her two messages but she never called back yet.

Leave her another one. What did you say in them?

That's none of our business, Virgil said as he scraped his oatmeal bowl clean and pushed it across the table. He studied Celeste's face and said, You tell me. What do we do about Julius now?

You call the Coast Guard and tell them about Jonah's boat.

The hell. Get a bunch of prepubescent hootenannies down here sniffing around like they're in a panty drawer and doing not a goddamned thing but spending my tax money? You think they'll do anything?

I don't know.

So tell me what we should do because you know damned well I'm right.

I don't know, she said. Isn't there enough room out there for you to all work? It's the ocean for God's sake.

Sure there is, said Bill. Only you got to follow the rules and that boy just plain don't.

That's right, said Virgil.

Why don't you talk to Osmond about Julius?

Julius's out of it, Jonah said. He wanted to go on but there wasn't anything else to say.

Virgil spread his hands flat on the tabletop and exhaled. It's all part of it, he said. It's all coming down.

Celeste reached down and grabbed one of Virgil's wrists and squeezed it. Part of what? she said then wished she hadn't.

Virgil didn't answer. He took her hand from his wrist and held it. I'll talk to Osmond all right. I've got a few things to say to him. But let's deal with the boat first. What're you gonna do, Jonah? It's your boat on bottom. First thing is we got to raise her up. You want to dive on her, Captain? That boat of yours will pull her ashore on a high tide and she'll drain out.

Bill's face and neck were white and covered in red splotches. He didn't take his eyes off Virgil. Course my boat and yours'll be sunk in the morning, he said.

Hard to sink a boat if your legs are broke, said Jonah.

Jonah, said Celeste. Can't you just warn him or something?

Let's get that boat up, Virgil said. It's high water first thing in the morning so we should get a line on her tonight. Go get your gear, Bill. And Celeste, breaking Julius's legs would be a warning.

Jonah cleared his throat. Let's wait on the *Jennifer*.

What?

Let's just wait. I'd rather wait.

Virgil eyed Jonah but didn't speak.

You ain't right, said Bill. If that was my boat I'd of had her up on dry land and had that engine stripped right down and flushed clean before Julius even finished sinking her. And I'd of broke his neck by now too.

And if I was you I'd have the girl I knocked up back with me by now.

Bill, Celeste said. If you don't love her that's one thing. But if you do then you better do something and do it fast.

Bill shuffled his feet. I will, he said.

The house felt more vacated than ever. The walls were bare and the air was cold. Bill turned the thermostat up. He checked his answering machine. He walked down the hall to his bedroom and stood before his bureau. He opened the top drawer and pushed his socks and his underwear out of the way and reached into the back corner of the drawer and found the small box. He set the box on the top of the bureau and after a pause he flipped it open and took the ring that had been his mother's from the cushion and held it pinched between his thumb and forefinger. He stuck the tip of his finger into it but the ring was only half the diameter of his finger. He put the ring in the box and put the box in his pocket.

He picked up the telephone in the kitchen and stared at the numbers and wondered what Erma Lee would say if she answered. And wondered what he would say. He felt the ring box in his pocket and wished it would do the hard part for him.

The doorbell rang. He spun around and saw the mailman through the window. He put the phone down and opened the door and signed for a certified letter. He sat at the table and watched the hard north wind toss waves across the harbor. The thermometer read eight degrees. The harbor was free of ice but the only thing keeping it free was the wind.

He tore open the envelope and tapped the check out onto the table. He slid the check in circles with his pointer finger and closed his eyes. Over a quarter of a million dollars. If he had his father's share in the pound he would most likely never make that much money. If he had a few good years of fishing and no boat payment and no truck payment he would. But the price was down and he had both payments and a house payment on top of it. Here in his hand was a quarter million that he didn't have to lift a finger for. Some of it would go to Jonah because the camp wasn't worth nearly that. Some would go to taxes and the rest would be gone in a heartbeat paying off his debts and then what? Then emptiness. Then him wishing he had the pound. It was a lot of money but he didn't want it. Dead money is what it was and it didn't mean a thing.

He stuffed the check into his free pocket and went out the door. He drove to the pound and sat in his truck. New ice gleamed white around the edges and the rest of the pound would be frozen by dawn. Ice cover would keep the birds and other predators out and the lobsters would all go dormant so Osmond wouldn't have to feed. He'd have a good product.

Several crows eyed Bill from their perch in a dead spruce. He watched as one of them leaned forward as if falling and dropped like a stone. Just before it hit the ground it flattened its wings and swooped over the pound and out of sight.

His truck idled. He worked the ring box out of his pocket but didn't open it. He thought about Erma Lee and for the first time found himself wondering what it was she saw in him. Jonah had asked him why she'd want to go back to him and he'd said security. He had a nice boat and he caught a lot of lobsters and he made good money. But maybe what Jonah had said was true. Maybe that wasn't enough for her.

He'd been there for ten minutes when Osmond pulled in and parked. Bill shoved the ring back into his pocket and got out of his truck. He waited as Osmond helped the two little girls out and led them across the driveway.

William, Osmond said. You remember my girls. Dolly and Rhonda.

Hello girls, Bill said.

Hello William, said Dolly. I remember you. Grandfather says the Lord is going to strike you down if you keep coming here.

Bill watched her face but it was stone. Rhonda made a hissing sound and Bill looked at her eyes and wondered if she were blind. Beyond her he saw the crows awaiting him. He wanted to leave. He turned to Osmond and Osmond had a slight grin on his face as if pleased by his granddaughters. The hissing continued like a pressure cooker.

Strike me down, Bill said and he was surprised to realize how scared he was of the little girl. He thought of a skunk that could spray him from afar.

Did you get your check, William?

Bill nodded.

Good. I faxed the insurance company some paperwork they needed. I hope the amount is satisfactory.

Rhonda kept hissing and Bill squeezed his fingers together until they hurt. He looked around the pound. His breath rose in the air. You aware that little shithead grandson of yours sank Jonah's boat last night? You aware of that? That little crowfucker.

Osmond lifted a finger into the air. One second, William. The hissing stopped. Osmond kneeled down and whispered into Dolly's ear. Dolly took Rhonda's hand and the two of them walked down the driveway and climbed over the ice-glazed rocks to the shoreline but Rhonda turned from the water. She held Bill in her gaze.

Now, what was that? Osmond said. He stepped closer to Bill and Bill could see the deep weather wrinkles on Osmond's face and the vertical folds on his forehead and his skin layered like granite shelves. He smelled like seaweed.

I said your little helper Julius owes my brother a fucking boat is what I said. Bill felt his heart like a hummingbird and cold sweat erupted on his temples. Osmond stepped closer and their chests touched and Bill was big but felt small against Osmond and Osmond was old but the age only added to his power. Sweat rolled down Bill's rib cage and he forced himself to take even breaths.

You're out of this pound now, Bill. You are history. I trust you understand that. But I will listen about your brother's boat.

Julius sank her like I said.

Why would he do that?

Bill hesitated. Osmond's presence was like the confused embrace of fog. He said, Julius set his gear on the Leviathan just like you done but he set his trap for trap on Virgil. We didn't cut a single one of them. Just moved them like we'd of moved our own gear.

But it's not your own gear, William.

It's our mountain you know as well as I do.

You don't own that ground.

We always fished it and that's that. Just like you always fished the southern edge off the Spencer and no one ever bothered you there. There ain't no difference.

Julius is young. You understand that. I suggest you realize that things in this world change, Captain. I'll discuss things with Julius, but I want to be certain that this isn't about Virgil's daughter.

It ain't about her unless it is for Julius.

I have work to do. I trust that the next time I see you it will be a social call?

Bill took the check out of his pocket and held it in front of Osmond's face. I want in the pound. Here's three hundred grand. I want the old man's share.

Osmond shook his head. I don't think so, Bill.

I do. Bill took out his pack of cigarettes and tapped one out and lit it.

You do? But you've got no say. Half will go to Julius and half to me. So scurry along.

Fuck yourself, Osmond. I ain't the smartest guy on the coast but I can put two and two together. I don't want to call the cops but by God I will.

Osmond's face was so close that their noses nearly touched. Too late for that, Captain Bill. Nicolas and I planned things so this scenario would never unfold.

He didn't plan for you to kill him you sonofawhore and you better tell Julius to stay away from me and Jonah or he'll be swimming in this same motherfucker pound.

Osmond put his hand over Bill's wrist and squeezed so hard that Bill dropped his cigarette. His eyes stuck to Osmond's eyes. They were black and red and in them Bill saw something that looked like a crow.

You are an infant, Captain Bill.

Fuck off, Bill said and he reared his head back out of sheer fear and bashed his forehead into Osmond's nose and felt the smash and crack but Osmond's grip didn't slacken. Bill stared stunned at the bloody smiling face.

That was a mistake, Osmond said in a voice low as ocean echo. Then like a piece of machinery he drove Bill back into the building and across the floor. Bill slammed against a post and Osmond held the wrist so hard that Bill's hand went numb.

Bill smelled diesel fuel. He looked into Osmond's eyes but they'd gone sheer black. Bill's heart smacked in his chest and his knees trembled and he thought he would actually die and the twisted notion that he should call his dead mother flashed into his mind.

Osmond let him go. An apron of blood covered Osmond's chest and he wiped his face but the blood only smeared across the mustache and filled the wrinkles like streambeds. His long black hair hung over his shoulders and eyes. It is now over, Bill.

Bill's hand began to tingle.

If I see you here again I will kill you. And I will feed you to those lobsters right there. Osmond pointed to the pound. Take a good look, William, because it is a rare thing to foresee one's death.

Just like you did my old man? You kill your only friend in the world for a fucking lobster pound? Then you go preaching about the Lord? You chickenshit sonofawhore.

Osmond drove back against Bill and his entire body pressed him to the post. His breath shot into Bill's ear and down his neck and it came ragged as if stemming from a torn chest but Osmond's voice was smooth and unhurried. He said, Nicolas Graves was the only friend I have ever had and you are his son and that is the only reason you stand here unhurt while I bleed.

Grandfather, came Dolly's voice. Osmond and Bill looked at the two girls in the doorway. Ice covered their boots and jackets.

I think Rhonda has to use the bathroom, she said.

Okay, Osmond said. I'll be right there. Osmond wiped at the blood on his face. Blood stained his worn teeth pink. This is over, Bill, or I will end it for you and your family. Do you understand? Tell me you understand.

Osmond waited and his frame still pressed Bill.

Fuck you, Osmond. And your whore egg granddaughters and their pirate pimp father and fuck Julius too.

William. You are getting very close.

Osmond went to the girls and lifted Rhonda into his arms as if his face and chest were not blood-smeared and his nose was not broken and gushing and his eyes not leaking tears. He turned back to Bill. You will excuse us, William. My granddaughter needs to use a bucket and we'd prefer privacy.

Bill crossed the room and went outside and got into his truck and left. His whole body quaked in the seat and his teeth chattered but he clenched them. He parked at the wharf and stared at the harbor and wished Erma Lee were there beside him.

Jonah drove fast up the hill to Julius's house. The maple and the alder whizzed by in a panic and the truck bucked over the frost heaves. The afternoon sky was red. His heart struck deep and sweat beaded like miniature marbles on his upper lip. He thought of his boat rotting on bottom and he thought of his father dead and he thought of Julius's hands on Charlotte and he wanted to beat him but even that wasn't enough. He wanted to hurt Julius the way Julius had hurt him but it seemed impossible to do so.

He parked in the snow bank beside Julius's truck and squeezed the steering wheel. He saw the blue light from the television flickering through the blinds. He hit the steering wheel with the butt of his hand. He climbed the steps and opened the door and walked into the house.

Julius was on the couch in basketball shorts and jersey. He sat up on an elbow and grinned as if a friend had arrived. Jonah grabbed Julius's ankles and pulled him across the couch and over the armrest and clubbed him with his right fist and Julius fell back and rolled onto the floor between the couch and the coffee table. Jonah went for his ankles again but Julius kicked at him and stood up on the far side of the table. His lips were split and bleeding. He spat a wad of blood like snot onto the floor.

Jonah pushed the coffee table away and Julius waited and when Jonah swung Julius ducked and hit him in the side of the stomach. Jonah bent and Julius hit him in the nose but he was off balance and the swing was weak. Jonah straightened and stepped back. Julius came again and hit him on the ear and it was like a club striking his skull and Jonah saw sparks and stars and darkness surrounding the stars. Another hit came and Jonah held his forearms over his face and fell to his knees then his side. Julius kicked him in the stomach and Jonah couldn't breathe and the darkness eclipsed the stars and the tunnel closed and he went out.

• • •

Julius stepped back and ran his forefinger across his nose to wipe the bloody snot. His chest pumped hard and he could barely breathe. He sat down as a wave of nausea struck him.

• • •

Strips of scarlet flashed in the sky as darkness fell on the harbor. Two gulls circled then landed on the shit-covered bow of the *Cinderella*. The sea surged and the water crinkled as it shifted into ice. Virgil tossed a cigarette butt out the truck window and coughed and rolled the window up. He put his truck in gear and drove around the harbor and up the hill along the east side of the river. It was black dark in the woods and the treetops shuffled in the east wind. Virgil came out of the woods and into the rolling white snowdrift fields.

He parked next to Jonah's truck and sipped his drink then got out with the drink still in his hand. He lit a cigarette. Everything was quiet except the wind streaking over the frozen grasslands. He flicked Chowder's ears and told her to stay. The dog licked her own nose.

• • •

Julius was still on the couch when he heard the truck. He eased the shade open and saw Virgil smoking his cigarette. He looked around the room. On the counter was a long black metal flashlight. He took it and stood at the side of the door waiting for Virgil. A surge of adrenaline displaced the nausea and he thought of the city lights he'd seen.

• • •

Virgil crossed the dooryard and climbed the three steps to the
door. There was a small wooden deck then one more step into
the house. He had a cigarette in his mouth and a drink in his
hand. He opened the door slowly and stepped into the house but
glimpsed Jonah on the floor. Out of instinct or surprise Virgil
stepped back onto the deck and as he did there was Julius like a
whir and something swished over Virgil's head and splintered the
doorframe.

Virgil swung his arm and the heavy glass hit the side of Julius's
neck. Julius's legs went out from under him and he looked at Virgil
as if he'd stepped into a world he'd never known. Virgil dropped
the glass. It hit Julius's forehead with a tink. He crossed the room
and knelt beside Jonah. Jonah looked at Virgil but didn't move
or speak and Virgil touched Jonah's chin then rested his hand on
Jonah's forehead.

I thought you were dead, Virgil whispered. I really thought
he'd killed you. Virgil still had his cigarette in his mouth and he
took a drag and released the smoke. He ran his hand over Jonah's
forehead and over his hair and he gripped Jonah's shoulder. Are
you okay?

Jonah's nose was bleeding and his ear looked frostbitten and
the side of his lip was cut. I'm fine, Jonah said.

You're sure?

Jonah nodded and Virgil helped him to his feet. They stood
facing each other as if embarrassed by their separate weaknesses
and each of them wondered what the other thought. Virgil
stepped over Julius and took his glass from the floor and went to
his truck and refilled the glass. The wind blew hard. Jonah was
standing over Julius when he came back inside. He handed the
drink to Jonah and Jonah took a swallow. Jonah's chest pumped
and his ears rang as he swallowed and he began to finish the drink
but Virgil took it back.

You shoot him?

I guess he's knocked out, Virgil said. The flashlight was on the ground next to Julius and Virgil kicked it across the floor. It's a good thing I'm a short fat sonofawhore. He near took my head off.

Jonah's breathing subsided but he shook all over. He lit a cigarette. A movie was playing on the television and Virgil shut it off. He nudged Julius with his toe and Julius shot upright as if waiting and he stood wild in front of them but his hands were steady as stone.

Easy, Virgil said.

Julius's face was gray. His neck pulsed.

Sit down, Virgil said. Both of you.

Neither moved.

Sit down, he said again and his voice sounded as if it came from a different man in a different room.

Jonah sat on the couch armrest near the doorway and Julius sat on a wooden chair.

Virgil held his cigarette in his fingers. You got a ashtray, Julius?

Julius glared at him. Color returned to his face and his lips swelled coal black. A worm of blood crawled down his chin and nested in the arrowhead of hair. No, he said.

Virgil went to the sink and ran water on the cigarette then dropped the butt on the counter next to a pile of dirty cereal bowls. He came back into the room and faced Julius. This what you want?

I don't want nothing.

You don't want nothing, Virgil said. He stepped to Julius and slapped him. Blood and spit sprayed from Julius's face. You must want something or you wouldn't be clamfucking around and setting gear on my traps. Then you sink Jonah's boat? You think that's funny?

It ain't your ocean and I ain't touched your traps.

Why'd you sink his boat?

Fuck off.

My wife says I got to talk to you so that means we got to talk. Tell me what you want, Julius. Tell me what your goal is.

The room was silent. They sat for a full minute and then the refrigerator kicked on. Julius didn't say anything.

Is it my daughter? Is that what it is?

Julius smiled. His eyes moved to Jonah then back. Virgil lifted Julius from the chair and gripped his testicles and squeezed and Julius's eyes bulged and the veins on his neck bulged. Virgil let go when Julius began to dry heave.

So this is over, Virgil said.

Julius didn't respond.

I said this is over, Julius.

Julius coughed and spat. This ain't never over, he muttered.

Virgil slapped him again. Julius smiled and the stretching of his lips made more blood gush and Julius formed a circle with his lips and blew. Blood sprayed Virgil and dotted his face like freckles. Virgil knocked him down with a single glance to the nose then fell on him and cinched his arms up behind his back. He breathed hard as he held Julius's face smeared into the carpet.

Get me some fucking line, he said to Jonah.

Jonah stared at Julius for a second then went out the door and took a coil of rope from the bed of his truck. The rope was frozen stiff so he put it in the sink and ran hot water over it to thaw then gave it to Virgil. Virgil tied Julius's hands behind his back and hoisted his feet up behind him and tied those to his hands and dragged him by the rope across the floor. Julius's baggy shorts slid down around his ass and his shoulders came out of his tank top.

Get him in my truck, Virgil said to Jonah.

What? Jonah stood over Julius. He imagined Charlotte's hands touching the skin and he felt his stomach drop out.

Get the whoreson in my truck.

Jonah stared at Julius's back until Virgil began pulling Julius by the feet. It took both of them to carry the bucking boy to the bed of Virgil's truck. It was full dark. Jonah shivered and said, He'll freeze to death back there.

Good, said Virgil.

We ain't going to kill him. Jonah went into the house and stripped the blankets off the bed and took one from the couch and piled them atop Julius. He took his truck and followed Virgil down the east side of the river to the harbor. He pictured Julius on top of Charlotte with her fingers raking his sides. Gray trees glinted past. He watched Virgil's truck bounce over potholes. His anger was gone. He hoped they would never get where they were going.

. . .

Virgil waited in his truck as Jonah rowed out to the *Charlotte & Celeste*. Jonah started the engine and brought the boat back to the wharf. Ice ringed the pylons. The harbor echoed with the roar of the single engine.

They dragged Julius onto the boat.

This ain't a good idea, Jonah said. He wore his hood up but his bruised ear stung in the night wind. His head was fuzzy and heavy as a hammer. His teeth chattered. It's fucking cold, he said.

Shut up, Jonah.

You thinking through this?

My dad'll fucking kill you, Julius shouted.

Jonah shoved an oil-soaked rag into Julius's mouth. He rolled him into a blanket then piled other blankets on top of him. They steamed out of the harbor and turned east along the shoreline. The north wind was hard and the sea choppy and everything was black save for the flasher buoy at Two Penny and the distant circling of the light on Drown Boy Rock. Virgil watched the numbers unfold on his GPS and he watched his compass as waves sprayed over the bow and pummeled the windshield and froze on the roof and baitbox and deck in a soft salt crust.

They rounded the fir-covered peninsula and heard the steady gong of the buoy marking the channel through the narrows and they saw its green flash every four seconds as they passed. They crossed the bay and waves crashed over a series of ledges. The ice was growing thicker on the roof and gunwales and deck. The lights of a small village and the Coast Guard station and the bridge to Mason's Island glowed in the distance. A lobster buoy shot by and Virgil throttled down and spun the boat around. He gaffed the buoy. He threaded the rope through the pot hauler and the rope coiled and froze at his feet. Freezing water sprayed his face and chest. He backed the hauler off. The rope stayed wedged tight in the hauler discs with the traps hanging somewhere in the water below them.

What are you doing? Jonah said. He couldn't see the color of the buoy Virgil had hauled and he didn't know whose traps they were.

Bring him over here.

What for?

Just get him, Jonah.

Jonah hesitated and wondered if Virgil actually intended to drown Julius but he dragged Julius across the iced floor anyway.

Get him up here, Virgil said.

Together they lifted Julius to an awkward position on the washrail. Virgil untied one of Julius's hands and one of his feet and held the hand out toward the pot hauler. Water slapped the hull. Virgil eased the hauler lever on and the hydraulic discs began to spin like gears with the rope sandwiched between them. He pulled Julius's hand toward the hauler. The fingers grazed the spinning steel discs. Any closer and the fingers would be sucked between rope and steel and the hand would come out a mashed and gnarled chunk no longer attached to a wrist.

Julius's eyes were red in the night. The boat's electronics glowed. The sea heaved.

You want to tell me about Nicolas now? Virgil said. He pulled the rag out of Julius's mouth.

Julius didn't answer. Virgil brushed the fingertips against the disc and Julius shrieked. Virgil pulled the hand back. A nail had caught and torn off and the finger bled but hadn't gone in.

My fucking God, Jonah yelled.

Julius here's going to tell us some things. What'd you do to Nicolas?

Fuck you.

What about Osmond? What'd he do? Which one of you did it? Or both of you?

Julius bit his lips. I didn't want that fucking pound.

Virgil hit the hand against the side of the disc and the spinning metal ripped the skin from his knuckles. Julius howled and shook like a rattle in Jonah's arms. Jonah felt beads of panic shaking within himself.

What about Jonah's boat? Virgil said. His voice whirled. Spit hung from his lips. You think you can run around and sink boats you little clamfuck?

Julius didn't answer.

What the hell happened to Nic?

He got done living.

You're a scared little clamfuck just like your father, aren't you Julius? You did it, didn't you?

Julius smiled. His muscles tightened with a shot of adrenaline. His jaw worked for a moment before releasing its words. So what if I did? Maybe I did throw the old cocksucker in the pound. I'll throw your fatfuck ass in there too.

Virgil seemed to shrink. He wiped his lips dry. Jonah watched him breathe in and out. Then just as fast Virgil puffed his chest and latched onto Julius's hand with renewed conviction and he shoved the fingers toward the hauler discs and the rope wound and Julius's hand hit the rope.

Jonah and Julius both landed on the floor and Virgil stood above them as Jonah worked his way out from beneath Julius. Julius stared at them and his mouth and nostrils and eyes all were black caves.

Christ, Virgil said. He sped up the pot hauler so the traps rose quickly then he stopped it and in the slight delay before the traps began sinking he pulled the rope free of the discs and block. He dropped the rope overboard and tossed the buoys with it and throttled the boat into the night.

Tie him back up, Virgil grunted to Jonah as he steered.

Jonah tied Julius's free hand behind his back again and shoved the rag back into his mouth and said into Julius's ear, You owe me.

Julius didn't respond. Jonah left him on the floor and stood next to Virgil.

I don't know, Jonah said.

I guess you didn't quite give us a chance to know.

That would've cut his damned hand off.

Virgil faced Jonah and there was a gentleness in Virgil's eyes. He shook his head and mouthed the word, *No.* Then he said, But don't you fuck with me like that again. I saved your ass and now you go clamfucking me.

They veered north into the cove that sheltered Osmond's house and wharf and moored boat. Virgil switched the GPS off and the slight neon glow that had lit their faces disappeared. Osmond's boat heaved in the chop. The hull was ringed with ice like a billowed skirt. The house and wharf were dark but Jonah could make out the gray cedar shakes and white trim breeched against the woods. He knew Osmond could hear them and thought, *This will be bad.*

They came alongside Osmond's boat and flopped Julius over the rails and onto the fiberglass deck. Jonah jumped over with him and wrapped him in the blankets and looked below and found several sets of oilgear and a few more blankets which he added to the pile. He pulled the bloody oil-soaked rag out of Julius's mouth and leaned in close and saw Julius looking childish and frightened. Jonah felt the same way and wanted to apologize and untie him but thought of Charlotte again and his boat again and his father again and said, Next time you will be in a fucking trap.

They pulled away and steamed downwind with the chop breaking against the stern. They both leaned against the bulkhead and wondered at the amount of ice forming on the boat. The engine grumbled. Virgil flipped the GPS on and watched the compass and steered south-southwest then west.

Jonah peered at Virgil through the darkness then looked back at the water. He looked at Virgil again before he spoke. You believe him then, Virgil? That he did it? Drowned the old man in the pound?

Virgil grimaced. No.

Jonah was surprised. No?

He's full of shit, Jonah.

I don't know, Jonah said. Doesn't seem full of shit to me. Why the hell would he lie?

The boat rumbled and between the rumblings came a hard silence. Virgil looked Jonah in the eye. It was me, Jonah. I put Nicolas in the pound.

Jonah shivered and clenched his hands and repeated to himself what Virgil had said but he knew he'd heard wrong.

I put old Nic—, Virgil began again but his voice was drowned by the groan of the gong buoy that burst from the darkness with a sudden flash that lit the boat. The groan was eerie and deafening and in that frozen instant Jonah saw Virgil grimace then deflate as if he'd lost some piece of himself.

The buoy disappeared as fast as it had come and Virgil spoke again.

JON KELLER

What happened was Royal James fished Nic up in his urchin drag. I took Nic's body. And I dumped him in the pound. I should have told you, Jonah.

Jonah put his palms on his ears and pinched his eyes shut. He didn't want to hear another word. They rounded the head of Stone Island.

Jonah?

Jonah didn't answer.

You okay, Jonah? I'm sorry I didn't tell you.

I'm just fucking cold, Virgil. I'm cold.

The boat swayed. Virgil put his arm around Jonah and pulled him close as if to warm him but neither held any heat. It'll work out, Virgil said.

I really don't care.

Imagine that, Virgil said.

Jonah let the words tumble in his head. He stepped away from Virgil. Imagine what?

Virgil rotated his head as if it were a saucer spinning atop his neck and he peered at Jonah through the electronic glow. The Highliner don't care.

Jonah ground his molars together. He clenched his fists and breathed a lungful through his nostrils. I don't care? I don't fucking care, Virgil? You feed my father to fucking lobsters and tell everyone Osmond done it? I know why you did it, you sonofabitch. I know you. It's because they never let you in the pound, ain't it? Because my dad partnered with Osmond, you sonofawhore. After this long?

No, Virgil whispered. The words leaked like bile from his mouth. No, Jonah.

The hell not. Then you near rip Julius's fucking arm off? And you say I don't care? Well fuck you, Virgil. Fuck you. You're fucking insane and you're a goddamned liar and that's it. I am done with you. Jonah looked off into the darkness. He could feel Virgil's

270

silence. Anger and adrenaline spiked like a cocktail through his body. And you know what, Virgil? I feel bad for Celeste. She don't deserve such a fucked-up husband as you and slut daughter like Charlotte. You and her both can go to hell.

Jonah, Virgil said but his voice was brittle and it fell as if frozen.

When they reached the harbor Jonah pulled himself up by the davit and walked the iced rail to the bow. He settled to his knees and gaffed the mooring and pulled the rope through the iced chocks and over the bit. The water looked like tar beneath him. He sat in the bow of the skiff as Virgil rowed them back to the float and when the bow touched the float Jonah climbed out and left Virgil in the skiff.

Jonah put his hood up and walked down the road. He didn't look back at the harbor where Virgil sat in the skiff with his head in his hands and his entire body shaking as the skiff carried him into the silent and frozen night. Jonah tucked his chin to his chest and clasped his hands together within his sweatshirt pocket. He walked toward the village. He looked at the few houselights. He pictured Virgil adrift in the skiff and felt a deep loneliness. He had nowhere to go and no one to go to. He'd lost both parents and he'd lost his girlfriend and his boat and now he'd lost Virgil. All that remained was his brother and for a moment he thought about Osmond and faith in blood but even from his brother he felt estranged.

Eventually he heard Virgil's truck start and climb the hill above the wharf and turn toward him. He thought of hiding behind a tree but didn't have the energy. He kept walking. He hoped Virgil would drive by but at the same time hoped he would stop. The truck approached. Jonah didn't turn then as it passed he thought with a satisfied fury, *Fine.*

Then the brake lights flashed.

Jonah reached the cab and the passenger side window rolled down.

I'm sorry, Jonah, Virgil said and the voice shook and struggled.

Jonah kept walking. Virgil waited a moment before catching up.

Jonah stopped.

We had that storm surge right after Nic went lost, remember? Those big tides and onshore winds. He would've sunk and those currents would've pinned him to the No Where Ledge that Royal drags. It all funnels into that ledge.

So what? So he fell the fuck overboard and washed into a ledge. That don't mean he was murdered, and it sure as shit don't give you reason to put him in the fucking pound. Are you fucking psychotic? Why didn't you call the police? They could've done a autopsy and found out how the fuck he died. Maybe he had a heart attack. Maybe he choked on a fucking cigarette butt.

Jonah, Virgil said again.

Jonah saw that Virgil was crying and it was a strange thing to see but he didn't care. Just leave me alone, Jonah said and he walked off the road into the snow and disappeared among the trees.

eleste was still up when Virgil stepped shivering into the kitchen. She waited for him to say something but he didn't. She saw blood spattered on his face and his face red and swollen and she said, Oh God, Virgil, are you okay?

He nodded but stood transfixed.

Are you sure? Where's Jonah? Is he okay?

Fine. He went back out to camp.

She reached out and wiped his cheeks with her two thumbs. Her skin blanched and shadows formed on her face as if cast from within. She thought for a moment. Whatever you've done, don't tell me yet, Virgil. Not yet. She pulled him into her grasp and as she held him she felt him begin to quake and soon his entire body shook.

He sobbed and said, I was wrong, I was wrong.

She gripped the back of his head in her palm and pressed her chin against the back of his neck. She closed her eyes and told herself that this was her husband.

When he settled she stepped back and lifted his chin and his big cheeks sagged red and white. She wiped his face with her cuff. She led him up the stairs and turned the shower on and helped him out of his clothes. She took her own clothes off then pulled him into the heat of the shower and lathered soap over both of their bodies.

When they reached the bed Virgil said, I was wrong about everything, Celeste. I'm sorry for you to go through this.

I know you are, she said. She pulled the covers over the two of them. Tell me what you did.

It starts with Nicolas, he said and he stopped and did not continue.

She clenched the sheet in her fist and she remembered the night he'd come home with the smell of death like rot upon him and she said, Just tell me, Virgil.

Virgil's voice came distant and methodic and each word was forced. When he was finished speaking Celeste crimped her eyes closed and said, Why? Why would you?

They couldn't of done a autopsy on him. I barely knew it was him myself.

That's not what I asked you, Virgil.

Virgil hesitated then spoke. I thought he would break. Osmond. I thought I could do that, and I was wrong.

Celeste didn't say a word. The grandfather clock in the hallway ticked.

Virgil spoke again. I'm so scared, he whispered. Julius is just a kid and I near took his hand off. I don't know who I am anymore. I need help. I need your help.

• • •

One hour later Celeste still held the sheet in her fist when she spoke. Tomorrow morning I am going to get up and make coffee and eat breakfast like I have done every single morning for as long as I can remember. But I am not going to remember what you told me tonight. I am not going to remember what you did because if I think of it for one single more second I am going to take my daughter and bring her as far away from her father as I can get and we are going to stay there. Do you understand that? Maybe you're right about Osmond. Maybe he murdered your best friend. I don't know, but what I do know is that the way you're going about this ends right now.

Virgil choked once. His pillow was soaked with tears and he squeezed his eyes shut as if a sledgehammer were slowly descending upon him and he wished for such a simple pain. He nodded to himself over and over but Celeste's back was still to him and he wished for one more thing and that one thing was to join his wife and daughter as they left him behind.

Osmond awoke to the rumble of the diesel engine. He lay motionless with his eyes open as the boat came closer and for a split second he thought of Julius's grandmother as if she would return from the heavens and would do so by diesel power across the sea. She'd had long black hair and white skin and a voice like tumbling beach rock.

He cast off his sheet and wool blanket and rose naked in the blackness. He could taste Laura as if she'd been standing above him as he slept. He thought of gills. He shook the strange image from his mind and it was replaced with the image of her smooth pregnant shape. Never for a second had he regretted his time with her even though it had reordered his life. He'd lost his brother and fallen from the church and his fall had been hard and had shattered his ideas but not his faith as if a gale had burst the windows but not broken the frames.

He moved silently across the room. The wood floor was cold and he stood at the window edge as the boat slid into the inlet. Osmond could not see his boat on its mooring but he could see the end of his wharf and the easterly chop cresting against the pylons and rocks and he could see the sheerness of the firmament.

He thought of switching on the wharf lights but he wanted to allow whatever was to happen to happen. He had nothing in this world to lose because all that mattered was either lost or in this house with him.

Except Julius.

Osmond did not know about Julius.

He held one hand against the window sash and listened. He pictured the boat approaching his own. He heard it shift into neutral and idle.

Virgil, he whispered as if he'd been awaiting this coming. In his mind rose Virgil's face burning amid the cold dark sea crests. He ran his fingers over his own broken nose but Bill did not enter his mind. Only Virgil whom Osmond could not help but think of as some judge sent to condemn him and he understood that the stabs of fear he felt were regret although he told himself over and over that regret was only distrust and distrust was only lack of faith.

He squeezed his fist tight around his own forearm. He'd done things in this lifetime that no man should and he'd been victim to things that no man should endure but one did not justify the other despite the fact that the two existed as parallels. He had not looked back at Nicolas as Nicolas drowned any more than he'd shown his brother mercy over Laura. Sin was only sin when allowed to manifest as such.

Now his grandson. Julius acted out of fear and out of conceit and out of vanity because Julius had no faith. Nicolas Graves's death was part of an alignment set into motion before the world began and its ramifications existed beyond any of them but nevertheless Osmond sensed that without his old system of beliefs Nicolas's memory would rise and break his faith in a single great wave.

He waited until Virgil's boat eased into gear then pulled away. He listened as the diesel engine grumbled and roared and disappeared into the gulf.

Osmond dressed. He turned on the wharf lights and was surprised to see his boat still afloat and still lashed to its mooring. Waves came like razors flashing in the flood. He stepped into the night and pushed his skiff overboard and rowed through the bucking chop that sprayed and froze to his back and neck and head. He pulled alongside his boat. He stood in the skiff and saw first a heap of blankets and oilgear then saw that this heap was his grandson.

Osmond tied the skiff off to the pot hauler and climbed aboard. He uncovered the boy. The skiff banged against the boat's hull. Julius's hands were tied to his feet and blood froze to his face. Julius glared at Osmond with hatred and loathing as if Osmond's hands had bound him there and the look struck Osmond like a cleaver.

Here was his bloodline. His grandson. His failure.

He cut the rope that held Julius and the boy rolled over and slowly straightened his limbs. His face was beaten and his lips crusted and swollen.

Osmond stepped forward and reached a hand out to the boy. Julius flinched but steadied himself as Osmond lifted him to his feet then held him tight to his chest as if saying goodbye. He was surprised at the thinness of the boy and the smell of the boy like the skin of a newborn. Osmond held him tighter.

Julius kept his hands at his sides and made no move to embrace his grandfather.

I see you had a long day yesterday, Osmond said.

Julius pushed away and kneeled over the open stern. He dipped his head into the frigid water and came up and wiped at his stinging broken lips. He dipped his head again then stood and ran both hands through his black freezing hair.

Osmond noticed the mangled hand.

Weren't bad, Julius said. He tried a grin but his lips refused. He shivered.

You finally pissed off Virgil and the boys.

Appears. Him and Jonah.

Not Bill?

I guess he knows me.

You sank Jonah's boat. Osmond's voice was tired. Why, Julius?

The wharf lights rocked and shimmered over the breaking ocean chop.

Julius wiped at his lips again. He didn't answer.

You must have a reason. Traps? Charlotte? Tell me.

Julius shifted himself so he could see his grandfather better. Don't worry, he said. I didn't tell them.

Julius's eyes held something like hope within them but Osmond was unable to see it. He felt his knees flex as if readying himself to kneel before Julius. His jaw locked tight. He did not want to ask but he did. Tell them what, Julius?

Julius's voice was almost playful. They think it was me.

Again Osmond did not want to ask but again he did. They think what was you, Julius?

Julius ran a hand over his frozen hair. He breathed in and out and the hope that had sparked in his eyes faded and left the familiar void. What happened to your nose?

Osmond covered his nose with a gloved hand. I had a run-in.

A run-in?

Yes, Julius. A run-in.

With who?

That is neither here nor there. What do they think you've done? I cannot protect you unless I know what is happening.

Seems you're the one needs protected, Julius said.

• • •

Back in the house Julius eased into Rhonda and Dolly's room and sat in the darkness on the bed beside Dolly and shook her shoulder until she awoke. She blinked her eyes until they focused on him then she sprung up and wrapped her small arms around his neck.

Get up, he said. Grandfather's making waffles.

Waffles, Dolly said. I'll awake Rhonda.

Let her sleep awhile. We'll get her up when breakfast is ready. Julius stood. You get dressed.

Dolly came out wearing pink overalls and a short sleeve shirt and she sat in a chair at the table. Osmond wore a red striped apron and he mixed waffle batter at the counter. Wind pelted the windows. The air had warmed enough that a few flakes of snow came.

What happened to you, Julius? Dolly said. Did you get hurt like Grandfather?

I got beat up, he said.

You got beat up?

Yeah. Can you imagine?

I can't, said Dolly. Why'd you get beat up, Julius?

I fell in love with the wrong girl and she already had a boyfriend.

Osmond stopped what he was doing and looked at Julius with his mouth open as if hearing for the first time something that he did not already know. He held the whisk in the air and let the egg whites flop back into the bowl and a light that had not been in him for a long time suddenly turned on and he allowed himself a brief moment of hope.

You fell in love with a girl? Dolly said.

I sure did.

Who is it?

Her name is Charlotte. Isn't that a pretty name?

It's beautiful, Dolly said and she said the word slowly. Are you going to marry her?

I hope so.

Enough, Osmond said.

Why, Grandfather? Dolly said.

Enough now. The Lord will decide those things.

Can't Julius decide who he loves?

The Lord has already decided. Long, long ago. Now awaken Rhonda and she will help cook these waffles.

I'll get her, Julius said and he went into the room and came out with Rhonda in his arms. Her arms were tight around his neck. White drool crusted along the edges of her mouth. He sat her at the table but she refused to let go of his neck. He tried gently to unwrap her handhold but she clung to him with locked fingers and from deep within her came a whining sound as he tried to free himself. He stood and she dangled like a drapery from his neck and she bucked and writhed and would not let go.

Osmond lifted Rhonda by her armpits and Julius slid from her grasp. Her whine increased and Osmond turned her in his arms and hugged her tight to his chest as the whine turned to a cry and a scream.

Dolly took a pencil from a jar of pencils and wrote her name over and over on a piece of scrap paper. Julius looked out the window and wished he had a magnet that could lift the water from the sea so he could see each lobster hidden there. Osmond danced the screaming girl around the room and whispered to her and she screamed and he danced and he whispered as her body shook as if gripped by seizure. He hummed to her and sang to her and danced her around and around and around the room and he cupped the back of her small head in his hand and touched his cheek to hers and he danced and he danced and she finally calmed. She held his neck in her arms. He wet a cloth and wiped her face. He pushed two chairs over to the wood cookstove and sat her in one. Dolly climbed on the other and Osmond poured batter into the cast-iron waffle iron and the girls watched.

They were all silent as Osmond drove Julius home. He watched Julius's bloodied face out of the corner of his eye. He felt silence heavy as chain. When they reached Julius's house they sat for a moment in the truck.

Osmond said, Please let this battle end before it is a war, Julius. We have the pound to worry about. The price won't get any better. I am old but you will need that pound to survive. Fishing alone will not last, Julius, and we will need to insulate ourselves. You will need the pound and you will need the market that Jason can organize. We don't need more problems with Virgil and the boys.

They ain't got the guts.

They nearly killed you, Julius. I don't believe guts are an issue for them.

Well, these things are up to the Lord aren't they?

The Lord is speaking.

Ain't He always.

Yes, Julius, yes He is. Always.

Does He always speak through you?

Osmond sighed. He speaks through you as well, only you do not listen. He speaks through everything. He is everything, Julius.

I thought He was a old guy on a cloud with a lightning bolt in His hand, Julius said. He put his fingers on the door latch but he didn't open the door.

This is the Lord, Julius. You and me and everything around. The Lord is not man nor woman, good nor evil. The Lord is what allows your chest to beat and the wind to blow. The Lord is the tides, Julius. You only need to be quiet long enough to listen and once you hear you will believe. You will have faith, Julius. You will be free.

Huh, Julius said. He opened the door and stepped onto the driveway. I suppose if He's diesel power then I'll start believing but till then the god I believe in is Mister John Deere and he's a lean mean diesel-sucking sonofawhore.

Jonah stood beside a birch tree. He leaned his head against the white flaking bark and he watched Virgil's taillights disappear in two red streams. A breeze fitted itself between the trees. He lit a cigarette but it tasted bad and he dropped it into the snow and watched the ember sizzle dead. He stepped onto the road and turned toward the wharf with the intention of walking to his camp but after a dozen steps he stopped. Through a break in the trees he could see Bill's house across the harbor. The lights shone over the snow and onto the water.

All was quiet as he walked through the village. The old farmhouses with barns attached by breezeways looked like vacant relics and Jonah had the feeling that time had ended.

He knocked once and opened Bill's door.

Bill stood halfway then sat back down. Jonah, he said. He shut the television off and dropped the remote on the coffee table. What're you doing? You seen a ghost? You get your highliner ass kicked?

Jonah touched a finger to his swollen ear. Near it. I seen Julius. And I seen Virgil.

Bill went to the kitchen and returned with two cans of beer. He handed one to Jonah. Jonah pulled his boots off and crossed the carpet and stood with his back to the wood stove. He knocked the stove damper open with his toe and the heat beat the shots of fresh air into flame.

What about it?

Jonah drank down half the beer and wiped his face although he didn't feel capable of tears. Fucking Virgil, Bill. He done it. This whole time it was him who done it.

Him what? Done what?

• • •

Bill didn't speak for a long time. His jaw muscles worked. He lit a cigarette and smoked half of it and the smoke lingered about his head. He said, Virgil's fucking nuts, Jonah, but I keep thinking maybe he's right about Osmond. Don't you think? What if he is? Jonah?

• • •

That night Jonah slept on Bill's couch. He dreamed of his father floating in a flat calm sea with his arms at his sides. Nicolas was emaciated but pumped with small and tight muscles the size of scallops. His veins rose into blue swollen tracks. A blanket of water spread over him. Their mother was in the dream and she floated beside her husband and she turned her eyes on Jonah and cried, *What have you done, Jonah? What have you done?* He awoke on the couch and he was glazed in sweat and the blanket was on the floor and flames piled against the glass door on the wood stove. He sat up and wiped his face and body down with his T-shirt then held the shirt on his knee. He heard his brother's snores come tumbling down the hallway.

• • •

The next morning. Wind blasted the house and sea smoke swirled and rushed in legions over the water. A bank of clouds like a mountain range stood at the other end of the sea. Jonah lay on the couch watching the flames in the stove. His face was sore from the hits Julius had dealt him. He felt a stabbing pain in his ribs. His head pounded and he was exhausted. He wanted to sleep the day through but he knew he couldn't sleep another minute.

He could hear the squawking and honking of eiders in the harbor and he hoped Julius wasn't frozen solid aboard Osmond's boat. He rolled to his good side and ran a hand over the couch cushion and looked out at the snow surrounding the harbor. It was high water and the tide was slack. The water was gold in the sunlight and rimmed with sheets of salt ice. A fox stepped out of the woods and ran across the ice and rounded a small spit of land. A flock of whistlers burst from the cove and flew overhead and even inside the house Jonah could hear the noise of their flight.

Jonah pictured Virgil dumping the body. He pictured the skull he'd found. He pictured swarms of lobsters like troops racing across the seafloor to join the frenzy of feeding on his father and his stomach turned and he tried to force the image away but still his mind filled with the silent and dark movement of lobsters.

He dressed. He sat at the counter and looked at the harbor. The *Cinderella* and *Gale Warnings* were on their moorings and the dream-image of his father with scalloped muscles and swollen veins came back to him and so did his mother's voice calling, *What have you done, Jonah? What have you done?*

Charlotte parked in Julius's driveway. She knocked on his door. He didn't answer and she knocked again. When he still didn't answer she opened the door and called for him.

Yeah, he said.

Can I come in?

Yeah, he said.

She stepped inside and shut the door and took off her jacket. The coffee table was upside down and two chairs were tipped over. She saw splashes of blood on the carpet.

Julius came out of the bedroom wearing sweatpants but no shirt. She saw his black lobster tattoo. His lips were swollen and cracked and the side of his neck was bruised purple and yellow and his wrists were burned where the ropes had chafed. His knuckles were swollen and crusted in blood and several fingers were wrapped in a bloody bandage.

He stood in front of her and smiled.

Oh my God, she said. Jesus Christ. What happened?

She stepped to him and ran her finger over his lips and stood up on her tiptoes and pressed her lips gently into his.

It ain't bad, he said.

She lifted his wrist and examined the bandage. Did Jonah do this? He did, didn't he? Oh my God, I'm so sorry. This is my fault.

No it ain't, he said. It's not about you.

Yes it is, she said. He still loves me and he's jealous. He wants to get married and have kids and things.

He thinks I sank his boat, Julius said.

But you didn't?

Julius sat on the couch and Charlotte sat next to him. He pulled the remote from the cushion and turned the television on. You don't want to have kids? he said.

Not now. Probably not ever.

What do you want now?

Nothing, I guess. I want to move. I want to be on my own. What do you want?

Just what I have. Just to go lobster fishing.

I bet you want your dad out of jail, don't you? Or your mom back.

No, Julius said. He flicked through the channels.

Charlotte pulled her feet up beneath her and put her hand on Julius's head with her fingers driven into his tuft of hair. She pulled slightly. Did you sink Jonah's boat?

He faced her. Them boys ain't as tough as they think.

That wasn't the question. She pulled his hair harder.

So you think I'd sink Jonah's boat because of you? You don't trust me.

Answer the question.

His tongue flicked out of his mouth and ran over his scaled lips. His pupils were small and dark despite the dark room. No, he finally said. I don't want a thing to do with them.

She released his hair and put her hands in her lap. Julius flicked through the channels on the television then dropped the remote on the cushion.

He said, So what do you dream about?

What do I dream about? I don't know, I guess. I dream about lots of things. I used to have a nightmare that my mom and dad got a divorce.

I dream about water, Julius said.

Water?

Like I'm underwater but there's no me. I'm part of the water or something. I just see water everywhere. And hear it too. Sometimes I think that's what the Lord is. The water and the tides.

Charlotte stared in disbelief. You always dream that?

All the time, he said. You just have to be quiet long enough to let it happen. As soon as my head hits the pillow the water turns on. I bet you never met anyone like that before. Who dreams he's water.

No.

Just me, Julius said. That's it.

What color is the water?

Blue and green. Like water is. No bubbles or nothing. Julius looked away and thought for a moment then turned back to Charlotte and put his hand on her knee.

So who sank Jonah's boat then? she said.

I don't know. You don't believe me. You think I did it.

You're the obvious conclusion.

Jonah's boat goes to bottom and everyone thinks it's me? Just because I just got my new boat is why. That's the only reason. Jonah acts all nice on dry land but get him on the water and he's a mean bastard. Hell, him and your father both broke down my door and did this. I don't want a battle to be a war.

I know, said Charlotte. She got up and went into the kitchen and came back with a wet paper towel. We should clean those lips up some, she said and stooped over him and held the wet towels out like showing a bone to a strange dog. Julius didn't move and she dabbed at his lips. He didn't seem to feel anything and when she finished wiping them clean he reached up and pulled her by the hips toward him. She leaned over him and her hair hit his shoulders. He pulled her knees apart and eased her down so she straddled him. He ran his hands up her back and beneath her shirt. She kissed the broken lips gently then kissed his cheek and he flinched as she approached the bruised side of his neck.

I don't want to talk about them anymore, she whispered into his ear.

Julius pushed her back so he could see her eyes. It's just me out there, Charlotte. I got no sternman and no friends. My old man's in prison and my grandfather's a nutcase.

Poor you, Charlotte said. She stood up. She took the pile of wet towels to the sink and was about to drop them when she recognized on the counter her father's cigarette butt with its always pinched filter. She'd known he'd been there but actual evidence of his trespass stung her. She dropped the towels on top of the cigarette.

She turned. She saw Julius. The black spark glinted in his eyes.

Charlotte stepped from the linoleum to the carpeted living room. She felt blood begin to pump in her chest and up her neck. She looked at Julius. He was beat up but still so arrogant. Her hand rose to her shirt. She turned around and faced the kitchen. The cabinets were open and her father's cigarette butt was on the counter. She undid the top button on her shirt. Her hand slid down the fabric and paused on the next button. She undid that one as well. Her breath came in a rush. She felt Julius on the couch behind her and her eyes stung with the image of his chest and the black lobster tattoo and she undid another button and smiled as if in disbelief. Her shirt slipped from her shoulders. She caught it around her hips and held it there for a moment then released. The room was cold and she felt the cold air climb her torso like a squall. She looked down at her shirt on the brown stained carpet. She closed her eyes and reached behind her back and undid her bra and held it there for a moment then dropped it. She undid her belt and slid her pants down and stepped out of them. She wore small red underpants and she hooked her thumbs in the thin hipline and ran them back and forth in a moment of final decision then pulled the red underpants down and Julius was suddenly behind her.

She straightened and felt a shard of air like steel against her skin. His hands slid around her rib cage and gripped her breasts hard. Her mind pulsed. She looked down at the two hands on her two breasts. The knuckles looked sharp. She pulled his hands free and turned and faced him. Her heart raced and she could feel his knees trembling. She bent and pulled his sweatpants from him and set her hands on his kneecaps to still them. She lifted her eyes to him and saw the black lobster tattoo like a shield on his chest.

Jonah started his truck and leaned back as it warmed. He looked down at the wharf and out at the harbor. The truck cab smelled like cigarettes and salt and gasoline and bait. He felt relieved to be done with Virgil and Charlotte but he knew not to trust that relief because now he was alone and his mother's dream voice reached through his loneliness and cried, *What have you done, Jonah? What have you done?*

And what had he done?

Nothing, he thought. *Not a goddamned thing.*

He rolled his iced window down and watched his breath cloud and rise. A black truck drove down the hill and parked. Osmond Randolph stepped out. Two girls' faces emerged from the back seat and stared through the glass like twin guppies within a tank.

Osmond glanced at Jonah as he walked down the gravel and ice drive toward the wharf but neither gave any indication that he'd seen the other. Osmond righted a skiff and untied it and slid it into the water and rowed toward Julius's boat. Jonah looked over his shoulder at the girls. Still they both stared at him. His engine idled and his truck shook. He put his hand on the shift lever and was about to leave when he saw Osmond pull alongside the *Cinderella* and climb aboard.

Jonah put his truck in gear and eased down the hill and onto the wharf. Water spread on three sides of him. Osmond ducked down forward and soon afterward returned. He looked around the boat and ran his finger up the bronze coaming then stood in the center of the deck and faced Jonah as if to say, *Here I am.*

Jonah waited. Osmond rowed across the harbor. His back and shoulders hunched over the oars and he rowed with short hard strokes that pushed the narrow skiff like a driven nail. He pulled the skiff onto the float and tied it off and started up the ramp. Jonah watched him through the side mirror and muttered, Fuck this. He slammed his truck into reverse and spun the wheels hard across ice and gravel until he blocked Osmond's passage.

Osmond didn't pause until he reached the top of the ramp. He gripped the rail on Jonah's truck bed and without looking at Jonah he said, Pull back so I can open the door.

Jonah glared at him through the back window then reversed.

Osmond opened the door and folded himself into the truck seat. His nose was purple and broken and his hair black and oiled and the truck cab suddenly smelled like something raw and earthen but Jonah knew not what. He rolled a window down and shook a cigarette out and offered the pack to Osmond who only shook his head once.

You're wondering what business I have aboard Nicolas's boat?

Jonah's throat crimped and he put one hand on his knee to still his shaking leg. He swallowed. That's right.

I've already discussed things with your brother, William.

I see that.

Osmond turned his head to give Jonah a frontal view of the damage. He is unhurt, Osmond said.

I'd say he's had plenty of hurt, Osmond.

Osmond's eyes shifted to Jonah then away. Your father and I were very close and I am sorry for the course things have taken, although I cannot see that I should apologize. I have done nothing wrong.

Jonah nodded. Osmond's voice was deep and certain. There was an undertone of authority and compassion that made Jonah believe what he was saying even as he told himself not to. Julius had been about to lose his hand in the pot hauler and still he'd lied and Jonah wanted so badly to say, *You killed my father you sonofawhore.*

He faced Osmond. He said all he could think to say. You set traps on the Leviathan first thing. You know that ain't right. You knew damned certain that would cause problems.

Correct, Osmond said. He let his chin dip to his collar line. For that I have paid, and I apologize. I was rash and greedy, and I was confused over the loss of a dear friend. Oftentimes when a loved one dies, the survivor attempts to emulate them. It is about comfort, and fear, you see.

Jonah nodded and the truck cab filled with silence as if it had blown in through the window.

What happened with Julius, Osmond continued, is unfortunate. You have to understand how his life has been.

I understand all right, Jonah said. But he sank my fucking boat.

Osmond nodded slowly. He ran a hand over his chin. You are an orphan as well, he said. Your paternal grandparents are in New Hampshire, are they not? Disavowed of your father long ago. Since Vietnam. Your maternal grandfather, long since dead—and that maternal grandmother is where? The Midwest, I believe.

Michigan, Jonah blurted but he did not want to exchange information with this man who should not know his lineage least of all speak of it.

Your father and I were close, Osmond said.

Jonah and Osmond watched Nicolas's boat twist on its mooring.

That boat needs to be bleached, Osmond said.

I guess she does.

Do you intend to use her? She's a good boat. I will reimburse you for your old boat. What Julius did was inexcusable, and I shall answer for him myself.

Jonah glanced at Osmond and puffed on his cigarette and as he released the smoke he said, I don't want your money.

Osmond didn't blink.

Jonah waited for Osmond to leave but Osmond didn't move. Jonah sucked hard on the last of the cigarette and dropped the butt out the window and gulped fresh air.

I saw you last night, Osmond said. You and Virgil. I was certain that I would find my boat on bottom, not my grandson beaten as he was. That was not easy to see.

Why'd you think we'd put your boat on bottom, Osmond?

Osmond took several breaths through his nostrils.

Julius is my responsibility, Osmond said.

Well, he's got a sight more coming to him I'd say.

Osmond reached out quick and grabbed Jonah's shoulder. Jonah tried to slide away but couldn't. He looked at the hand and the skin was red and white and scaled. The fingertips landed on his breast. The nails were yellow. The thumb jammed into his shoulder blade and he had no doubt that if Osmond so desired he could clamp that hand like a jaw.

I will handle Julius and I alone will handle Julius. I do not want any interference. Is that clear? If you have something to say to him, you come to me.

How about this, Jonah said. He squirmed beneath Osmond's grip. How about you let Bill buy back into the pound? He's got the insurance check. And Julius is poison, you know as well as I do. You sell to Bill, we let Julius alone for you to deal with.

Osmond released Jonah and folded his hands on his lap. We all have things in this world that we should do, Joshua. Things we know we should do that we do not, and so often we would feel so much better if we only did them. Sometimes it is as simple as allowing ourselves to believe in something, but we do not. No matter how little effort these things may take, we do not do them. We keep secrets from ourselves. We create reasons and justifications to hide behind when all the while all we have to do is follow our own path, yet we believe that we find comfort in these justifications and so we stick to them. Do you understand what I'm saying?

I understand that you know damned well you should let Bill back in the pound, insurance deal or not. It's what's right. You know as well as I do.

Bill is not who I am talking about.

Then what in fuck are you talking about?

Look, said Osmond.

With a slight movement of his fingers like a card dealer he motioned toward the harbor.

Jonah looked at the *Cinderella* but his eyes went back to the hand that Osmond now held draped over one knee. Jonah focused on the fingers and wished he could reach behind the seat and take his father's skull from there and place it in Osmond's lap. Osmond's words repeated in his mind and he was tempted to say, *Yes, Osmond, I do understand exactly what you're saying.*

Osmond shook his head slowly. The pound and its future are not up for discussion, Jonah. As I've said, I apologize for your losses.

It took Jonah a while to speak and when he did his words were deliberate. I'm not worried about the pound anymore.

I see.

Jonah lit another cigarette and blew the smoke out the window. He stole a glance at Osmond and Osmond appeared to have lost track of the conversation. Jonah made himself continue. But all that talk don't answer what you were doing aboard my father's boat.

Just looking, Osmond said.

Looking for what?

Osmond's eyes flashed back and forth. Nicolas was my friend, and I wanted to be aboard his boat one last time. To take a last look, that is all.

A last look for what, Osmond?

Osmond opened the door and began to step out and Jonah very nearly shouted, *You, Osmond, you*, but instead said, You think he did it, don't you?

Osmond pulled his foot back in and shut the door. He turned to face Jonah again. Would you care to explain that?

Jonah coughed and rolled the window down another inch and spat into the harbor. He rolled the window up. His pulse raced and his mind pounded as it tried to keep up with his mouth. He thought about Julius. He took a few more breaths then said, He wasn't supposed to end up in the pound, was he?

Those things are not up to us, Jonah.

Jonah resisted the urge to open the door and run. He said, Julius didn't put him in the pound, but he killed him, didn't he?

Osmond faced forward and his body relaxed in the seat. He leaned his head back into the rear window and Jonah heard the thud of skull on glass as Osmond closed his eyes. There it is, Osmond said with his eyes closed. There it is.

Jonah tried not to stare at him but he couldn't pull his eyes away. He wished for his father's rifle. Osmond's tongue came out of his mouth and wetted his lips then slid back in. His hands remained folded in his lap. When he spoke his voice had changed as if it now sounded from below. You were surprised by what I know of your family. Your father loved you dearly, Joshua, and he lived and died regretting that you did not know that.

How the hell do you know that?

I knew him well. He was a stubborn man, and stubborn men die with many regrets. Did you know that I named you, Jonah? Did you know that?

What?

Yes. Don't you remember? Nicolas drowned his son, Joshua, don't you remember? And out of the sea came Jonah, ready this time to accept the Lord?

Jonah spun and reached fast for the door handle and tried to push the door open but Osmond grabbed his bicep and spun him back and held him pressed into his seat. Jonah heard his own heartbeat.

But you, Jonah, you still seek to flee the Lord. You have yet to learn that no matter where you flee in this world, one is with you and one is after you. *He* was with you as you drowned, but you don't remember, do you?

I remember that you're fucking nuts, Jonah said and his face shot red and sweat rolled and he grabbed Osmond's wrist with all of his strength but even with two hands Jonah could not begin to move Osmond's one. He looked up at Osmond's face and Osmond looked saddened.

It's true, Jonah. Don't you remember being underwater? Your mother was dead only a short while, but you heard His voice and climbed from the pit. Soon you will believe, will you not? The Lord shall deliver us all. The path, Jonah. The Lord is the path.

Jonah worked his hand around Osmond's index finger and tried to bend it back but Osmond only gripped tighter.

Then Osmond relaxed. He sighed. Let go, Jonah, and I will let go.

Jonah let go. Osmond's hand left Jonah's arm but slid overtop Jonah's eyes and squeezed the temples. The palm became a screen on which Jonah saw himself as a child dipping beneath the waters. He saw his father and brother standing aboard the boat watching. His father held the gaff at his side and hollered something which the winds would not allow Jonah to hear and now Jonah writhed under Osmond's embrace and again he reached for the door but Osmond held him. Jonah saw his brother leap into the water and swim to him and he felt the cold skin of Bill's arm wrap around his neck and he heard his father's distant screams but could not understand the words.

Osmond's hand released Jonah's head. Jonah sat for a moment and tried to dismiss the uncanny notion that he'd been raped but did feel as if his mind had been somehow penetrated and before he recovered he blurted, Blood and blood alone, right?

Once more Osmond reached out and he took Jonah hard by the jaw and lifted and Jonah's ass came out of the seat and his head hit the cab ceiling. Osmond's eyes were red with veins like arc welds. Jonah gripped Osmond's arm and it was like squeezing oak. Jonah choked and scrambled and his knees hit the dashboard. He reached for soft tissue. His hand landed on Osmond's face and the broken nose was cold plastic so Jonah pulled his hand away and instead gripped the hand that held him as if he were holding a microphone. Osmond held him in the air with a hand like a crusher claw and with an icy finality Jonah understood right then that death was on its way.

Julius is innocent, Osmond said with a voice strangely fervent. Do you hear me? I believe that Julius is innocent.

Osmond released him and opened the door but before he could get out Jonah said, You *believe*? What do you *believe* Julius told us last night, Osmond? Tell me that.

Osmond paused then lifted himself out of the truck but before he shut the door he bent over and faced Jonah and said, He did not tell you a thing.

Now Jonah grimaced. Do you believe that? You think he's as tough as he pretends to be? You ever had your hand in a pot hauler, Osmond? I'll tell you this: The next time he goes on the water, he ain't coming home. We gave him a chance, and you know as well as I do that he didn't take it. So now it ends.

Osmond blinked once then eased the door closed and walked up the hill and it was not until the black truck was gone that Jonah began to shake.

• • •

Jonah drove past the harbor and up the hill into the maple woods. He followed the east side of the river. He didn't know where he was going. His stomach muscles clenched with confusion. He crested the hill and saw Charlotte's car in Julius's driveway and the confusion spun away like a column of wasps.

He slammed the truck to a halt and stuffed an unlit cigarette in his lips and he opened the truck door. He crossed the frozen driveway and went up the three steps and stood under the small roof and peered through a window. It felt like years since he'd been there but it was only a matter of hours. The kitchen was still a mess and the coffee table was upset and the television was on and there was no one in the room. He gripped the doorknob and everything was silent and in that silence he heard either a gasp or a plea and couldn't tell but it was as if the walls were shaking. The noise shot into his ears and down his neck and torso. His mind flicked to his mother reading him a children's story about the sky falling down.

He held his breath. The gasp echoed. He needed sleep and he needed food. His brain felt charred. He managed to light the cigarette and he heard another noise and he looked down at his legs shaking and he couldn't stop them and he couldn't interpret the nature of the noise. It occurred to him that he should just get in his truck and run far from it all and leave her to get what she'd come for.

His thighs and hips and back clenched. He held the cigarette in a shaking hand. A car passed like a silent film and he saw the woman driving the car and she was pale and obese with a skinny bearded man whom Jonah recognized as a local clam digger slumped and grimacing beside her. Another noise and he thought, *The hell with it*, and he gripped the doorknob. The latch clicked quiet and he stepped into the house. It smelled like tomato sauce. He held the door in his hand and he heard Charlotte's throat sounds clearly now and his throat constricted. He saw her clothes piled in the middle of the room. Her red underwear and her red bra. He crossed the floor. He couldn't catch his breath. He stopped opposite the bathroom door and the toilet seat was up and a half roll of toilet paper sat on the sink and several towels were strewn about the stained floor. He heard skin smacking skin and Charlotte's grunts and still he knew not if the grunts were born of pleasure or pain.

He took another step and stood framed in the bedroom doorway.

He saw Julius's back and his bare thin white ass working and Julius's skinny muscled legs. Julius stood on his tiptoes at the end of the bed and beyond him on the bed Jonah saw Charlotte's white skin. She was on her hands and knees and her black hair hung onto the white bed. He could see her chin atop the pillow and her legs spread and quaking on either side of Julius. A single breast dangled and swung.

Jonah's mind flashed. He stepped out of the doorway and stood with his back to the wall. He slid down the wall like a bloodstain and sat with his legs out straight. He held his burning cigarette in his fingers and it burned down to ash and Charlotte grunted deep and primal and the ash fell on the carpet and he heard her manage *I want to be on top now* then a brief rustling and they did not stop and did not stop. Jonah leaned his head back against the wall and stared at the ceiling and his ribs throbbed and tears ran down his cheeks and caught on the edges of his mouth. He tasted saltwater.

Bill drove fast through the maple woods and over the empty sweeping fields. He crossed the river clutched with ice and turned south down the western shore. He stopped at a double-wide trailer with a broken-down swing set beside it.

Erma Lee's car was in the small driveway. He looked at it for a moment before getting out. He crossed the dooryard which was ice and dog shit and he climbed the few plywood steps to a sagging off-level deck. He knocked on the door. It rattled with each knock. Through the window he could see the television set flickering and he heard voices and footsteps and finally the door opened.

It was Erma Lee's cousin Josephine. Her bulk filled the door space. She looked Bill up and down before saying, Erma Lee, you got yourself a visitor.

She shut the door and left Bill standing on the deck. He examined the rusted framework of the swing set and the swing with no seat but only a length of rope to balance on. A dog barked somewhere down the street. He stuffed his hands in his pockets and stamped his feet and wondered if Erma Lee had any intention of coming to the door. He was preparing himself to knock again when it opened and she stepped out.

She wore a hat and mittens and a heavy jacket. She moved past him and down the steps and got in the driver's seat of her car. He stood in front of the car wondering what she intended to do. She opened her door and said, Get in if you got something to say.

He sat in the passenger seat. The car smelled of air fresheners and fast food. He concentrated on the ratty siding on the trailer walls and swallowed several times before he said, Erma Lee. His voice cracked and he repeated himself. Erma Lee. I love you and I love that we've got a baby coming.

He paused and looked at her but she was stone-faced. He pushed his feet into the floor mat. He blinked several times over. He took his glasses off and rubbed his eyes raw then put them on. He faced her. I know I don't deserve it for the way I been but here I'm asking you to believe in me. That's all. I ain't asking for you to love me or even trust me just yet. Just believe in me because I know I ain't got everything you need but I'll get it, Erma Lee. I will get it.

Erma Lee glanced at him then blew a breath of air out and opened her door. She started to get out and Bill grabbed her arm.

We got a chance here, Erma Lee. Don't we?

You tell me. I done gave you a chance, Bill. I gave you plenty.

I know it.

Then what do you want?

She stuffed her hands between her thighs and hunched her shoulders then settled.

You. I want you. But not just you and not just me but us and the baby all as one. I ain't been like that before.

All of a sudden you want all that, Bill? I don't see nothing different except it's winter and you ain't been on the water every day so you're bored is all.

Bill shook his head no. He moved his mouth as if chewing the words he was trying to speak. It's always been me and maybe Jonah. Ever since our mother died in that wreck. I never figured on more than that. You know?

No, Bill. I guess I don't, she said. She nodded toward the trailer. You think this is how I figured my life? Living at my cousin's trailer?

I guess not. Maybe it took me a long time to learn it. Maybe even too long for you. But either way it's learned. It sunk in. I know it.

You know *what*, Bill? I don't know what you're saying.

He cleared his throat and when he spoke the words came fast as if they'd been piled up in his throat. I know it ain't me and you and a kid is what I'm saying. We're one and that's what I want. That's what I need. There ain't no other way and I'm sorry it took me so long. And I'm sorry for the hurt I caused you for it but I learned it and that's what matters. From here on out we got us nothing but open sailing.

She turned her head to him. Nothing on her face moved as her eyes dug into him like barbs which he could not pull out. He felt his pulse in his throat like the thump of railroad tracks.

Erma Lee got out of the car. She leaned forward as if to say something to him but instead she shut the door. She took a step back and hesitated then turned away. He watched her climb the steps and disappear into the trailer. The old storm door slapped in its framework behind her.

Bill slumped back in the seat and watched the door. He took out his cigarettes and turned the pack in his hands over and over and read everything written on the pack then leaned his head back and shut his eyes and wondered if loneliness was something he would get used to. When he opened his eyes it was dark and lights shone from the trailer windows. He saw a movement out of the corner of his eye and at first thought it was a dog probing the shadows but the car door opened and Erma Lee stuck her head in.

You're still here, she said.

I guess so.

Why don't you go home, Bill?

I'm waiting for you to come with me.

Now?

Now.

Erma Lee straightened. All he could see was her hips and torso and he focused on the spot he figured the baby to be. He reached a hand out to touch it but as he did so she shifted and he withdrew his hand. He expected the door to shut and her to go back inside but she bent and he saw her eyes wide. He rolled his hips and dug into his pocket and brought the ring out.

This ain't where I wanted to do this and this ain't how. But it's why and it's you and that's all that matters to me. He held the ring out between two big awkward fingers and the diamond sparkled in the residual trailer lights. Erma Lee sucked in her bottom lip but her eyes didn't leave Bill's.

Later, she said. She put her hand on his cheek and leaned in and kissed him. You do this later, Bill.

The house was empty when Charlotte got home. She stood in the shower with the water hot and her eyes closed. She felt a tight pain in her guts and remembered the pain of Julius squeezing her breasts. The black look in his eyes. The recent memory tolled like the sound of a faraway bell and there was a hidden part of her that had been proud of the pain but now that pride disgusted her.

Her parents came home. Her father stumbled into the living room and collapsed into his chair and stared at the television that wasn't even on. Charlotte wished she could go to him but she did not. Instead she slipped out the door and drove to the Irving station and bought a small heat-lamp pizza. She ate a slice as she drove and tossed the rest out the window. She thought about her father and she didn't feel the anger she had earlier. She felt sorry for him as if she'd not been there for him when he needed her and it dawned on her that she'd never before thought her father would need anything from anyone.

Darkness had settled by the time she passed her own driveway. She skirted the harbor and bounced down the two-track road and parked at the pound. It was a calm night and the moon was full and the spruce trees were covered in snow. The pound was frozen over and the ice gleamed in the moonlight. She dug through her glovebox and found her small flashlight and turned it on and got out of the car. She put an extra sweatshirt on and stepped into the trees.

The trail was canopied by spruce and fir boughs and the snow came to her shins. Her flashlight beam bounced yellow over the white expanse. She walked quickly and warmed with the exertion. The woods were silent but she heard the steady crashing of waves on the rocks and the gong buoy ringing and between the crash and the ring she could hear the empty beckon of the sea. She hadn't walked the trail since she was a young girl and now in the moonlight she remembered taking this trail with her mother and father to visit Nicolas and in a single shocking moment she understood that her childhood was far behind her and there in the nighttime woods she had to stop moving in order to reorient herself as if a new person had entered her body.

• • •

Jonah's camp was dark when she stepped into the clearing. The sky was clear and without the tree canopy she could see everything. The ocean was white and still. She shut her flashlight off and crossed the small clearing and opened the door. She paused with the door latch in her hand and turned her flashlight on and there sat Jonah only two feet from her like an apparition and her heart skipped and she nearly screamed.

He was at the table. He didn't have a shirt on. I got lights, he said.

She shut the flashlight off and stayed motionless. It was quiet inside and she heard his breaths and she heard the ocean.

After a minute he said, What do you want?

I thought you had lights?

I got a candle, he said but made no move to light one.

Jonah, she said and as she said his name she thought maybe she'd lost her closest friend.

Jonah flicked his lighter and held the flame to a candle in front of himself. Charlotte watched the flame slide along his thumb and the skin darkened but he didn't move until the wick caught.

Sit down if you want, he said. I don't care.

I'll go, she said. She waited and took a few breaths then stepped back but still held the door latch.

The cold air bent the candle flame over and put it out.

Either stay or go but shut the fucking door, Jonah said. He flicked the lighter again and lit the candle and held his hand blocking the wind.

Charlotte didn't move. She felt a rush of anger. You got no reason to be an asshole to me.

Jonah glanced at her in the candlelight then back to the candle. She heard his breathing.

Fine, she said and stepped outside and shut the door.

He dumped a few cigarettes out of a pack onto the table and took one and put it in his lips and leaned forward and lit the cigarette with the candle flame. He shielded the flame with his palm. His hands shook. He leaned back and blew smoke out of the sides of his mouth.

He let his hand fall to the table and he stared at the candle's reflection in the window and within that reflection he saw his own face and naked shoulders shuddering in the light. He couldn't see Charlotte standing beyond the window and wasn't sure if she was there or not. He looked around the room and felt a strange surge of energy like he was surfacing from a long time underwater.

He let the candle go out. He saw Charlotte on the far side of the glass.

• • •

Charlotte stood alone amid the darkness. She held her hands in her pockets. She watched the calm moonlit waters push across the patch of cobblestone below. As the water receded the stones tumbled together and created a hollow knocking that filled the air. She wondered what her life was going to be from this point on. It was as if she were staring out to sea with the intention of walking across it and was only now judging the possibility of such a feat. There'd been a time when she'd envisioned a life with Jonah and children but that vision had evaporated and all that remained was the air and the space that the vision once filled.

She reminded herself that air and space was what she wanted. She heard the door open and Jonah stood in the doorway. He spoke to her and his voice was tired but carried over the sea. My old man used to say that everyone in this world wants to be treated like whoremeat at least once and I'd say you done treated yourself to a shark's portion.

Why are you telling me that? Her voice was proud and defensive and hollow.

Julius used you like a whore or you used him like a whore.

You followed me? she said and the words had slipped out and her voice had no strength and she remembered her fear and she remembered Julius's hands like vices.

Jonah looked at her. He saw her on the bed with Julius behind her and her clothes piled on the dirty stained carpet and dirty towels sprawled on the dirty bathroom floor. He still heard her grunts as if they'd burrowed like mites into his head. A single breast swung. He closed his eyes and tried to separate the girl he knew from the girl he'd seen but he didn't know if separating them was possible or even right.

He heard her quick breaths.

Her eyes were wet but she didn't cry.

Neither spoke for several minutes and both hoped the ocean would somehow through size or power or age remove their two brief histories.

Come the spring of the year, Jonah finally said with a grin, I'm taking myself clamming.

Her look lost its severity and her skin looked like ivory in the starlight. No you aren't either, Jonah. You'll keep saying that and saying that, then my dad and Bill will talk you into lobster fishing again. Just like always.

The hell they will. But if they do, I'm thinking I might take the *Cinderella*. I'm starting to like the sound of it. Jonah motioned to the mouth of the cove. I got her here now.

You have the *Cinderella*?

Jonah nodded.

Why'd your dad even name it that? I always wondered.

A smile spread across Jonah's face. He never told me, but Bill said that's what he used to call Mom. I don't know.

I like it, Charlotte said. It's sweet.

Yeah. Well I'm going to leave the *Jennifer* right where she is. Right in the belly of this godfucked ocean. I think the old man might like having her down there. It'll be his gravestone.

Underwater? With his wife's name on it, Jonah?

It does seem so.

Charlotte drew in a deep breath. She brushed her hand over Jonah's then put it back in her pocket. I was so mad at my dad, Jonah. But when I was driving around today, I all of a sudden felt sorry for him. He always seemed so big and now he doesn't.

Jonah listened but the words were far off. The ocean echoed in his head and a remote piece of his father echoed in his head. As he listened the echoes merged and took shape as a truth that Jonah felt he could almost touch. He looked out at the water that covered the *Jennifer* then out to the mouth where he'd left the *Cinderella* at anchor.

This is it, he said. His voice carried a force he didn't recognize.

This is what, Jonah?

Jonah stared a while at the silver ocean. Never mind, he finally said. Just that I'm leaving the *Jennifer* right there on bottom. Jonah nodded his head as he spoke. I think the old man will like having her down there with him.

He turned and opened the door and stepped inside. He lit the candle and the flame cast an orange shadowed glow across the spruce walls. He breathed in heavily through his nostrils.

Charlotte moved in behind him and put her hand on his shoulder. He turned and held the candle shielded by his palms.

Her chin and nose and forehead gleamed in the soft light. She put her hand on his cheek. I'm sorry, she said. I'm so sorry.

They stared at each other through the flame.

Charlotte sucked in her cheeks.

Jonah looked at the window and his reflection still flicked on the glass. Waves rolled against the ledges as the moon pulled against the Atlantic. Eventually Jonah said, I'm hungry. You hungry?

No.

I'll make pancakes. You want pancakes?

No.

I got syrup. I know you love that.

She smiled and her smile turned into a yawn and her yawn turned into a stretch. No, she said.

Jonah lit a lantern and stoked the fire. As the fire grew he took a box of pancake batter from the cupboard. He mixed the batter and set a griddle on the stove. Charlotte stood with her back to the fire and held her hands behind her and her chin was over her shoulder as she watched Jonah. When the pancakes were finished he gave her a plateful and she thanked him. They ate in silence and when they were finished Jonah put more wood on the fire. They sat on the small couch together with just the light of the candle burning. Soon Charlotte fell asleep and her head slid to the side and landed on Jonah's shoulder. He didn't move. He sat there listening to her breath as he thought about Osmond Randolph.

Jason Jackson left the city early in the morning. Turtle rode with him and they drove a small Japanese car and they drove in silence along the broken coastline. Turtle sat cross-legged and held a small handbag in her lap.

They went first to the harbor. Jason pulled onto the wharf. The wind blew hard from the north and stretched the fleet's mooring lines. Ice hung from the bridles and hulls and riggings. Jason spotted Julius's new boat and pointed it out to Turtle.

I'd like to see that little prick come to Honolulu, she said.

Settle down, Jason said.

He looked out to Ram's Head and nodded then backed off the wharf and drove to the pound. The car dragged its undercarriage over the rocks and snow and frozen ruts but Jason didn't seem to notice. They stood at the edge of the pound with the air at their backs as Jason surveyed the ice and the causeway and the pound house and the dam. He turned and faced the east where the tidal stream eased through the frozen marsh grass. Beside the marsh stood the piles of Nicolas's traps.

They drove to Osmond's house. Osmond was in the bar when they arrived. Jason held two bottles of sake tucked in his elbow and he gave them to Osmond.

Where's your boy Julius?

He'll be here.

What happened to your face?

I had a run-in, that is all.

Jason grunted. What does Julius think of things?

He's young, said Osmond. He thinks his boat is the only thing he needs in this world.

He doesn't understand connection, Jason said. But he is quite a lad. Gwen spoke very highly of him.

Osmond nodded.

Turtle's never been this far north, Jason said. What do you think of the north, Turtle?

It's a dump.

Show Osmond your new jacket.

Turtle stood and turned around. Her jacket was glittering red nylon and on the back was the silhouette of a woman on a motorcycle with her hair trailing in the wind and the jacket said *Hell's Bitches*.

Daniel found that at a vintage clothing place.

You see that? Turtle asked Osmond.

I see, said Osmond.

I know, she said.

Jason shook his head. What are your plans, Osmond? If Julius isn't interested in our ideas, what are your plans?

He'll be interested. This is for him.

I understand that. You don't want him to grow up like his father. I didn't want to grow up like my father either because he beat the shit out of me but that's not the point.

Julius respects his father.

Jason turned to Turtle and whispered something into her ear and she said, Fuck off, Big Man.

We agreed, he said.

That was before I knew this was the fucking Arctic Circle up here. I'll freeze to death.

Turn the car on.

Fucker, she said. I'll be out there thinking of all the shit you owe me for all this shit you pull.

She walked out the door.

Jason shook his head again. He looked out the window and waited until he heard the car door shut. Then he spread his hands on the marble bar top and faced Osmond. Tell me this—How did Nicolas Graves die?

Are you asking me something in particular?

Jason laughed and wiped his hand along his black and white beard. Yes I am, yes I am. I'm asking you exactly what I asked you.

Be careful, Jason, Osmond said. He tucked his hair behind his ear as he watched Jason.

I am careful. I'm careful about investing a lot of money in a partnership with someone I don't trust.

Osmond's face gave away no emotion but his eyes were small and dark and he spoke more quickly than usual. And what do you base this lack of faith on?

Jason swirled his hand around the bar top. No, no, Osmond. I'll put it this way. I trust my Japanese friend because he is a ruthless bastard. To him, I am a means to an end. Just like I am to you and you are to me. I trust him because that is on the table. I fuck him over and he sends some little ninja slob to slice my throat. What I don't trust is your boy Julius. I don't trust what motivates him because it's not money and it's not pussy. You tell me what it is, Osmond, because it's not your God either.

Osmond watched the ocean froth white outside his windows. He watched his boat buck in the chop. He thought about Chimney and knew that to be the only thing in the world which motivated Julius in a sheer and lucid way and as he thought Jason spoke.

His father, Chimney, isn't it? That was Gwen's take as well. She's a quick one, Osmond. She understands. I don't keep her around for her looks.

Osmond didn't know what to say. He felt heat rise in his face and it wasn't a feeling he was used to.

I don't trust him because I believe that when Chimney is released Julius will be at his command. And even before then. I am not going to invest my money in an endeavor with someone whose motivations are so dubious.

That's enough, Osmond said but his voice was quiet.

Do you understand me? Jason said.

They heard Julius's truck come down the driveway and stop. Jason nodded.

I understand you, Osmond said. And you must understand me. Nicolas was my friend and that is all I will say.

I know he was, Jason said. He was a good man. And Julius killed him, is that right?

No, said Osmond but his voice did not listen to him as he told it to speak surely. No, he said again and again he remembered Julius's voice that he had shut from his mind and the voice said, *They think it was me*, and finally like a gut-shot Osmond understood something he should have understood long ago. This boy who he had been trying to save for so long was now trying to save him and the realization left Osmond so breathless and so shocked by regret that he had to brace his physical structure in order to carry on.

No? I think so, Jason said as the door opened and Julius came in with his broken lips and bruised neck. Jason turned and nodded. Julius, he said.

Julius went behind the bar and opened a can of cola. He held the can away from his lips as he drank. Osmond watched him and wanted to lift him into his arms and run and never stop.

Tell me a story, Julius, Jason said.

I don't tell stories. I say it like it is and that's that. Julius peered out the window. Why's Turtle in the car?

She likes it, Jason said.

She'll freeze. I better go get her.

No you won't, Osmond said.

Give her a moment, Jason said. She's got a new jacket. Right now I want to hear your story.

Julius's eyes flicked to Osmond. Osmond watched the lobster in the tank. He's wondering about Nicolas, Osmond said. His voice was flat.

He's dead, said Julius.

I understand that.

What do you care anyhow?

I don't care. I wonder. That is what one does when one is in business. You wonder about the men you do business with. You wonder until you know.

And you wonder about me, Julius said to Jason but faced his grandfather.

Yes. And so does your grandfather.

Jason, Osmond said but that was all and he felt Julius's betrayed eyes on him and a feeling of deep and absolute exhaustion spread through him and if in that moment he could have closed his eyes and never opened them again he would have done so without hesitation.

Jason leaned back and laughed. Go get Turtle, Julius, would you please? Tell her to come in here before she freezes to death. It's cold out there. And ask her to bring the food with her.

When Julius went out Osmond poured a glass of scotch and tipped it back and looked at Jason and said, Don't fuck with us, Jason. I know you are big and I know you have friends and that is good and that is fine but you shall not interrupt my family life.

Business is family, Osmond. Settle down.

The vertical lines on Osmond's face were deep and lined with glistening sweat like flooded irrigation ditches. He could smell his own sweat like pesticide and it repelled him.

Julius came back followed by Turtle. She had a white cardboard box of sushi with her. She smiled and nodded at Jason then set the box on the bar and opened it. Jason plucked two out and swallowed them one at a time.

Big eye from Hawaii, he said. Caught two days ago. Goddamned Filipino crews down there pay attention. It's all quality.

Jason slid a glass of sake to Turtle and she drank it down in one gulp and said, Are you boys done with your little private talk? Fuck me waiting in the car.

We're here to come to an understanding, Jason said.

Understanding of what? Julius said.

Of you. First off, I'd like to know what happened to your face.

None of your business.

Virgil and the boys, Osmond said.

Virgil, said Jason. Virgil Alley did that? What for?

Caught me fucking his daughter is why. Julius glanced at Turtle but she was looking at the lobster in the tank.

Jason grinned and Osmond leaned over and whispered into Julius's ear, Please watch yourself here and now, Julius. Please do it for me.

I ain't got to watch nothing, Julius said. His voice was loud.

Was this fucking similar to what you did to my friend Gwen?

Julius sipped his cola.

They had a disagreement over traps. Territory, Osmond said and wished he hadn't spoken. He sat down and he looked at the bar then at his grandson then at his own palms. He tasted scotch. He looked at Jason sitting quietly in his white lab coat. Jason looked big and oafish but he was peeling back the layers that covered Julius and seeing Julius so exposed had exposed him as well and within that exposure Osmond saw so incredibly clearly that he had stepped to the side as his grandson Julius Wesley took his fall.

Jason leaned over and spoke to Turtle. She nodded and said, I think so too.

Jason turned back to Julius.

Julius put his empty cola can on the bar. Me and my girlfriend are none of your business.

That's right. I don't care about you and your girlfriend. I do care about you and Gwen, but we'll deal with that one later.

Osmond stared at a thin slice of tuna. He couldn't look at Julius.

Julius watched his grandfather then said, Fuck it, and walked out from behind the bar and began out the door but Jason held a hand up to stop him.

I'll walk you out, Jason said. He rose and put his hand between Julius's shoulder blades and gently pushed Julius toward the door. Osmond started to say something but his jaw felt locked and his throat too dry. Turtle stood before him staring at him with eyes that made him want to leave his own home.

Soon Jason returned. He sat at the bar and finished the bottle of sake. His neck gleamed with sweat. He watched the big lobster and Osmond watched him and on Jason's white lab coat Osmond saw a smear of wet blood that he could not take his eyes from. No one spoke and it was almost ten more minutes before they heard Julius's truck start and spin around and run down the long clamshell driveway. Osmond pictured the boy in the truck now beaten once again and he wished he could chase Julius down and hold him in his arms and tell him that someday soon they would start over.

Go, said Osmond.

Maybe we'll talk later.

No. Go away from here.

Jason stood. He slid the box of sushi toward Osmond. He took Turtle by the hand and left.

Osmond sat at the bar and listened as Jason's small car started and drove away. He looked around the empty room. His gaze settled on Julius's empty cola can. Something was perched atop the can and Osmond stood and took two steps and there atop the can sat a single gray tooth. Osmond lifted it into the air. He knew it was Nicolas's and he understood it to be the last words of a hangman so without pause he turned and dropped the tooth into the lobster tank.

All that remained was the ocean.

Hours before daylight. Jonah alone walked the dark woods to Nicolas's wharf. He paused at the edge of the trees. He lit a cigarette and his unshaven face flashed orange against the night. Before him spread the small cove shot silver from the moon. The wharf like a thumb jutted toward Stone Island with planks heavy and glistening with frost. With one hand he climbed the ladder down to the float and with his other he held his father's rifle.

His skiff was upside down on the float and caked in ice. He slapped at the ice with a single palm and the cakes broke off in soft sheets that slid to the float planks and crumbled. He reached beneath the gunwale and righted the skiff then slid it into the water. Tails of kelp swished and frames of ice glowed and the small waves shifted white then silver then gray as the water tilted and swung beneath the sky.

He braced the rifle against the stern and fitted the oarlocks into their sockets then the oars into their locks. He spun the skiff and rowed stern-first to the mouth of the cove. The *Cinderella* lay at anchor with the beggar gull perched on the bow. The skiff banged against the fiberglass as Jonah climbed aboard. He opened the baitbox and tossed a herring to the gull and watched as the gull batted its wings then swallowed the fish in a single choking gulp. He fired the engine and tied the skiff's painter off to the anchor rode. The big diesel grumbled in the cold air then settled into its easy throaty rhythm.

Jonah throttled south to open sea. Water sprayed from the chines. Wake tumbled like snow from a plow blade. Two Penny flashed and Drown Boy revolved and beyond both and beyond the bright shining moon lay Orion perched in the sky as if guarding the holds of the sea with bow and arrow and Jonah wished for such simple weaponry.

The sea was plate steel. An archipelago of islands like thrown stones spread to the south and to the east the bridge with its archway of lights led to the village on Mason's Island. Jonah ran the *Cinderella* at half throttle. The rifle was on the bulkhead before him and he nested his left hand atop it. He rounded the point that sheltered Osmond Randolph's home. A single light in the end window cast a smooth glow on the surrounding snowpack. Jagged points of spruce and fir pressed the skyline. Osmond's boat floated a black shadow atop the water and beyond the boat the small wharf stood silhouetted against the granite ledges.

Jonah stopped less than a hundred yards off. He took three cartridges from his pocket and fitted them into the magazine. He chambered one. The working of the bolt clicked against the sound of the diesel. He held the rifle to his shoulder and peered through the scope at Osmond's home. In the crosshairs he saw a bedside lamp. He pictured Osmond reading beside it then pictured the bulb shattering.

With the boat in neutral and the rifle butt braced on his hip he slammed the throttle wide open for a breath. The engine howled and ripped. He watched. Sweat beaded in his armpits and rolled down his ribs. He leaned against the wheelhouse wall and tried to sight on the lamp as the boat rose and fell with the movements of the water. He reached down with one hand and pumped the throttle again and the noise was like a hole punched in the nighttime. A flaw of wind pushed him toward shore so he spun a quick circle to keep the boat off the rocks and just then he saw Osmond glide like a bird past the window.

Jonah aligned the boat with the bow facing the house. He cranked the windshield open and pointed the rifle through the opening. He reached down and flipped the overhead lights on and blasted Osmond's house with light and suddenly there in the window stood Osmond Randolph naked and white and frozen in time with his black hair wrapped along his jawline and his arms spread like the reaches of a cross. Jonah's blood surged and he heard pistons slide in his ears. He struggled to catch his breath. He tried to settle the crosshairs but his mind flashed to Osmond's hand upon his face and he remembered feeling from that palm that death was on its way.

The crosshairs danced over Osmond's body. Jonah shouldered sweat from his forehead. He jammed his eyes closed then open and felt the salt sting. He thumbed the safety off. He smelled gun oil. He worked his finger against the trigger and even with the rise and fall of the sea and the shaking of his body the crosshairs found Osmond's trunk.

The *Cinderella* drifted toward shore.

Jonah whispered to himself, *You, Osmond, you.*

He thought of his brother. He blinked over and over and tried to refocus. He felt the stock now warm against his cheek. He told himself that Bill would have shot by now but in truth he doubted it. He tapped his finger against the trigger and the barrel end wavered out in front of him. He wished Osmond would duck or run or charge but all Osmond did was stand like a target with his arms spread wide.

Jonah lifted his head to see Osmond through naked eyes. Osmond leaned forward and pressed his body against the window and with that slight movement Jonah understood what Osmond was after. The *Cinderella* rose sharply on a steep wave and Jonah looked around and saw that he'd drifted into shoal water. Waves lifted from beneath him then curled and broke. He faced Osmond. He held the rifle vertically out over the water with its barrel pointed skyward and with a last glance at Osmond he released it. The rifle fell with barely a splash.

Jonah shut the overhead lights down. The engine rumbled in the darkness. Then easy like a coyote backing across a snow white plain he reversed the *Cinderella* until all that remained of Osmond's home was a distant shining light holding the shape of a man.

• • •

Osmond Randolph moved. He stepped naked from his house into the bitter dark. He eased the door closed. He walked the ledges to his wharf and his bare feet melted tracks into the frozen granite and into the frosted wharf planks but the footprints quickly glazed with ice making it appear that his passage had been long ago.

Osmond made his way to the end of the wharf. He watched the *Cinderella* round the peninsula but the echo of its engine still throbbed across the waters. He held a pistol in his hand. He stood with the toes and balls of his feet out over the end of the wharf. He looked first to the unclouded heavens then to his boat and last to the ebb and swirl of seawater. He said something that nobody heard.

• • •

Jonah slammed the throttle down. He sped east with Orion off to the south and the moon easing into the west and gradually his breathing slowed and his heart settled but the image of Osmond begging for end burned in his mind.

When he reached the harbor mouth he slowed to an idle. He saw to the north the few lights of the small village and the shape of the wharf with its bait house roof sheathed in frost and moon. He looked east to the shape of Stone Island and saw the faint glow of a lantern burning in his camp like the soft reflection of flame on rock.

He looked south and considered the world out there. A smile cracked across his face. He spun the *Cinderella* and charged offshore with Orion over his bow and the full open eye of the moon sliding beneath his starboard rail. A pair of auks bobbed off Ram's Head and scattered as he passed. He swung tight against the ledges off Two Penny and a flock of sandpipers lifted from the rocks and their white undersides flashed in a single wave. The abandoned lighthouse rose in the moonlight and he saw first the reflection of the moon in the glass dome at its peak and then the passing glint of the *Cinderella*.

He held an unlit cigarette in his lips. He braced his hand on the brass wheel that was worn to fit a dead man's fist. The Drown Boy Rock lighthouse rose like a steeple out of the water and far beyond stood a mountain. As he steamed south the mountaintop began to burn with the first trace of sunrise and soon it appeared not that the light descended the mountainside but that the mountain itself rose to the light.

• • •

Clouds came with the sun. Jonah drifted above the Leviathan Ground. The moon had sunk and all was gray and he could not tell where the sea ended and the clouds began. He thought of his father down below. He thought of his brother on dry land. He thought of Osmond with his vertical wheals of skin like ruts and his eyes like rust holes. He thought of Virgil and of going and taking the man in his arms and telling him all was forgiven. He thought of Charlotte asleep at his camp and he knew that the girl he'd known was gone from him forever.

He dropped his fist onto the throttle and spun the wheel. The bow of the *Cinderella* arced through the waters until it faced north and eclipsed the vacant lighthouse on Two Penny. Beyond Two Penny was an island called Burnt and within the grip of Burnt Island stood a slat-wood dam and a riprap causeway which together formed a lobster pound. He sailed north for home and the diesel engine echoed but Jonah heard only the gentle slide of water like voices calling and his eyes searched the mist that sprayed from the chines as if he would find a loved one there. He felt he understood something although he could not say what so he knocked his fist against the boat's bulkhead as if to reaffirm the center of the earth.